The Coverup

Copyright © 2006 William Daniel
All rights reserved.
ISBN: 1-4196-4309-6

To order additional copies, please contact us.
BookSurge, LLC
www.booksurge.com
1-866-308-6235
orders@booksurge.com

WILLIAM DANIEL

THE
COVERUP

2006

Dedicated to
Jackie Hawkins
And
Mina Daniel

FIRST ENCOUNTER
Chapter One

I t was a quiet little town just north of the Mexican border and twenty miles east of El Paso in a little place called Quasar Villa where Josh Hernandez lived on his small chicken farm. Josh raised laying hens and sold the eggs in town to the local people. He was a quiet man, didn't bother anyone. He just sold his eggs and worked his farm for what little he could make. Josh was known all over town as the egg man and was very friendly with most people. He was an honest man who lived by his wits and the sweat of his brow.

One morning around 2:00 a.m., Josh was awakened by some loud noises coming from his chicken house. Leaping from his bed, he got dressed quickly, thinking there must be a fox in his chicken house. He knew that a fox in your chicken house could kill all your chickens. He hurried to get his shotgun and out the door he ran to the front porch and down the steps. As he was leaving the front porch steps, he noticed an object lying in the front yard about twenty feet from the house. Carefully he walked over to the object, and the closer he got, the better he could see that the object was his old dog, Bull. Holding a flashlight on him, he called out, "Bull!" but the old dog didn't move. He moved closer to the old dog, constantly looking around to see if anything was out there in the yard. The squawking from the chicken house had Josh jumpy as he approached the old dog. When he got to Bull, Josh looked down at his dog, only to discover he was dead. The old dog's lifeless body lay still before him. Josh became very angry as he turned and stared at the chicken house. Bull had been a good friend to him for ten years. Mumbling to himself, Josh swore to get who or whatever killed his dog. He stormed off to the chicken house, his fear replaced by anger. He opened the door to the chicken house, and chickens went flying out the door around him. When the feathers and dust cleared, he could see that the east wall had a big hole in it.

Suddenly some noises coming from just outside the hole in the chicken yard startled him. The noises made fear run through his mind again. "What could that be?" he thought to himself as he entered the chicken house. He made his way over to the hole in the wall. When he got to the hole, he raised his shotgun in order to get off a quick shot. He wanted to make sure whatever it was didn't get away. Josh pointed the flashlight and his double-barrel shotgun out the hole. He was trying to spot what was out there before he stepped out into the chicken yard. He moved the flashlight around on the ground until he came upon some feet with claws on them. His nerves went into shock as he raised up the flashlight. At the top, he found a hideous creature standing in front of him. Pale in color with big black eyes, the creature stood about four feet tall with long blood-drenched fangs snarling at him. As quickly as he spotted it, the creature flew off into the black sky before he could get a shot at it.

Sheriff John Barton raised his head from the pillow. Looking at the clock, he let out a sigh. As the phone rang, he whispered, "Who the hell is this calling me at two-thirty in the morning?" He staggered out of bed, grabbing his head in pain and thinking to himself, "I wish I hadn't drunk all that

THE COVERUP

tequila last night." He walked over to the phone and picked up the receiver and said, "This had better be good." He recognized the screaming voice on the other end. It was Josh Hernandez.

"What can I do for you, Josh?" he asked as he rubbed his eyes. Josh proceeded to tell the sheriff about the creature that had broken into his hen house and killed old Bull. "What kind of creature was it, Josh?" John asked as he yawned.

Josh described the creature in great detail to John. He explained how the creature flew off into the darkness faster than you could bat an eye.

"Now, Josh, have you been in the liquor cabinet? Did you see any pink elephants out there, too?" John sarcastically asked.

"You don't believe me. You come out and see for yourself. My Bull, he is dead, I tell you. It killed Bull and some of my chickens. I'm not drunk. You come see what I tell you is true!" screamed Josh.

"Calm down, Josh," John said as he fumbled around the kitchen table for a cigarette. "What do you think it was?"

Silence fell upon the receiver as Josh gathered his thoughts. "I think it was El Chupacabra," Josh replied.

"Oh, for God's sake, Josh. There's no such thing as El Chupacabra, and you know it!" John screamed.

"Please, Sheriff, I don't know what it was! I'm frightened! Please come see!" cried Josh.

"OK, Josh, just sit tight. I'll be there as soon as I can. Stay inside and keep your door locked. I'll get there quickly as I can," John replied.

John let out a low groan as he hung up the phone. "Is this the kind of day I'm going to have? Great, just great," he said. He walked over to the stove and began to make coffee as he mulled over the conversation he just had with Josh. "Old Josh must have gotten into some hard liquor or some wacky weed last night," John thought. He reached up into the cabinet to get a coffee cup and began to pour a cup. Then he sat down and lit a cigarette as he picked up the phone and began dialing a number.

The phone rang a few times when Deputy Tom Bowman answered, "Who is this?"

"It's John," John answered. "I need you to get the squad car and come pick me up. We've got a disturbance out at the Hernandez farm. Josh says something broke into his hen house. I'll fill you in when you get here."

"All right, I'll be there as soon as I can get awake," Tom replied.

John hung up the phone and started to sip on his coffee, wondering just what he was about to get into. Being a sheriff of a small town, you don't get many strange cases, mostly chicken thieves, moonshiners, and family fights. This was the reason John became a small town sheriff. Once an FBI agent in Dallas, Texas, he had seen all the murders and drug busts he wanted to see. This, coupled with a suspension over something he didn't do, convinced him to make the move to a small town. He reached over to the counter and opened a box of doughnuts, pulled out one, put out his cigarette, and staggered off to the bedroom to get dressed.

BOWMAN ARRIVES
Chapter Two

At three-thirty a.m., Deputy Tom Bowman pulled into the driveway, stopped the car, and stepped out, stopping for one moment to collect his thoughts. Then he slammed the door shut on the car.

"My God! What a mess!" Tom thought, as he looked at all the toys lying in the yard while he was walking to the front porch. "I'm glad I don't have kids," he mumbled to himself. He stepped onto the porch and walked over to the door. John was buttoning his shirt when he heard someone knocking at the door. "John, it's Tom!" shouted Tom.

"Come on in, Tom," John replied as he continued to button his shirt.

"Early in the morning, John," Tom quipped.

"Yeah, I know. You want some coffee?" asked John.

"Yeah, cream and two sugars," Tom replied as he sat down at the kitchen table. "What's up with Josh this morning?" he asked.

"Well, it seems that Josh has had a visit by El Chupacabra, or rather, he thinks he has," John began. "Now, I don't believe in this unholy devil that the Mexicans believe in, but the way Josh described this thing, it sounds like some of the other stories I've heard. Josh claims to have seen a creature about three feet to four feet high, gray-skinned with claws, and it just took off right in front of him," John said while biting his lip to keep from bursting out laughing.

Tom beat him to it. "Ha!" he whaled. "You've got to be kidding me."

"No," John answered. "Josh was kind of upset when I talked to him."

Now John was, by far, not a fool, but Josh sounded really upset about something.

"Josh a drinking man, John?" Tom asked.

"No, I already asked Josh about that and he nearly bit my head off. Besides, I don't believe he drinks much, if any at all," John replied.

"Long as I have known him, I don't think I ever saw him take a drink," Tom said. "It's just Josh and that old dog, right?"

"Far as I know, he never married, nor does he have any kin folk around here," John replied.

"I think I remember he had a wife years ago, and she died. Someone told me that," Tom answered.

"Well, I have only known him for ten years, and he has always been alone, just him and that dog delivering eggs and chickens," John replied.

"Yeah, he always had that dog with him every time I saw him," Tom remembered.

"He was kind of proud of that old dog. You never saw them apart. They went everywhere together. I don't think I ever saw him without that dog with him," John said.

THE COVERUP

"Gosh, with Bull dead, Josh is not going to have anyone left. That's sad, you know," Tom remarked.

"Well, I expect he will find himself another dog, and maybe he will get over Bull. Who knows?" John said.

The two men went on talking about stories they had heard about people who saw the creature, so-called El Chupacabra. Tom began telling about a goat that was taken away, right out from in front of an old Mexican farmer.

John finished dressing and turned to Tom and said, "Well, let's go see what he's talking about," as the two men headed for the door.

Tom asked as he slid in behind the wheel, "Should I call for a backup?" as he was trying not to laugh.

"Don't make me laugh. It's too early. Let's go," John said

THE HERNANDEZ CHICKEN FARM
Chapter Three

Tom started the car and began to back out of the driveway slowly, driving toward the highway. The drive to Josh's farm was about 20 miles. First you had to drive through town, then get on Highway 4 South for five miles, then turn onto Farm Road 2423 for 10 miles before getting to Josh's driveway. John thought about the papers lying on his desk back at his office. Several years ago, an old friend, Mike Holmes, offered him a job as a police officer in Dallas, Texas. He and John grew up together in Dallas. They went to the police academy together. But to John, the city life was just too fast for him. He liked the quiet of the country life and the fact that he was in charge.

Tom turned the car into Josh's driveway and began driving up the long narrow road to Josh's house.

"Well, I guess we are here," Tom said as he drove the car up to the house. The two men scanned the area to see if Josh was outside.

"Look," John whispered. "There's the dog in the yard."

"Yeah, I see him," Tom replied. "What is our next move?"

John sat in silence for a moment and replied, "You go check out the dog. I'll see if I can get Josh to the door."

As John started to the door, he looked back and whispered, "On second thought, you'd better come with me. Look at the front door."

Tom turned his head to the door, only to find out there was no door there. The two men began to walk to the door very slowly as they stepped onto the porch. John suddenly noticed the door had been torn off the frame and was lying on the floor.

"Look at that, Tom!" John said.

"My God! What the hell happened here?" Tom asked.

"I don't know, but it doesn't look good," John replied as he turned his head to look at Tom.

Both men drew their guns. John motioned for Tom to go to the other side of the door. Then he motioned for Tom to go first, and Tom jumped inside the door, wheeling his pistol to the left as John turned to the right side of the room. The room was a shambles, furniture turned over, lamps lying on the floor, and pictures hanging crooked.

John turned to Tom and said, "Kitchen," as the two men searched through the front part of the house very slowly. The two men searched but found no signs of Josh in the front part of the house, so they moved to the hallway and headed for Josh's bedroom. John went first, and Tom followed, covering their backside as they slowly moved down the hall. When they arrived at Josh's bedroom, they noticed the door was wide open, so they moved into the room scanning it with their flashlights. John noticed Josh lying on the floor.

"Josh!" he cried out, but there was no response. He moved into the room and reached down to check for a pulse on Josh's wrist. He then turned to Tom and shook his head indicating that he was dead. He holstered his gun and turned to Tom.

"Go see if you can get an ambulance out here and call Rocky. Tell him to bring his dogs. I want to search the woods around the chicken house."

THE COVERUP

"Oh," he snapped, "Better see if you can get the judge up. We need him to certify Josh is dead."

Tom turned and very quickly went out the door and headed for the car. John knelt down beside Josh's body and started looking for signs of what might have killed him. He then started looking around for any kind of evidence that might explain what could have happened. He began trying to remember what Josh had said when they had talked on the phone earlier that morning. Now he wished he had listened better to what Josh had said. John turned to the door and walked out, being careful not to disturb anything as he was leaving the room. As he reached the front door, Tom was walking in.

"Well, I got Rocky on the way. The judge was already on his way," Tom said.

"The judge is already on the way?" John asked.

"Yeah, his wife said he got a call to come out to Josh's farm," Tom replied.

As the two men stood at the door and pondered what that was all about, John said, "I guess we should check the chicken house. That's what Josh was complaining about."

Tom looked at the chicken house and turned to John. "What was that Josh was saying, something about 'El Chupacabra'?" Tom stopped to watch John's reaction, and went on, "You don't believe that, do you?"

"Well, to tell you the truth, Tom, I don't know what to believe right now," John replied. "But I will tell you this. I know what I heard Josh say."

"Well, I guess we better go see what we can find in the old chicken house," Tom answered.

As the two men walked to the chicken house, they scanned the ground for any signs of strange footprints. When they arrived at the door, Tom shined his flashlight into the house and stepped inside. "John, look at this!" Tom shouted. John quickly stepped inside and looked where Tom was pointing his flashlight. He couldn't believe what he saw. The wall had a very large hole in it, like someone had crashed through it.

"What do you make of that?" Tom asked.

John walked over to the wall, scanned his flashlight around the chicken yard, and stepped out through the hole with Tom following behind him. "Look at all the dead chickens!" John exclaimed.

"That's nothing. Look at the scratches on this wall," replied Tom.

"My God!" John said. "It looks like bear claws did that!"

"There aren't any bears around here," Tom replied. Being an avid hunter, he knew it couldn't be a bear.

"What the hell could have done this, then?" John asked.

"I don't know, but it had to be big, whatever it was," Tom replied. The two men looked at each other, and then back at the wall, and then looked back at each other with a confused look.

After searching around the chicken yard for any signs of what might have done this, they came upon a set of tracks that neither man had ever seen before. No doubt this had to be what caused the hole in the wall. These tracks could not have been made by man or chicken. They were more of a reptilian type, and there were no reptiles that big in this area. By looking at the prints, John could see what Josh was talking about when he described what he saw. Three or four toes and claws about three inches long was the description by the many people who had seen El Chupacabra and reported it. The two men continued to search the pen for more clues but found nothing more than the two tracks. John and Tom were

THE COVERUP

trying to figure out why there were only two pairs of tracks left in the chicken yard.

"Well, I don't have a clue. You got any suggestion, Tom?" John asked.

"I don't know, either, John," Tom replied.

"Maybe we better make a plaster cast of them for evidence," John said. "Check around the dog for prints."

As they headed out of the chicken house, they heard a loud rumble coming from down the driveway. "That must be Rocky," John said.

Down the road came a rusty old truck bouncing around the road, loaded down with redbone hound dogs. Rocky Boyd was a tracker for the county, and his hounds were the best at tracking down escaped convicts. As Rocky drove up to the house, Tom and John walked out to meet him. The three men exchanged greetings, and John began explaining to Rocky what had happened while he unloaded the dogs from the truck.

"What do you want me to do?" Rocky asked.

John explained to Rocky how he wanted him to take the dogs to the chicken house and see if they could pick up a scent. Suddenly a car came roaring down the road. It was the Judge. John told Rocky to go ahead and take the dogs to the chicken house and for Tom to go with him to make sure they didn't destroy the tracks.

JUDGE ROY JONES
Chapter Four

J udge Roy Jones was a hardnosed man that had been in controversy all his political life. Many convicts knew him for passing out life sentences in the past. His view on criminal behavior kept all criminals in fear of facing him and regret when they did. His under-the-table deals were controversial. However, nobody could discover his method. Judge Jones always covered his tracks so well that nobody could find out what he had done.

"Judge Jones, how nice to see you again," John said sarcastically as the Judge stepped out of his car.

"John, how are we doing?" Judge Jones replied as he stood up from the car. "How are the kids and the wife?"

"Fine, Judge, just fine," John answered.

"John, we have a controversial matter at hand here," the Judge said as he walked up to John.

"Well, you would know more about that than I would, Judge," John answered somewhat sarcastically.

"I'm going to need your cooperation on this, John. I hope you will give it to me," the Judge said, sounding very cold and stern.

"Long as we are talking about the truth, Judge."

"Damn it, boy, this kind of thing could get out of hand," the Judge said as he began looking around the yard. "You know, someone else could be wearing that badge of yours."

John, stunned by the words the judge said, replied, "Okay, Judge, it's your call."

"I would remember that if I were you, Sheriff," the Judge said as he turned and walked into the house.

John's attention turned to the chicken house. "Tom, Rocky, let's go!" John hollered as he headed for the path leading behind the house. John, Rocky, and Tom disappeared behind the chicken house with the bloodhounds in the lead.

The three men searched the whole area but came up with nothing, so John decided they would go back to the house. As they came up the path, John noticed a black sedan in the driveway. "Looks like we have company," John announced. Tom and Rocky were too tired to say anything when they arrived at the black sedan. John began to walk toward the house when a tall man wearing dark glasses stepped out to greet him. John took one look and recognized him. It was Jack Riley, FBI director, from Dallas.

"Hello, John," Jack said. "Been a long time."

"Not long enough, I'm sure," John replied.

"You sound like you're not happy to see me, John."

"I would rather tangle with a rattlesnake," John replied. "Probably a cousin of yours."

"Now, John, is that any way to talk to an old friend?" Jack asked.

John knew Jack was a dirty FBI agent who would get things done one way or another. Years ago when John was with the FBI, Jack had fired him from the agency.

"You're not still mad about that little incident that happened years ago, are you?" Jack asked.

"Wouldn't you be?" John replied.

"Well, it's a hard world we live in, John. You've got to get

THE COVERUP

with the program or be left behind, and that's what happened to you," Jack explained. "You were too soft to be an FBI agent."

"And you bend the rules a lot," John replied.

"I get things done," Jack said.

"And what is your version of what happened here, Jack?" asked John.

"Josh's neck is broken. That's how he died," Jack began. "There is a convict on the loose who has a file full of people he's killed in the same way. We think he's in this area."

"And that's your idea of what happened?" John asked.

"That's the way I see it," Jack answered.

"And what does the Judge have to say?" asked John, turning to the front porch where the Judge stood listening to the two men argue.

"That's right, John. I'm sure Josh died of a broken neck," the Judge replied. "And this convict that's on the loose could be the one who did this."

John knew it would be better to keep quiet for now and figure out what happened on his own later. The chance that anyone was going to believe him without proof was very unlikely, and John knew this to be true. The whole thing sounded so wacky that even John had trouble believing it. The best thing for him to do was back off for now and look into this thing without anyone knowing. At least they wouldn't think he was crazy if they didn't know.

THE NEXT MORNING
Chapter Five

The next morning at 8:00 a.m., John awakened to the sound of dishes banging together in the kitchen. Sitting on the side of the bed, he fumbled around on the bed stand for his cigarettes, pulled out one to light it, and stretched his arms to the dresser for his robe. As he was dressing, John's thoughts turned to what he should do next about last night's incident. He staggered off to the kitchen to get a cup of coffee. This day was not one that John was looking forward to, for he knew that the Judge and Jack were covering up something. He could see it in their eyes, tell it in their voices, and knowing their past, John knew those two were up to something.

"Morning, babe," John announced to his lovely wife, Regina, when he walked into the kitchen. He walked over and put his arms around her, kissed her neck, and staggered to the coffee machine to pour himself a cup.

"You want some breakfast, honey?" asked Regina.

"Yeah," John replied as he took his coffee cup and walked down the hall to the spare bedroom where his computer was. After pushing the on button, he leaned back in the chair and waited for it to boot up. When the computer was ready, John punched the internet key and punched in one of the animal web sites. When the web site came up, he typed the word, "Chupacabra" in the key word box. Several pages appeared on the screen in front of John, and he began to read them. Some of the information he was receiving was kind of comical, but others were interesting. John decided to print the information on paper so he could read it later. Suddenly the phone rang.

"Hello," John said as he picked up the receiver.

"Hey, John." came a voice from the phone.

"Hey, Tom. What's up?"

"What's our next move?" Tom asked. "Are you going to check out this thing further?"

"Well, I'm thinking about it," John replied.

"Have you seen the paper this morning?" Tom blurted out.

"No, I just got up," John replied.

"Well, you'd better look at it. Someone is making us look like fools," Tom answered.

"What are you talking about, Tom? Hang on a second."

As he walked into the kitchen to look for the paper, he met his wife at the door. "Your breakfast is ready," Regina said.

"Yeah, okay, hon. Where is the paper?"

"Still in the yard, I guess," Regina answered.

John stepped out the front door and into the front yard. There it was lying in the grass. John picked it up, unfolded it, and began to read the article on the front page. The further he read, the madder he got.

THE COVERUP

'The perpetrator of this hideous crime is an escaped convict named Richard Whitehead, commonly called Whitey,' the article quoted Jack Riley. 'We believe that he was in the area at the time this crime occurred and not an alien or an unknown animal like the local sheriff believes.'

John headed back into the house reading how Jack was heading a massive manhunt for this escaped convict. Jack informed the press that he would not rest until Richard Whitehead was caught or killed. John walked into the bedroom where the phone was and told Tom he would get to the bottom of this as soon as he could catch up with Jack. Then he stepped into the kitchen and sat down at the table with an empty stare.

Regina noticed that something was wrong. She walked over to where John sat staring into space and asked, "Want me to fix you a plate?"

John did not answer her, so she fixed his plate and laid it in front of him, and still he said nothing. She walked over to the other side and sat down, all the time looking at John.

"John, what is the matter?" There was still no response, so she tried again. "John!" she shouted.

Startled, John turned his eyes to Regina and handed the newspaper to her as he went back to his stare. Regina looked at him and then turned her eyes to the paper she now held in her hand. She quickly scanned the headlines and began to read the article.

"Not him again," she said. As she read the part about Jack Riley, the more she shook her head. "I thought we were rid of him when we came out here," she added. She then turned her eyes to John who was still staring into the table. "What are we going to do now?" Regina asked.

John raised his head and said, "I don't know."

Suddenly the phone rang. John walked over to the phone and picked up the receiver and said, "Hello."

"Hey, Sheriff!" screamed a voice from the phone. "Where can I find me one of those aliens?" he shouted. "Ha, ha, ha," he began to laugh.

John quickly hung up the phone and reached down to unplug it. Then he looked at Regina and said, "We'd better leave this unhooked for now." As John started to sit down, the doorbell rang. He stood up and walked over to the door and looked out the peephole and saw Tom standing at the door. John opened the door.

"Tom, get in here," John whispered as he grabbed him by the arm and pulled him into the house.

"What is going on, John?" Tom asked.

"Jack has made me look foolish in the paper. I want you to go and keep an eye on him."

"There are some reporters wanting to talk to you. Shall I get rid of them?"

"Yes, tell them I'm busy right now. Keep an eye on Jack and let me know what is going on."

"OK, Chief, I am on him like white on rice," Tom answered.

"I have to get hold of this professor at the University, and then I'll meet you at the office at noon," John said.

"All right," Tom answered as he turned and went out the door.

John headed back to the computer and began to scroll through the numerous pages on the Chupacabra. He came to an article that Professor Donner from the University of El Paso had written on the creature. At the bottom of the page was a phone number to the University. John plugged the phone back in and began to dial the number. A young lady answered.

THE COVERUP

"University of El Paso. My name is Terri. How may I help you?" she announced.

"Yeah, this is Sheriff John Barton. I need to speak to Professor Donner, please."

"OK, Sheriff, I will connect you with Professor Donner's office," the girl answered.

"Thanks," John replied. The phone began to ring as John waited.

"Hello," a voice said.

"Professor Donner, please?" John asked.

"Hold on. I will get him," the voice said.

John began to think of what he was going to say to the Professor.

"Hello, can I help you?" asked Professor Donner.

"Phil, how are you? It's John Barton."

"Johnny, how nice to hear from you. It has been a long time since I heard from you."

"Yeah, well, I am no longer with the FBI," John replied.

John had called the Professor many times when he was an FBI agent.

"Oh, really? What are you doing now?" Phil asked.

"I am with the sheriff's department in Quasar Villa now," John returned.

Professor Donner had studied fossilized prehistoric bones for years before he became a teacher at the University of El Paso. He also studied u.f.o.'s and strange creatures. John met the Professor early in his career as an FBI agent. He would call the Professor whenever he came across old bone remains or u.f.o. pictures. John knew the Professor had studied the Chupacabra years earlier.

"Well, Johnny, it is nice to hear from you," Phil said. "What can I do for you?"

"We have a farmer who claims to have seen the Chupacabra."

"Oh, really? How did he describe the creature?"

John gave the Professor the description Josh had given him the night he was killed.

"Yes, that is the exact description I always got when I interviewed individuals who claimed to have seen the creature," Phil replied. "All the cases I interviewed seemed to point toward this creature being of reality," Phil continued, "but there has been no scientific evidence to back this theory so far."

"Yeah, I would have to see one myself to believe it," John answered.

"Bring this farmer to the University so I can talk to him," Phil said.

"I can't. He is dead."

"Oh my. What happened?"

THE COVERUP

"I'm not sure. I only know that his neck was broken," John answered. "However, Jack Riley believes an escaped convict killed him. Do you think this thing could have done this?"

"That is not possible. In all my investigations, this creature has never attacked a human being," the Professor replied. "In all the interviews I have conducted, the creature has had ample opportunity to kill the individual, but did not do so."

"Never?" John asked.

"No, the alleged creature is more concerned with escape rather than killing. You see, he only kills for food. Apparently, he has a need for the blood of animals, especially for goats. That is why he is called the goat sucker."

"Maybe Jack is right. Maybe the two of them were there at the same time," John answered.

"One thing I can tell you is that Jack Riley is always around these sightings," Phil replied. "Johnny, there is a gentleman who investigates these sightings for me. I would like to send him there to help you."

"That would be great, Phil. Thanks. I owe you one."

"Richard Cooper is his name. He will be there as soon as possible," Phil said. "Richard knows as much or more than I about the Chupacabra."

"Thanks, Phil," John replied.

"OK, Johnny. Bye, now," Phil answered.

John hung up the phone, unplugged it, and started to get dressed. As soon as he was dressed, he headed for the kitchen. He stopped to inform Regina that he would get to the bottom of this and for her not to worry about it. He grabbed the car keys, and as he was headed out the door, he kissed her on the cheek and told her not to talk to anyone about it.

John arrived at the office, only to find it swarming with reporters and concerned citizens. He quickly drove to the back and entered the office. As he walked into the room, his secretary, Sue Brock, said good morning to him. She then relayed the messages that he had received and informed him that a Jack Riley had called looking for him. John informed Sue not to tell Jack anything, just to tell him she did not know. John sat down at his desk and looked over his messages. He looked up at Sue who was staring at him.

"All right, I will tell you," John said. He began to explain the events that happened the day before and how Jack was trying to set him up to keep him from the truth.

"Josh is dead?" Sue asked.

John told Sue not to worry. There was no killer running about loose. He knew she would believe him over some stranger from out of town.

"See if you can reach Tom on the radio, and tell him there is a group of reporters here asking questions," John said. "Tell him to come to the office and handle the situation, but don't tell him I'm here."

Sue nodded her head. "Yes, sir." Then she stepped out of the room toward the dispatch radio to call Tom and relay the message.

John stood up from his chair and walked over to the coffee machine to pour himself a cup. He returned to his seat, lit a cigarette, and began to think about the events that happened the day before.

First he thought of how he had found Josh lying in the floor. He hadn't seen any visible evidence that Josh had been attacked by the creature. Then there was the house, how it

THE COVERUP

was torn apart, as if someone was looking for something. Now this could indicate someone breaking into the house, killing Josh, and rummaging through the house for weapons, food, or valuables. Then he thought about the chicken house, the hole in the wall, the footprints in the chicken yard, the scratches on the outside wall of the chicken house, and not to mention the dog, dead in the front yard. John remembered the phone call he had received from Josh. Josh had told him about the dog being dead, and the hole in the chicken house, and had given him a description of this creature all before he was killed. Could there have been two attacks that night, one by the creature, another by the escaped convict? Then there was Jack. Why was he always around these sightings, what was he up to, or what was he hiding? And what about the Chupacabra? Was this a real animal or a figment of peoples' imaginations? Suddenly John remembered something that happened that night which hadn't crossed his mind since. "The Judge," John whispered. Then he stepped out of his office and asked Sue if she had contacted Tom yet.

"Yes," she said. "He's on his way now, Sheriff."

"Thanks." John replied as he turned and went back into his office and sat down behind his desk.

Around 12:30 p.m., Tom arrived and ran into the Sheriff's office.

"John!" he shouted at the top of his voice. "They caught him. Jack's taking him to El Paso."

"You mean the convict, they caught him?"

"Yeah, Jack's taking him to the sheriff office in El Paso," Tom said. "His name is Richard Whitehead, that's what Jack called him."

"So, there really was a convict on the loose," John replied.

"It appears so."

"Tell me something, Tom. Did you notice anything odd about this guy?"

"Well, I thought he was very clean for someone who had been hiding in the woods."

"Tom, this is very important. The night we were out at Josh's farm, did you get hold of the Judge?"

"No, I told you the Judge was already on his way."

"Well, how did the Judge find out?"

"That's a good question."

John stood there pondering the situation while Tom looked on. "What does that mean?" Tom asked.

"I don't know," John replied.

"Sheriff, Wayne Faulkner calling on line one!" Sue shouted.

"Thanks," said John as he headed to the phone and picked up the receiver. "Hey, Wayne, what's up?"

"Hello, John. I got a calf out here that's been shot in the neck a couple of times."

"Did you see anyone around, Wayne?"

"No. Funny thing, though, there didn't seem to be any blood around."

"OK, Wayne, we'll be out as soon as we can. Don't touch anything."

"OK, Sheriff."

John hung up the phone, and then he and Tom started talking about everything he had thought of earlier. Tom agreed

THE COVERUP

on every little detail that John mentioned. He even came up with a few of his own, like the footprints. One pair of footprints was all they found, and unless he was wearing a pair of funny shoes, they did not belong to the convict, Richard Whitehead. Then there were the dogs. They never did pick up on a scent the whole time they were there.

"Get the squad car and bring it around back," John told Tom. "I will meet you there, and we'll go out to Faulkner's Ranch." Tom dashed out of the office and headed for the car.

THE FAULKNER RANCH
Chapter Six

It was two-thirty p.m. when John and Tom arrived at the Faulkner Ranch. They met with Wayne Faulkner, the owner, and his ranch foreman, Wayne's brother, Joe Faulkner.

"Hey, John," Wayne greeted.

"Where's the calf?" John asked.

"Over on the west end of the ranch," Wayne answered. "Come on. I've got a jeep waiting for us."

"Good, let's go," John replied.

The four of them walked to the back of the house and climbed into the jeep waiting for them. As they drove across the pastureland, John noticed Wayne had a lot of land. There must have been three or four thousand acres. Wayne Faulkner and Joe were the richest men in the area. They owned most of the land around Quasar Villa. Most of their riches came from their father, John Faulkner, who had settled there back in the thirties. Big John Faulkner had a lot of money, and he spent it wisely when he moved there. Big John, as he was often called, was six feet, seven inches tall, and two hundred fifty pounds. He was, however, a very nice man, who liked to mingle with the little people. He was the kind of man who would sit down at a bar and drink beer with just about anybody. John had settled here with his young wife, Maria, and started buying all the land around the farm. Maria was a Mexican girl John met in El Paso when he was a Colonel in the U. S. Army. She was a very happy woman, and all the people in and around Quasar Villa, Texas loved her. Wayne and Joe were a bit quieter when it came to socializing. The two brothers kept to themselves most of the time. Every now and then, they would step out and visit with the local residents. They did, however, throw parties, mostly holiday gatherings and church socials and a few birthday parties. Mostly, they stayed on the ranch working with the many horses they owned. Wayne and Joe liked to train cutting horses and sell them to the highest bidder, and they raised a few cattle as well.

"How many cows have you got now, Wayne?" John asked.

"Oh, we have about twenty-five hundred, depending on how many calves hit the ground last night," Wayne answered.

"Oh, really?"

"Really," Wayne replied.

"How does it feel to be that rich?" John asked.

"Real good," Wayne answered, while making a funny eyebrow move like Groucho Marks.

"I could only imagine," John replied. "What's that over there?" he asked as he pointed toward a building in the distance.

"That is our grain plant. We grow our own corn and make our own feed. We've got a lot of stock to feed, you know."

They drove on across the pastureland heading for a wooded section of the ranch. Wayne explained to John that the calf

THE COVERUP

was in the woods. That's where he found the calf earlier this morning, in the same woods they were headed. Wayne drove the jeep down a small hill and across a creek, down a path that led into the woods. As they entered the woods, Wayne turned the jeep to the right and drove through the woods until he came to a clearing. He stopped the jeep, stepped out, and turned to John and said, "Over here in the bushes is where I found him."

John stepped out of the jeep and walked behind Wayne as they headed toward some bushes in front of them. Joe and Tom followed a bit behind them, cautiously looking for snakes. As they broke through the bushes, Wayne pointed to the calf lying on the ground in front of them. John knelt down beside the dead calf and pulled back the fur to look at the holes.

"Tom, give me your pocket knife," he said.

Tom pulled out his knife and handed it to John. John took the knife and began to probe the holes on the other side. John looked up at Wayne with a confused look on his face. "I don't think these holes are bullet wounds, Wayne," John said.

"You're probably right," Wayne replied. "Your creature, right?"

"You know about that?" John asked.

"Saw the creature myself once," Wayne began to explain. "It was about two years ago, close to these same woods. Yeah, I know about it, read it in the paper," he continued.

"You never told me you saw this thing," John said as he stood up.

"Didn't tell me, either," Joe added.

"Sorry, Joe. I didn't want you to think I was crazy or something," Wayne replied.

"Well, tell us what happened," Tom said.

Wayne cleared his throat and began to tell a story about what happened. It was a warm summer night about two years ago. Wayne was having a hard time sleeping, so he got out of bed and went downstairs. He decided to go for a ride on one of his four wheelers and maybe take a look at his cows at two o'clock in the morning. Maybe this would tire him out enough so he could sleep or at least get his mind off his problems. He started the bike and drove off into the dark. Wayne was known for his spur of the moment antics. He headed for the pastureland and drove the bike out into the middle of his herd. The cows paid little attention to the bike. They were used to it. Wayne always rode the bike when he checked on the herd. He turned off the bike and sat enjoying the clear night. There was a full moon that night. You could see real well. The ground was lit up all around as Wayne sat there watching the calves stare at the four-wheeler in somewhat confusion.

Suddenly, as he watched one of the calves jump about, the creature swooped down and grabbed the calf and flew off into the dark sky. Wayne sat there confused as to what just happened. He rubbed his eyes in case he was seeing things that didn't happen. Then he became angry and confused at the same time. He started thinking of what it was that just carried off one of his calves. Suddenly he realized, from all the stories he had heard, that must have been El Chupacabra, and that made him even madder. Then he realized something even scarier than the calf being carried off. He was out here all alone. His anger turned to fear, as he jumped on the bike and took off

THE COVERUP

in a hurry. Constantly, he looked back to see if the thing was chasing him as he rode the bike back to the ranch house. Once there, he jumped off the bike and ran into the house, barely taking time to open the door. Inside, Wayne quickly went to his office and pulled a 44 magnum from his desk and went to the living room. As he walked into the room, he opened the revolver to make sure it was loaded. He sat down in his favorite chair, shaking like a scared rabbit. Sweat was running down his face as he constantly watched the door and the windows. When morning came, he was sleeping in his chair. Melissa came downstairs and found him sitting there with that gun in his lap. She became frightened at the scene she was witnessing. She began to shake Wayne to wake him up. Wayne, groggy at first, quickly grabbed the gun lying in his lap. Then he realized it was Melissa. He laid the gun down and looked up at Melissa and told her not to ask. She never did nor did she worry. Melissa knew that Wayne would have a good reason for doing something like this. There was no reason for her to question him.

"Well, that's some story, Wayne," John remarked.

"Yeah, how come you never told me that story?" Joe asked.

"Well, I didn't want you to worry about me. Besides I wasn't sure it actually happened," Wayne confusingly replied. Joe started to walk away.

"Joe!" Wayne cried as Joe was headed for the jeep.

"I'm very disappointed that you couldn't tell me about this. I'm your brother. You can tell me anything. I would have believed you," Joe said as he turned to face Wayne.

"Okay, let's go. I think I have seen enough," John remarked.

Tom and Joe hopped into the back seat of the jeep, and Wayne slipped behind the wheel.

"I want all of you to keep what we saw and heard today to ourselves," said John as he walked up to the passenger side of the jeep. "No sense everybody getting into trouble like me." They all agreed to not say anything until John found out what was going on with this creature.

John was afraid that people would get paranoid if they heard about this creature. Until he had proof, there was no way he could confirm that the creature even existed. John climbed into the jeep and they headed back to the ranch house. When they arrived at the ranch house, John reminded them not to say anything. They again agreed not to say anything about the creature.

THE ARRIVAL OF RICHARD COOPER
Chapter Seven

Tom and John walked over to the police car and climbed in. Tom got behind the wheel and started the motor. "Where are we going now, John?" Tom curiously asked.

"Back to the office," John quickly replied. Tom drove the car down the driveway and turned onto the highway toward town.

"Base calling Sheriff Barton," came a voice on the police radio. "Base calling Sheriff Barton. Come in." It was Sue calling John on the police radio.

"Barton here. What is it Sue?" John asked as he picked up the microphone.

"Jack Riley is looking for you. I told him I didn't know where you were at this time."

"Okay, thanks, Sue."

"Also, your wife is trying to get a hold of you," Sue returned.

"Yeah, I'll call her as soon as I get back. We are on our way back now," John replied.

"Ten-four, Sheriff."

John hung up the microphone and looked at Tom. "You know, this thing with Jack could get ugly," he remarked. "If you wanted to bow out or something, I could say you went on vacation."

WILLIAM DANIEL

"No way. I'm sticking with you on this," Tom replied.

"Okay, but don't say I didn't offer," John remarked.

Upon arrival at the office, they noticed that Jack was nowhere to be seen. They stepped out of the car and headed for the door to the office. John walked in first with Tom right behind him. He walked over to Sue's desk. "Sue, would you get my wife on the phone, please?" John asked politely.

"Sure thing, Sheriff," Sue replied.

Suddenly the door to the office opened. In stepped a short man with a scraggly beard, wire-framed glasses, and curly blonde hair. He walked over to where John stood staring at him.

"Can you tell me where I can find Sheriff John Barton?" he asked.

John looked at him from his dirty tennis shoes to his curly blonde hair.

"Who are you?" he asked.

"Richard Cooper is the name," the stranger answered.

"What do you want? We are kind of busy here, sir," John asked.

"Well, I'm looking for Sheriff Barton. Professor Donner told me to get in touch with him. Do you know where I might find him?" Richard asked.

"Oh, yeah. I'm John Barton. The Professor said you would be coming," John replied.

38

THE COVERUP

"Nice to meet you, Sheriff," Richard said as he shook his hand.

"Yeah, the same here. So you work for Professor Donner?"

"No, actually I'm a crypto-zoologist. Professor Donner calls me to check out strange encounters of unknown species," Richard answered. "I'm kind of a private investigator."

"Oh, they must call you a private dick," John sarcastically replied with a grin on his face. Richard started laughing with this funny little giggle.

"Well, I've never heard it quite put that way, but I guess I am a private dick," he answered.

"Sheriff, I have your wife on the phone!" Sue shouted.

"Okay, thanks Sue," John replied. "Have a seat in my office, Richard, and I will be with you in a minute." He walked over and took the call on Sue's phone. He told Regina that he would be on his way home soon. Regina told him that Jack had been there looking for him. She did not tell him where to find him. John figured that Jack would be looking for him all day. Before the day was out he would see him. He informed Regina not to worry about Jack Riley. He would probably be leaving soon. John hung the phone up and went into his office where Richard was waiting for him. As he walked into the room, he closed the door behind him, went over to his desk, and sat down in his chair.

"What do you need first?" John asked.

"First, tell me everything that you know and don't leave out anything," Richard said.

John began with the phone call he had received from Josh the night he was killed. He told him about the description Josh had given him and about his old dog, Bull, being killed. Then he got to the chicken house. He told him about the scratches

39

on the wall, plus the footprints in the chicken yard. He then got to Jack Riley and the Judge. He explained what happened there. Then there was the escaped convict that Jack supposedly caught that might have killed Josh. Richard asked how Josh was killed, and John told him his neck was broken. Then he asked if anyone else saw the creature that night.

"No," John told him, "Josh was the only one to see this thing that night. However, there is a rancher who saw it about two years ago." John told Richard about the calf, which he just saw out at the Faulkner Ranch earlier in the day. He explained how it looked like the calf lost all its blood. It had holes in its neck about the size of a pencil.

"So, what do you think?" John asked

"First, I would like to go out to the Hernandez Farm and take a look before I make any comments about the case," Richard replied.

"Okay, how about first thing in the morning?"

"That will be fine. Now can you tell me where I can find a decent hotel and a good restaurant?"

"You can stay at my house. My wife is a very good cook."

"I don't want to be a burden."

"Nonsense. We would love to have you," John replied as he picked up the phone and dialed his house.

"Well, if it's not an inconvenience."

"Not a problem. Hey babe, I've got a gentleman, Richard Cooper, here who's going to stay with us," John said as Regina answered the phone.

"I'll get the guest room ready," Regina replied.

"Great. See you soon," John said as he hung up the phone. Then he got up from his desk and motioned for Richard to follow him. As he walked out of his office, he turned to Sue and told her to lock up. Then he told Tom to give them a ride to his house. When he turned to the front door, it opened. A young man stepped in the door holding a large envelope and a clipboard.

WILLIAM DANIEL

THE COVERUP

THE MEETING WITH JACK RILEY
Chapter Eight

Hello. Can you tell me where I can find Sheriff Barton?" the young man asked.

"That would be me," John replied. He reached out for the envelope and the young man handed him the clipboard, showing him where to sign. John took the clipboard and started to look for a pen. The young man pulled a pen from his pocket and handed it to John.

"Here, use this one," the young man said. John took the pen and signed the clipboard. He started to hand back the pen to the young man.

"Keep it," the young man said. Then he turned and walked out the door quickly.

"Wonder what this is?" John asked as he opened the package. John pulled out a report and began to read it.

"What is it?" Richard curiously asked.

"It's the coroner's report on Josh," John replied. He read the report and handed it to Richard for him to read it.

"Read it for yourself. It says Josh died of a broken neck," John said.

"Yeah, it also says your man was very drunk," Richard remarked.

"What? Josh doesn't drink," John replied.

"According to this, it says he was dead drunk. He had a four point zero alcohol level. He must have been dead before he was killed," Richard remarked as he read the report.

John was somewhat confused. He knew that Josh didn't drink much, if any at all. About that time, the front door opened again. This time it was Jack Riley who walked in the door.

"Hello, Richard. It's no surprise that you are here. On another bug hunt, are you?"

"Funny how I'm always running into you, Jack."

"Not funny to me, bug hunter."

"Have you two met?" John sarcastically asked.

"I sent the prisoner to the Macon County jail house," Jack said.

"What? Our jail too small for you, Jack?" John asked.

"Well, I wouldn't want him to get eaten by a fictitious bug. Besides you and Barney Fife here might let him get away," Jack replied as he took the pen from John's hand and placed it in his shirt pocket. John motioned for Tom to stay so he wouldn't hit Jack and get himself into trouble.

"See you around, John," Jack said as he turned and walked out the door.

"Well, that was pleasant," Richard remarked

"About as pleasant as a visit with a rattlesnake," John replied.

"I think I would like to see the Hernandez farm now, if you don't mind," Richard said. John agreed, as did Tom.

The three men got into the squad car and headed for the Hernandez farm. As they were driving down the road, John kept asking questions about how Richard met Jack. Richard told him that Jack always seemed to be around when he was investigating a sighting of El Chupacabra. Richard told him he would explain the whole thing later.

WILLIAM DANIEL

THE COVERUP

INVESTIGATING THE HERNANDEZ FARM
Chapter Nine

When they arrived at the Hernandez farm, they turned and drove up the driveway to the house. Tom noticed the dog was gone from the front yard. The three men got out of the car and headed for the house. As they entered the house, John remarked how it looked the same as the night that Josh was killed. Tom looked around the room and agreed with John. They searched through the house room by room. Nothing seemed to indicate to Richard that El Chupacabra had been there.

"Well, let's take a look at the chicken house," John said. They left the house and headed for the chicken house.

"Wait till you see this," Tom remarked. Along the way they stopped at the place where Bull was lying the last time they saw him.

"I wonder what they did with Bull?" John asked.

"Maybe someone buried him," Tom remarked.

"Maybe, but who and why?" John asked.

They turned and walked to the chicken house. Tom opened the door. John and Richard stepped inside the chicken house.

"Where is the hole that was in the wall?" John quickly asked as he pointed to the wall on their left. The hole in the wall was gone. It was like it was never there.

47

"What the hell is going on here?" shouted Tom as he stood at the door. He turned and looked outside and noticed a black sedan parked on the road in front of the farm.

"Don't look now, but I think we are being watched," he said as he turned and looked at John.

John walked over to the door and looked outside. "I don't see anyone," he said as he turned to Tom.

"Where did he go?" Tom curiously asked. "There was a black sedan parked out on the road in front of the farm."

"Well, he's gone now," John replied.

"Say, fellows, come here," Richard commanded. John and Tom walked over to the wall where Richard was standing.

"What?" John asked.

"These boards are the same as the others, only if you would notice, they have new nails in them," Richard explained. These were the same boards where the hole was when Tom and John were there before.

"Somebody replaced these boards," Richard said.

"Why would they do that?" John asked.

"To cover up what really happened, that's why," Richard replied. "Let's go. I don't think we are going to find any evidence here. They have covered it up."

The three men went back to the car and got in. Richard suggested that they go see the calf before it got dark. John told him that Jack didn't know about the calf because it was never reported. Only John, Tom, Wayne, and Joe knew about the calf. Nobody else was informed.

"Let's go home, get something to eat, and get a good night's rest, and then get a fresh start in the morning," John said. They all agreed.

Tom drove them to John's house, and John and Richard got out. John told Tom to pick them up first thing in the morning, and for him to stay away from Jack. He and Richard headed for the house and Regina met them at the door.

John introduced Richard to Regina and asked what was for supper before he sat down in the living room. Regina told them supper was ready.

"I hope you like roast beef," she said to Richard.

"I love roast beef," Richard replied. "Where can I wash up?" he asked.

"Down the hall, first door on the left," she replied.

John got up from his chair and walked into the kitchen with Regina. Richard headed down the hall to the bathroom to wash up, stopping for a moment to look at a painting on the wall in the hall. In the kitchen, John gave Regina a big hug and a kiss and asked how her day was.

"Fine, with the exception of having to see Jack again," she said.

John apologized to her. He didn't think that Jack would come there to look for him. Then he went to the cabinet and pulled out the plates for them to eat on. Regina placed the food on the table and pulled out a bottle of wine. She gave it to John and told him to open it while she got out the wine glasses. John went to the cabinet and got the wine opener and began to screw it into the cork on the wine bottle. Richard walked into the kitchen about the same time John popped the cork on the wine. John told him to sit at the end of the table as he began to pour his wine.

"Thank you," he said. "Mrs. Barton, this food smells delicious."

"Well, thank you, Richard. I hope you like it," she replied.

"Let's eat," John said.

They filled their plates and began to eat the food Regina had fixed for them.

"This roast is delicious," Richard proclaimed.

"Do you really like it?" Regina asked.

"Yes, I haven't had roast beef this good since my mother died," Richard replied. "See, I'm always on the go, so I don't eat much home cooking, mostly restaurant food, or I'll make myself a sandwich to take with me."
"When did your mother die?" Regina asked.

"Mom died about three years ago," Richard replied.

"Oh, I'm sorry," Regina, said.

"No, it's okay. She was very old," Richard said.

John decided to change the subject. The conversation became more personal.

"How did you become a private investigator of strange creatures?" John asked.

"That's funny I like that, strange creatures," Richard replied. "Well, I guess you might say that I had a close encounter of El Chupacabra once, about ten years ago."

THE COVERUP

RICHARD TELLS HIS STORY
Chapter Ten

Richard began to tell the story of his life, beginning with the time he got out of high school. He moved around to different places looking for his life's ambition, a place where he could be happy, and still be himself. One day after he had been in California, he met this girl who was an anthropologist studying under Professor Donner. She was so cute that Richard could not resist being around her, so he enrolled in college under Professor Donner. He wasn't interested in anthropology; he was only interested in this girl. Her name was Helen Drake, and he was crazy about her. She was only interested in anthropology, and in order to get close to her, he had to excel in the class. He dated her for about a year, and then one day she disappeared. He never saw her again. She had been seeing a football player who graduated and was picked by the Dallas Cowboys in the NFL draft. He had called her and asked her to marry him, and she did. I mean, why not? He was a football player. He decided to stick with the classes, and he found that he liked it. Professor Donner was a nice man and he learned a lot from him. He was on a dig down in Mexico one day when he discovered some ancient Indians. He spent about three months trying to excavate the bodies from the site. One night he could not go to sleep, so he returned to the dig in the middle of the night. While digging that night, he decided to take a nap, so he turned off the lights to get some

51

rest. He lay down on a blanket right where he was digging for the Indians and fell asleep. About two hours later, he heard a noise and rose from the blanket to see what was going on. Right before his eyes was this creature sucking blood out of a goat. Richard froze. He didn't know what it was at the time, and he was afraid he would scare it away. He stood there looking at it in the dim light from the full moon. As he stood there looking at it in great awe, he was wondering what this creature was. Then it hit him. The four foot structure, the wings, the pale gray skin, the claws, and those sharp blood-sucking fangs... There was no doubt, from all the stories he had heard down here, it was El Chupacabra. He didn't believe in those stories. To him it was a lot of folklore nonsense. But seeing the thing himself, he believed in those stories now. The creature finished with its meal, and started looking around until its gaze came upon Richard. It folded out its wings and flew off into the moonlit night. He knew right then this was his dream-come-true. This was his destiny, the thing he was looking for all his life, to be a part of the growing number of people who had the privilege of seeing El Chupacabra. That was when his life changed into being a crypto zoologist investigator. He followed up on every story he came across, hoping one day he could prove it existed.

"That is what I have been doing ever since," Richard finished.

"What do you think it is?" John asked.

"There was a story that came out years ago about an alien space craft that crashed in New Mexico," Richard began. "There were four aliens that were found. Three were dead, the other one was alive."

"You think that this is the alien?" John asked.

THE COVERUP

"Yes, I do," Richard replied. "But that happened about fifty years ago."

"Could this thing be alive today?" John asked.

"We are talking about aliens. Who knows how long they live," Richard replied.

"Sounds a bit far fetched to me," John returned.

"Not really, listen to this," Richard said. He began to tell the stories that he had dug up over the years. In 1947 an alien spacecraft crashed in New Mexico. The soldiers that were the first to arrive at the site saw dead bodies lying around and one little alien running around holding a box and screaming. One of the soldiers hit the little alien with the butt of his rifle to shut him up. There were parts of the ship scattered all about, but the main part of the ship was embedded in the side of a hill. It was reported to the American public that the army had recovered an alien spacecraft. The army released this information shortly after it happened. Later it was changed to a weather balloon. They even showed pictures of the balloon. But soldiers who were there told a different story to their relatives. Richard had interviewed a woman whose father was one of the first soldiers to arrive at the scene. She told him what her father had told her about what he saw. According to him, there was an alien spacecraft that had crashed in the desert that night. There were alien bodies lying around. He had picked up some of the spacecraft that was scattered about and stuck it into his pocket. When he got home, he brought this stuff out and showed it to her mother. There was a tin foil-like substance that he showed her. It looked like tin foil, but you could not cut it with a knife or a pair of scissors. She said her father tried

WILLIAM DANIEL

to cut it and could not penetrate the material. He then wadded it up into a ball, but when he released it, the material folded back into its original form.

There was a piece of the ship that looked like a small metal beam, about the size of a ruler. It had these raised figures on it like the Egyptians put on their walls. Only they were different. The beam itself was light as a feather and stronger than steel, in the same size portion. Her father tried to bend it, but he couldn't. He took a hammer and tried to bend it that way, but the beam would not bend. This woman saw these things when she was a little girl. The next day the cover up began to unfold. The report about the spaceship turned into a weather balloon, and the pieces were picked up before anyone else saw them. The ranch owner who found it first was told to keep his mouth shut. He never told anyone anything about what he saw out there that day. The pieces of the ship that her father had kept somehow disappeared, and she never saw them again. This man came to their house and told them they did not see anything, and if they told anyone, they would take them out into the desert where no one would ever find them.

There were other accounts of the events that happened that night. "There wasn't any evidence of El Chupacabra before the so-called Roswell incident," Richard noted.

"So you think that this alien who survived the crash is El Chupacabra?" John asked.

"There's more," Richard replied.

A man Richard met some years ago told him a story that was totally unbelievable. The Government had a team working on the spacecraft that crashed in New Mexico. According to him, they uncovered evidence linking these aliens to the beginning of man. They found records of a monkey that these aliens were using as slaves to dig minerals from earth. The

THE COVERUP

females of the species were often used for sexual favors by the aliens. The monkey they were referring to was the legendary Big Foot. When they did the autopsy on the dead alien bodies, they found the same organs that we have. All evidence points to this possibly being the origin of man's existence on earth. A team of geologists searching for geo rocks in California found a round rock that had an electrical device inside of it. This rock was found to be millions of years old, a long time before man existed here on earth.

"I believe that El Chupacabra is the link to this theory," Richard said.

"So this is why Jack is always around when El Chupacabra is seen?" John asked.

"Yes, I think he is covering up the tracks of El Chupacabra," Richard replied.

"Well, I don't doubt it," John answered. "Jack's the kind of person to do something like that."

John got up from the table to get the wine. He picked up Regina's glass and began to fill her glass with wine. He reached over to Richard's glass and filled it for him. He sat back down and filled his own glass before continuing to eat his supper.

"What about Josh?" John asked. "Do you think Jack had anything to do with his death?"

"I don't know, but I would love to talk to that convict he arrested," Richard replied.

"Yeah, me too. Let's go talk to him tomorrow," John answered. "First, however, I want you to see the calf, and then we will go to El Paso."

"Where is the calf?" Richard asked.

John told Richard where the calf was located and what he should expect to see when he got there. He explained how he measured the holes with a pencil, and how he probed the holes for a bullet, but found nothing. Then he told him about Wayne seeing the creature some time back.

"So, the creature has visited Wayne's ranch more than once," Richard figured. "If the creature has been there more than once, there's a good chance he could return tonight."

John thought it might be a bad idea to visit Wayne in the middle of the night. Wayne would gladly lend them his jeep, or take them himself.

"Let's wait until morning, and we can tell him we are coming," John said.

"There's no need to call him at all. We will be in and out before he realizes we have been there," Richard replied. "Don't worry about getting there. I have better transportation."

"Yeah, like what?" John asked.

"Trust me," Richard answered.

John gave in to Richard's demands and agreed to go along. Richard told John to call Tom over to give them a ride. John looked at Regina and shrugged his shoulders as he picked up the phone receiver. He dialed the number and waited for him to answer.

"Hello," came Tom's voice on the receiver.

"Tom, bring the car. We are going now," John said.

"Now?"

"That's right, we're going now."

THE COVERUP

"Okay, I'll be there as soon as I can."

John hung up the phone and walked over to Regina and gave her a hug. "All right with you if I go out and play?" John asked.

"Do I have a choice?" Regina asked.

John looked over at Richard who shook his head, no.

"Guess not," John replied, "and don't wait up for me either."

"Well, in that case, I guess you can go, but please be careful, okay?" Regina said.

John walked over to the table and picked up the bottle of wine. He looked at Richard. "How about one more before we go?" he asked as he poured the wine into his glass.

"None for me. I'm driving," Richard replied.

John downed the glass of wine like it was water. He walked over to the cabinet and opened the door and reached in to retrieve a pack of cigarettes.

"Is there anything we need to bring with us?" John asked.

"No, I have everything we will need," Richard replied.

Richard looked over at Regina and smiled. "Don't worry, I'll take care of him," he told her.

"Thanks," she replied.

"Say, I don't mean to pry, but I noticed that you have a lot of toys in your yard. Only, I don't see any kids," Richard remarked.

"Yes, the kids are staying at my parents' house for a while," Regina answered.

"Grandparents are wonderful when you have kids, aren't they?"

"Yes, they give you some relief from all the screaming,"

"What are their names, if I may ask?"

"Well, let's see. There's John, Jr. He's eight years old, and Jenny, our little one, she's five years old."

"That would account for all the toys in your yard."

"Well, they are a handful, but we love them."

"I'll bet they are. I hope I get to meet them before I leave."

A horn began to blow outside John's house. It was Tom in the squad car. "Tom's here, let's go," John announced. "Sweetheart, I will see you later."

John and Richard headed for the door, grabbing their coats in case the night air became cool. Richard turned to Regina as he was heading out the door and thanked her for a delicious dinner. John walked out the door behind Richard and shut the door behind him.

Richard had walked to the car and was climbing into the back seat when John arrived at the car. Tom pulled the car out of park and backed out of the driveway. "Where to, boss?" Tom asked.

"I don't know. Richard, where are we going?" John asked.

"Okay, do you know where the Greene farm is?" Richard asked.

"You mean Johnny Greene's farm? Yeah, I know where it is," Tom replied.

"That's where we are going," Richard said.

Tom turned the car onto the highway and headed south to a farm road called Greene Road.

"Why the Greene farm?" John asked.

"You will see when we get there," Richard replied.

WILLIAM DANIEL

THE GREENE FARM
Chapter Eleven

After a few miles down the highway, Tom turned the car onto Greene Road. He drove the car down the road for a couple of miles before turning into the Greene farm driveway.

"Does Johnny know we are coming?" John asked.

"I told him that I might be back late at night," Richard replied. "Turn into the first gate you come to."

"Do you know Johnny Greene?" Tom asked.

"Well, let's just say he's a recent acquaintance of mine," Richard answered.

Johnny Greene, a Mexican American, was a co-owner of Greene's Farm. His farm produces six percent of the produce sold in the surrounding area. He also grows 70 percent of the corn that is made into flour tortillas, a food that is used in Mexican restaurants in south Texas. They also make corn tortillas, corn meal, and sell the shucks to make tamales. He employs some fifty percent of the Mexican Americans in the county and runs his own airport. He has three airplanes and employs four pilots who fly the planes used to dust the crops on his farm. Johnny Greene's father, a Mexican immigrant, moved to Texas in 1958. He settled here in Quasar Villa and built the Greene farm, which was a small shack at the time. He had six kids, five girls, and one boy. Together they built this farm to what it is now. Johnny took over the farm in 1989 when his father died of cancer. His five sisters married and moved away but still own part of the farm. Johnny sends them their percentage of the farm income every month. He owns fifty percent of the farm and runs the farm himself, along with fifteen Mexican Americans.

Tom turned the squad car into the first gate. As he drove down the road he headed for a large building. He stopped by a guard walking toward them. Tom rolled down the window as the guard walked up to the car.

"Good evening," Tom said as the guard stooped down to look in the car. He was holding a shotgun in his hands. He was poised to use it if necessary. This was part of Johnny's security measures since the fall of the New York City Twin Towers. Security measures have been beefed up to assure that terrorists would not tamper with the food he sells. Johnny may be a Mexican American, but in his heart he was a true American patriot.

"What are you doing here, gringos?" the guard asked.

"Deputy Tom Bowman and Sheriff John Barton. We have a passenger that asked us to bring him here," Tom replied.

"Who is this passenger visiting the Greene farm this late at night, and what is the nature of his visit?" the guard asked.

"I will handle this, Tom," Richard said as he leaned forward to speak to the guard.

John looked out of his window on the passenger side of the squad car. He saw a figure standing on the other side of the fence holding a shotgun pointed at his window. It was another guard who was motioning to another guard to move up to the back of the car.

"Yes, please handle it, Richard, before we all get shot by a bunch of trigger-happy guards!" John said abruptly.

THE COVERUP

"Don't worry, I'm on top of it," Richard replied. Richard leaned toward the window as far as he could so he could see who the guard was.

"Uh, Manuel, is that you?" Richard asked. "It is I, Richard Cooper, you know, the owner of the bird."

Manuel looked into the back seat of the car and shined his flashlight.

"Oh, si, Senor Cooper, I'm so sorry. I did not see you back there," Manuel said.

"That's okay, Manuel," Richard replied.

Manuel stood up and ordered the other guards to return to their posts. Then he stuck his head back into the car window to talk to Richard.

"Senor Cooper, you come for your bird?" Manuel asked.

"Yes, I did," Richard answered.

"Senor Cooper, your bird, she is in good shape. I watched it very close for you," Manual said.

"Thank you, Manuel, I really appreciate that," Richard replied.

"Oh, and the men and I would like to thank you for the case of beer you gave us," Manuel returned, "and I hope you don't mind we took some pictures of ourselves beside your bird."

"That's okay, Manuel. Uh, you didn't touch anything, did you?" Richard asked.

"No, we just took the picture and looked at it. We no touch it, though," Manuel replied.

"Good. May we come in now? We are kinda in a hurry," Richard asked.

"Oh, si," Manuel said as he ran over to the gate and let them in. Tom drove the car through the gate and down the driveway leading to the hanger. When Tom turned the corner to get in front of the building, he noticed a helicopter sitting in the runway.

"Gentlemen, there is my bird," Richard announced.

John and Tom stared at the helicopter for several seconds, and John turned to Richard and said, "Lot of money in the private eye business."

"Actually, I paid for that on my own," Richard replied.

"Are you rich or did someone die and give it to you?" Tom asked.

"Actually, yes I am," Richard replied.

Richard's father had left him a great deal of money when he died, and he was very rich. He made all his money in steel production and wire hangers. Richard did not want to run a big corporation, so he sold the family business and made off with a lot of money.

"Well, gentlemen, shall we fly?" Richard asked.

"I can't go up in that thing," John said. John was afraid of flying in an airplane, but helicopters do not look like a flying machine to him. The problem he had with a helicopter was the blades that rotate above the machine. If these blades should stop while you are flying, the machine will fall straight to the ground. With an airplane, you have the wings you can at least glide to the ground. In a helicopter, you're going to fall with no way to stop or control it.

"Trust me, it's safer than a car," Richard told him.

"Are you kidding? That thing could fall out of the sky! You can't even jump with a parachute!" John screamed.

"It's not going to fall out of the sky," Richard answered. "I have flown all over the U.S.A. and I have never had a crash landing."

Richard had logged about 25,000 hours in a helicopter. He also had logged about 15,000 hours in an airplane. Being rich had its advantages, and Richard had taken advantage of every opportunity that he could. First he took flying lessons and received his pilot license, and then he bought himself an airplane. After a few years flying all over the place, he decided to learn to fly a helicopter. He bought himself a helicopter and hired a retired helicopter pilot to teach him how to fly it. The helicopter proved to be more efficient in the field. He could fly just about anywhere and land without a runway.

"Come on. You will like it," Richard said.

"I'll go, but I won't like it," John replied.

John turned to Tom and told him to go back and keep an eye on things in town. He and Richard headed for the helicopter while Tom turned the car around and left. Richard walked over to his helicopter and opened the door. He climbed into the craft and told John to get in on the other side. John walked to the other side and opened the door before climbing in. Richard started flipping on switches all over the helicopter. Then he turned a key that started the blades to turn very slow, and then they started to turn faster. Suddenly the blades started to move even faster as the motor started to run. Richard put headphones on John's head and another pair on his head.

"Now, we will be able to talk over the noise of the engine," Richard told him. "We are going to be flying low to the ground, so don't get nervous."

"Are you sure this thing won't fall?" John asked.

After laughing a few seconds, Richard assured him it would be okay. The blades on the helicopter started to turn even faster as the engine got louder. Then the craft began to lift off the ground, straight up into the night sky. As the helicopter got off the ground, Richard turned the lights on to see where he was going.

"Which way to the Faulkner ranch?" he asked.

WILLIAM DANIEL

THE COVERUP

THE FLIGHT TO THE FAULKNER RANCH
Chapter Twelve

John pointed, and Richard flew the helicopter in that direction. The craft hummed like a fine tuned machine as they flew into the dark sky. John held onto his seat with a vise-like grip and closed his eyes.

"I take it you have never flown in a helicopter before," Richard said.

"No, I never had the opportunity to, nor did I want to," John answered.

Richard called on the radio to the closest airport to report the altitude and direction they would be flying. Then he looked over at John who still had his eyes closed.

"You need to open your eyes, John, so you can tell me where the ranch is," Richard remarked.

"Okay, but if you kill me, I will never speak to you again!" John replied.

"Promises, promises," Richard replied.

"Hey, there's the ranch over there," John said as he pointed to a house in the distance.

"Which way from here to the calf?" Richard asked.

"South," John replied.

Richard turned the helicopter to the south and flew on into the darkness. After a few minutes of flying south, John spotted the section of woods where he examined the calf. He pointed to the area where Wayne had driven the jeep into the woods the day before. Richard flew the helicopter to the area where John had directed him. He found a flat area and began to bring the helicopter down slowly. When he landed the helicopter, he began to turn off the switches, and the blades on the propeller slowed to a stop.

"Okay, let's go see your calf," Richard said.

John opened the door and climbed out and walked to the other side. Richard, grabbing a bag behind his seat, climbed out of the helicopter. He laid the bag on the ground and opened it. He reached inside and pulled out a flashlight. Taking the flashlight in his right hand, he turned it on and began to pan it around the area to see what was there. He took the flashlight and handed it to John and told him to hold it shining down on the bag. Richard reached into the bag again and pulled out a small black case, which he laid down beside the bag. He reached inside the bag again and pulled out another flashlight and turned it on. He reached down and picked up the small black case lying on the ground.

"Which way do we go?" Richard asked.

"Over here," John answered.

They walked over to the woods and started to search the ground as they walked into the dark wooded area.

"Hope there aren't any snakes out tonight," John whispered.

"Are you afraid of snakes?" Richard asked.

"I'm not afraid of them. I just don't like them," John answered. "How about you, are you afraid of them?" he asked.

"About two years ago, I helped some people catch a twenty foot giant Anaconda down in South America," Richard replied.

THE COVERUP

"I guess that was a no on that question," John answered.

"Yeah, well, they don't scare me, but I prefer to stay away from the poison kind," Richard replied.

"I don't blame you. As for me, I just as soon not see any kind of snake," John said as he waved his flashlight around on the ground.

"Most snakes would just as soon get away from you as you would them," Richard replied.

"I just as soon they did, too," John answered.

They walked on into the dark dense woods slapping at mosquitoes and brushing away spider webs. John led Richard to an area that was dense with bushes and trees. He pushed through the bushes to the other side as Richard followed.

"Here it is," John said as he pointed to the calf lying on the ground in front of them. Richard walked over to the calf and knelt down beside it on his knees. He began examining the holes in the calf's neck.

"I forgot my probe. Have you got a pen on you?" Richard asked.

"Yeah, here you go," John replied as he handed the pen to him.

Richard took the pen from John, and using it like a probe, he inserted it into the holes in the calf's neck. The pen seemed to go very deep into the holes and was much larger than the pen in diameter.

"I thought you said these holes were shallow and the same size as this pen," Richard said.

"They were. Why do you ask?" John returned.

"Well, because the holes are much deeper than you said, and they are bigger around than this pen," Richard replied.

"They were when I checked them yesterday," John answered.

Richard grabbed the calf by the head and tried to lift it. The calf was getting stiff from rigor mortis that had set in. Richard tried to pick up the whole calf by himself. He found this to be difficult and asked John to give him a hand. John reached down and grabbed the calf by the head and lifted it so Richard could look underneath. Richard bent down to get a better look at the neck of the calf. Shining his light on the calf's neck, he reached over to feel what might be on the other side.

"There appears to be two holes on this side, too," Richard said. He stood up and told John to help him lift the calf and turn him over to the other side. As soon as the calf was on the other side, Richard knelt to the ground so he could examine the other holes. He noticed these holes were about the same size as the holes on the other side. He leaned back and sat down on the ground. He looked up at John. John noticed a confused look on Richard's face.

"What?" he asked as he sat down beside Richard.

Richard looked over at John and said, "This calf appears to have been shot at close range."

"That's not possible! The holes were not that deep yesterday!" John screamed.

John stood up and went into a rage, screaming and cursing. "It had to be Jack!" he swore. "How could he possible know about this?" he screamed as he began to kick the ground below him. "You, me, Tom, and the Faulkners are the only ones who knew, and I don't believe that Wayne and Joe would tell!" he said.

Richard sat there looking at the calf as he reached into his bag to get a rag. He took the rag and began to clean the pen he was holding in his hand. As he wiped the pen, he noticed a faint inscription on the side. He grabbed his flashlight and shined

THE COVERUP

it on the pen. It read, "Property of the U.S. Government." He sat there staring at the pen as the wheels of thought began to turn in his head. First, where did this pen come from? He got it from John. Second, where did John get it? He got it from the delivery boy. Third, Jack entered and took the pen from John's hand and placed it in John's shirt pocket.

John walked over to Richard and shouted, "What are we going to do now? He's beaten us! Are you going to just sit there like a knot on a log? What are we going to do now?"

Richard put his finger to his lips to warn John to be quiet as he reached into his bag and pulled out a notepad. He wrote on the notepad, "Follow my lead," and handed it to John. John looked at him in a state of confusion as Richard held the pen up while shining the flashlight on the inscription on the side. John stood there for a moment before his brain kicked in. He suddenly realized the same things Richard did. He nodded his head in agreement as Richard began to take the pen apart. He carefully unscrewed the top of the pen and pulled it apart to expose what was inside. A little chrome wire was attached to the ink cartridge inside. He put the pen back together and placed the pen in one of the holes in the calf's neck.

"I'm sorry, Sheriff, but nothing you have shown me has any hard evidence that the Chupacabra was even here," Richard began. "You must be wrong about this. I give up. You have no evidence for me to follow. I'm wasting my time here," he said. "Let's just get back in the chopper and I will leave here in the morning."

"I'm sorry, Richard. I don't know what to say," John replied.

"I doubt that even Jack would perpetrate something as devious as this," Richard claimed. "Let's just go. I have some packing to do before I leave."

71

John and Richard walked away from the calf toward the helicopter. When they arrived at the helicopter, Richard turned to John and said, "That is what we are up against."

"He bugged that pen so he could keep up with what we were investigating," John replied.

"He just doesn't want us to follow this thing for some reason," Richard answered.

"So what do we do now?" John asked.

"Okay, here's what we are going to do," Richard explained. He began by telling John to go home and act like the whole thing was over. Following the statement he just gave Jack through the bug, Richard would go back, pack his belongings in the helicopter, and leave. Only he wouldn't be gone for more than a day. Then he would return under the cover of darkness tomorrow, and the two of them would stake out in the fields. If he could get close enough to the Chupacabra, he had a tracking device that he could dart him with, and they could follow it.

"If we could find out where it is hiding in the daytime, we might just be able to answer some of the questions we have," Richard said. "And I'll bet you Jack is going to be right in the middle of it."

"I don't doubt it," John said, as he and Richard got into the helicopter.

"I got a better idea. Are you up to taking a vacation?"

"Well, it has been a while since I've had some time off."

"Here's what I want you to do. Plan a vacation to Galveston and take Regina with you to make it look real. Keep the ink pen with you at all times except when you need to talk to Regina. Book a room at the Mariott Hotel two days from today. I will meet you there and we will get together in my room. I want you to leave the pen in your room."

"How are you going to contact me when I get there?"

"Don't worry, you will know when the time comes. Now go back, get my bag, and put the pen back in your pocket."

John got out of the helicopter and walked back into the woods. He retrieved Richard's bag and the pen. Returning to the helicopter, he climbed in and buckled his seat belt laying the bag beside him. Richard cranked the helicopter up and they flew off of the ranch.

John remembered how Jack had set him up when he was an FBI agent. Jack had become a very powerful man in the agency. He took advantage of his office to set John up.

When they arrived at the Greene Farm, John got out, and Richard flew off.

WILLIAM DANIEL

THE VACATION
Chapter Thirteen

John looked up and saw the familiar blue Oldsmobile, which belong to Regina, coming down the Greene farm driveway. He told Manuel it was his wife coming to get him and said goodbye. He walked out to meet Regina as she drove up. Regina pulled the car up to where John was standing. He opened the car door and sat down in the passenger seat and reached over to give her a little kiss and said, "Hello, baby."

"Want to tell me about it?" Regina asked.

"No, I don't want to talk about it," John replied.

"It's Jack again?" Regina curiously asked.

"Yeah," John replied.

"I guess we are never going to get rid of him," Regina said as she turned the car around and drove down the driveway to the highway.

"Well, I just want to forget the whole thing. Hey, how about you and I take a trip up the coast? Maybe to Galveston for a week or two," John said.

"Are you kidding? I would love to," Regina excitedly replied.

John began to point at his pocket. He was pointing at the pen and moving his lips without making a sound. He began to utter the word, "bug." Regina looked at the pen in John's pocket. She looked up at him and shook her head to indicate that she understood. John gave her the thumbs-up as if to say, "Okay."

"The Greene farm sure looks good this time of year," Regina said trying to make idle conversation.

"Yes, they have a very nice farm," John replied. Silence returned between them as Regina drove down the highway.

"I can't wait to get to Galveston," Regina said, smiling as if she believed they were really going. John sat there for a moment smiling back at her.

"Me too," he replied. He turned his head to gaze out the window.

He was thinking to himself what he would need to do to get ready for this trip. When he turned back to look at Regina, he noticed she was in her own thoughts. "She probably is thinking of the same things," he thought to himself. As Regina pulled the car into their driveway, John reached into the back seat to get his jacket. When the car came to a halt, he opened his door and stepped out. He walked over to the other side and opened the door so Regina could get out. He put his arms around her and they walked up the steps on the front porch. John took the keys from Regina and opened the front door. He stood back and let Regina walk in first. He followed her in and closed the door behind him. He walked over to the closet and pulled a hanger out to hang up his jacket and closed the door. Walking down the hallway he headed for the bedroom. He walked into the bedroom and over to the dresser. He pulled the pen from his shirt and placed it on the dresser. Turning around he walked out of the bedroom and closed the door behind him. He then walked down the hall to the living room. Walking over to Regina he put his arms around her, giving her a kiss and a hug.

"I left the bug in the bedroom so we can talk," he whispered to her.

"What is this all about?" Regina curiously asked.

THE COVERUP

"Jack has been listening in on all our conversations."

"You mean he knew all the time what you were doing?"

"Yeah, I'm afraid so."

"That asshole. That low life sack of dog shit!" Regina screamed in a low tone.

"Whoa," John said, surprised at her reaction.

"How could he do something like this? No, why would he do something like this?" Regina angrily asked.

"Well, Richard and I think he's trying to cover up something," John answered. "Like maybe El Chupacabra."

"The nerve of that man. You need to kick his ass," Regina angrily replied.

"We will, believe me, we will," John answered.

"I could use a drink, how about you?" Regina asked as she headed for the kitchen, still steaming.

"Yeah, me too. Say, do you actually eat with that mouth? I should wash it out with some soap. You're becoming a regular potty mouth," John playfully replied as he followed her into the kitchen.

Regina walked over to the kitchen cabinet and pulled out a bottle of whiskey. Then she reached back in and pulled out two glasses that she placed on the table. She walked over to the refrigerator and took out a bottle of coke. Taking the coke over to the table, she grabbed the bottle of whiskey. She poured some of the whiskey in both glasses. Then she poured coke in both glasses until they were full. She went back to the refrigerator and took out an ice tray. She brought it over to the table and put a couple of cubes in both glasses. John grabbed one of the glasses and took a drink. Regina did the same with the other one.

"So what is our next move?" Regina asked as she sipped on her drink.

"We wait for Richard to make the first move," John replied.

"When will that be?" Regina curiously asked.

"Soon. What we have to do is play out this trip like we were really going on a vacation," John answered.

"I wish we were," Regina said as she took another drink from her glass.

"Maybe we will after this thing is over. Let's go into the bedroom and start planning our trip. I want Jack to hear everything we do," John said as he turned and headed for the bedroom. Regina followed him into the bedroom and walked over to the bed and sat down. John retrieved the ink pen that was on the dresser where he left it. He walked over to the nightstand and opened the drawer to get a piece of paper. He then sat down on the bed and began to write down the things that needed to be done before they would leave.

First he needed to call the office and inform Sue about the vacation.

1. Call Mom and Dad.
2. Call Regina's Mom and Dad about keeping the kids longer.
3. Call airline and get tickets.
4. Get travelers' checks.
5. Call Tom.
6. Call about a rental car in Galveston.
7. Pack cloths.
8. Call paper boy and cancel paper for a week
9. Call hotel to make reservations.
10. Call the Post Office to hold the mail.
11. Shut off gas.

John looked up from the notes he was writing, and read them out loud to Regina.

"Can you think of anything else we need to do?" he asked when he was done reading.

"Not at the moment," Regina replied. John got up from the bed and walked over to the window to open the curtains.

"It'll be dawn in about an hour. Why don't you get some rest?" John told Regina as he closed the curtains.

"What about you? I think you need it more than I do," Regina asked.

"I'll be all right. I'll get some sleep later today," John answered. Regina agreed and got undressed. She slipped under the sheets to try and get some sleep.

John walked out of the bedroom and headed for the kitchen. He walked into the kitchen and found the whiskey on the counter. He poured himself another drink and sat down at the table. He knew he was going to have a hard time convincing Tom that this thing was over. "What am I going to tell him?" he thought to himself as he sipped on his drink. He thought it would be best for Tom, to leave him out of this. No sense in both of us taking a chance on losing our job. Besides, Tom was a bit of a hot head. He might blow the whole coverup. Anyway, someone would have to stay and watch the town while he was gone. Tom would not understand, John was sure of that. He knew it was going to be tough convincing him.

"I'm just going to tell him that I gave up on the chase," he thought to himself. The main thing he had to worry about was Regina. How would she handle being alone in Galveston while he and Richard chased a legend?

The sun began to peek through the cracks in the blinds. John got up from the table in the kitchen. He walked over to the refrigerator and opened the door. He was hoping to find some leftovers he could nibble on. Otherwise, he would have to make breakfast or wait until Regina got up to cook breakfast.

He found the leftover roast that Regina cooked for Richard. He pulled a knife out of the counter drawer to cut a piece for a sandwich. He pulled a plate from the cupboard and laid it on the counter. Cutting a slice of roast beef, he placed it on the plate. Grabbing a loaf of bread from the counter, he opened it and took out two slices. He went back to the refrigerator and got the mayonnaise. He layered the bread with the mayonnaise and roast beef and placed the other slice of bread on top and cut the sandwich in half with the knife. He took the sandwich to the table and sat down to eat it.

The sun broke the horizon at six a.m. that morning. It was going to be a clear day with a high in the mid eighties. There was a light covered fog in the early morning that would burn off by mid-morning. It was going to be an interesting day for Regina and John. They didn't know if their plan was going to fool Jack. And what about Richard? When will he return and how will he get by Jack? If Jack is not fooled, Richard will have a hard time getting together with John and Regina, that is, without getting caught or recognized by one of Jack's agents. However, if he does know, their plan will never work. The element of surprise is the only way to make this plan work. If Jack does not know what they are doing, then he will be unable to stop them. John and Regina must put on a good show in order to fool Jack.

THE COVERUP

THE GULF OF MEXICO
Chapter Fourteen

Eight a.m., June 26, 2002, Richard sat in the boat he had rented watching the waves roll in and out. He had rented a boat in Corpus Christi, Texas and took himself out into the Gulf of Mexico. He already had a plan for sneaking back to John and Regina. Out on the ocean was where he planned to make his move. He sat there sipping on a glass of wine waiting for the sun to hit the horizon. He wondered if John and Regina were able to fool Jack into believing they were really going on vacation. He knew he was going to have to be very careful because Jack was no fool. Every move he made, he would need to check to see if anyone was following him. He had his fishing pole rigged and in the water. This was to give the appearance that he was fishing. Actually he was fishing and planned to do so all day, at least until sunset had fallen upon the ocean's horizon when his plan would start. Who knows, he might even catch himself a boatload of fish while he was there.

Eight fifteen a.m., June 26, 2002, John walked to the phone and picked it up while Regina was making breakfast. He dialed the number to his office and waited for someone to answer. He lit a cigarette and took a puff as the phone began to ring. A voice came over the receiver.

"Cook County Sheriff's office, Sue speaking. How may I help you?" Sue asked as she answered the phone.

"Sue, it's me. Anything going on today?" John asked.

"Not much, Sheriff, just a few prank calls," Sue replied as she sat down a cup of coffee on her desk.

"I expected that to happen," John said as he puffed on his cigarette.

"Are you coming in today?" Sue asked as she searched for some notes she had.

"No, I'm starting my vacation today. Tell Tom for me, will you?"

"You know he is going to want to talk to you."

"Well, I will be right here today. Tomorrow we are flying to Galveston for a week."

"I've always wanted to go to Galveston, myself."

"So why didn't you?"

"Are you kidding me? On my salary, I couldn't afford it," Sue replied as she took a sip of her coffee.

"Yeah, I know what you mean. Regina and I need some time away from here. Besides, I have promised to take her there for a long time," John said as he put out the cigarette in the ashtray beside the phone.

"Well, I hope that you and Regina can enjoy your trip."

"Thanks, Sue. I will be in touch with you before we get back. Maybe I will bring you something back from there."

"That would be sweet of you, Sheriff, but you really don't have to."

"I know I don't, but you have been a good secretary. I just want you to know how much I appreciate you."

"Thanks, Sheriff, and don't you worry about anything. I will take care of everything while you're gone. Just enjoy your vacation and tell Regina I said hi."

"I will, Sue. Talk to you later," John said as he hung up the phone.

John was playing his role as fine tuned as he could. The next step would be to convince Tom that the case was closed. Even though he knew he was lying about the trip, he would still have to convince Tom. Tom was a sensitive man, and he hoped he would forgive him for it. He can take things hard when you leave him out like you didn't trust him, but John hoped he would understand once he explained what was going on. He knew he would take this hard, being left out, because in a small town you just don't get many serious crimes to investigate. John was sure he would have to find a way to make it up to Tom. That in itself would prove to be a challenge. Tom was a hard man to please. That was probably one of the reasons why Tom never married. No one could put up with him. But John knew he would have to come up with a solution to the problem.

WILLIAM DANIEL

THE NEXT MORNING
Chapter Fifteen

Eight thirty a.m., Regina entered the room and informed John that breakfast was about ready. It was time for John to figure out what hotel and airline he would call. He would have to get reservations and tickets for the trip, so he walked over and grabbed the phone book. He headed for the kitchen where Regina was setting his plate on the table. He sat down and began to eat his breakfast. He thumbed through the El Paso phone book for the airline that he would be calling later. Regina laid down her breakfast plate and sat down in the chair across from John. She watched John looking through the phone book as she began to eat her food. John took the pen from his shirt pocket and underlined the number to one of the airlines. He looked up from the phone book at Regina.

"I'm going to call the airline in a few minutes. Then I'll call and get us reservations at the hotel where we will be staying," John said. Regina just nodded her head as she continued to eat her food.

"What do you want me to do?" Regina asked.

"Call your parents to make sure it's okay with them for the kids to stay while we are gone," John replied.

"I'm sure it will be. Anything else?" Regina asked.

"Yeah. I need you to go to the bank and get some travelers' checks. Then stop by the Post Office and have them hold the mail," John replied.

"Do you want me to contact the gas company?" Regina asked.

"No, I'll cut that off myself and I'll get a hold of Jimmy about holding the paper," John answered. Regina got up from the table and walked over to the coffee pot to pour herself another cup. "Do you want some more coffee?" she asked.

"No thanks, I've had enough," John replied. Regina poured herself another cup and returned the pot to the machine. She sat back down and returned to eating her food without saying a word. John could see the disappointment on her face. The whole trip was just an act. He wished he could actually take her to Galveston for a vacation. He pulled out his checklist. He began to mark off what he had already done and what Regina was about to do. When he had finished his breakfast, he got up from the table and walked over to Regina. He bent down and gave her a little kiss on the cheek.

"That was a good breakfast. Thank the chef for me, will you?" he said.

"You're talking to the chef," Regina answered as she took a sip of coffee.

"Well, for a chef you sure do have pretty eyes," John said as he stood above her.

"Flattery will get you everything," Regina replied.

"You know I love you very much," John remarked passionately as he held her face in his hands.

"I love you, too," Regina replied. John reached down and gave her a passionate kiss on the lips. He stood up and smiled as he walked out of the kitchen and into the living room. He walked over to the phone and began to dial a number. He waited quietly as the phone rang on the other end.

"El Paso International. This is Sissy. How may I help you?" asked the young lady on the receiver.

"Yes, I would like to book a flight to Galveston, Texas, please," John replied.

"Okay, sir, I can do that. How many will there be?" Sissy asked.

"Two, round trip," John replied. John pulled out a credit card and gave the number to the young lady. She took the information from the card and told him the departure time before she hung up the phone.

WILLIAM DANIEL

THE COVERUP

RICHARD FISHING IN THE GULF
Chapter Sixteen

At 9:00 a.m., Richard sat in his seat on the boat. He was sipping on a glass of wine when suddenly his fishing pole began to swing up and down. He jumped from his seat and grabbed the pole. He began to reel it in feeling it pull back on the other end very hard. He fought the fish on the other end for about fifteen minutes. Finally he pulled the fish over the side of the boat. It was a large sea bass weighing about six pounds. Richard reached down and picked up the fish and put it in the live well at the back of the boat. He walked over to his wine and took a big drink as if he was celebrating a big victory. After he was finished patting himself on the back, so to speak, he baited the hook again. He threw the line back out into the salt water. He sat back into his chair and poured himself some more cold wine. He leaned back against the chair and took a sip from his wine as the morning sun grew in the eastern sky. He reached under his chair and pulled out some sunscreen and began to rub it on his exposed skin. He sat back in his chair to absorb some rays from the bright sun.

The morning was passing by very slowly and Richard was getting very relaxed. He began to dose off into a nap as a light breeze blew across the salty gulf sea. He hadn't drifted off to sleep for very long when another fish hit his line. He woke up to the sound of the pole swishing up and down. He jumped up from his chair and began to reel in yet another sea bass. This one was about the same size as the other one. He placed him in the live well, then baited his line and threw it back into the water. He walked over and settled back down into his chair. He reached over and retrieved his glass of wine and took a big gulp. Taking the bottle from the ice bucket, he poured himself some more wine. As the boat rocked back and forth from the small waves of the ocean, he settled back into his chair. What a life it would be, he thought to himself, to do nothing but fish and drink wine all day. But to Richard a life of frolicking in the sun all day and every day would get very boring. He needed excitement more than the money his rich family left him.

Nine thirty a.m., Richard had dosed off to sleep in his chair as his fishing pole began to flop up and down again. He had caught another fish on his line, but this time he did not wake up. He had drifted off into a dream about El Chupacabra that included John and Jack. In his dream Richard had caught the creature in a net he had set up. It was the kind of net that is used to catch very large creatures. The net was set up across a field in which you would catch a large flock of birds. An explosive charge is set off that propels the net over the creature as it passes by. The net was set up by Richard to catch the creature before he could escape. By chance he got lucky. He was in the right place at the right time. John was there to help with the capture. He was at one end of the net when the creature was caught. Richard had the other end and together they were trying to hold the creature down. They thought the creature would tire soon as they held it down. Only El Chupacabra had other plans, like not getting caught. He ripped through the net like it was paper that was holding him down. He turned toward John and slashed out with his front claws ripping open John's neck. John fell to the ground, blood gushing from his

THE COVERUP

slashed open neck. At this same time, the creature turned to Richard and gave him a cold angry stare. He then leaped into the air with his kangaroo-like legs and flew away. Richard stood there in shock. He watched as the life- giving blood ran out of John's neck. Suddenly he noticed someone coming toward him as he watched John lying on the ground. It was Jack walking over to him with an angry look on his face. Richard was still in shock, and he could not move a muscle. Jack walked up to him and looked him in the eye.

"I told you and John to stay out of this," he said in an angry voice. "Now look what you have done."

"He's never killed anyone before. Why did he do it now?" Richard asked as he trembled in fear.

"You cornered a wild creature. What did you think was going to happen?" Jack replied.

"I didn't think this would happen!" Richard remarked in anger.

"I told you two to stay away. You should have listened to me," Jack replied.

"John is dead! What are you going to do about it, Jack?" Richard excitedly asked.

"There is nothing I can do for him now. I can't let you leak this information out," Jack replied as he pulled his gun from his shoulder holster. He pointed the gun at Richard and began firing several times.

Ten thirty a.m., Richard woke up suddenly with sweat pouring from his face. He wiped the sweat off with the sleeve on his shirt. He began to rub his eyes with his hands. He was trying to clear his head of the nightmare he just had. He stood up and walked around shaking his whole body to help wake him. He reached down for the glass of wine he had sitting on the floor beside his chair. He found out that his wine had turned hot, so he poured it out and got the bottle resting in the ice bucket. He poured his glass full and placed the bottle back into the bucket. He took the glass and drank a big gulp. He was hoping that would drown the thought of the dream he just had. When he had swallowed a couple of gulps, he noticed something was missing. For a few seconds he was baffled as to what was missing. Then it hit him like a sack of bricks. His fishing pole was gone. He walked over to where the pole was the last time he saw it. The fishing pole and the bracket that held it were gone. He began to scratch his head and look around as if he were looking for the person or persons who stole his fishing pole. When he turned to the starboard side he noticed something in the water coming at him. What he saw were two fins about six feet apart. That's when it hit him. It was a shark. This wasn't a little reef shark. This was a very big shark, and it was coming right at him. He stood there in awe as the big creature swam by the boat. Stunned, he watched as the fish swam past the end of the boat. Standing there with an intimidating look on his face, he noticed something trailing behind the shark. His face turned to anger as he realized it was his fishing pole the fish was pulling behind him.

The shark had appeared to swim away only to reappear on the aft side of the boat. This time he was heading straight at his boat. Richard watched in anger as the shark came closer and closer to the boat. Suddenly as if a light bulb turned on in his head, he realized this fish could turn the boat over. The anger on his face turned to fear as he ran to the controls of the boat and tried to start it. By this time the shark had reached the boat. He slammed into it very hard, knocking Richard to the deck. Quickly as he could, Richard got up and began to crank the motor over again. He quickly looked around the boat for the shark while the motor was turning over. He saw the shark coming at him on the starboard side. He looked back at the controls and noticed the gas gauge was on empty. Stunned for a moment, he looked up and grabbed hold of the steering wheel. The shark slammed into the starboard side. The force slung him to the aft side leaving him hanging halfway over the side. He could see the shark as it turned the boat over on the edge of the aft side. The shark, a great white, gliding under the boat, swam past the aft side. As the boat fell back flat, Richard gained his senses. He ran to the back of the boat, picked up the spare can of gas, and opened the gas cap on the boat. He began pouring the gas in as he watched for the shark. When he had finished pouring the gas, he ran to the control panel. Still watching for the shark, he began turning the ignition over to start the engine. The engine began to spit and sputter as it started. Richard looked up from the panel to see if he could spot the shark. He pulled the gearshift to the forward position. He could not see the shark anywhere around the boat as he pushed the throttle down.

Richard guided the boat out of the cove he was in. He headed up the coast a few miles before stopping. He waited a few minutes before turning around and heading back into the cove. Looking all around the boat for the shark, he went back into the cove. Suddenly he spotted the fins of the shark off the starboard bow. It was heading out to sea as he was heading back into the cove. When he was back in the cove, he turned the boat engine off. He watched the shark swim out to sea. He was relieved that the ordeal was over. He sat there thinking of the events that just happened. He had just been killed in a dream only to wake up to a real life-threatening situation.

"My God!" he thought, "What is going to happen to me next?"

He gathered his senses and walked over to the ice bucket to get the wine bottle. The ice was all over the bottom of the boat and the wine had spilled out. He quickly retrieved another bottle from his ice chest and opened it. He poured himself a glass and took a big drink. As he sat back down, he wondered if the shark would return. He decided to return to port for repairs and get some lunch. There he would report the incident to the Coast Guard. He knew he would have to report the shark before it reached one of the many swimming beaches. He started the engine and put it into forward gear. He pulled the throttle to full and headed out of the cove. He decided to pick up the radio and call the Coast Guard. When he reached them on the radio, he told them about the shark. They asked him which direction the shark was heading. The Coast Guard told him to return to port as soon as possible. There he could fill out the report. They thanked him for the information and told him that he may have saved a life. Feeling proud for doing a good deed, he told the Coast Guard that he was heading in right now. He turned the boat around and headed for Corpus Christie where he had rented it earlier in the day. The boat whirled around and churned the ocean water up as it pushed the craft across the water.

THE COVERUP

CONFRONTATION WITH TOM
Chapter Seventeen

Eleven a.m., John sat in the front yard in his favorite chair under a shade tree. He was sipping on a cool lemonade drink. He was still trying to come up with the right words to tell Tom. Regina was in the house packing clothes for the trip. John had everything in place for the trip that he could think of. Regina had taken care of the paper, travelers' checks, and the mail was stopped. Now it was a waiting game for John and Regina. They would find out if anyone were watching them before they left. He was sitting there thinking of his next move. A car came wheeling into the driveway. It was Tom. The moment that John was not looking forward to just became reality. He was not ready to face Tom, but he had no choice now. He sat back in his chair and waited for Tom to walk over to him. Tom got out of the patrol car and walked over to where John was sitting in the shade.

"What is going on, John? Why are you taking a vacation in the middle of an investigation?" Tom excitedly asked.

"Hey, Tom, how nice to see you," John replied.

"Don't you avoid the question. Why are you giving up on this case?"

John knew he was concerned and had to think quickly. Tom stood in silence waiting for an answer from John.

"Well, I tell you, Tom, the case is closed," John conservatively replied.

"What do you mean it's closed? What were the results? What conclusions did you come to?" Tom quickly asked.

"Well, Tom, Richard and I decided there was nothing to investigate, so we let Jack have the case," John replied.

"I don't understand. The other day you were sure Jack was up to something," Tom said. "Now you say that there is nothing to investigate."

John could see Tom was becoming more frustrated with every word that was said. He knew he was going to have to make Tom forget about it and get on with his job.

"Look, Tom. Jack is just going to cover up everything we try to look into. So why even try?" John told him.

"I just don't believe this," Tom said in disgust.

"Besides, life is too short to be wasting it on lost causes. Now you go on and take care of the town while I'm gone. You are in charge now," John explained.

"Okay, but I would never have thought you would give up so easy," Tom said in disbelief.

Tom turned and walked away muttering to himself. As he walked away, John grinned as if he had won the battle but not the war. He hoped that he had convinced Tom enough to keep him out of it. The game was being played at all cost, especially when it meant putting his friendship with Tom on the line.

Regina opened the door and walked outside where John was relaxing in the shade.

"Well, how did that go?" she asked him.

"I think I might have gotten through to him."

"I hope he doesn't get mad at you."

"Yeah, me too."

"I have some lunch ready for you. Do you want to eat out here?"

THE COVERUP

"No, I think I'll come inside," John replied as he got up from his chair. They walked toward the house together. John took her hand in his until they came to the door to the house. John opened the door and let Regina go in first. Then he followed, walking in behind her. They walked into the kitchen where John sat down at the table. Regina fixed him a plate and placed it in front of him. John looked over at the clock and noticed it was twelve o'clock. He got up from the table and walked over to the refrigerator to get himself a drink. After getting a soda, John returned to his chair and sat down to eat. "Everything packed to go?" he asked Regina.

"Yeah, I think I got everything we are going to need."

"Good. We are booked to fly out at six thirty in the morning."

"That's early. What time will we be in Galveston?"

"We should reach Galveston shortly after sunrise."

"I hope you got us a good hotel and not one of those roach motels."

"We're staying at the Marriott. Is that fine enough for you?" John asked with a smile on his face.

"Oh my gosh! The Marriott. Can we afford that?" Regina excitedly asked.

"Well, I have been saving up for such an occasion. I think we have enough to go first class. Besides, nothing but the best for my lady," John replied smiling from ear to ear.

"Oh, John, this is wonderful! You deserve something special for this," Regina said as she got up from the table to give him a big kiss. "You know, I really do love you," she said passionately.

"Yes, me, too," John replied.

"You really love me?" Regina asked.

"No, I meant I really do love myself," he replied.

"Oh, you trickster. You probably do love yourself more than me."

"Now, babe, you know I love you more than anything in this world."

"Well, you never say anything, makes me wonder."

"You can take my word for it."

"I don't know. Some people think you are crazy. I don't know if I can take your word for it."

John reached over and grabbed Regina by the waist and pulled her close to him. He then gave her a passionate kiss. "Does that convince you now?" he said when he was finished.

"I'm not sure. I think it needs more research," she replied.

John pulled the pen that Jack gave him from his shirt pocket and placed it on the table. "Maybe you're right," he said as he gathered her up in his arms and carried her off to the bedroom.

It was 12:30 p.m. when Richard docked the boat from where he had rented it and proceeded to climb out after he tied down the boat. He walked over to the rental office, opened the door, and walked into the office.

"I just got attacked by a Great White shark. You might want to check out your boat. I'm supposed go to the Coast Guard and fill out a report," Richard told the man behind the counter of the rental office.

"You say that a Great White shark attacked you?" the man asked.

"Yes, there might be some damage to the boat," Richard said. "However, I would like to keep that boat if you don't mind."

THE COVERUP

"Why, sir, there hasn't been a Great White around here for years," the man answered.

"Well, there was today, about a twenty footer. He slammed your boat a couple of times pretty hard," Richard told him. "Would you have it checked out? I'm going to get some lunch after I report the shark. Then I would like to go back out."

Laughing out loud with some other customers, the man agreed to check his boat. Richard walked over to the pay phone to call a cab for a ride to the Coast Guard. He sat on a bench outside the boat rental office waiting for the cab to pick him up. He noticed the caretaker had not made a move to check out his claims about the boat being damaged. He began to wonder if he had taken him seriously about his claim, seeing how he laughed at him when he told him the story. He got up from the bench and walked into the office to seek out the young man behind the counter. When he found him, he asked if he was going to check out the boat. If he was not going to check out the boat, he would have to rent another boat somewhere else. The young man reassured him that the boat would be checked out as soon as one of the workers returned from lunch. Convinced that the young man would do the job, Richard returned to the bench and waited for the cab. He began to think to himself about what he was going to have for lunch. While he waited, a Coast Guard helicopter flew over the rental dock. He figured they were on their way to check out his claim. He sat on the bench waiting for the cab to arrive. As he was waiting, he noticed a young man walking into the rental office. He got up and walked over to the pay phone to call the cab company again. The dispatcher answered the phone, and Richard asked how long before the cab would get there. The man told him he would check and put him on hold. While he was waiting, the young man returned from the rental office.

He walked over to Richard's rental and began to check out the hull above water level. After he had walked around the boat, he pulled his shirt off and jumped into the water. He had a facemask in his hand, and he placed it on his face. Then he went under the boat to check out the underside of the boat. After a short moment, he returned to the surface and began to shout at the young man in the office.

A cab pulled up to the rental dock, and Richard got up from the bench and walked out to it. As soon as he reached the cab, the young man from the office walked out to the man in the water. He could hear them talking about the hull on the boat being cracked, as the cab began to pull away. He turned and looked back at them, and they looked up at him as he was leaving. He turned back around with a grin on his face and told the cab driver where to take him. Then he asked the cab driver where there was a good place to get some lunch. The cab driver told him of a small restaurant that was next door to the Coast Guard main office. He told Richard it was within walking distance, and if he didn't like that one, he would recommend another to him that was a little farther away. Richard didn't care, as long as they had good food to eat.

The cab driver pulled up to the main office of the Coast Guard and stopped. Richard paid the driver, got out of the cab, and walked through the door. He walked up to the front desk and asked the girl where he needed to go to report a shark attack. The young lady behind the counter informed him he was at the right place. She picked up some forms for him to fill out and told him how to complete them. Richard took the forms and sat down at a table to fill them out. When he was finished, he gave them back to the young lady, thanked her, and walked out the door.

It was 1:30 p.m. when Richard walked down the busy street to the restaurant the cab driver had told him about. He walked into the restaurant, found an empty table, and sat down to order some lunch. The waitress asked what he would like to drink as she handed him a menu to read. He took the menu and scanned over the meals to order and asked her for a glass of tea. Richard picked out the meal he wanted while the waitress brought his drink. When the waitress returned with his drink, he told her what he wanted. As the waitress carried off his order, Richard took out a pen and paper and began to write down what he needed to do before going out again.

WILLIAM DANIEL

THE COVERUP

JACK RILEY AT HIS OFFICE
Chapter Eighteen

Two pm. Sitting at his desk, FBI agent Jack Riley picked up the phone and began to dial a number. With a cool and calm look on his face, he waited for someone to answer on the other end.

"Yeah, Jack," answered the party on the other end.

"Where are they at right now?" Jack asked.

"Well, the sheriff is away from the mike right now, but he is at home," the party replied.

"Okay, what else?" Jack asked.

"He has booked a flight to Galveston, Texas, and he reserved a room at the Marriott Hotel," the party continued. "They have packed and plan to leave in the morning from El Paso International."

"What about the other one?" asked Jack.

"He was fishing in a cove in the gulf and was attacked by a large shark that he just reported to the Coast Guard," the person on the other end of the phone line said. "Now he is sitting in a restaurant eating lunch and plans to go back out later."

"Is that all?" Jack asked.

"That's about it. They seem to be through with their investigation," the party answered.

"Keep the surveillance on. I don't trust those two," Jack replied as he hung up the phone.

103

Jack sat at his desk staring at the notes in front of him for a few moments before picking up the phone and dialing another number. Holding the phone to his ear, he waited for someone to answer.

A young lady answered the phone with a polite voice. "Hello, Jack."

"Is he in?" Jack asked.

"Yes, he is. Just a minute," she replied.

A few moments passed before a voice came on the phone. "Hello, Jack. I hope you have good news for me," the voice said.

"Well, so far, so good, sir," Jack replied.

"Good. Keep me informed of the progress," the voice answered as he hung up the phone.

Jack returned the phone to its cradle, and then picked it up again and dialed another number.

A lady's voice answered, "Hello."

"Get me Tom Jackson," Jack said.

"One minute, please," she answered.

"Hello, this is Tom Jackson."

"Tom, Jack. I need you to go to Galveston tonight."

"Yes, sir, Mr. Riley. Who do I contact?"

"I need you to be at the airport where John Barton and his wife will be arriving," Jack replied.

"What do I do?" Tom asked.

"I want you to search their luggage when it comes off the plane," Jack informed him.

"Yes, sir. What am I looking for?"

"Anything that doesn't relate to someone on a vacation. Let me know what you find."

"Yes, sir. I will be on the next flight," Tom replied.

Jack hung up the phone and returned to looking at the

notes on his desk. Then he got up from his chair and walked over to the window and opened the shades. He walked over to a cabinet against the wall and opened the door. He pulled out a file, walked over to a liquor bar in the corner of his office and fixed himself a drink. Opening the file, he poured a glass about half full and walked over to his desk. He sat down and sipped on his drink while he viewed the file in front of him. Jack had a stone cold look about him, as if he was an old soldier who was left in the trenches for the whole war. Each move that he made was as if he studied it before he made it. Jack knew his job was on the line on this one, but this one was personal. He never could forgive John for taking Regina away from him, and he vowed to get even. He believed that if John had not come into the picture, Regina would have given in to his desires. Regina only hung out with Jack because she was new to the Dallas area. She wanted to meet new people and figured Jack could introduce her to them. However, Jack took it as if she had a feeling for him. His life might have been totally different if she had married him instead of John.

It was 3:00 p.m. when the phone on Jack's desk rang as he was signing some papers. He reached over and picked up the receiver and said, "What?"

"Our boy just bought some scuba gear. Is that something we should be worried about?" the voice replied.

"Well, he could be going dive fishing. Did he buy a spear gun?" Jack inquired.

"Yes, sir, he did," the voice answered.

"All right. Get some people down there who can dive to keep an eye on him," Jack told him.

"Sir, do we stop him if he makes a move?" the voice asked.

"No, just follow him, and keep me posted," Jack replied.

"Yes, sir, Mr. Riley. I will take care of it," the voice replied.

"See that you do. I don't want any slip-ups in this operation," Jack replied as he hung up the phone.

Jack's loss of Regina was making his blood run cold with jealousy. Cold and heartless, he wandered through life with no feeling for anyone, although it made him a better FBI agent than he would have been if she had married him. No one to go home to, he spent his life working to be the best agent ever in the history of the FBI or any other branch of the government. Only he did not do it honestly. He used his mean side to manipulate people into his way of thinking. Jack was bound and determined to take John Barton down, one way or another. As for Richard Cooper, it would be a blessing in disguise to take him down with John. Jack had the upper hand because he had nothing to lose but his pride. John, however, could lose Regina, and Richard had his family wealth to look after. It would be nothing to Jack to take away the things they loved. Richard had been a thorn in Jack's side for a long time. Ever since he saw the Chupacabra, he would show up every time someone claimed to have seen the creature. He was obsessed with finding the creature and exposing its existence to the public. Jack needed him out of his way, but because of his family money and their political pull, he needed Richard to do something wrong. This way he could put him away for a long time. Richard, on the other hand, needed to find the Chupacabra to prove his theory, that the creature was indeed the alien from the spacecraft that had landed in 1947. Jack saw this whole situation as an opportunity to get rid of the two people he despised the most.

THE COVERUP

GOING BACK OUT IN THE GULF
Chapter Nineteen

Richard arrived at the boat dock at 4:30 p.m. where he rented the boat that he had used earlier in the day. As he walked down the walkway, he noticed that the boat was gone. He walked straight for the office to find out where his boat was. As he opened the door to the boat rental office, he saw the young man he had talked to earlier.

"Where is my boat?" Richard asked.

"We had to take your boat over to the repair dock. It was damaged badly enough that it will have to be pulled out of the water," the young man said.

"But I love that boat," Richard replied.

"I'm sorry, sir, but it was too dangerous to allow it to go out. But we have you another one, and we moved all your stuff onto it."

"Well, I suppose it can't be helped."

"I am sorry, sir, that we didn't believe you, but sharks of that size haven't been around these waters in years."

"Okay, I have some more gear to stow away."

"I will have Joe put it on your new rental. Again, I am sorry."

"That's all right. Uh, where is the new boat?"

"Joe is fueling it as we speak."

Richard was disappointed in not having the other boat. He felt much safer in it.

Richard walked outside the rental office and began to check his gear before he put it on the boat. As he was finishing his check of his gear, his boat pulled up to the dock. Joe stepped off the boat and told Richard he would stow his gear for him. Richard thanked him and stepped onto the boat to check it out. As he walked around making sure everything he needed was on the boat, Joe loaded his gear. He noticed that Richard had scuba gear with him. Joe was puzzled. How can a guy that's been attacked by a shark go scuba diving later? He just had to ask. "Are you going scuba diving after being attacked by a Great White shark?"

"Well, it's just a fish, a very large fish, but just a fish," Richard replied.

"Yeah, that is true, but a fish that can eat you, too," Joe said.

"Yeah, but you can't blame him. He was just looking for a meal," Richard replied. "Besides, I have been attacked by sharks before."

"You have more balls than I do, sir," Joe answered. Richard laughed at his response and continued getting ready to sail.

At 5:00 p.m., Richard started the boat motor and began to maneuver away from the boat dock. He noticed that this boat was a couple of feet smaller than the other one. Going scuba diving did seem a bit out there, he thought to himself, but he figured the shark would be gone from this area by now. Then, of course, there was the Coast Guard who was out looking for the shark. He felt somewhat safe, but not totally safe, going scuba diving. However, Richard had a plan that was about to go into effect at sundown. He was going to have to dive in order to make it look realistic. Everything had been put into motion long before he sailed earlier that morning. The shark attack was something he did not count on. He just survived it, that's all there is to it. As the boat puttered out of the dock and toward the open sea, Richard pulled out a can of beer and opened it. He was trying to give the impression to those he was sure were watching that he was on vacation. He grabbed the throttle and pushed it all the way to full power, and the boat took to bouncing across the waves. He turned the boat toward the small cove he was in earlier that day.

Arriving at the cove, Richard stopped the boat about the same place he was earlier. He got up from his seat and walked over to the bow to drop the boat anchor. As he watched the anchor drop to the bottom of the cove, he noticed a glimmer coming from the shore. He knew they would be watching his every move, so he had to play his part as close to perfect as he could get it. What he had planned would keep them watching this boat all night. This would be his diversion that would allow him to sneak away. He walked back to the stern of the boat and pulled out a new fishing rod he had bought. He put a hook and bait on the line and cast it out. Then he sat back into his fishing chair.

WILLIAM DANIEL

THE NIGHT BEFORE DEPARTURE
Chapter Twenty

As the hot summer sun began to set low in the sky, John was about to sit down to watch some TV. A knock came at his door, and he walked over to the door and opened it. It was Tom.

"John, I have got to talk to you."

"Tom, there is nothing more to say. This thing is over. Let it go."

"You can't tell me that you are not the least bit suspicious of what is going on," Tom answered.

"No, I'm not."

"You saw what I saw. You know Jack is covering this up. How can you turn away?"

"Look, Tom, Jack has the upper hand, and we don't have any proof. I don't want to lose my job."

"Your job? What about Josh's death? Doesn't that mean anything to you?" Tom screamed.

"Josh's death has been solved."

"And that is the way you see it?"

"I'm sorry, Tom, but I don't have any choice."

Tom stood there for a few moments confused and shocked.

"I am very disappointed in you. I guess you have your reasons," Tom said.

"Believe me, Tom, it will all blow over in a few days. The best part is you and I will keep our jobs."

"That is all you care about, your job? What about the truth?"

"I have a family to worry about, and my job is what feeds them," John quickly replied. He turned away from Tom and walked over to the table by his chair. He reached down and picked up a pack of cigarettes. Pulling one out and lighting it, he turned to Tom and said, "My family means more to me than my job."

"The Sheriff Barton I used to know would not let things like that get in his way," Tom replied as he turned to the door and walked out.

"Tom, don't be mad at me," John pleaded.

Tom walked down the steps and got into the patrol car. He backed out of the driveway. John watched him drive away, walked over to his chair, and sat down. He felt very sad at what he was doing to Tom. However, he knew it was necessary. He could only hope to make it up to Tom when this was all over. Right now he had to concentrate on the job at hand.

Regina walked into the room while John was sitting in his chair smoking his cigarette.

"Was that Tom I just heard?"

"Yeah, he's not very happy with me," John replied.

"Well, Tom doesn't have a family to worry about. He will get over it."

"I hope you are right," John said. "Tom's a good man. I would hate to loose him."

"Don't worry. I'm sure he will see things your way when he has time to think about it," Regina remarked.

"Yeah, maybe you're right," John answered with a smile.

"I know I am," Regina replied with a smile.

"Yeah," John confidently said.

THE COVERUP

"I'm going to fix us some supper. You just relax and watch some TV," Regina said as she headed for the kitchen.

"Okay, call me when it's ready."

"I will," Regina replied as she walked through the kitchen door.

John began to search for the remote to the TV so he could turn it on. He looked all around the furniture but did not see the remote. "Have you seen the remote?" he shouted to Regina.

"Try looking in your chair," Regina replied. John reached his hand into the side of his chair cushion.

"Did you find it?" Regina asked. John didn't answer her as he continued to look for the remote in his chair. Finally he came across it lodged deep down the side of the cushion.

"Did you find it?" Regina asked again.

"Yeah, I found it," John replied. He turned the remote toward the TV and turned it on. He sat down in his chair and began to flip through the channels to see what was on. He came upon a documentary about strange creatures and decided to watch it.

"Would you like a beer while you wait for supper?" Regina asked as she popped her head out of the kitchen door.

"Sure, thanks, babe," John answered. Regina went to get the beer while John sat in his chair watching the program. Suddenly the announcer said the next thing they would talk about would be El Chupacabra. John's attention focused on the TV as he waited for the beer Regina was bringing him. Suddenly the documentary about El Chupacabra came on the TV. John could not believe what he was watching. The creature appeared to look just as Josh had described it to him before he was killed.

"Here you are, John," Regina said as she walked into the room with the glass of beer.

"Thanks, babe."

"What is that?" Regina asked, referring to the picture on the TV.

"That would be El Chupacabra. The creature that we are looking for."

"It sure is ugly," Regina said as she looked at the picture.

"Yeah, he is that. Now this is not a real picture of the creature. This is just an artistic drawing from eyewitness accounts. No one has an actual picture of the creature."

"Well, if he looks anything like that, he must be an alien," Regina remarked.

"I agree," John replied giggling.

Regina returned to the kitchen to get supper ready. John had his eye glued to the TV watching the program on the creature. He thought this program might better prepare him for an encounter with the creature. But in reality nothing could prepare him for the real life creature that he would soon meet. How can you prepare yourself for an encounter with a creature that is not supposed to exist? Without seeing one in real life, it is hard to believe in their existence. All that John had to go by was the evidence he found at Josh's farm. Then there is the fact that someone covered up that evidence. Richard believed the only way to prove their theory was to capture the creature. This was exactly what was happening with the legendary Big Foot of the northwest. Sasquatch or Big Foot has been reported by many to be a real animal. Most people have a problem believing in a legendary creature like Big Foot. If the scientific world cannot prove that it exists, how can anyone believe in it? John knew this was going to be hard to prove. There are no fossil remains that have been found to prove the existence of

Big Foot or El Chupacabra, but on the other hand, there are so many people that have seen these two animals.

As John continued to watch the program on TV, he wondered if they really did exist. He did not know Richard Cooper, but he did believe in Professor Donner. However, the professor believed in Richard's story, and that was all John needed. The program continued with stories of individuals who have seen the legendary Big Foot. John watched as people explained what they saw. So many reported seeing the same kind of animal and described it the same way. John thought to himself, how could so many people see a creature that does not exist? To believe or not is in the eyes of the beholder. Most people believe that it is a product of a wild imagination.

John continued to view the program on TV. He could not believe the number of stories about El Chupacabra. So many people had claimed to see the creature and so many pictures of blood-drained animals. It was very hard not to believe something was going on here. Is it a hoax or does this creature really exist? John heard Regina call him to come eat. He got up from his chair and walked into the kitchen still baffled by what he had seen on TV.

WILLIAM DANIEL

THE COVERUP

THE MINI-SUB ARRIVES
Chapter Twenty-One

Six thirty p.m., Richard got up from the fishing chair and walked over to the storage compartment in the back of the boat. He opened the compartment and pulled out the scuba gear he had bought earlier. He began to check out the equipment as a safety precaution measure. After he finished, he got up and walked over to the fishing rod he had set out. He began to reel it in so he could store it.

As the warm summer breeze blew across the cove, he began to put on the scuba gear. He placed the air tank on his back and sat down to put on the flippers. As soon as he was geared up, he put the ladder over the side and jumped into the water. Diving down to the bottom of the shallow water in the cove, he began swimming to deeper water. Soon he came across a small submarine stationed in fifty feet of water. He swam over to the sub and began to bang on the diver's hatch. After a few seconds a green light came on indicating the diver's room was now flooded. He began to turn the wheel that opened the hatch to the diver's room. After opening the door he swam into the sub and closed the hatch. He pushed the button that would empty the room of all the water. As the water receded, Richard began to turn the handle on the inside hatch. This was the door that went inside the sub. When the water was all gone, he opened the door and stepped inside the pilot room.

"Mike, I see you made it," Richard said as he entered the room.

"Yeah, what is all this about?" Mike curiously asked.

"The less you know the better you will be, trust me."

"Okay. Now what do we do?"

"Put this diving suit on and swim up to the boat on the surface."

"Then what?"

"All right. You are going to act like you are me on vacation," Richard explained. "So just fish, drink some wine or beer, and relax like you were on a fishing trip."

"I can do that," Mike remarked.

"Good. If anyone should ask you, tell them nothing."

"That should be easy seeing as how I don't know anything," Mike replied.

"Good. Get dressed," Richard said as he started to remove the air tank and suit.

Richard handed the scuba gear to Mike and sat down in the pilot seat so he could check out the sub's gauges. Mike began to put on the equipment as Richard piloted the sub toward the boat on the surface. When Mike was ready, he walked over to the diving hatch and began to turn the wheel to open it. Richard maneuvered the sub as close to the surface boat as the shallow water would allow. He climbed out of the pilot seat and helped Mike get on the air tank. When Mike was ready, he began to open the door to the diving room. He walked in and began to put on his fins. Richard began to close the hatch but stopped just before he shut the door.

"Oh, by the way, there is a very large shark swimming about. I suggest you swim to the boat and never leave it again," Richard explained.

"A shark!" Mike exclaimed as Richard shut the hatch.

"Good luck," Richard said as he pushed the button to flood the room. He climbed back into the pilot seat and waited for Mike to exit. Richard turned the sub around and headed for Galveston at full throttle.

By eleven pm., Richard had arrived at the shores of Galveston. He stopped the sub a few hundred yards off the swimming beach. He shut the sub down and grabbed the microphone on the radio. He began to call out to someone waiting on the shore.

"I'll be waiting for you," he said. He shut off the radio and opened a storage compartment over his head. As he opened the compartment, he found three small air tanks and two sets of fins and masks. He closed the compartment and sat back in the pilot seat to take a nap. Richard's plan was working like a charm. There was a lot more to come, though. He had no way of knowing if his plan had fooled Jack Riley. He felt good about it and the report from shore was no FBI agents had been sighted. Everyone was in place like he had planned. The worst part was about to unfold as morning came to Galveston.

WILLIAM DANIEL

JOHN AND REGINA ARRIVE IN GALVESTON
Chapter Twenty-Two

The plane landed at eight a.m. in Galveston, about thirty minutes behind schedule. John and Regina got off the plane and headed for the terminal to collect their baggage. John gave the young man his claim ticket to get his baggage. The young man returned and informed John that his baggage would be delayed a few minutes.

"What seems to be the problem?" John asked.

"I'm not sure, sir," the young man replied, "but I will find out for you."

"Thank you," John said.

"What is the problem?" Regina asked.

"I don't know. He's going to find out," John replied.

"I hope they didn't leave them in El Paso," Regina remarked.

"That would be a fitting start to our vacation," John remarked as he waited for the young man to return. The young man came walking out from the back room.

"Sir. Uh, Mr. Barton," he called out.

John walked over to the counter where the young man stood.

"Yeah," John replied.

"They are having some trouble with the compartment door. It will be a few minutes."

"Yeah, okay."

John walked back to where Regina stood and told her what the young man had said.

"How long do you think this will take?" Regina asked.

"Not long I hope."

"I am starving for some breakfast," Regina remarked.

"Yeah me, too." John replied.

"Want to get something here at the airport?" Regina asked.

"I guess we could. I will tell him to call us when they get our luggage." He walked over to the counter where the young man stood.

"We are going to get some breakfast at the restaurant," John said. "Call us when you get our baggage."

"Yes sir, I will, and I am sorry for the delay," the young man replied.

John and Regina walked over to the restaurant. They found an empty table and sat down. A young waitress came over and asked them what they would like to drink.

"Two coffees, please," John said as he and Regina looked at the menus.

"I think I will have the cheese omelet," John said.

Regina kept looking at the menu while the waitress came back with their coffees and set them on the table.

"Have you decided what you would like?" she asked.

"Yes, I would like to have the cheese omelet with the hash brown potatoes. Give me some sausage and a biscuit with that," John ordered.

"And how about you?" the waitress asked Regina.

"I think I will have the same."

The young waitress wrote down their orders. "Your orders will be out in a few minutes," she said and walked over to put their orders into the kitchen.

THE COVERUP

John reached over and got two of the artificial sweetener packets. He opened them and poured them into his coffee, got a packet of cream, and poured it in. "What would you like to do first?" John asked as he took a spoon to stir his coffee.

"When we get checked into the hotel, we can get a local paper and see what events they have today," Regina replied.

John continued to stir his coffee and took a sip to see if it tasted the way he liked it.

"I guess it is too cold to go swimming right now," John said.

"Yes, I would like to see what museums they have," Regina replied.

"Okay, or maybe just walk on the beach," John suggested.

"I think I will go to the ladies' room. Be right back," Regina said as she got up from the table.

John sat at the table sipping on his cup of coffee and looked around the room. The young man from baggage claims walked into the restaurant and began to look around for John. John stared at him, not knowing if he was looking for him or someone else. The young man scanned the room until he came upon a pair of eyes staring at him. He quickly walked over to where John was sitting. He informed John that he had his luggage and wanted to know what he wanted to do with it. John told the young man that as soon as they finished eating, he would pick it up. The young man apologized for the inconvenience, thanked him, and left the restaurant.

John noticed the restaurant was full of people. He had always believed that a restaurant full of people meant good food. While he waited for his food, he began to wonder what Richard was doing at that moment. He started to think about the events from the last few days. Everything that happened was stored in his memory, like a movie or video. He believed that Jack was going to do something to him. After all, Jack had hated him ever since he took Regina away from him, and vowed to get him for it. John was sure Jack would not hurt Regina, but he could try to get rid of him. The thought made him nervous, and he knew he had to do something. He was confident that Richard would come up with a good plan. He just didn't know what it was or when it would happen. John knew he had to bust Jack to get him off his back before he did something drastic.

Regina returned from the ladies' room and sat down at the table with John. The waitress returned to their table with their breakfast, and set it down in front of them.

"Mmm, that looks good!" John said. He placed his napkin in his lap and began to eat. Regina took a sip of her coffee, and began to eat her breakfast.

"Have they called about our luggage yet?" Regina asked.

"Yeah, he just came in. We can pick it up when we're ready," John replied.

"Good. I would like to change into something more comfortable," Regina said.

They continued to eat their meals. The events of the day were about to unfold. Little did John or Regina know what was going to happen in the next few hours.

As John and Regina continued to eat their breakfast, Richard was preparing to meet with them in a clever disguise. With his family money, he had gathered together friends and professionals to help pull off his plan. John and Regina had no idea what Richard planned to do. All they could do was wait for him to contact them. When they finished their food, John got up from the table and went to pay the ticket. Then he returned to the table where Regina was waiting for him. They

THE COVERUP

left the restaurant and headed for the baggage claims. After retrieving their luggage, they walked to the front exit to get a cab. John called out to one of the cab drivers and asked him to take them to their hotel. The cab driver opened the trunk to his car and put in their luggage. John and Regina got into the cab and put on their seat belts. As the cab pulled out of the airport terminal, John put his arm around Regina's neck. "This is going to be fun," he said.

"Yeah, to finally take a vacation," Regina said.

"I'm sorry we didn't do this sooner," John replied.

"Me, too."

"I wish I could take you somewhere every year, but being sheriff of a small town has its disadvantages."

"I know, and I have no regrets. I married the man I love. That is all that matters."

"Do you miss the big city life?" John asked.

"Not really," Regina replied.

"Me, either. I married the woman I love, and that is all that matters to me."

"We should bring the kids down here sometime," Regina said.

"Yeah, I bet they would love it."

"When we get to the hotel, I think I will call them."

"Yeah, I'll bet they are driving your mother and dad crazy."

"I'm sure they are."

"I wonder how Tom is making out. You know, he's never been in charge before," John said.

"You should give him a call. He was not very happy when we left."

"Yeah, I know, but I will make it up to him someday."

"I don't think he will ever forgive you for backing out on the investigation."

"He'll get over it."

The cab driver continued to drive up one street and down another, arriving at the Marriott Hotel. The cab driver told John the fare was $25.50. Then he stepped out of the cab to open the car trunk. John and Regina got out of the cab and walked to the back of the car. John reached into his back pocket and pulled out his billfold. He opened it up and got $30.00 and gave it to the cab driver. They picked up their luggage and walked into the hotel to register. When they got to the registration counter, John asked the bellhop to take his luggage to their room. Regina began to register while John handed the key to the bellhop.

"We will be right up," he said.

The young man answered, "Yes, sir," as he carried the luggage to the elevator. John noticed an old man with a beard and a younger man with a beard walking up to the counter. He greeted them with a smile as the older man asked the man behind the counter for his key. John noticed the old man had a Scottish accent as he rattled on about something. When the old man was done, he turned to John and said, "Tis a fine day, isn't it, lad?"

"You must be from Scotland?" John asked.

"Ah, that I am, laddie, from the southern part of Scotland," the old man replied.

"Well, I hope you enjoy our country," John said as he and Regina walked to the elevator.

"That I will, laddie, that I will," the old man replied as he, too, walked to the elevator. When they were all in the elevator, John asked the old man what floor he wanted. The old man told him he wanted the fifth floor as John pushed the button for that floor.

THE COVERUP

"So, you are staying on the fifth floor, too?" John asked the old man.

"That I am, laddie. Maybe we could get together for a bit of Scottish whiskey."

The elevator lurched as it climbed upward to the fifth floor. John and Regina stood silently as the old man rattled on about Scotland. When the elevator reached the fifth floor, John and Regina waited for the old man to get out. When he was out of the elevator, John and Regina stepped into the hall. The old man, still rattling about Scotland, turned to John and asked, "Would you like to be having that drink now, laddie? I have a fine bottle of Scotch whiskey in me room right now," he whispered.

"Maybe later. We would like to get settled in right now," John replied.

"Ah, I be sure that you would now," the old man said. "Let me give you me room number. May I be borrowing your pen, young laddie?"

"Sure, here you are," John replied as he pulled the ink pen from his pocket. He handed it to the old man. The old man looked at the pen and began to look for some paper. After looking in all his pockets, the old man looked up at John and asked, "Would you be having any paper on you, laddie?"

"No, I don't. Regina, do you?" John asked.

"Yeah, I've got some paper," Regina answered as she reached into her purse. She pulled out an envelope and handed it to the old man.

"Ah, thank you, my dear," the old man said. He took the paper and walked over to a small table in the hall. He laid the envelope down and began to write something on it. John and Regina didn't know what to think of the old man's persistence about having a drink with him. John thought the old man was eccentric or maybe lonely. They watched as the old man continued to write on the paper. When the old man was through, he turned to John and held up the envelope for him to read. John took the envelope and read the following: "Meet me in room 510 in fifteen minutes. Richard."

John looked at the note, looked at the old man, and handed the note to Regina. She took the envelope, read the note, and looked at John. They stared at each other as if they could not believe what it said. The old man took the envelope and placed it in his pocket. John and Regina turned and looked at the old man, still not believing what they read. The old man, looking at them, winked with his right eye. John and Regina, looking at the old man, began to smile. Richard took the ink pen and gave it back to John. Then without uttering a sound, he said, "Leave the pen in your room."

John read his lips and nodded. He and Regina walked away.

"Okay, sir, we will see you later," John said as he was walking away. They walked to their room, number 506, and stepped inside. The young man who brought up their luggage was waiting for them. John thanked the young man and gave him $2.00 as he was going out the door. Regina placed their suitcases on the bed and began to unpack them. She left a blouse and pair of shorts out for changing into, hung some clothes in the closet, and put the rest in the dresser. She began to undress so she could change into the clothes she had laid out previously. John walked into the bathroom to wash his face and hands before they left. He placed the ink pen on the sink, along with his ring and watch. When he finished washing his hands and face, he put on his ring and watch. He left the bathroom, leaving the ink pen on the sink. When he walked into the room, Regina was brushing her hair.

THE COVERUP

"I saw a gift shop downstairs. Want to go find something for the kids?" John asked.

"Okay, let me fix my face, and I will be ready to go," Regina replied.

"Okay," John replied as he pointed to his watch, indicating that time was running out. He walked over to the TV to pick up the remote and turned it on. He began to flip through the channels while he waited for her. Regina sat down in front of the dresser and began to fix her makeup. John continued to flip through the channels while he waited. After a few minutes, he checked his watch. He turned and walked over to Regina. He bent down and looked at her in the mirror. "You are gorgeous," John said.

"And you are one handsome man," Regina replied.

"You ready?" John asked.

"Yeah," Regina answered. She got up from the chair and turned to face John as he took her hand, and together they walked into the hall. She waited for John to follow. He took one last look at the room and walked out the door, closing it behind him.

As Regina and John walked down the hall, they talked about what they thought Richard had planned. When they arrived at room 510, John knocked three times on the door. The door opened, and there standing in front of them was Richard. He was still made up to look like an old man. "Come in," Richard said as he stepped aside for them to enter.

"Man, am I glad to see you," John said.

"Did you think I wasn't coming back?" Richard asked.

"Well, I was a little unclear what you had planned. What is with the makeup?" John asked.

"It was the only way I could meet you without anyone noticing me."

"They sure did a good job. I didn't recognize you under all that makeup."

"Let me introduce you to our makeup artist," Richard said as he turned to a woman standing beside him. "This is Elizabeth Jones. And this is John and Regina Barton."

"I am pleased to meet you," Elizabeth said as she held her hand out to shake John's.

"Yes, nice to meet you, too," John replied.

"I am happy to meet you," Regina said as she held out her hand.

"Okay, over here is Ike Marten. He is an actor, and he is playing my Scottish nephew," Richard said. Ike walked over to them and held out his hand to greet them.

"Nice to meet you both," he said as he shook their hands.

"Now, I am sure that you are wondering what this is all about," Richard said.

"Well, I am a little curious," John replied.

"Okay, the plan is to have Elizabeth make you up like Ike here, and to make Ike look like you. Then you and I can slip away without anyone noticing us," Richard explained.

"You can make him look like me?" John asked.

"Ike is the same build as you. All I have to do is make the face features the same," Elizabeth explained.

"Now, don't worry, John. Ike is an actor, and he is gay," Richard said.

"That is true, sir. I am a professional, and I do like the boys," Ike replied.

"Great, someone has to play me, and you go and get a gay guy!" John shouted. "No offense."

"John, trust me. It will be just fine," Richard answered.

"Sir, I assure you. I will play your part just like a straight person, and the best part, I will not fool around with your wife," Ike told him.

THE COVERUP

"Well, I don't know. What do you think, Regina?"

"I guess it will be all right, John."

"See, Regina's okay with it. Trust me, John. I would not do you wrong," Richard added. "Without trust, this whole plan will not work. Come on, what do you say?" he asked.

John stood there for a moment mulling over the whole idea of a gay playing him. The thought of another man with his wife made him nervous, even if he was gay. He wondered if this whole thing was worth it, but the thought of starting over again turned his stomach. He always thought Regina saw him as a coward for walking away from the FBI without a fight. John knew if he did not take Jack down, he would never get rid of him, so maybe it was best to go through with Richard's plan.

"All right. Let's do it," John replied.

"That's the spirit!" Richard shouted.

"Richard, what exactly am I supposed to do?" Regina asked.

"Just be your natural self. Go out, have fun, like you were out with your best friend," Richard replied.

"Okay, but it's going to feel really weird," Regina replied.

"Ike is going to take you into the other room. I want you to sit down and get to know him. He is a likable guy. You will love him," Richard told her.

Ike and Regina walked to the other room while Richard and Elizabeth got ready to fix up John. First, Elizabeth took pictures of John from all sides. Then she clipped some of John's hair for a color match for Ike. She began to prepare John's face for the mask he would wear. She took the pictures and put them on a scanner so she could download them into her computer. Once all the pictures were in the computer, she started a program that would match John's face with pictures of Ike. The computer took those images and turned them into graphics. These graphics would show just where to place the plastic to change John's face to look like Ike. When it was ready, Elizabeth went to work putting on John's face. While she worked on the face, Richard went into the other room to check on Regina.

"Have you ever been to Soul Falls before?" Ike asked Regina.

"No, I have never been there."

"Oh, dear, you must go. It is so beautiful there."

"Really? I must get John to take me there some day."

"When you get there, go to Tony's Restaurant. They have the most divine linguini you ever did taste."

Richard could see that Regina was starting to like Ike. She was getting more relaxed with every word he said.

"How's it going, guys, or should I say girls?" Richard remarked.

"Okay, enough with the queer jokes, Richard. He's been picking on me ever since he called me to do this job, but I still love him, like a brother, that is," Ike quipped.

"I'm sorry. Sometimes I just can't help myself," Richard replied.

"Yes, it's like a disease with you, isn't it?" Ike returned.

"Okay, I will leave you two alone," Richard said as he walked out of the room.

"I have a great idea. Why don't I treat you and John to a trip? Better than that, I will take you there myself. If I can get Carlos to go with me, we will make it a fun weekend," Ike said.

"Oh, I don't know if John would like that."

"Why not? Does he hate gays or something?"

"Well, let's just say he is uncomfortable around gays."

"He doesn't have to worry. I won't bite, you know."

"I'm sure he knows that."

"To each his own, I guess, but the offer still stands if you should change your mind."

"Well, thank you, Ike. I will talk to John about it."

"Good. Now tell me a little something about John, you know, what he likes and doesn't like."

"Well, he doesn't like going to art exhibits, but I drag him along anyway," Regina answered.

"Oh, and you do like to go to them, right?"

"Yeah, I like to go to the museum, too, but John thinks all that stuff is boring."

"Does he have any noticeable habits, like maybe a nervous twitch or something he might do all the time?" Ike asked.

"No, not that I have noticed, except he does put his hands in his pockets and rocks back and forth sometimes when he is trying to talk romantic."

"Okay, give me an example."

Regina put her hands in her pockets and began to rock back and forth. She began to talk and act like she saw John do on several occasions.

"Okay, like this?" Ike asked. He began to rock back and forth on his heels. Then he started to talk in a romantic way to Regina.

"Yeah, that's exactly how he does it," Regina answered.

Regina and Ike continued to work on copying John's actions while John and Elizabeth worked on his face.

WILLIAM DANIEL

AT FBI HEADQUARTERS
Chapter Twenty-Three

FBI headquarters in Dallas. Jack was checking upon the progress of the surveillance. He picked up the phone and began to dial a number. The phone started to ring on the other end.

"Hello," said a voice on the other end.

"Have there been any changes?" Jack asked the agent on the other end.

"No, sir. He's just sitting there fishing and drinking beer," the agent replied.

"Were the divers in the water when he went diving?" Jack asked.

"No, sir. They did not get here in time to go in," the agent replied.

"So, what you are telling me is we have no way of knowing what happened when he went into the water?" Jack asked.

"That is pretty much it, sir," the agent replied.

"Okay, continue the surveillance and keep me posted." He hung up the phone and began to dial another number. While the phone rang, he began to write down some notes of the last conversation.

"Yes, sir," said a voice on the other end of the line.

"Any changes since we last talked?" Jack asked.

"No, sir. He was last reported in his room with his wife. However, they did meet some old man who invited them to his room for a drink," the agent reported.

WILLIAM DANIEL

"Did he go?"

"I'm not sure, sir. The last thing we heard was the water in the bathroom when he went to wash his face and hands."

"And nothing since then?"

"No, sir. It has been quiet ever since."

"The equipment working okay?"

"Yes, sir, everything's working. I think he may have left the pen on the sink in the bathroom."

"Hmm, do you think he knows about the bug?" Jack asked.

"Could be, sir, or maybe he just forgot the pen when he left."

Jack mulled over the situation for a few moments. Then he began to see a possible pattern in the back of his mind.

"Continue the surveillance. Let me know of any changes," Jack said as he hung up the phone. He began to think of all the possibilities that might be going on. He knew these two quite well, and he was positive something was wrong in Denmark. He quickly picked up the receiver of his phone and began to dial a number.

"Yes, sir," the agent answered at the other end of the phone line.

"Get a boat and go out to see if that is really Cooper on that boat," Jack commanded.

"Yes, sir. Right away," the agent replied.

"Get someone to replace you at your post before you go."

"Yes, sir. Right away."

"You know what he looks like. That is why I want you to go yourself. Do you understand?" Jack asked.

"Yes, sir. I met him a couple of years ago. I know what he looks like. I will take care of it myself," the agent replied.

THE COVERUP

"Make it look like you are going fishing. Then ask for a fishing report."

"I will take care of it, sir."

"Wait a minute. Did you say that you met him a couple of years ago?" Jack asked.

"Yes, sir, I did."

"Send someone else. He might recognize you," Jack ordered.

"I'm not sure anyone else knows what he looks like, sir."

"Change your appearance, send a picture! I don't care what you do! Just get it done!" Jack screamed.

"Yes, sir," the agent replied as he hung up the phone.

Jack sat motionless, staring into space, while he mulled over the situation. After a few moments, he picked up the phone and dialed a number. While he waited for the party to answer, he began to write down some notes in a folder. He wrote down the information he got from the agents. As he was writing, a voice came across the phone line. "Is he in?" he asked.

"Yes, sir. One moment, please," the President's secretary answered.

"Jack, how are you?" said a voice over the phone receiver.

"Fine, Mr. President."

"Jack, we are old friends. You can call me Ted. Besides, if this story gets out, I will not be President for very long."

"Just trying to respect your position in office, Mr. Pres...I mean, Ted."

"That's better, Jack," Ted answered. "General Rumsfield is on the line with us."

"Jack, James Rumsfield here. What is our situation now?"

"Well, to tell you the truth, I'm still gathering information from the field," Jack answered.

137

"Tell us what you have right now, Jack," Ted said.

"Well, we know that John and his wife are in the hotel in Galveston, Texas, but we are not sure if he knows about the bug."

"What about the other one?" James asked.

"I ordered some divers to go in the water at the same time Cooper did, but they did not get there in time," Jack continued. "I sent a boat out to see if it is really him on the boat."

"That was a good idea, Jack," James said.

"However, the other one has met some old man in the hotel," Jack explained. "I'm not sure if something is going on here or not, but I am going to find out."

"Do what you have to, Jack. We must keep this thing a secret," Ted said, "Even if it means killing them."

"I understand, sir," Jack replied.

"Jack, we trust your judgment on this. I hope this personal thing between you and John Barton doesn't cloud your thinking," James said.

"I assure you, General, I have the interests of national security in mind," Jack answered.

"Good, Jack. Let us know if there are any changes," Ted replied.

Even though Jack told them he was not out for revenge, in reality, he was. Jack's jealousy had taken over his ability to choose right from wrong. All along, he had planned to kill John and Richard, and it was a matter of when and how. He had baited John and Richard with the Chupacabra, and planned to use the creature to kill them. He knew that Richard would fall for this setup. After all, he had been following the creature for a long time. Every time the Chupacabra was sighted, Richard was there. The little rich kid, poking his nose in things he shouldn't have. With all his family money, he could get into things and buy his way out. Jack hated him, and he wanted to get him off his back. John, however, would be a little harder to sell without the help of Richard. He knew Richard would talk John into it if given the opportunity to do so. All he had to do was get the two together and let their suspicious minds take over. He knew Richard's curiosity would sucker him in without a problem, but he knew that John would be suspicious of anything he was involved in. In order to get him involved, he would have to kill someone in his county. He was sure John would take things personally if he knew what he was up to.

WILLIAM DANIEL

THE COVERUP

BACK IN GALVESTON WITH THE MAKEUP ARTIST
Chapter Twenty-Four

Elizabeth was working on John's face. Changing John's appearance would not be that hard for her. She had changed many an actor's face over the years, and John's was no different from theirs. A rubber mask and a little makeup here and there, and John would look just like Ike did.

"What's your plan, Richard?" John asked as Elizabeth continued to work on his face.

"I have everything in place. Let me bring you up to date on my plan," Richard answered.

He began to explain what they were going to do. First, John and Ike would change identities, which was why Elizabeth was hired. Then Ike would leave with Regina, as if it were she and John on vacation. John and Richard would stay and carry on as the old man and his nephew. Regina and Ike would tour the town like tourists. John and Richard planned to board a plane headed for El Paso, Texas. Richard wanted to see Professor Donner at the University of El Paso tomorrow. The Professor had some important information that would help in their investigation. This information was very important, and had been kept a secret by Professor Donner. From El Paso, the two men would travel by car.

"The rest of the plan will be kept secret for now," Richard explained.

The less John knew, the better off he would be if things should go wrong. After Ike was made to look like John, he and Regina would retire to their room and stay there for the rest of the day. That evening they planned to dine out on the town and return to their room for the night.

John's face was taking shape as the nephew of the old man while Regina and Ike continued to go over John's habits. It was very important for Ike to be able to look and act like John, to fool Jack. He would need to learn all of the hand jesters and body movements. Also, he needed to know anything John liked and disliked. Ike needed to feel the part, as well as look the part, to act like John. The timing was important to keep Jack on the wrong trail. Richard knew Jack would be watching them all the time. The transformation must go smoothly so he and John could slip away before Jack knew what was happening. He knew it would be hard to fool Jack, but if he could get a small window of time, he and John could slip away. His plan was to stay ahead of Jack's thinking so they could reach their destination before Jack knew what was happening. By the time Jack could figure out what was happening, they would have their evidence to nail him.

It was 11:00 a.m. when John's face was finally finished and Elizabeth was satisfied with the work she had done. Richard stepped into the next room to ask Ike to come into the room with John. As the two men stood side-by-side, Regina, Richard, and Elizabeth compared John's face to Ike's.

"You are good," Regina said to Elizabeth as she studied the two men.

"Thanks," Elizabeth replied.

Richard already knew what Elizabeth was capable of doing. After all, he did hire her.

THE COVERUP

Regina walked over to John and put her arms around his neck and asked, "Doing anything later, stranger?"

"Don't get used to this disguise," John replied. "As soon as this is over, this is coming off."

"Too bad. I kinda like it," Regina replied.

"Okay, let's go into the other room so Elizabeth can work some more of her magic," Richard said as he led them into the next room. It was time to transform Ike into John. This was a crucial job for Elizabeth. In order to fool Jack, she must make Ike look like John down to the least little detail. For many years, she had worked on lots of actors. Changing their appearance was what she was good at. Now she must use her experience to make one man look like another without any flaws.

In the other room, Richard was going over Regina's schedule for the day. He had planned for her to have a day of visiting art galleries. This would keep her and Ike busy for most of the afternoon. Richard and John would be boarding a plane bound for El Paso.

"Why are we going to El Paso?" John asked.

"You and I are going to see Professor Donner. He has some very important information for us," Richard answered.

"What kind of information?"

"The kind that is going to lead us right to the Chupacabra without even looking for him."

"So it really does exist?"

"Oh, yeah. It exists all right. Believe me, I have seen it."

"Well, if you say so, but I have my doubts."

"Trust me. It has all been set up. All we have to do is slip past Jack long enough to get to your destination. When we get there, we will then be able to expose the whole thing to the public. Jack will not be able to touch us after that. The President

WILLIAM DANIEL

will have to arrest Jack for the murder of Josh Hernandez. Then an investigation will probe into the disappearance of other people who have witnessed the creature. This will also open up the investigation into the Roswell crash of 1947. To actually prove that the crash did happen is going to be big on its own. But to prove that the Chupucabra is one of the aliens of that crash will be even bigger. To prove that our government covered it up all these years will be even bigger. You just don't know how many people want to believe. They are afraid of being called crazy for believing in something this bizarre. To be frank, I have had my doubts myself. Until I saw it myself, I didn't believe that the Chupacabra existed either. But I saw it, and I know that it was real. I have spent a lot of time and money trying to prove it is real. Now I'm about to prove that I was right. I have seen the same fire in your eyes ever since you and I met. You want to prove this thing as much as I do," Richard explained.

"That is where you are wrong. I could care less about this creature or proving that it exists. All I want to do is solve the murder of Josh Hernandez. If that means having to prove your creature exists, then that is what I will do," John replied.

"Oh, come on, John. Don't you have a desire to solve a fifty-something year old case that has been swept under the rug by our government?"

"Actually, no. I am afraid of what it might do to this country if everyone knew aliens existed from other planets. What about the Bible, the good book? Will it destroy that faith in God, as well as our country? What about all the people who believe in the Bible and all that it has taught us? Do we throw all that away, too? What are people going to believe in if all that is no longer the truth? How will they go on with their lives?" John screamed.

THE COVERUP

"Proving that aliens exist is not going to destroy the Bible. For all we know, God created these aliens as well as he created us. In fact, I would be a little disappointed if God created human beings only. That would make this a very lonely universe that we live in. I don't want to destroy the Bible or what people believe in. I would like to prove that God created other creatures besides what is on Earth. The Bible is a good book to follow throughout your life. Right or wrong, it is still a good book to follow because it teaches only good things. I don't want to destroy the Bible. I just want to prove that I am not crazy, that what I saw was real!" Richard screamed back at John.

"Well, I guess you have a right to prove your sanity, but when it comes to exposing this to the public, I think we should use some consideration. Maybe we can handle it in a different way," John replied.

"Like what?" Richard asked.

"I don't know. Maybe we could bring it to the President of the United States, instead of telling the public point blank."

"John, where we are going, we will not have a chance to bring evidence to the President. Jack will kill us before we ever get close. Besides, we are not going to be able to tote the Chupacabra out of this place we are going. The only thing we can do is expose the whole thing from there, show it to the public and get them to stand beside us."

"And what makes you think they will believe us?"

"They won't, but there are scientists inside this place that are wanting to expose this thing, so they will believe. That is why it is important for us to get there, to help them bring this thing out. Otherwise, more people will die at the hands of Jack. I know you do not want that to happen."

"No, I don't want that to happen."

145

"Then you have got to believe me," Richard said as he walked over to the small refrigerator to get himself a drink.

"The whole thing sounds so bizarre," Regina added. "I mean, how could this thing be real and our government cover it up?"

"You think I don't know how crazy this thing sounds? Do you think I don't wonder if I am crazy myself?" Richard replied.

"Richard, I didn't mean to imply," Regina started to say before Richard interrupted her.

"That I sound a bit crazy, or maybe this is the product of a wild imagination? You can't imagine how many people think that same thing. You don't know how many times I have told this same story only to become an outcast by my own family? Everyone in my family thinks I have lost what little brains I once had. I'm not even allowed to join in on family get-togethers anymore. They are afraid of exposing their lives to a crazy notion of aliens from another planet. You know I have never worked for money in my entire life. My parents have never worked for money. My entire fortune is family money that has been passed down over the years. When I graduated from high school, I went straight to college. When I graduated from college, I put together my own team of anthropologists and archaeologists," Richard continued as he took a drink from the water bottle he got from the refrigerator.

I financed every dig I went on. No one paid me to dig in the ground for old relics or bones of strange creatures. But to bring back the past, to unearth creatures that once roamed the earth, to find and dig up things that mother earth has kept secret for millions of years, has fascinated me. When I was in junior high, I had to bring to school a current event for class one year. I found this article on a giant octopus that

THE COVERUP

had washed up on this beach years ago. This creature was so bizarre, that they took a photo of it. It was like three hundred feet long, the length of a football field. Even though I had a photograph in my hand of this creature, they did not believe me. They all laughed at me and made jokes about it. No one wanted to believe that an octopus could grow to be the size of a football field. Even though I had a photograph in my hand, proving it did exist, they did not believe me. The creature was buried in a field that is now a football field for some local high school," Richard explained.

"Why don't they dig it up and show them?" John asked.

"Because an octopus doesn't have a skeleton. It is nothing but flesh and a beak that it eats with. You see, flesh and cartilage will not leave fossil remains for you to dig up. In a situation like this, you only have a photograph as evidence that this creature existed. Years ago, a legendary anthropoid called the mountain gorilla did not exist in the scientific world. Yet, it was discovered in Africa in the last century. People reported seeing the creature, but nobody believed them. No one believed the Tasmanian tiger existed, and it only went extinct in the 1920's. Big Foot, and the Loc Ness Monster are two creatures that people have seen, but nobody believes them to be real. Until they find one alive or dead, no one will ever believe they existed. The same goes for the Chupacabra. No one is going to believe in its existence until it is exposed to the public," Richard explained.

Elizabeth opened the door to the next room where John, Regina, and Richard were waiting. She walked into the room and told Richard she was finished with Ike. Then she walked over to the refrigerator and took out a bottle of water.

"Ike, you can come in now," she said as she opened the bottle of water.

All eyes turned to the doorway where Ike was entering. No one said a word as Ike walked into the room and stood in front of them. Silence remained in the room as they gazed upon her creation. Everyone sat there staring at Ike for several seconds.

"You are good!" Regina said as she broke the silence. John stood up and walked over to Ike to get a closer look. As he stood there looking at Ike, Regina got up and walked over and put her arms around Ike.

"Hi, honey. Where have you been?" Regina asked just to tease John.

"Now, wait a minute," John said as jealousy took over his mind.

"John, it's just an act," Regina replied as she let go of Ike and put her arms around John.

"Well, make sure it's just an act."

"Elizabeth, you are the greatest makeup artist ever," Richard announced.

"Why, thank you, Richard, but I just did what you paid me for. That's all."

"And it's worth every penny, too."

Richard turned his attention to Ike. He was convinced Ike now looked the part, but what about his acting?

"Okay, Ike, how is the voice copying coming?" Richard asked.

"Well, I can't answer that question. You tell me," Ike replied as he spoke in John's voice.

"Very good, very good. I think that will pass the test," Richard replied.

Several hours had passed since John and Regina had landed in Galveston. It was now 1:00 in the afternoon, and all was going as Richard had planned.

THE COVERUP

"Okay," Richard said as he looked at his watch, "I'm going to order us some lunch to be sent up. Then it will be time for John and me to depart for El Paso."

"Yeah, lunch, that's what I've been missing," John said as he looked at his watch.

"Is it that late already?" Regina asked.

"Actually, it is 1:00 in the afternoon," Ike answered while looking at his pocket watch.

"Well, I'm starved. What are you going to order, Richard?" Elizabeth asked.

"Whatever you guys want."

"Steak and baked potato for me," John said.

"Me, too," Regina said.

"I think I will have a chicken salad," Ike announced.

"Hey, that sounds good. I'll have the same," Elizabeth said.

Richard walked over to the phone and called the front desk. In his Scottish voice, he asked for the restaurant. The hotel clerk got the restaurant on the phone for him. Richard turned in the order for everyone. He told the waiter who took his order to put the bill on his tab. Then he walked back to his chair and sat down. As he watched Regina and Ike talking, he smiled. He felt quite confident that he had put together a good crew. He listened as they discussed some of the habits John was always doing. He turned his head in the direction of John and Elizabeth, who were discussing John's makeup. His plan was falling into place just like he wanted it to. All he had to do now was get Regina and Ike out into the public. In this way, Jack's agents would be watching them so he and John could slip away. He would send Regina and Ike out on the town to shop and visit museums. While they were doing that, he and John would slip off to the airport. He began to envision how his plan would go. First, Ike and Regina would leave the hotel for the museum. After they had left, Elizabeth would depart for the airport. John and Richard could slip out of the hotel into a cab and get on a plane before anyone knew what was going on.

It was 1:30 in the afternoon as Richard sat quietly in his chair listening to the others talk. Suddenly a knock came to the front door. The room became silent as everyone stopped what they were doing. Richard jumped from his chair and ran to the door in the other room. As he approached the door, he motioned to the others to stay out of sight. He opened the door to see who it was.

"Good afternoon, sir," said the young man standing in the hall. The young man was tall and skinny with long black hair. He was wearing a black waiter's suit and had a cart behind him with their food.

"I have your order here, sir," the young man said. He walked toward the door pulling the cart behind him. Richard stepped back and allowed the young man to enter.

"Ah, thank you, laddie," he said as he opened the door all the way.

"Where would you like me to put it, sir?" the young man asked.

"You can be sure you can leave it right there," Richard answered.

"All right, sir. Just sign right here," the young man said as he held out the bill.

Richard took the bill and signed it. He reached into his pocket and pulled out a twenty-dollar bill. He placed the money on top of the bill and gave it to the young man.

"And this is for you, laddie," he said.

THE COVERUP

"Why, thank you, sir, and if you need anything else, you just call me. My name is Scott," the young man said as he walked out the door.

"Well, you can be sure that I will, laddie," Richard replied. He closed the door and walked to the other room. "Food's here. Come and get it," he told the others as he walked into the front room and began lifting the lids on the servant cart.

"John, you and Regina had steak, right?" Richard asked.

"Yeah, that would be mine," John replied.

"Here you go," Richard said as he held the plates out to him.

"Thank you," John said as he grabbed the two plates.

"Let's see. This one is chicken salad, and I guess this one is too. Elizabeth, Ike, these are yours," Richard said as he turned and gave them their plates.

"Thank you, Richard," Elizabeth replied.

"Here you go, Ike," Richard said as he gave the plate to him.

"Thanks, Dick," Ike replied.

"Don't be calling me that. Somebody might get the wrong impression!" Richard screamed.

"Why? It's your name, isn't it?" Ike asked.

"Be as that might be, but when you say it, it sounds wrong," Richard answered.

"Why, Richard, I do believe you are blushing," Ike returned.

"Not while I'm eating, please," Richard begged.

"Can't a guy have some fun around here. Besides, you're not on my list," Ike replied.

"I thought all men were on your list," Richard said.

"Not bosses," Ike replied.

"He has a list? I hope I'm not on it," John said.

"Oh yeah, cowboys are at the top," Ike replied.

"Oh, God, that is all I need, to be on your list," John said.

"I didn't say you were on my list. I said cowboys were at the top. Nothing I like better than riding a horse," Ike replied.

"Oh, God, I think I'm going to be sick," John said.

"Please, people, I'm eating!" Richard screamed.

"This is ironic," Elizabeth said as she was putting the dressing on her salad. "Earlier today, John was worried about his wife being with Ike. Now he's worried Ike is fantasizing about him. Now, that's funny."

"I'm not fantasizing about him, unless you want me to," Ike replied.

"Oh, God!" John moaned.

"It appears to me that you should be the one worrying," Elizabeth said to Regina.

"Believe me, I'm not worried," Regina replied.

"I don't know. Ike's pretty cute," Elizabeth said.

"Yeah, but John's a man's man," Regina followed.

"That's just what I like, a man," Ike said.

"Oh, God!" John moaned again.

"People, please I'm eating!" Richard screamed.

"I might change your life, John," Ike said.

"Oh, God, no thanks. Now I know I'm going to be sick," John replied.

"I'm just teasing you, John. I don't see you as an attractive man," Ike replied.

"I'm not attractive to you?" John asked.

"Nope," Ike answered.

"Now wait a minute. Maybe the light isn't right or something," John replied.

"Doesn't do a thing for me," Ike said.

THE COVERUP

"Well, I tend to grow on people when you get to know me better," John replied.

"If you say so," Ike replied.

"Here, let me give you my card," John said.

"John, what are you doing?" Regina asked.

"I was just going to give the man my card."

"I don't think so," Regina said.

"People, please!" Richard screamed as he walked out of the room with his plate in hand.

"Call me," John said to Ike.

"John!" Regina screamed.

"I'm just kidding him. I didn't mean anything by it."

"He's a lot of fun," Ike said.

"Yeah, a barrel of monkeys by himself," Regina said sarcastically.

Richard sat down in a chair by the window. He set his plate of food on the windowsill. With his fork in hand, he began to eat his food in privacy. While eating, he stared out the window at the people walking down the sidewalks. It was not that Richard hated gay people. He just didn't want to hear about it while he ate. He knew what Ike was before he hired him. Gay people didn't bother him. What they believed in was not what he believed in.

Suddenly a sense of urgency came over him as he watched the people walk by. He began to look more closely at each and everyone who was outside the hotel. Something wasn't right. He could feel it. The more he looked at each individual, the more he felt it. Somewhere deep down inside, he knew someone was watching them. Like an investigator looking for clues, he stared at each individual as if they were an FBI agent. He noticed a man standing in a doorway across from the hotel. This man seemed to be watching everyone coming and going from the hotel.

"FBI agent," he thought to himself.

A moment of caution fell upon his mind as he watched the man standing in the doorway. The thought had not occurred to him. Maybe Jack knew what they were up to. How could he know this? He had checked the room thoroughly for bugs when he first got there. He knew John had left the pen with the bug back in their room. Could it be that this man was told to watch every move John made? He began to scan the area for more suspects. He figured when Ike and Regina left the hotel, this man would follow them, but what he didn't know was whether or not there was another one watching.

"How can we be sure this was the only agent watching?" he thought to himself. What would be the next move to take? Should he and John go out separately so the other one could watch what happened? Maybe he should have Elizabeth watch so she could report what happened. He figured he had better inform the group so they could discuss what to do.

"Yeah, that's what we will do," he thought, "but not until they finished their meals. Why upset them now when they were enjoying themselves so much?"

In the other room, the group was still talking and laughing. As they were finishing their meals, they were asking each other questions about their lives. Ike was interested in John's and Regina's kids. He asked how old they were, what their interests were, what school they attended. He wanted to know all about them in case he was asked any questions later. Regina informed Ike of every detail about them. Just like a good mother, she was proud of her kids. John was asking Elizabeth about all the actors she had worked with. He was amazed at how many big name actors she had worked with. Naturally, he asked what each one was like. It kind of shocked him that each one was not like they seemed on film.

THE COVERUP

"You mean to tell me that he is an asshole?" John asked.

"Yeah, he is a great actor, but in real life he's not a person you want to know," Elizabeth answered.

"Really? He seems so nice in his movies."

"You would be surprised at the different attitude they have when not in front of a camera," Elizabeth explained.

"To each his own, I guess," John replied.

"I'm sure that if you were put in front of a camera, you would change, too," Elizabeth said.

Richard heard the conversations and laughter getting louder from the other room.

"Well," he thought to himself, "I guess it's time to get this show on the road."

Richard got up from the chair and walked into the other room. Everyone looked at him as he entered.

"Okay, people, we have some issues to deal with before we go our separate ways," Richard announced.

He turned around and switched off the lights in the other room as he walked over to where John was standing and asked them to gather around. Regina walked over to John and put her arm in his. They faced Richard from his right side. Elizabeth and Ike faced him from his left side.

"Okay, I just noticed from the window in the other room there is a man standing in a doorway watching the hotel. I am sure he is an agent sent here to watch John and Regina. We must decide how we are going to leave here and keep them off guard. I don't know if there are more of them, but there could be. John can give us some input as to how they handle their operation," Richard said as he turned to John.

"Well, they probably have a car somewhere with two agents watching. This is in case someone takes a cab or a car when they leave. If I know Jack, he will probably have one or two agents in the lobby. We are looking at maybe four or five agents watching from somewhere. There will be a van set up for communications. That's standard procedure in a stakeout. They will follow each one of us with one or two agents. They will probably have someone watching the back, also. That's the way I would handle the situation, and I'm sure Jack will, too," John explained.

"So we are covered from all sides?" Richard asked.

"Most likely, and I don't see any way of getting out without being seen. But if we could cause a scene, a distraction, something that would cause them to pull some of the agents away, this might give us time to slip away," John explained.

"What kind of distractions are you talking about?" Richard asked.

"Well, we all know about the terrorist attacks on nine eleven," John stated.

"Yeah," Ike replied.

"Who could forget that?" Elizabeth said.

"You mean call in a terrorist threat of some sort?" Richard asked.

"That's a felony, you know," Ike said.

"Yes, I know, but a fire, a bank robbery, car accident, or any other kind of incident will not pull them off. The only thing Jack would have to respond to would be a terrorist threat. This would get some of the agents off the case in a hurry. I don't know how you could pull this off, but this is what I would do," John explained.

"Okay, how about an airplane in a no-fly zone at NASA?" Richard asked.

"No, this would draw the Air Force in. We need something that would draw ground attention. It would have to be something Jack would have to send some agents to investigate.

THE COVERUP

Something that would force the government agents in on," John said.

The group began to mull over ideas of how they could pull the FBI into an investigation. What would cause such a scene that Jack would have to pull some of his agents off of the group and into an investigation? This scene would have to be very dramatic, something everyone could see happening, something that could cause a quick response from the FBI and local law enforcement. John knew, whatever they decided, it would have to involve lots of American citizens, something that would cause national attention to the scene. A quick response was what they needed. This would allow John and Richard to slip away without notice. This would prove to be the group's hardest decision.

"Okay, people, think. We must come up with a solution now," Richard said.

"What if we park a yellow rental truck in front of a federal building?" John inquired.

"That's not a bad idea, John," Richard said.

"We could have someone park the truck and walk away quickly," John said.

"Yeah, tell me more," Richard requested.

"Okay, we get an Arab man to park a box van in front of a large federal building. We put a large lock on the back door, have the Arab man wearing sunglasses step out of the box van and walk away. Maybe have a car pick him up as soon as he steps out of the van," John explained.

"Why a big lock on the back door?" Ike asked.

"It will take longer for the agents to open the door. This, in turn, will keep them there longer. They will have to wait for a bomb squad to open the door," John explained.

"And the Arab will make it more realistic, right?" Ike asked.

"Well, it would be more believable if we had an Arab to do this," John replied.

"What do you think, Regina?" Richard asked.

"Well, I would believe it if I were standing there," Regina replied.

"How about you, Elizabeth?" Richard asked.

"Oh, yeah. I would, too," Elizabeth replied.

"Ike, what do you think?" Richard asked.

"I guess if I were standing there and saw an Arab man pull up a box van to a federal building, get into a car that pulls up and drives away in a hurry, yeah, I would believe it and run like hell," Ike answered.

"I think it would be better if we have someone on the street to call it in," John added.

"You mean have someone there on purpose to call the FBI from the area?" Richard asked.

"He could use a pay phone in the area and be a witness when they show up," John said.

"Not bad, not bad at all," Richard added.

"He could explain everything he saw and be totally innocent," John explained.

"Good input, John. I know just the man to pull this off. Abdul Jamjar, he owes me a favor, and he is good at pranks. John, come with me and help with the planning," Richard said.

"Is there anybody this guy doesn't know?" John whispered to Regina.

"Doesn't seem like it," Regina replied.

"Say he owes you a favor, Richard?" John asked.

"Yeah, I lent him some money when his wife was in the hospital. He's an Arab who moved here years ago. He didn't have any insurance and was in debt up to his ass with hospital bills," Richard answered.

THE COVERUP

"And you paid his bill? What a nice guy you are," John replied.

"Yes, I know."

"So he's going to do a favor for you that could get him thrown out of the U.S. Is that your plan?"

"Yeah, he'll do it."

"What, you're not going to pay him?"

"Of course I'll pay him."

"You're kidding me."

"No, I always pay for the services I need."

"Just how rich are you?"

"Very rich."

"Want to adopt me?" John asked jokingly.

"No way. You're too old and ugly to be my son."

John and Richard walked into the other room where the phone was. Richard picked up the phone and dialed the front desk clerk. John walked over to the window to scope out the scene to see if he could spot the agents. He turned to Richard and said, "I wouldn't use the hotel phone. It might be bugged, you know."

"You're right. I'll use my private cell phone."

He hung up the hotel phone and began to look around the room and walked over to a table in the corner and picked up a wireless. He began to dial a number while John continued to look out the window. He was calling information to get Abdul's phone number. When the operator gave him the number, he wrote it down on a notepad on the table. When he was finished, he looked up at John who was still staring out the window.

"See anything else we need to deal with?" he asked.

John turned to Richard and shook his head, "No."

After a few rings, a voice answered, "Hello."

"Abdul, how are you?" he asked. "This is Richard Cooper."

"Mr. Cooper, how nice to hear from you," Abdul answered.

"Listen, I need a favor from you."

"For you, anything you want, Mr. Cooper."

"I need for you to rent a van, put a lock on the back door, park it in front of a federal building, and have someone call the F.B.I," Richard explained.

"What is in van, Mr. Cooper?" Abdul asked cautiously.

"Nothing, just an empty box van."

"What is purpose of parking van in front of building?"

"How's $100,000 sound?"

"Sounds like I'm renting van and parking in front of federal building," Abdul answered.

"You really are rich," John said.

"I'll explain it to you later, Abdul," Richard said.

"Whole thing sound risky, but I'll do it," Abdul replied.

"Don't you worry, I'll take care of you, Abdul."

"You're my best friend, Mr. Cooper. For you, I will do anything you ask. If it were not for you, I would be out of America. I love America."

"Soon as you park the van, get someone to pick you up. Then get away from there, and don't come back until tomorrow. It is very important that you get away as quickly as possible."

"Yes, Mr. Cooper, I will take care of it right away."

"Thanks, Abdul. You are a good man. Say hi to your wife and kids for me."

"Yes, I will, and you will come see us soon?"

"You can count on it. I want some more of your wife's cooking."

"Oh, very good. I will tell them you will come soon."

THE COVERUP

"All right, Abdul. 'Bye now," Richard said as he turned off the phone. He turned to John, who was still looking out the window. He walked over to the window where John was standing.

"His wife's cooking, huh?" John said.

"Yeah, well, she's not that good a cook, but they are great company," Richard replied.

"You are just an old softy, aren't you?"

"Yeah, well most of my friends hang around because I have money."

"Money isn't everything, you know. I can't believe I just said that," John remarked.

"That's what I like about you, John. Money doesn't impress you. You may be the only real friend I have now," Richard replied.

"Well, I don't want to work for you. But if you change your mind, I'm still available for adoption," John said sarcastically.

The two men laughed out loud. After the laughter died down, they turned their attention to the street.

"So, I guess we wait now, huh?" John asked.

"Yeah, but we should see some results in about thirty minutes," Richard replied.

As they watched the streets for results from Richard's plan, the others walked into the room and took a seat.

"So, what are we doing now?" asked Ike.

"Well, we are waiting for a plan to take effect. As soon as the results happen, I want you and Regina to take a cab and go visit a museum. Here is the address of the museum. Now you will have to call a cab from John's room. Stay at the museum for about an hour. Then return to the hotel and make plans for the evening. Regina, treat this just like you and John planned it," Richard explained.

"I understand," Regina answered as she got up and walked over to where John was sitting.

"You will be careful?" Regina asked.

"You can count on it babe," John replied.

John reached over and gave Regina a little kiss, and turned to Ike and said, "Take good care of her for me, and no funny stuff."

"Please, John," Ike replied. "The very thought of being with a woman sickens me. I'm an actor. I only play the part of being straight. The very notion that I would lower myself to being straight is unappealing to me. However, if you should want to change your style, give me a call."

"Now cut that out!" John shouted as he backed away from Ike.

"I'm just teasing you."

"All right, you two, knock it off. We have work to do!" Richard shouted.

Richard stepped away from the window and turned to Elizabeth. "Thanks for everything, Liz. Your check is in the mail already."

"Thanks, Richard. Will I be hearing from you soon?"

"Sure, I'll call. We'll have dinner."

"Yeah, I've heard that line before. Well, then, I will be on my way. Good luck, guys."

She walked into the other room, grabbed her bag, and out the door she went. As she was leaving the room, everyone said goodbye.

Richard walked over to the window to take a look at the agent watching the hotel. The agent was still there watching everyone coming and going. John walked over to the window to look for himself. "Are they still there?" he asked as he peered out the window.

THE COVERUP

"Yeah, they're still there," Richard answered.

"So, how long do you think it is going to take to put this plan in motion?" John asked.

"Shouldn't be long now," Richard answered.

"Think it's going to work?" John asked.

"Sure it will. I have every bit of confidence in Abdul getting the job done. He's a good man, you know. I trust him with every little thing I own."

"Well, I don't know him at all, but I do trust you."

"Thanks. That means a lot to me, John."

"Do a lot of people trust you, or is it just your money they trust?"

"Most people want my money, that's it. Abdul wouldn't give me the time of day if I hadn't bailed him out that day. There's something about money that makes people go crazy. I don't know what it is. I have had money all my life, and it hasn't changed me a bit. But I'm glad to have a friend like you who really trusts me and not have to pay for it."

"I do, as long as you don't screw it up," John said jokingly.

Richard and John waited by the window while Regina and Ike talked about John and how he would react to certain things. Meanwhile, Abdul had contacted a friend to rent a van for him. He knew it would be hard for him to rent one because he was an Arab. His friend was an American and would have no trouble renting the van. Abdul waited by a street corner while his friend signed the papers on the van. As soon as he was finished, he was to drive to the corner where Abdul was waiting. He would then get out and walk away. Abdul would take the van to the federal building and park it. He would run from the van, making sure lots of people could see him. Abdul had called another friend to pick him up at the corner of the street across from the federal building. The two men would take off making as much noise as they could. They would call the police and alert them of a strange van parked there. They would, also, tell them an Arab man ran from the van.

At 4:30 p.m., back at the hotel, Richard and John waited for Elizabeth to exit the building. Keeping their eyes on the agent below, they watched for his reaction to her leaving. Elizabeth walked out of the hotel, turned to her right, and walked down the sidewalk. She was heading for her car parked in the garage down the street.

"There's Elizabeth," Richard said as he and John watched the agent across the street. The agent looked at Elizabeth as she walked out of the hotel but had no reaction as she was leaving.

"Well, she's clear. He doesn't recognize her," John said.

"Yeah, I guess she will make it," Richard answered.

His plan was unfolding as he had hoped it would. Next thing to do was to get Regina and Ike out of the hotel. They had to wait for Abdul to set the plan into motion.

The tension in the room was so thick you could cut it with a knife. Each person was sitting with his own thoughts. Richard was thinking he was about to crack the case of the Chupacabra and expose those involved, and he was thinking of all the times he was accused of being crazy. What was this thing that drank blood from animals? Could it be an alien from another planet that landed here more than fifty years ago? Could it be that what he saw was just a figment of his imagination? Could all the evidence he uncovered be fabricated by willing jokesters or pranksters? What about all the eyewitnesses that claimed to have seen it? In Richard's mind, it was real. All his emotions were focused on finding the truth. John, on the other hand, just wanted to solve the murder of a citizen. He had not thought of what might really be this creature that stalks animals in the nighttime. There have always been legends and monsters that have never been explained. Bigfoot, loc ness, giant squid, giant octopuses, and sea serpents, legends of monsters are rarely seen, yet documented over the years by sailors and adventure seekers. John did not think of these things. He just wanted to get Jack Riley off his back and out of Regina's life for good, so the thought of making that a reality was all he needed to keep going. Maybe somewhere deep inside, he really did want to believe in aliens from another planet. Regina just wanted to be with John. Her only thought was of him and what he believed in. She, too, wanted to get Jack out of the picture forever. If this were what John wanted to do, she would see it through with him. Not once did she ever think of what might be lurking in the darkness of night while she slept. Ike had no interest in strange unknown creatures. He was an actor, and his thoughts were always on the performance. His mind stayed focused on the job at hand, how to act like John and make people believe he was John. He was constantly watching John's every movement so he could repeat it as perfectly as John did. Everyone sat quietly waiting for the phone call from Abdul.

Sitting with their innermost thoughts, they were roaming their eyes to see what everyone else was doing. Suddenly Richard's cell phone began to ring. Everyone jumped in their seats as if they were watching a scary movie. Richard walked over to the end table where his cell phone was and picked it up to answer it.

"Yes," he said into the tiny phone.

Richard stood silently as he listened to the voice on the other end. All eyes in the room were trained on Richard.

"Good, thanks," Richard said as he pulled the phone down and turned it off. "Well, the game is about to begin."

"What do you mean?" John asked.

"That was Abdul. He has placed the van in front of the federal building. Now he will call the FBI and notify them of his intentions. We will soon see if this plan is going to work."

THE ESCAPE
Chapter Twenty-five

As soon as Richard said that, everyone turned his or her attention to the window. After a few seconds of staring at it, they all walked over to see what was happening outside. Everyone stood silently looking out the window at the FBI agent on the sidewalk. They were waiting for him to make a move. The tension in the room had risen to a new high. They were like thoroughbred horses waiting for the gates to be opened. Their nerves were about to explode as they waited for something to happen.

"There, he just got a call from someone," John said as he pointed out the window.

"Looks like it," Richard said.

The FBI agent stood on the sidewalk talking to someone on his radio. Suddenly a black sedan drove up and stopped where he was standing. He opened the door and stepped into the car. The car sped away at a high rate of speed.

"Well, there he goes," Richard said.

"Think they took the bait?" John asked.

"Looks like they did," Richard answered.

"So, now what?" John asked.

"Okay, let's go. Ike, go over to John and Regina's room and get that pen he left over there. Then you and Regina meet us at the elevator," Richard said.

"We are out of here," Ike said as he grabbed Regina's arm and walked with her to the door.

"Don't say anything about where you are going! Let them figure it out!" Richard shouted as they were leaving.

"John, grab that duffle bag and let's head for the elevator," Richard said.

John grabbed the bag that was lying on the bed. He noticed the bag was quite heavy as he lifted it off the bed.

"What is in this thing? It's kinda heavy."

"Something we are going to need, trust me."

"Well, okay, let's go," John said as he threw the bag over his shoulder.

The two men hurried out the door. They walked down the hall until they came to the elevator. John set the heavy duffle bag down on the floor.

"They should be along soon," Richard remarked as he turned and looked down the hall where their room was. He turned back and said to John, "Remember, let me do any talking."

"You got it."

"What is taking them so long?" Richard asked.

"I don't know." John replied.

"Here they come," Richard announced as he watched Regina and Ike walk down the hall to the elevator. Richard turned to the elevator and pushed the down button. As soon as Regina and Ike got to the elevator, the door opened. The four of them stepped into the elevator, and Richard pushed the first floor button. The doors closed and the elevator started to move downward.

The four of them stood silently in the elevator as it lowered to the first floor. John, looking over at Regina, gave her the thumbs-up sign. Richard took out a notepad he had in his pocket and began writing something on it. When he was finished, he handed the note to Ike. Ike took the note from

THE COVERUP

Richard and read it to himself. Then he handed it to Regina so she could read it. She took the note from Ike and began reading it to herself.

'Regina, Ike, if you do not hear from us in five days, call this number, 1-800-266-5999. This is my lawyer's number. He will know what to do. If you get into any trouble, call him, and he will take care of it. Memorize this number, and give it back to me so I can destroy it. Good luck. We will call you in five days.'

Regina looked at the number and began saying it to herself over and over to memorize it and gave it back to Richard. He took the note and put it in his pocket.

The elevator finally reached the first floor and came to a stop. The doors opened and Regina and Ike stepped out and headed for the front door. Richard, with his hand on John's chest to hold him back, waited a couple of seconds. He took his hand off of John, and they walked out of the elevator. This gave Regina and Ike time to reach the front door. At the front door, Ike opened the door, and Regina walked out to the sidewalk. They turned to the right and began walking down to the corner. Ike was constantly looking up and down the street for a cab. John and Richard walked out the front door of the hotel, turned to the left, and walked down the sidewalk to the corner.

"Well, so far so good," Richard said as they were walking.

"Looks like it. What do we do now?" John asked.

"I have a car waiting for us in that parking garage across the street," Richard answered.

He and John looked both ways and walked across the street to see if anyone was following. When they reached the other side, John looked to see if anyone was following them. He noticed Ike and Regina getting into a cab and driving away.

"They got a cab," John said as they walked into the garage.

"Good. Now let's get our car," Richard replied.

He walked into the parking garage and began looking for the attendant. He saw an office over to the left and motioned for John to follow him. They walked up to the office and stepped inside. There was a man sitting at the desk writing on some papers.

"Excuse me, laddie. Could you be getting me car for us?" Richard asked as he held out his ticket.

"Sure thing, sir. Be just a minute," the man said as he looked up at them. He went back to writing on the papers. When he was finished, he looked up at Richard and asked for his ticket. Richard handed him the ticket. The man took it from him and looked at the number. He walked over to the corner of the room where a microphone was. He turned on the microphone and said, "Tony, get number 411 and bring it to the front." He walked over to Richard and told him it would be just a few seconds. Richard looked at the man, a short, fat, stocky man who walked with a limp and had a short cigar in his mouth.

"Thank you, my good man," he replied. He and John walked over to a place beside the office and sat down on a bench. They waited silently, occasionally looking to see if the car had appeared.

"Here it comes," Richard remarked as an old Chevrolet Impala came roaring down the upper ramp.

"An Impala? I was expecting a Corvette or a Ferrari," John remarked.

THE COVERUP

"We want to go unnoticed, not run up a red flag so they can find us."

"At least we could have outrun them."

"If they don't notice us, we won't have to outrun them."

"I hope I don't have to push this thing to get it going."

"Have a little faith. The Impala is a reliable car."

The attendant pulled the car up to where John and Richard were standing. He got out of the car and walked around to the other side. He gave the keys to Richard and looked at John.

"I didn't think there were any old Impalas still around," the attendant said as he walked away.

"'Tis not the looks of a car that makes it run well, laddie," Richard remarked as the attendant walked away. He looked over at John who was smiling at him. "You guys just don't know a good car when you see one," he said as he walked around to the driver's side.

John walked over to the car and opened the door on the passenger side. He sat down on the seat and put on his seatbelt. Richard opened the driver side door and sat down. He put the key into the ignition and started the car. He put the car into drive and pulled out of the garage. When he hit the street, he reached down under the dash and flipped a switch. The old Impala began to lope like a hot rod with its headers uncapped. He stomped on the gas, and the car started to spin its wheels with tremendous force. A huge cloud of smoke from the burning rubber tires covered the car. When gravity finally caught up with the spinning wheels, the car took off. Like a bullet fired from a gun, the Impala sped away. John, pinned against the front seat of the passenger side, was in total shock. He turned and looked at Richard, who had a big smile on his face. He realized at that point that Richard enjoyed going fast. He looked as if he enjoyed speed like a drug addict. The faster he went, the more he loved it, and the more he wanted it.

John turned his eyes to the speed odometer, and he saw it had reached one hundred miles per hour. "I thought we were trying not to attract attention!" he shouted at Richard.

Richard began to slow the car down. He turned to John and said, "Sorry. When it comes to fast cars, I sometimes lose control."

"Yeah, well, I think you have lost your mind," John replied. "You can let me out at the corner."

"Relax, Holmes, I got it," Richard replied.

"No, that's okay. I'll walk from here," John said as the car slowed to the speed limit.

"All the way to El Paso?"

"Is that where we are going?"

"Professor Donner has some information for us. It is very important that we meet with him, or we will never accomplish our mission."

"It is going to be tough to get in to see him with Jack on our trail."

"John, you don't have any confidence in our plan."

"Jack is very smart. He could be ahead of us right now, you never know."

"Have a little faith, my friend. It is a very good plan we have put into play here."

"Don't get me wrong, Richard. Your plan is perfect, but Jack is always a step ahead of everyone. The guy studies crime all the time. He has caught a lot of criminals that way. He seems to know exactly where you are going to be before you get there. The guy never married. I guess crime is his whole life."

"Ah, come on. Jack dates, just may not be the opposite sex that he is dating."

"Not since Regina and I got married."

THE COVERUP

"Well, maybe he just hasn't found the right girl, or guy, or transvestite that does it for him."

"I know one thing. He has tried several times to break up Regina and me."

"So with you around, he has a personal vendetta, as well as professional?"

"Seems that way."

"Well, that does make for a bad combination."

Richard and John continued to talk about Jack as they drove down the street. Turning onto a main street, they were unaware of a black sedan pulling in behind them.

"You know that you will never get rid of him," Richard said as they continued to talk about Jack Riley.

"Yeah, I figure one of us will have to die first. I hope it's him," John sarcastically replied.

"Me and you both, my friend, me and you both."

They continued down the street not realizing they were being followed. They came to a red light and stopped. Richard glanced in the rear view mirror, and then looked up at the traffic light. Suddenly his brain registered something he saw in the rear view mirror. He casually looked back in the mirror to see what was there and noticed the black sedan following them.

He looked over at John and asked, "You remember that black sedan at the hotel?"

"Yeah, what about it?" John asked.

"I think he's behind us right now."

"What do you want to do?"

"I'm going to make a right turn just to see if he's following us. You look out the right side and see if you can spot them out of the corner of your eye."

Richard turned the Impala to the right onto another street. As he made the turn, John glanced out the right side of the car. He noticed the black sedan slowing down to make the same turn. "Yeah, that's the FBI, all right," John said as he turned his head back toward Richard.

"Didn't take them long to figure out what was going on at the federal building," Richard said.

"My guess is they never went there," John replied.

"You think they were waiting for us to leave so they could follow us?"

"I told you. Jack is smart. He may be a slime ball, but he's a smart slime ball."

"Got any suggestions as to how to handle this?"

"Well, we could stop and ask them what they want," John sarcastically replied.

"Very funny. Do you think we can outrun them?" Richard asked.

"You're just dying to light the wheels on this hot rod, aren't you?"

"I think I asked an intelligent question which should have got an intelligent answer."

"You're not going to admit that you just want to mash on the gas of this thing you call a car."

"Well, do you think we can outrun them?" Richard asked again.

"I'm not going to talk you out of this, am I?"

"My guess is no."

"I don't want to die in a piece of shit Impala."

"Have a little faith, my friend. It's a beautiful car."

"It's a piece of shit."

Richard maneuvered the car into the outside lane. He began to look for an opening that would give him an advantage when

THE COVERUP

he took off. He saw an opportunity coming. A young woman and her child were about to cross the street at the corner in front of them. Richard sped up to cut her off so he could get in front of the sedan. The young woman began to shout at him. The sedan following them was forced to stop for the woman. When they stopped, Richard slammed the accelerator to the floor and made a right turn. The sedan was forced to wait for the young woman to cross in front of them. Richard drove a couple of blocks before the sedan could make the turn.

"We got them now," Richard said as the Impala roared down the street. John was glued to his seat. The Impala continued to scream down the street as Richard made several turns.

"You have any idea where you are going?" John asked.

"Yeah, I know right where I'm going," Richard replied as he drove the car up one street and down another. When he came to an intersection, he turned the car to the left and drove down the street until he came to a beach house. He pulled the car up to the beach house and stopped.

"Why are we stopping here?" John asked.

"Get out quick!"

"What are we doing? Can't we just keep going?"

Richard opened the driver side door and stepped out. John grabbed the door handle and opened the passenger door, jumping out and screaming at Richard, "What are we going to do here, hide out or something? They are going to catch us if we stop! They will find this place in a matter of minutes!"

"End of the line, John. Now we make a stand."

"Make a stand? We don't have a chance against them. Have you lost it or something? They are going to be on us in a matter of minutes. This is a bad idea, Richard. It's not going to work!"

"That's a chance we are going to have to take, John," Richard said as he calmly looked at John.

"You're crazy! Okay, what the hey. We got nothing to lose now," John said as he closed the door to the car.

"Hey, John!"

"What?"

"Grab that bag out of the back seat!" Richard shouted as he stepped onto the porch of the beach house.

"Oh, yeah, the bag." John had forgotten the bag he had put in the car. "What is in this thing?" he asked as he pulled the duffle bag out of the car.

"You'll find out real soon," Richard replied. He noticed a black sedan roaring down the street. "Let's get inside," motioning for John to come on.

John ran over to the porch where Richard was standing. Richard turned to the door on the beach house and opened it. Walking inside he looked around the room. It was starting to get dark outside, so it was hard to see. Richard turned to John and grabbed the duffle bag from him. He reached inside of the bag and pulled out a flashlight. He turned on the flashlight and shined it inside the duffle bag he was holding. He reached inside and pulled out an object. John stood there watching Richard and saw what he had pulled from the bag. It was a gun, and a very large one at that. Suddenly fear and disappointment hit John's face. He couldn't believe Richard had plans to shoot it out with the FBI. He was sure Richard had lost his mind. After all, he didn't know Richard that well. In fact, he had only met him a couple of days ago. Richard took the gun and walked over to a window in the front of the house. He took the flashlight and broke out the window and after pointing the gun at the two agents who were exiting the sedan, began firing two rounds at them. The agents ran behind the sedan to keep from getting shot. They pulled their weapons but did not return fire. Richard watched as one of the agents got out a radio. The agent began calling someone, possibly for backup. Richard turned his head toward John. He could see him standing there very still.

"What?" as he could see some confusion on John's face.

"What do you think you are doing? How do you think we are going to shoot this out?"

"It's just a starter pistol. I had it made for starting the relay race for the Boy Scouts I sponsor at camp every year," Richard answered.

"Oh, well, that makes things better. They will still kill you over it!" John shouted in a low tone.

"Are you always going to be like this?"

"Like what?" John asked.

"A worry wart," Richard replied.

"I'm not a worry wart. I'm just concerned about my life."

"You know, you're just like a woman."

"And how is that?"

"Well, you nag all the time."

"Oh, so now you are an expert on women."

"I have dated hundreds of women. I should be an expert, but never did I ever find one I could marry."

"What? You couldn't buy one somewhere?"

"Now that hurt."

"Sorry, I couldn't help myself."

"You can't possibly know what it is like to be me. Constantly dating one after another, hoping this is the one. Only you find out they are around just for the money, not because you are sexy, handsome, or smart, to be loved just for the money you have. You just can't believe how many I thought was the one. I would find out they just wanted to marry a rich man. I mean, I would give my entire fortune to find the right one. How do you know when you have found the right one?" Richard said, his eyes beginning to tear up. He turned to John and asked, "How can you tell?"

"You will know," John answered.

"Yeah, but how will I know? What signs do I look for?" Richard asked.

"I'll tell you how it was with Regina. When I first met her, I knew she was the one. My stomach began to get those butterflies. I found myself unable to take my eyes off of her. I had to force myself to go up to her and introduce myself. When our eyes met, it was like we had known each other all the time."

"I never felt that way about anyone I have met. Most of the women I meet are beautiful and sexy. They don't seem to have a problem sleeping with me. It's all about the money and that's it," Richard replied.

"Let me ask you something, Richard. If you had a choice between the right one and the money, tell me, would you give up the money and take the girl?"

"Not on your life. I sleep with gorgeous women. What more could you ask for?"

"Yeah, well, how about buying us out of this situation. We are trapped here, you know."

"Have a little faith, John. We will make it."

"Well, you have been right until now. Okay, let's do it."

"Good. Now grab the duffle and follow me," Richard instructed.

THE COVERUP

THE SMUGGLERS' TUNNEL
Chapter Twenty-six

John grabbed the duffle bag and followed Richard into the next room. Richard walked into the room and headed for a closet door. He opened the door and walked inside. John followed him, dragging the duffle bag behind him. Once they were inside, Richard began to run his hand over the inside wall. He found a hidden handle and pulled a door open. John stood there with his mouth open with a surprised look on his face.

"What?" Richard said as he turned to face John.

"What is this place?" John asked.

"Oh, I bought it from a drug smuggler years ago. He retired and moved to India to live. It has a tunnel that leads into the ocean. The guy brought drugs into the country from a ship offshore. He never got caught, so the feds don't know about it. I thought I might use it for something legal," Richard explained.

"And I thought you were crazy. What are we going to do, swim to El Paso?" John asked.

"Oh, ye of little faith trust me. I do have a plan."

"Yeah, you're right. I have a problem with that faith thing."

"Come on, you will see," Richard said as he walked into the tunnel.

John followed, still dragging the duffle bag behind him. The tunnel made a sharp left turn. As soon as they made that turn, there were some stairs going straight down. Richard took the flashlight and shined it on the stairs. He began climbing down the stairs while John waited for him. He lowered himself onto the stairs, pulling the duffle behind him. They climbed down about ten feet and came upon a small room. Richard helped John pull the duffle bag into the room. He set the bag down on the floor and opened it and began pulling out two pairs of snorkel fins and masks. He reached back inside and pulled out two small air tanks with mouthpieces.

"I'll say one thing about you. You always seem to be prepared for every occasion," John remarked.

"Well, one never knows what might happen," Richard said as he checked both tanks to see if they were working right.

"No, you didn't guess on this one. You had this planned all the time."

"Well, let's just say I figured if we drove, we would get caught."

"So what are we going to do? Swim out and thumb a ride with the first ship that passes?"

"Not exactly."

"Then what? Surely we are not going to swim to El Paso?"

"No, I have a boat waiting."

"And what makes you think they won't send the Coast Guard?"

"Actually, it never crossed my mind. See, we're not going on top of the water."

"So you have a submarine waiting for us offshore?"

"Well, not exactly. It is a mini-sub."

"How did you know things were going to happen this way? I mean, how could you do this and not really know what was going to happen? You never intended to drive to El Paso, did you?"

THE COVERUP

"Look, John, if I told you we were going to scuba dive into the ocean, would you have come?"

"No, I wouldn't."

"Let me tell you something, John. I knew we would never make El Paso on land. Jack is going to figure out where we are every step of the way. The best thing to do is to change everything as we go. It's the theory of the hunted and the hunter. The prey constantly changes his direction in order to outmaneuver the hunter. The more things you throw in the way, the more likely you will get away. While Jack is figuring out what has happened here, we can slip away in another direction."

"Yeah, but doesn't the prey always get caught?"

"Most of the time."

"So, chances are we are going to get caught, right?"

"We have the upper hand at this moment. By the time Jack figures out what has happened, we will be in El Paso. Besides, Jack's the least of our worries right now."

"What?"

"Well, sharks," Richard said in a very low tone.

"Sharks? Oh no! I'm going back! I'm going to take my chances with Jack," John said as he started up the stairs.

"I wouldn't do that, if I were you."

"And why not?" John asked.

Suddenly a loud boom rocked the tiny room where they were standing.

"That is why," Richard replied.

"What was that?"

"Well, that would be the explosives I had set before we came down here," Richard explained.

"What explosives?"

"I had placed some plastic explosives in one of the walls some time back before we started this quest."

"So you blew up the house?"

"Yeah, I set the timer off with a switch on the wall in the closet, just before we came down the tunnel. We can get out of here now."

"Look, Richard. I have never scuba dived, let alone ride in a sub. I don't know if I can do this."

"Don't worry. I'll be right there with you. Just breathe normal. There is more than enough air in these tanks for where we are going. Take maybe ten minutes tops. There's at least thirty minutes on these tanks."

"Breathe normal, he says. I'm going under the water where I have never been before, not to mention facing sharks. And what about the sub? Are we just going to bump into it or something?"

"Don't worry. I have a locator beacon. Soon as we hit the water, I will turn it on. The sub should find us real fast."

"I hope you are right."

Richard started putting on the gear and told John to do the same. As soon as they were ready, Richard led the way down the tunnel that went to the ocean. Soon they came to a place where water filled the tunnel. They put their masks on and turned on each other's tanks. With Richard leading, they walked into the water and swam under. As soon as they were underwater, Richard pulled the beacon out of his pocket. He pushed the button on the top to turn it on. They swam a good distance until they came to an opening into the ocean. They swam out for several minutes. Richard looked back at John every few seconds to make sure he was okay. After they swam straight out from the tunnel, Richard stopped. He shined the flashlight all around them. With the sun nearly down, things were getting dark.

THE COVERUP

Suddenly a light came shining out from the dark. Richard motioned to John and pointed at the light coming toward them. John knew he was telling him it was the sub. They waited for the mini-sub to come to them. When it finally arrived, Richard motioned for John to follow him. They swam under the sub to a hatch. Richard waited for a green light to come on beside the hatch. He opened the hatch and pushed John inside. He closed the hatch and pressed a red button. John stood in the tiny room as the water began to recede. As soon as it was gone, the inside door opened. There stood an old gray haired man who opened the door all the way.

"Come in," the man said. He reached inside and took John by the arm to help him into the sub.

"Thanks," John said as he took off the mask and air tank.

"Kelly Winthrop," the man said as he held out his hand to greet John.

"John Barton," John replied as he shook the man's hand.

"Excuse me, John," Kelly said. He maneuvered around John so he could close the door to the hatch. He pressed a green button to fill the diver's chamber for Richard. Richard opened the latch as soon as the green light came on. He climbed inside and waited for the water to subside inside the little room. As soon as the water was gone, Kelly opened the door.

"Hey, boss," Kelly said.

"Hey, Kelly. I'm glad you found us," Richard replied.

"No problem, boss," Kelly answered as he changed places with Richard. The sub was only big enough for two people. Kelly had to get in the diving room so Richard could get into the sub. Richard handed his facemask and fins to Kelly.

"Thanks, Kelly," Richard told him as he handed him his air tank and flashlight.

"Catch you later, boss. Nice to have met you, John," Kelly said.

Richard closed the door and pressed the green button. He climbed into the pilot seat and began checking out the sub. John sat down in the other seat and watched Richard. As soon as Kelly had cleared the sub, Richard pushed the sub into maximum speed. He pulled out some charts and plotted a course that would land them near El Paso.

"How long before we get there?" John asked.

"Well, in a normal mini-sub, we wouldn't make it, but I have modified this one so it can run much faster and farther. See, these subs run on battery power, but I added a twist to this one. It also has a small gas powered engine that will recharge the batteries and push the sub. The only thing is to run on the gas engine. We must surface. Two problems come into play. One, we will be exposed to any traffic on the surface. Two, we will have to deal with the weather conditions. If the sea is rough, it will take us longer. The gas-powered engine will only push us about fifteen knots, and it only holds two gallons of gas, which is not going to last long. It should be enough to recharge the batteries. Then we can make the rest of the way under water. Once we get there, we will have to exit the same way we came in," Richard explained.

"Yeah, but how many hours?" John asked again.

"I don't know exactly how many hours. My guess is maybe twelve to fifteen."

"That's a long time from now. I'm getting kind of hungry. Got anything to eat?" John asked.

"Yeah, there are some granola bars in the overhead compartment to your right," Richard replied.

"Granola bars? I guess that will have to do."

"It will, 'cause that is all we have on board."

THE COVERUP

"I was sure you would have a barbeque grill somewhere on here."

"Wouldn't that be nice? I could go for a nice grilled steak about now."

"Yeah, and a six-pack of beer would hit the spot."

"Give me one of those bars. All this talk about food is making me hungry, too."

The sub was flying through the water like a graceful seal. Richard had turned the lights down to a minimum to conserve power. He was now piloting the sub by its radar and depth finder to avoid objects on the sea floor. Staying close to the shore, he would have to watch for coral extensions and man-made objects. Richard was staying close to the surface in order to clear objects on the ocean floor. He knew he was going to have to resurface and recharge the batteries sometime soon, and he knew the sub would only run for a few hours at top speed, but at the moment, the gauge read ninety per cent. They would be able to run a couple of more hours before the batteries would go down.

Richard flipped on a radio to check the weather report. He needed to know what the conditions were like on the surface. The weather report stated that winds had picked up considerably. This would last for several hours and diminish by midnight. The sea in the Gulf of Mexico would be rough until then. This was not good news for them. Richard knew the tiny engine he had added would not push the sub very fast in rough waters. Their only bet was to get as far as they could on the batteries, and then surface and recharge the batteries while they fought the sea.

"Well, that was a really good steak. How was yours, John?"

"I prefer mine to be hickory smoked. Otherwise, it tastes like a granola bar."

They began to laugh as the sub flew through the water. Suddenly the sonar picked up on an object straight ahead. Richard quickly slowed the sub down to avoid a collision with the object.

"What is it?" John asked nervously.

"Probably a ship that sunk some time ago," Richard replied.

As the sub got closer to the object, it got bigger. Suddenly the object appeared. It was a large shrimp boat that had sunk. Richard piloted the sub around the shrimp boat.

"See those nets on that ship?" Richard asked.

"Yeah, I see them."

"They're very dangerous. Get caught in one and you could be trapped for a long time."

"Look at that!" John shouted.

"Yeah, it's a reef shark. Looks like he found the net. Once they get hung up in them, it stops their motion. Sharks can't breathe when they stop like that. They have to swim to keep water flowing over their gills. Once he gets hung up in that net, he will drown," Richard explained.

"That is sad. You're born and live your whole life in water, only to drown in it," John said.

"Yeah, those nets should be cut loose. I'm going to mark where this ship is and notify someone about it."

"Tell me something. How is it you know about everything?" John asked.

"Well, I have done a lot of traveling. Sailed around the world three times. Scuba dived all around the world. When I'm home, I read a lot of books. I took a lot of classes at several colleges. I don't have a nine-to-five job. It can get very boring with nothing to do, so I stay busy doing something. Keeps my mind off the loneliness."

"All that money, and you are lonely."

"I never said I was lonely. I just don't like being alone. I like to stay busy, that's all."

"All right, whatever you say."

The two men talked on as the sub continued to whirl through the water. The batteries had dropped to sixty per cent, but for the time being, the sub was running good. Richard knew the power would drop much quicker now. He kept one eye on the batteries while he piloted the sub. Suddenly another object came up on the sonar. This time it was on the surface. He figured it was a ship passing over, but to be on the safe side, he stopped the sub until it passed. Then he took off in full power.

Thirty minutes passed, and the sub's power dropped to forty per cent. Richard figured now was as good a time as any to surface. He powered the sub up to the surface, started the little engine, and took off across the gulf. The sub bucked and swirled around as the little engine purred on. The waves, which were slamming against the sub, pushed it closer to the shore. Richard turned the sub into the waves to keep from hitting the reef. For every minute he went forward, he would have to go out the same amount. The progress was very slow, and they weren't making much ground, but it was necessary to build up the charge on the batteries.

WILLIAM DANIEL

JACK AT HOME
Chapter twenty-seven

At 8:30 p.m., Riley residence, Plano, Texas, Jack sat down in his favorite chair and turned on his stereo. He picked up a magazine and started to thumb through the pages. The cd player loaded the music he had selected. Orchestra music was Jack's favorite music, so it was no surprise when Johann Sebastian Bach's music started to play. He leaned back in his chair that was made of fine leather. His eyes trained on an article in the magazine. Quietly, he sat reading to himself while Bach played. His thoughts were far from the job he performed everyday. Jack was a high-class man. Nothing but the highest quality products was in his house. If it were the best of the line, Jack would buy it. He was quite content and tame when he was off duty, not the mean, underhanded backstabbing agent he was on the job. But with Richard and John preying upon his closest secrets, he was on duty all the time. Constant surveillance was his way of dealing with this case. He worked hard to get where he was. Nobody was going to take it away without a fight.

Suddenly the phone began to ring. Jack put down the magazine he was reading. He picked up the cordless phone lying on the table beside his chair. He looked at the number on the caller ID. It was one of his agents calling him. It was the agent he had sent to find out who was on the boat. Jack pushed the talk button and said, "Hello."

"Mr. Riley, this is agent thirty-four. We have completed our visit to the boat."

"And you have concluded it is not Richard."

"Uh, yes, sir."

"Continue your surveillance of the boat. Report to me if there are any changes," Jack ordered.

"Yes, sir," the agent replied.

Jack hung up the phone and went back to his magazine. He knew Richard was not on that boat. For several years now, he had been following Richard's every move. It was like he knew what he would do next. Some of the agents believed he was psychic, but it was really just years of observation. It was experience that told Jack what could happen, but by the same token, it was a guessing game. If you could guess what the quarry would do next, you would catch him at his game. If not, you would only trail behind him. It was like a chess game. You had to know what your opponent's next move was. If not, you would be on your heels defending your own territory. One way or another, Jack would always come away the victor. If he could not beat you legally, he would kill you, or at least have you killed because there was no way Jack was going to fail.

Bach continued to play on the stereo while Jack read the magazine. After he finished the article he was reading, he placed the magazine on the table by his chair and walked over to the bar in the corner of the room. He picked up a glass and opened the ice bucket sitting on the bar in front of him. He put some ice into the glass, reached for a bottle of Crown Royal, and poured himself a drink, and replaced the bottle on the shelf.

The phone began to ring again as Jack walked back to his chair. He placed the drink on the table and picked up the phone. The caller ID read Charles Goodwin, a friend of his. He

THE COVERUP

pushed the talk button and placed the phone to his ear. "Hey, Charles, what're you up to?"

"Jack, how's it going?"

"Okay, I guess. Just this darn case I'm dealing with is keeping me up."

"Yeah. Who's involved? Do I know them?"

"You know I can't tell you about a case I'm on, so don't bother asking."

"Still the hard-nosed FBI agent, huh, Jack?"

"What do you want, Charles?" Jack asked in a perturbed tone.

"Okay, okay, don't get your feathers ruffled. Bobby and Bill came over to visit. The three of us are going to the Nasty Lady for drinks. Thought we would see if you wanted to come, too."

"No, I'm busy," Jack replied with a cold tone.

"Come on, Jack, loosen your tie up. Get out and socialize. You're in dire need of stress relief!" Charles shouted.

"Not tonight, Charles. I've got some things to attend to."

"That job of yours is going to kill you. You haven't been out with us in three months. The stress is going to give you a heart attack!" Charles screamed.

"Goodbye, Charles," Jack said as he hung up the phone. He picked up the glass of whiskey from the table. Swishing the ice around in the glass to cool the drink, he raised the glass to his lips and took a drink. He sat the drink back on the table and picked up the magazine. He started to flip through the pages when the phone rang again. He picked up the wireless phone and looked at the caller's name. It was the agent he had stationed in Galveston. He pushed the talk button and said, "Yes."

"We have a bit of a problem here, Mr. Riley. We were called to a disturbance at the federal building. Someone parked a yellow van in the front and walked away. I have one of the guys trying to find out who it was, but on the way, I got a little suspicious and turned back. I saw the Bartons get into a cab and drive away. I sent Pete in a car to follow them. When I was heading back to the stakeout, I saw two men crossing the street. I called Joe in from the back, and we followed them. It was just a hunch, sir, but it turned out to be Cooper and Barton dressed up," the agent explained.

"What happened?" Jack asked.

"Well, they tried to run, but we caught them. One of them took a couple of shots at us. We ducked behind our car, and I called for help. They climbed into an abandoned beach house. A couple of city police cars pulled up. I informed them we had some suspects in the house. I told them to block off the area. After a few minutes went by, the beach house blew up."

"It just blew up?"

"Yes, sir, it exploded into an inferno!"

"What's the status now?"

"At this moment, I can't confirm they are alive or dead."

"Get that fire under control as soon as possible. I want that entire building searched for clues. I need to know if they died in that fire. Have someone search the beach for footprints. They may have escaped out the back. I need to know what happened as quickly as possible," Jack ordered.

"Yes, sir, Mr. Riley."

Jack hung up the phone and placed it on the table. He picked up his drink and took a sip. Slowly, a mean, sinister grin came to his face. The thought of the two of them dying in a fire brought happiness to him. He downed the rest of his drink and got up from his chair. He walked over to the bar and lay

THE COVERUP

down his glass. Pulling the top off of the ice bucket, he began to refill his drink. Reaching behind him, he grabbed the bottle of Crown. He took off the cap and began to pour. As soon as he poured a little into the glass, he laid down the bottle. He picked up the glass and began to dance around like a ballet dancer, humming to the music of Bach the whole time.

Suddenly he stopped dancing and laid his drink on the table by his chair. His face had gone completely blank. A frightened and confused look took the place of the happiness. The thought of the beach house and the ocean behind it filled his mind. He knew Richard was a diver. "Could he have planned the explosion to cover up his escape?" Jack asked himself. He quickly grabbed the phone and began to dial. "If they did go into the ocean, where would they go?" he thought to himself. Then it came to him like a flash of light. The ocean would be a quick unsuspected way of getting to El Paso. They're going to meet with Professor Donner, he thought.

"Yes, sir, Mr. Riley," came the voice at the other end of the call. He had called the agent who was watching Richard's boat.

"Get someone to take your post. I want you to go to El Paso immediately. Stake out at the University of El Paso. Keep a close eye on Professor Donner. Our suspects may be heading there to see him," Jack ordered.

"Yes, sir, right away."

"Report to me if you see them there."

He hung up the phone and laid it on the table again. He picked up his drink and took a big gulp of the whiskey. Fear had replaced the emotions on his face. The thought of the two of them pulling off a great escape plan had him worried. He sat down in his chair sipping on his drink. He got up and walked into the next room. He walked over to a desk in the middle of the room. Reaching down, he opened a drawer and pulled out an atlas map. He opened the map until he found the Gulf of Mexico. He began to study the map, noticing there were several places they could dock. He figured they would not go back to Corpus Christie. Richard would know his agent was there and would probably avoid him.

"Port Lavaca or Angleton is where he will hit land and run to El Paso. If he is headed to see Professor Donner, why?" Jack asked himself. Donner must have some information for Richard. Jack knew Richard and Professor Donner were working together. The phone, which Donner used to talk to Richard, was bugged. Jack ordered it after Richard was seen at some of the sightings. He knew Richard had studied under Donner.

Jack walked into the living room and got the phone lying on the table by his chair and dialed a number. He sat down in his chair waiting for someone to answer.

"Yes, sir, Mr. Riley," said Tom Bradley. Tom was Jack's special agent to the President, and his link to the White House.

"Is he in, Tom?"

"Hang on. I'll get him for you, sir." Tom put Jack on hold while he paged the President.

"Yes," answered the President.

"Sir, Jack's on line one," Tom answered.

"Okay, Tom."

"Jack, how are you?" Ted answered.

"Fine, Ted, and how are you?"

"Great, Jack."

"The situation is heading in the direction we were afraid of. I think they are heading to talk to Donner. I'm not sure what information he has for them."

THE COVERUP

"Are you sure, Jack?"

"They were seen entering an abandoned beach house. The house exploded into flames. I am not sure if they got out or died there. My agents are checking it out as soon as they get the fire out. I have a hunch they are not there."

"What makes you say that?"

"Well, we have an abandoned house. Most likely the gas and electric are turned off. There doesn't seem to be any reason for that house to catch on fire. The only way would be if someone set it ablaze."

"So you think Barton and Cooper set it on fire to escape?"

"It's possible. Richard could have staged an escape."

"Do you have some proof, or is this a theory of yours?"

"Richard is an accomplished diver. He could have had the equipment stashed or brought it with him. I don't have any proof of that, but it is possible. One of my agents saw the Bartons leave the hotel they were staying in. That was after someone reported a van parked in front of the federal building in Galveston. My agent had a hunch, and instead of checking out the report, he went back and spotted them leaving the hotel. He also spotted two men leaving at the same time. On a hunch, he followed them and had his partner follow the Bartons. These two men tried to run but wound up at the beach house. He is sure it was Barton and Cooper who entered the beach house," Jack explained.

"You think maybe he had a boat waiting for them to escape in?"

"As you know, sir, he is rich. It's just a theory, but I have a strong feeling about it."

"Well, what do you want to do about it?"

"I could have Donner picked up before they get there."

"Jack, you know Donner has a lot of political pull. The man has a lot of congressmen and senators who are his friends. If we move on him, we had better have some good evidence he is involved in something, and it had better be something besides this. We don't want any national exposure to our situation. It is in the best interest of all involved that we keep him out of it."

"Yes, sir, I understand. I have a man heading there to watch for them. I will let you know as soon as we have them. I just thought it would slow things down if we could get to Professor Donner first and detain him. This would give my men time to catch John and Richard, but I will send some men over to stop them on the way. Maybe they will get lucky."

"I hope so, Jack. Our whole careers are riding on this. Also, I will deny any involvement in this operation. You will take the fall if it happens. I suggest you get the job done right the first time."

"I understand, sir," Jack answered as he hung up the phone. He was sure something was going on with John and Richard. He also knew they would have to cross on land to meet with Donner. He started dialing a number on the phone.

"Yes, sir, Mr. Riley," answered the party he called.

"Get over to the local news station. Put out a statement that says John Barton and Richard Cooper died. They were killed in a mysterious fire at a local beach residence. Then have them run it on every station nationwide. Report to me when it is done. I want to watch it on the ten o'clock news tonight. Go now. Get it done, like it already happened!"

"Yes, sir, Mr. Riley."

Jack was putting together a plan. If they were to think we believe they are dead, maybe they will relax and let down their guard. He called his office and had them station men in every airport, bus station, town or road between the coast and El Paso. His plan would get the public to thinking these two were involved in criminal mischief, owning explosives and using them without proper notification. That is what he would pin on them. He could show them as terrorists involved in a plot. He could release a press conference in the morning. Then he would have reason to kill them. Wait a minute, he thought to himself. I could let them go all the way in and record everything they do along the way. I could even pick the time I can kill them. Maybe I could even do the job myself. Oh, what pleasure that would be for him, to be able to take out the two people causing most of his problems. Plus he could involve Professor Donner and take him out of the picture. This plan was looking better and better to him. The more he thought about it, the more he liked it. It was just a matter of time before he would have them right where he wanted them. All he had to do was watch Professor Donner.

Somewhere down the line, these two were going to contact him. All he had to do was catch up to them and follow them wherever they were going. He had a pretty good idea. After the press conference, he would get on a military helicopter and be there waiting for them. This plan was bringing an evil smile to Jack's face. He called General Rumsfield to ask him to help in the search. He also needed to get a helicopter to carry him to the site.

Rumsfield answered the phone, "What is it, Jack?"

"Sir, I need some of your men to help look for the two suspects. I think they are making a move to the site. I also need one of your helicopters to take me to the site."

"Okay, Jack. I will get you some men to look for them. Where were they the last time you saw them?"

"Galveston, sir."

"How did they leave there?"

"I'm not sure about how they got out of there. It may have been by boat. I do believe they are heading to the site, though."

"Okay, Jack, this is starting to get out of hand."

"I assure you, sir, it is not out of hand. I am going to let them walk in and then dispose of them. They are walking into a trap I have set for them. I need your men to make sure they are heading in the right direction. It's the only way I can stop them from pursuing this further."

"I hope you are right, Jack. The old man is going to have your head if you fail."

"I have never failed before, sir. I will not fail now. Put your soldiers in El Paso. Make sure they get on the bus to Nevada. If they don't, I want to know as soon as possible."

"Okay, Jack, but this had better go away soon or it's your neck. Do you understand me, Jack?"

"I understand perfectly, sir."

"Goodbye, Jack."

"Goodbye, General Rumsfield," Jack replied as he hung up the phone. He continued to sip on his drink as he pondered the situation.

"Wouldn't it be nice if I could get that wimp Rumsfield in the mix?" Jack thought to himself. "Then I could kill three birds with one stone. I just may have to invite him down for the show."

THE MINI SUB
Chapter Twenty-eight

At 12:30 a.m., Richard finished charging the battery on the sub. He took the sub down and headed up the coast.

"How much longer is it going to take?" John asked.

"We should be there soon," Richard replied.

"What are we going to do when we get there? Have you got a plan?"

"Don't I always have a plan?"

"Yeah, but it hasn't always been a good one."

"Have a little faith, John. We are still alive and free."

"Yeah, well, the night is not over yet."

"Don't worry about it. I have friends who will help us."

"You and your friends."

"Look, all we have to do is get to Professor Donner. He has someone we need to see. It's all been arranged."

"Yeah, and that's what's worrying me."

"What do you mean?"

"What if Jack is watching Professor Donner? How are you going to get in to see him?"

"Professor Donner and I worked out a plan a long time ago. It was right after the first time I met Jack. A locker will have a note in it for us if we can't see him," Richard explained.

"Yeah, but how will you know? We could be walking right into a trap."

"Professor Donner will leave us a clue. We have it all worked out, trust me."

"I hope you are right. I just don't trust Jack. He is very smart, you know."

"Don't worry. I have a surprise waiting for Jack in El Paso. It will keep him busy for a while."

"What kind of surprise?"

"Well, let's just say he'll never know what hit him."

"You wouldn't. Are you going to kill him?"

"No, but he'll be out like a light."

"And what does that mean?"

"It all depends on how repressed Jack is."

"You want to elaborate on that so us lower educated people can understand?"

"You are like a little monkey wanting all the bananas. Okay, you want details, you got them. I found a woman who looks so much like your wife, I intend to sic her onto Jack so his attention is away from us," Richard explained.

"Wait a minute. You're not going to try and get him to believe she is Regina. Jack will never go for it. He's much too smart for that."

"No, no. I'm not trying to get Jack to believe Regina has changed her mind about him. Our girl is going to bump into him and let him make the first move. Then she is going to explain who she is. All I'm looking for is a little window so we can disappear."

"I don't follow you," John said.

"Okay, let me see if I can explain. By now Jack has found out we are not in that burning house. He probably knows we left by the ocean. No matter how we left, he knows where we are going. He is going to have men stationed all the way to El Paso. Now, as you know, nobody makes a move without Jack's

THE COVERUP

permission. If I can get our girl in bed with Jack, his men will be stalled. We will simply slip by them without any problems. We'll get our information from Professor Donner and be on our way," Richard explained.

"And you think Jack will go for that?"

"Jack hasn't been laid in a long time. If you were in his shoes and ran into a woman who looked a lot like the one you love, wouldn't you want to get her in bed? And if she flirted with you, wouldn't you take the hint?"

"Well, I guess, if I were in his shoes."

"Well, there you have it."

"But what if Jack doesn't take the initiative? He may see that as a trap," John inquired.

"Don't worry. I always have a backup plan."

"Does your backup plan include some grub? I'm starved."

"Oh, yeah. I'm sorry. There are some sandwiches in that cooler over there. Get me one, too."

"Here, which one do you want?" John asked.

"What are they?"

"Well, I think this one is pimento cheese. This might be ham salad."

"I'll take the pimento cheese," Richard said.

"Good. I never liked pimento cheese," John replied.

"Oh, man, I love pimento cheese."

"I figured you for a steak sandwich."

"Why? Because I'm rich?"

"Well, I figure rich people like finer things."

"I'm only rich because I have to be."

"What does that mean?"

"My family left me all this money. In my opinion, the good things in life are free."

"Only someone with money could say such a thing."

"Yeah, well, being rich is not what it's cracked up to be."

"Oh, really? I'll gladly trade places with you."

"I didn't say I was stupid."

"Well, I thought you might want to try the poor life."

"Why did you become a cop?"

"When I was young, some boys stole my bicycle. I had just got that bike for my birthday. They took it while I slept that night. Next morning when I got up, it was gone. My old man tore up my tail end for leaving it outside. This policeman came to the house to investigate. He was a real nice man. He assured me he would leave no stone unturned. He told me my bike would be returned. He had that certain confidence that makes you want to believe him. That is when I knew I wanted to be that kind of policeman," John explained.

"And what about the bike? Did you get it back the next day?" Richard asked.

"Actually, it was about two weeks before he found it. That feeling of doing something good is what drove him to be a policeman. He would always talk to me when it came to the subject of the bike. I guess you could say he treated me like an adult. I could see how proud and happy he was for doing something good."

"I know that feeling you are talking about. I get it every time I help someone," Richard said.

"Yeah, I have had a few moments in the sun, myself."

"Yeah, but you earned yours. I can only buy mine."

"Doesn't matter if you work for it or buy it. It's the fact you are doing something for someone else, as long as you feel good about what you did."

"Sometimes I wonder if I'm doing it for the right reasons."

THE COVERUP

"What do you mean by that?"

"Sometimes I think I do it just to get back at my relatives."

"I don't understand."

"When my parents died, they left everything to me. All my relatives hated me because I would not give them a share. All of them mooched off of my parents for years. They would borrow money and never pay it back. Some of them got into trouble and my dad would bail them out. Never did they ever repay him, not even with a thank you. Dad always believed in helping out the family. He would build them a house or factory. It got to where Dad was sending them all monthly checks. They became like leeches sucking the very essence of life from his bank account. When I took over, I cut them off. Now they have to fend for themselves. That is why they hate me. I just thought it was time for them to take care of their own problems. When I do something for someone, I'm not sure if I am doing it for the good. I don't hate them, though, but it seems I'm getting back at them," Richard explained.

"Wow, I'll bet it's a happy time around you during the holidays."

"It's a lonely time for me. I never got invited to anyone's house for the holidays."

"That is sad, Richard. If you want, you can come to our house for any holiday. You don't even have to bring presents. I know Regina and I would love to have you."

"Thanks. I just might take you up on that, but I am not coming without presents."

"I'm not going to argue with you about that, but you don't have to. We would love to have you just the same."

"As long as you let me bring the food."

"Whatever makes you happy, man."

"You're good people. I felt that the first time I came to your house. I could feel the down-home life in your home. You're wife is a good cook, too. Yeah, and Regina is a lovely lady. You're a lucky man, John Barton. I envy you."

"Ah, come on. You envy me? Hell, man, you have everything money can buy, but you act like the loneliest man alive."

"I am, John. You don't know how hard it is to find someone real," Richard said emotionally.

"Well, you know what they say. There is someone out there for everyone. You just have to find them."

"Things will change when they find out you have money."

"Well, money isn't everything. What am I saying here? I'm starting to talk like you. Man, what a bummer."

"I am going to make a rich man out of you yet."

"Don't push it. Let's take it a step at a time," John replied laughing.

John and Richard chuckled for a few moments. Then the tiny cockpit went silent as they were engulfed in their own thoughts. You could hear a pin drop in the motionless silent little cockpit. John broke the trance they were in by stretching his arms yawning.

"Why don't you take a nap? We are about two hours from where we will stop," Richard said.

"Yeah, you got a bed in here somewhere?"

"Just lay your chair back."

"Oh," John said as he pulled the lever on the side of the chair.

"That better?" Richard asked.

"Yes, much better, thank you."

"Get some rest. You are going to need it."

THE COVERUP

"Why? Are you expecting more fun?" John asked sarcastically.

"It is sure going to get interesting."

"I was afraid you might say that. Well, wake me when the fun begins," John said as he drifted off to sleep.

The night posed no more threats to the two men. Richard piloted the sub through the dark ocean, taking it up to the surface a couple of times to charge the battery.

3:00 a.m. "John, wake up," Richard said as he shook him.

"What's up?" John asked as he wiped the sleep from his eyes.

"We are here."

"And where is that?"

"Port O'Connor."

"Now what?"

"We're going ashore and take a car to Cuero. We will catch a plane I have waiting for us. Then we'll fly to Horizon City where we will get transportation to El Paso," Richard explained.

"How did you get a plane in Cuero?"

"I made a call while you were sleeping."

"Oh, some more friends."

"Well, someone owed me a favor."

"I hope you have a lot more of them."

"If I don't, I'll create some new ones."

"So are we going ashore the same way we got in this sub?"

"Yes, we will have to swim to the beach and walk to the city. Then we can rent a car and go from there."

"You think there is enough air in these tanks to make it?"

"No, but I have some more in a lower compartment on the floor there."

"Where? In this one?"

"Yes, just pull up the lever and twist it to the left. There should be two tanks in there that are full."

"Okay, here goes," John said as he opened the door to the compartment.

"Grab two of them."

"Uh, Richard, there's nothing in here."

"What?" Richard shouted.

"It's empty," John replied.

"Let me see." Richard leaned over the back of his seat to look in the compartment. "Damn, I thought there were two small tanks in there."

"Now what?" John asked.

"That's all right," Richard replied.

"That's all right? We have no air tanks, and he says that's all right?"

"Have a little faith, John. I have another plan."

"You always have another plan. So what is this plan?"

"Well, it's simple. We just refill the ones we have."

"You can do that?"

"Sure, it's not a problem, except for one thing."

"And what is that?"

"I will have to spend another thirty minutes in this compartment with a whining baby," Richard remarked smiling.

"I wish I had as much confidence in you as you do."

"Ah, hell, it's just knowing what to do in a situation like this."

"Oh, and I guess us land lovers wouldn't know what to do when it comes to drowning," John remarked sarcastically.

THE COVERUP

"That's not what I meant."

"Well, I can't wait to hear the real meaning."

"Look, when you spend as many hours in a sub like this, you learn what to do. I had a real good instructor teach me. I paid him enough money for this thing. I told him to give me every situation he could think of. Some people are so touchy," Richard explained.

"I know I feel so sensitive. You know, you spend all this time in a small compartment with a guy. Well, I'm not sure you will respect me in the morning," John answered in a feminine-sounding voice.

"All right, enough of that. I need you to get me the tanks we used earlier," Richard ordered.

"Just like a man, always giving out orders," John said out loud to himself.

"Will you stop?" Richard said with humor.

"I'm not talking to you, you beast, you," John replied, laughing slightly.

"Not going to give it up, are you?"

"Okay, here are the tanks," John replied as he handed the tanks to Richard one at a time.

"Now, get me that hose in the wall behind you."

"How do you get it out?"

"Just pull on it. It will come out far enough to reach here." Richard reached over to the panel in front of him. Then he pushed a button on the panel. A loud gurgle noise rang out.

"What the hell was that?" John asked.

"Just the snorkel. It will float to the surface so we can get fresh air for the tanks."

"Oh, for a minute there, I thought we were taking on water."

WILLIAM DANIEL

"Push that red button behind your head, John."

"You mean this one?" John asked as he pointed to a red button on a panel behind him.

"Yes, that one."

John pushed the button, and an electric motor began to whirl. Then a pumping sound could be heard.

"This is going to take a little while," Richard explained.

"How long?" John asked.

"Oh, about thirty minutes," Richard said as he hooked the fill hose to the tank in his hand.

"Ah, man, you mean I have to be in this sardine can with you for thirty more minutes? I'm a land lover. I need something solid under my feet!"

"Calm down. It's only thirty more minutes."

"Sorry, I guess I am losing it."

"Don't worry. We will be out of here soon."

"Say, you never told me why you got into paleontology, or is it anthropology?" John asked.

"Actually, it's both. I took a lot of courses in college."

"Why?"

"Oh, I don't know. I guess I had a lot of time on my hands when I was younger."

"So you spent your time on a college campus?"

"By the time I was eighteen, I owned five cars, a yacht, a sail boat, six apartment complexes, two restaurants, and a gym. I was so bored with buying things that I could not stand it anymore. I met this guy at a frat party that I went to with this girl. He got me stoned on grass. It made me think about my life. I suddenly realized I was no different than my relatives. I was mooching off my parents. I was taking the family money and buying anything I wanted. I began to realize I didn't like myself. The next morning I suffered a large headache. I'm sure

THE COVERUP

it was from the pot. As soon as I was able to think again, I began to do the right thing. I called my father's accountant and began the process of changing my life. I got him to access all my properties to determine their value. Then I had him sell everything and pay back my father what I had borrowed from the family money. My father was very surprised when he heard of this. We had a long talk about what was going on. I told him everything from the frat party to what I had planned for the future. He was very impressed with what I had planned. I think at this point he became very proud of me. Then he offered to help me with anything, even if it was just business. I think we became closer than we had ever been before. I thanked him but explained that I wanted to do it all on my own. Anyway, I took the profits I made from the sale of all my properties and built a couple of factories. I expanded those into even more factories with the profits. By the time I was twenty-one, I had my own franchise all over the world. Then I sold the whole thing to a group of millionaires. By the time the sale was over, I was a multi-millionaire. I donated a lot of the money to the University of El Paso. I took the entry exam and got into Professor Donner's class, and you know the rest," Richard finished.

"So you smoked pot, did you?" John asked sarcastically.

"What? You going to arrest me now? It was just that one time," Richard explained.

"Well, this is a good thing," John replied.

"My whole life changed, and all you can remark on is the fact I smoked some pot. That's just like a cop."

"I am sorry. That is some kind of story you have there, Richard."

"It's not a story to me. It's my life."

"Oh, well, that is one of them things where you got to be there to understand."

"Look, don't cry for me. I don't need your pity."

"Well, now, who the hell said I feel sorry for you? To you, money may be the root of all evil, but try not knowing if you can pay your bills next month. Try having to get a second job to buy Christmas for your family. Try paying hospital bills when your kids get sick. No, you have had it too good, my friend," John explained.

"You're right. I have had it too good. I was born a rich kid, and I will die a rich kid. I can't change that. Wouldn't want to either. I like being rich and not having to worry about those little things, but I also like helping people who need help. Did you know that every person I help never has to pay me back? I ask them to help me out sometimes, but they don't have to. I don't mind helping people who really need a helping hand, but as for my family, they could get a job. You know, it really is a good feeling to do good," Richard said.

"And you know the best part. It's good on both ends," John remarked.

"What do you mean?" Richard asked as he removed the hose from the tank he was filling. He put the other tank in his lap and hooked the air hose to it.

"Well, you know that feeling you get when you do good?" John asked.

"Yeah," Richard replied.

"Well, that is the same feeling that the people you help get when you help them. You can see it in their eyes, just to know there is someone out there who really cares, not someone screwing you over for a percentage. You, my friend, have it bad," John explained.

"Have what bad?" Richard asked as he turned to look at John.

THE COVERUP

"You, my friend, feel guilty for having all this money dumped into your life. You don't feel like you deserve it, but you don't want to give it to a family you don't like, so you go out and find some poor needy person. Then you give him a bunch of money, and you think this makes you feel good. However, the real problem is you are scared."

"I'm afraid? What, exactly, do you mean?"

"You are afraid of being alone, so you go out and try and buy yourself a friend. This makes you feel better or so you think, but in reality, you are still somewhat lonely. You would just like to be able to sleep in the same room with someone, a person you can trust."

"Yeah, it's a family thing. I inherited it," Richard replied sarcastically.

"Most men are just looking for sex. You, my friend, are looking for something a little deeper than that. You are looking for someone really special," John said.

"What are you, a psychiatrist or something?" Richard remarked.

"No, but I did stay at a Holiday Hotel once," John replied laughing out loud.

"Wow, that must be some hotel. You have got me pegged to the tee," Richard said.

"Yeah, well, it's a gift."

"You must be psychic."

"Just a little on my mother's side. You won't hold that against me, will you?" John asked as he chuckled.

"Uh, no. I would, however, like to know how you know this stuff."

"Simple observation," John replied.

"So you have been studying me or something?"

"I just took a course once on word study."

"Word study? I don't think I ever heard of it," Richard said.

"It's where you study the words someone is saying. See, sometimes we don't realize what we are saying. We will say things that give out hints as to the truth. Take a woman who comes in claiming she was raped. You ask her questions on what she wore when she went out. Things like, 'Where did you plan on going when you went out? How did you introduce yourself?' Then you evaluate what they answer and study the words. 'Now let's see. You went out in this sexy short dress. You had on a see-through blouse and a sweet smelling perfume. You went to a bar, and you smiled real big at this guy. Then you go home with him and have sex. Maybe it got rough, or maybe you liked it that way. Maybe you wanted him to pay you money to keep quiet.' Things like that can come from listening to every word they say," John explained.

"I believe the psychic thing, myself," Richard remarked as he took the hose from the tank he was holding.

"Observation, my friend, simple observation," John replied.

"Well, let me observe you putting that hose away, and let's get geared up. I think you have been in here too long already," Richard said.

John put the hose back in the wall of the sub. Richard pushed the button to retract the snorkel. They put on their diving equipment and headed for the diving chamber. Richard put John in first. The chamber was only big enough for one person. He told him to go out the hatch when the water filled the room. He explained how to open and shut the hatch. When John acknowledged his understanding, Richard closed the door. Then he filled the chamber with seawater. He waited for John to exit and entered the chamber himself. He grabbed

THE COVERUP

a mesh bag on his way in and filled the chamber with water and exited the sub. When he was outside, he closed the door and motioned for John to follow him.

They were only about a hundred yards from the beach. Richard had parked the sub in twenty-five feet of water. This was so they could follow the floor of the gulf to the beach. Since John was an inexperienced diver, it would be easier for him. Richard knew the right directions to go and John could follow him. They swam along the ocean floor. When they reached shallow water, Richard stood up. He looked across the beach to see if anyone was there. Since it was early morning, he figured no one would be there. John came up behind him, stood up, and took off his mask.

"See anything?" John asked.

"No, the beach is empty. Okay, let's put our equipment into this bag. Then we will walk to the shore," Richard ordered.

"You just going to leave the sub there?" John asked.

"Someone will be along to get it as soon as we are out of here," Richard explained.

As soon as they had the gear in the bag, John set it down and began walking toward the shore.

"You just going to leave the gear there?" John asked.

Richard started to answer him, but John interrupted him and said, "I know. Someone will be along to get them."

"Why, John, are you catching on?" Richard replied.

"I may be slow, but I'm not dumb," John said.

The walk to shore through the water was slow, but as they got closer, it became shallower. This made it easier to walk, and they could pick up their speed. When they finally made it to the beach, they stopped and caught their breath.

"Now that we have landed, what now, Captain?" John asked.

213

"Now we walk to the nearest car rental," Richard replied.

As they began to walk toward the main part of town, John realized they were soaking wet. They made the swim in their clothes, which would take hours to dry.

"We just going to walk in with wet clothes on?" John asked.

"I'm hoping to pass a laundry mat," Richard replied.

"I was just thinking it might draw some attention if we show up wet with no shoes. Hey, we don't have shoes," John remarked.

"It's always going to be something with you," Richard remarked.

"Well, I just thought it would look funny going in to rent a car, being wet, with no shoes. People might think something is not right with this picture."

"I know. I'm working on it."

"What are you doing? Figuring this out as you go?"

"Yes, basically."

"I hope you have money."

"All my folding money is wet, but I do have plastic. Only thing is, plastic will not work in a dryer."

"Let me guess. You don't have change on you."

"Have you got any change on you?"

"I think I might have some quarters," John replied. He reached into his pocket and pulled out five quarters. "I have five quarters on me."

"That will have to do," Richard replied as they continued to walk toward the town.

When they made it to the main portion of town, they began to look for a laundry mat.

"There's one," John said as he pointed at a sign down the street. They walked down the street, which was mostly

THE COVERUP

vacant at the time. As soon as they arrived at the laundry mat, Richard asked John for the quarters and told him to go into the bathroom and take off his clothes.

John walked into the bathroom and removed his clothes and handed them to Richard through the door opening. Richard took the clothes and put them in the dryer, put some quarters in and turned it on. The dryer began to spin as he walked over to the bathroom.

"You might want to take the time to take care of business while you are in there," Richard said.

"Way ahead of you, partner," John replied.

"One other thing. You might want to wipe the salt water off with a wet paper towel," Richard said.

"Got it," John replied.

"I am only going to dry your clothes a little, so the pockets might still be wet. We don't have enough time to do a good drying," Richard explained.

"That's fine."

"We need to get out of here as quickly as we can," Richard explained.

"Are we going to get something to eat before we rent the car, or after?" John asked.

"You just ate a couple of hours ago."

"Yeah, well, I burn up a lot of energy just talking to you," John replied sarcastically.

"Yeah, just remember who has your clothes," Richard said as he began to laugh out loud.

"Oh, yeah. Sorry."

"Look, we'll grab something at a fast food restaurant on our way out. There's bound to be one around here somewhere. I mean I'm sure they don't eat fish all the time," Richard said.

"I hope you are right, partner."

"I'm going to check on your clothes," Richard said as he walked over to the dryers.

He opened the dryer that had John's clothes in it and reached inside to pull out his pants. He began to feel of them to see if they were dry.

"This will have to do," he thought to himself. He pulled out the rest of the clothes and walked over to the bathroom. "Hey, this is the best I can do."

John opened the bathroom door and took the clothes. He began to put them on. "These pants are going to be hard to get on wet like this."

"Just do the best you can. I have to get in there myself," Richard replied.

"Okay, okay, keep your panty hose on. I'll be right out."

"Just hurry."

A few minutes later, John opened the door and walked out. "All yours, my friend."

"It's about time," Richard replied. He stepped into the bathroom and began to take off his clothes. Suddenly it hit him, the most awful smell he had ever encountered. "They need to check your ass to see if someone died up there. What have you been eating, rotten eggs? Man, that stinks!" he screamed as he removed his clothes.

"And after all I did just to make sure I left that there for you. I am totally disappointed in you," John replied giggling.

"They should have had you in the war. We would have won and never fired a shot," Richard remarked.

"It's not that bad," John replied laughing.

"Remind me to stop at a car wash. I need to give you an enema!" Richard shouted.

"All right. Just give me your clothes and the change."

THE COVERUP

Richard opened the door and gave John his clothes. "The change is in the pocket of my pants."

John took the clothes and walked over to the dryer. He reached into Richard's pants pockets and pulled out the change. He placed the clothes in the dryer and put in the change to turn it on. He walked over to the front window of the laundry mat and looked out. The streets were beginning to get active as people began to stir. He watched for several minutes. People were going about in their normal routines. He began to wonder what Regina was doing at that time. He wished he could find out if she was okay, but he knew his wife could take care of herself. His train of thought broke when an old woman smiled at him as she walked by. He walked back to the dryer and looked in the door window.

"Wonder if these are dry," he thought to himself.

Suddenly the door to the bathroom opened. Richard walked out of the bathroom and looked over at John. "I couldn't stand another minute in there."

John looked at Richard standing there. He had wrapped himself with toilet paper. "What is this?"

"I had to get out of there. You know, you stink more than anyone I know," Richard replied.

"You look like a girl with a skirt on."

Richard had wrapped the paper around his waist several times.

"Well, I didn't want to come out naked," Richard replied.

"Are we a little unsure of our masculinity?" John asked sarcastically.

"All right, enough of that," Richard said.

Suddenly the door to the laundry mat opened. A middle-aged woman pulling a laundry cart started in the door. She struggled with the door as she pulled the little cart in with her. When she got the cart in the doorway, she looked up and saw Richard standing there in a toilet paper skirt. She looked over at John.

"Oh, my," she said as she pushed the cart back out of the door in a hurry. She quickly started up the street taking one last look to see if they were following her.

John looked over at Richard and then down at his paper skirt. Richard looked at John and then down at the paper skirt. Then they both looked up at each other. Without saying a word, Richard dashed to the bathroom. John ran over to the dryer and pulled open the door. He grabbed Richard's clothes and carried them to the bathroom door.

"Here!" he shouted through the door. Richard opened the door and took the clothes. He quickly shut the door and began to put on his clothes. John ran over to the window to see if anyone was coming. He was sure the woman would head for the police. He knew the one thing they didn't need was the police asking questions.

Richard finished putting on his clothes and opened the door. "Let's go," he said as he walked to the front door.

"I don't see anyone coming, yet," John said as he opened the front door. They walked out into the street.

"This way," Richard said. They walked in the opposite direction the woman had run and darted down an alley behind some buildings.

"Now what?" John asked.

"There is a car rental agency north of here. I rented a car there once sometime back when I visited here. Come on. It's this way."

They walked down the alley until they came to a street. Richard led the way as they walked up the street. They came

THE COVERUP

to an intersection and took a right. After walking several minutes, they came upon a car rental business.

"Ace Car Rental. This is the place," Richard said as he read the sign.

"We'd better get inside before they spot us," John remarked. They walked into the rental place and up to the counter.

"Good morning," greeted a young man as they walked up to the counter. "How may I help you?"

"We would like to rent a car," Richard replied.

"Okay. Fill out this form, please. Have you ever rented from us before?"

"Yes, but it was a few years back."

"Okay, what is your name?"

"Richard Cooper."

The young man began to type on his computer the name, Richard Cooper.

"Ah, yes, here it is. What kind of car would you like this time, Mr. Cooper?"

"I prefer a Chevrolet."

"Let's see. We have a Caprice or a Cavalier."

"The Caprice, please," Richard said as he filled out the form.

"Would you like the insurance package you had last time?" the young man asked.

"Yes, that would be fine."

The young man began to type in the information on his computer. "How would you like to pay?"

"Plastic," Richard answered as he gave him his credit card. The young man took the card from Richard and entered the information and ran the card through a machine. He received the information he needed on Richard's card and returned his card. Then he gathered all the papers needed to finish the rental agreement and gave Richard his paperwork. After he finished filling out the information on the computer, he turned to the board behind him and removed a key. He excused himself so he could inspect the car before he gave it to Richard.

When he returned, he gave the key to Richard. He looked down and saw Richard wasn't wearing shoes. He looked over at John's feet and saw he wasn't wearing shoes, either. Then he looked up at Richard as if asking for an explanation.

"We had our shoes stolen while at the beach," Richard explained after his and the young man's eyes met.

"Oh," the young man said, as he seemed satisfied with the explanation. "Can I recommend a good shoe store?"

"Man, that would be great," Richard replied.

The young man wrote down the information and gave it to him. John noticed something outside and walked over to where Richard stood. "Time to go," he said as he indicated with his eyes for Richard to look outside. Richard turned and looked outside. He saw a police officer talking to some people on the corner.

"Gotcha," he said to John as he turned to the young man and thanked him.

"Thank you, sir. Have a great day," the young man answered.

John and Richard walked out of the rental building and got into the car.

"Don't look at him. Just start the car and drive away normal," John explained.

"Time to get out of here now," Richard said.

"No, don't act like you are running. This can cause him to be suspicious of us. Take that road in front of us," John said.

THE COVERUP

Richard started the car and eased it onto the road and drove off in the opposite direction.

"Go down a couple of blocks and turn left," John ordered.

"When we get on the right road, we are outta here!" Richard remarked.

"Bad idea. Stop at the first fast food restaurant you see. Hey, look. A shoe store. Stop there and let's get some shoes and socks. They will be looking for us in the wrong places. By the time we get that done and grab a bite to eat, they will have given up on catching us."

"You don't think they might road block us?"

"No, after a few minutes, they will think we left. Then they will backtrack to see if we are still around. By that time, we will be on our way out of town."

"Not a bad plan. I knew I brought you along for something."

"Yeah, well, don't expect me to get you out of trouble every time."

"Oh, like this is my fault!"

"It is your fault!"

"How is it my fault?"

"If you hadn't come out of that bathroom with a toilet paper dress, we would not have been in this mess," John answered.

"If you hadn't left that bomb in there, I wouldn't have come out of there!" Richard shouted back at him.

"You didn't want to stay in that bathroom," John said giggling.

"Do you blame me?"

"Well, no, I guess not. You looked real cute in that paper outfit."

"Don't start with me."

"You should have seen the look on your face. Man, when that woman came in the laundry mat, I wish I had a picture of that. Regina would have loved to see that," John remarked.

"Oh, man, I guess I'm going to hear about this one forever."

"Okay, I understand. It was a very embarrassing moment for you. I promise I won't tell anyone, with the exception of Regina. I don't keep secrets from her, but that would be the only one."

"I guess, but she can't tell anyone else."

"Oh, come on, man. You are spoiling all the fun," John said laughing.

"No one else!" Richard shouted.

"Okay, okay. I get the picture."

"Good."

"Party pooper."

"Let's just get the shoes and go," Richard ordered as he parked the car.

They stepped out of the car and walked into the shoe store. John walked over to the boot section while Richard browsed the tennis shoes. They made their selections and walked to the counter.

A young woman standing at the register asked, "Can I help you?"

"Yes, we would like these, please," Richard replied as he handed her his credit card.

The young woman took the card and ran it through a credit card machine. She punched some buttons on her register and returned the card to Richard. Richard took the card and put it back into his pocket. The young woman gave Richard a receipt, which he signed and returned to her. Then he grabbed

THE COVERUP

the sack with their merchandise as she gave him his copy of the receipt, and they left the store.

As they got into the car, Richard opened the sack and said, "Put your shoes on, John."

"Well, so far, so good. I don't think anyone noticed," John said. He put on the socks and pulled on the new work boots.

"I noticed," Richard said.

"And what is it you noticed?" John asked sarcastically.

"I noticed that cute little lady behind the counter. Did you see her smile at me?"

"She probably noticed your big fat wallet."

"Hey, maybe she thinks I'm cute. Did you ever think of that?"

"Yeah, well, when she hears about that paper dress you were wearing, I'll bet she changes her mind," John said laughing.

"Just can't let it go, can you?"

"Well, you know," John said laughing.

"You know, there's something about her. I just can't put my finger on it. Like I know her from somewhere," Richard explained.

"Get down here much, do you?"

"No, I have only been here maybe once. But I'm sure that I have seen her before. I can't place where it was."

His mind went into a trance trying to remember her. Suddenly his face went blank. He turned to John and said, "I know where I know her from."

"What? You look like you just saw a ghost."

"That's Jack's secretary," Richard said as he turned to look out the front windshield.

"No, that's not possible. Jack's secretary? Are you sure? Maybe she just looks like her."

WILLIAM DANIEL

"No, I'm sure of it."

"Why, what makes you think so?"

"Did you see that mole on her mouth by her lips?"

"Yeah, so?"

"I met a young woman in New York last year. It was at a social gathering for a local science fair. They invited people to try and get donations from them. Phil, Professor Donner, introduced her to me. The first thing I noticed was that mole. Then I noticed the rest of her. She was very cute and built to match. We talked for a few minutes. She was interested in paleontology. Anyway, I excused myself and walked over to the bar. I ordered a drink and walked into the next room. I had a conversation with a professor from Germany. Then I walked around, kind of mingling with different people. I was floating around the room when I saw her. She was walking into one of the rooms with Jack."

"You've got a hell of a memory there. Well, if you are right, Jack knows we are here."

"I'm going to take a glance to see if she is looking."

"All right, but be subtle."

Richard turned his head toward the front window on the shoe store. He saw the young woman on a cell phone behind the counter. She wasn't looking at them, but she was pointing in their direction.

"I think Jack knows now."

"Damn, I told you that man is everywhere. Okay, let's try and move out of town. Put your shoes on and let's go," John said.

Richard reached into the sack and retrieved his shoes and hurriedly put them on. John glanced at the store window and quickly glanced down at Richard's shoes.

"Is that the shoes you bought?" he asked.

THE COVERUP

"Yeah, why?"

"They're red,"

"And your point is?" Richard asked.

"Why don't you just run up a flag? Are you trying not to be noticed? Out of a store full of shoes and boots, you bought these ridiculous looking things."

"Well, I like high tops, and these were the only ones they had in my size."

"Man, you are going to stick out like a sore thumb."

"Why? Because I have red tennis shoes?"

"Didn't you see The Red Shoe Diaries?"

"Yeah, well, a lot of people wear red shoes nowadays."

"Just start the car and let's get out of here."

"All right, just hang on. We'll be out of here in no time."

"I'll say one thing," John began.

"What's that?" Richard asked.

"Those shoes would have been perfect with that paper dress," John said laughing.

"There he goes again with the paper dress."

"Sorry."

Richard turned the key and started the car. He put it in reverse and began to back out slowly. When he was in the street, he put the car in drive. He slowly drove down the street until he came to a stop sign. He stopped, looked both ways, and turned left. He drove down the street until he came to the highway, turned right, and headed out of town.

"Hey, there's a hamburger joint! Pull in!" John shouted.

"All right, all right."

"I'm starved."

"What do you want?" Richard said as he pulled up to the menu.

"I don't care as long as it is dead."

"Okay," Richard said as he waited for someone to ask him what he wanted.

"Sausage and biscuit, if they are not serving hamburgers now," John said.

A young man turned on the speaker and said, "Welcome to Billy's Burger Barn. Can I help you?"

"Yes, are you serving breakfast or lunch now?" Richard asked him.

"Anything you want, sir," the young man answered.

"Cheese burger, fries, and a coke," John said. "Make that a diet coke."

"Yeah, give us two cheese burgers and fries, a diet coke, and a Dr. Pepper," Richard said to the young man.

"Anything else, sir?"

"No, that's all."

"That will be $11.97, please. Drive up to the next window. Thank you."

Richard drove the car to the window and waited for the young man to open it. When he did, he handed him his credit card. The young man ran the card through his machine and gave the receipt to Richard for his signature. Richard signed the receipt and gave it back to the young man. The young man tore off his copy of the receipt and gave it to Richard. A few minutes later, the young man brought their food. He gave it to him and thanked him. Richard took the food and handed it to John, thanking the young man as he drove off.

"All right! Food!" John said as he reached inside the sack.

"Which one is the Dr. Pepper?" Richard asked.

"This one, I think."

"Let me see," Richard said as he took a drink from the cup.

THE COVERUP

"Well, is that it?" John asked.

"Yeah, that's a Dr. Pepper all right," Richard replied.

John opened the sack again and got out the burgers. He gave one to Richard and laid the other in his lap. Then he retrieved the fries and gave one to Richard. They began to eat as Richard pulled the car back onto the highway.

"Time to get out of here," John remarked.

"We are on our way now," Richard replied.

"Where to now?" John asked as he munched on some fries.

"I've got a plane waiting on us up the road a piece."

"You know, you always have a plane or a sub waiting for us somewhere. How do you do that?"

"Connections, my friend, connections."

"You might as well connect to Jack. He is going to be everywhere we are."

"Yeah, looks that way, but we still have that little diversion I have planned."

"I hope you are right, partner."

"You will see. I think it's a good plan."

"I think we're in trouble."

"Hey, it's a good plan," Richard said defending his plan.

"I'm not worrying about the plan," John replied as he finished his hamburger.

"Then what?" Richard asked him as he polished off his last french fry.

"Our fearless leader wears paper dresses," John replied as he started laughing.

"Rubber room, that's where you belong. I should get you a monkey and an organ so you can stand on the corner."

"If I had a monkey, I would train him to pull off paper dresses," John remarked as he began laughing loudly.

"I knew I wouldn't live that down."

"Okay, I quit. I'm going to take a nap. Wake me when you want me to drive," John said as he laid his head against the door.

"Yeah, you take a nap. Maybe that will shut you up for a while."

"Just don't put that dress on while I sleep."

"You are about as funny as a barrel of monkeys."

"Ho, a barrel of monkeys pulling that paper dress off. Look out, candid camera time. Or should I say that's incredible," John remarked sarcastically.

"Never give up, do you? Sleep, my friend, sleep."

"Tell me a bedtime story, Mommy."

"Shut up and sleep."

After about an hour of driving, Richard pulled the car over to the shoulder and put it in park. Then he got out and stretched while looking both ways on the road. He walked over to the passenger side of the car, grabbed the door handle, and opened the door. John almost fell out of the car before catching himself.

"Hey!" he said as he wiped the sleep from his eyes.

"Your turn to drive," Richard replied. He opened the door all the way and helped John get out and asked him if he was awake enough to drive.

"Yeah, yeah, just give me a minute to get my bearings rolling." He stretched his arms to get the kinks out. He walked around the back of the car and looked both ways for traffic. Then he got into the car from the driver's side and sat there looking around at the gadgets on the car. He turned to Richard who had laid his head against the door. "Any last minute instructions?"

"Just watch ahead for a city called Yoakum," Richard replied.

"There is such a place?"

"Oh, yeah. You can't miss it. There are signs that will tell you how to get there."

"So you say there is."

"Just keep thinking Yoakum. You'll find it," Richard said as he closed his eyes to sleep.

"Yeah, I got a joke-m-yoakum, just for you," John replied sarcastically.

"Just drive, will ya?" Richard said.

WILLIAM DANIEL

THE CROP DUSTER
Chapter Twenty-nine

John drove the car down the highway for a couple of hours. He followed every sign which pointed toward Yoakum. When he came to a sign saying, "Yoakum, sixteen miles," he pulled the car over into a rest area park. He got out of the car and stretched his arms and legs. He began to scan the park for patrol cars. He noticed where the men's restroom was. He knew he needed to go. He figured he would let Richard sleep a little longer, so he walked over to the park facilities. As he started in, he began to think to himself, "Don't read the writing on the wall. Don't read the writing on the wall." He went in and found the place empty. "Good," he thought to himself as he took care of business. If John had one phobia, it was getting close to a gay person. He was as straight as they came. He loved his wife and kids more than anything, but on the other hand, he believed in letting people do their own thing, as long as they stayed within the law. John washed his hands and headed back to the car to wake Richard. When he got outside, he noticed Richard outside the car. He was talking to a big, tall man. He started walking over to them to see what was going on. As John got closer to the car, he could hear their conversation.

"Look, all I asked is what time it was!" Richard shouted.

"Why don't you go buy yourself a watch?" the tall man replied.

"Okay, okay. I'm sorry to have bothered you!" Richard shouted.

About this time, John had walked up to them. "What's the problem, big guy?"

"This queer your friend?" the tall man asked.

"Well, he is a friend, so why don't you go somewhere and sleep it off?" John replied.

"Why don't you sleep this off," the tall man said as he swung a punch at John. With his cat-like reflexes, John moved out of the way of the man's fist. Then he dropped the tall man on the ground with one leg kick. The tall man lay on the ground groggily with his nose bleeding. John walked over to him and picked him up.

"Sorry about that, man. Why don't you go on about your business now?"

"All right. I'm going, but you haven't heard the last of me," the tall man said as he staggered away.

"Now what was that all about?" John asked Richard.

"I don't know. I just grabbed his arm and asked him what time it was."

"Man, don't be touching people around here. We'd better get out of here before he brings some friends."

"All right. Just let me take a quick wiz."

John noticed the tall man leaving in his pickup truck talking on his cell phone. "Better make it a quick one," John said.

As Richard headed for the restroom, John got in the car on the driver's side and started the car as Richard walked into the restroom. After a few minutes passed, John backed out the car and drove closer to the restroom and parked. He left the car running and began to watch the entrance to the park. He figured the tall man would be bringing some friends. Richard

THE COVERUP

came out of the restroom and got into the car on the passenger side.

"Man, that was some drop kick you put on him," he said as he sat down and closed the door.

"We'd better get out of here. I think he went for some friends," John said as he drove the car out of the parking space.

"Are you thinking he might come back with some friends?" Richard asked.

"Trust me, he will. His pride has been hurt. He is drunk and mad now."

"Well, let's get out of here, not that I wouldn't want to stay and kick his ass."

"He would kill you," John replied as he drove the car out of the rest area and back onto the highway.

"Hey, I can hold my own. You don't think I can take him?" Richard asked excitedly.

"He would kill you."

"I would kick his ass and his friends'!" Richard replied loudly.

"He would kill you and your paper dress-wearing ass."

"Keep it up, fuzz ball."

"What?" John asked laughing.

"You should get a red rubber nose and pointed hat. Join the circus in the center ring."

"All right, I will stop," John said as he drove down the highway.

"How close are we to Yoakum?" Richard asked.

"About six miles," John replied.

"Okay, good. About two miles from Yoakum, there will be a farm road we need to take."

"You know the number of this farm road?"

"Yeah, it's FM 2516," Richard answered.

They drove down the road toward Yoakum. About three miles down the road, they passed a pickup load of men.

"Uh oh," John said as the pickup passed them.

"I'm with you. Just keep going until you see FM 2516," Richard said.

He quickly turned around in his seat to watch the truck.

"They are turning around!" he shouted.

John noticed they were going up a small hill. On the other side, he saw the farm road they were looking for. Quickly he spun the car off the highway onto the farm road. Then he stomped on the gas pedal. The car spun its wheels and took off real fast. As they drove down the road, Richard continued to watch the highway behind them.

"There they go!" Richard said as he watched out the back windshield.

"Are they turning or going on?" John asked as he sped the car down the farm road.

"Looks like they went on."

"I hope so. This road is coming to an end."

"What?" Richard asked as he turned to look out the front windshield.

"Looks like there's just a gate. That's it. The road ends at a gate. What kind of road ends at a gate?" John asked.

"A private one. Slow down. I'll open it."

"When were you going to tell me about this one?"

"It's not necessary to tell you every little detail."

"It is when you have a truck load of drunks wanting to kick your ass. I needed to know every detail there is!"

"Chill out, bro, I got your back."

"You got my back? The guy would have killed you if I hadn't stepped in."

THE COVERUP

"I can handle myself."

"He would have killed you."

"Hey, I took a few lessons. I know how to take care of people like that."

"Knowing how and having the physical ability is two different things."

"Are you trying to say I couldn't take him?" Richard asked.

"I'm saying he would have killed you," John replied.

"I tell you what, I can kick his ass and yours, too," Richard remarked.

"You know what you are? You are a banty rooster. Put you in with the big roosters, and you think you are better even though the big boys would kick your ass. You would still think you could take them."

"I could," Richard answered.

"Tell you what. The next time a drunk wants to kick your ass, I'm going to let him. Then I'm going to congratulate him as I drag your scrawny ass away," John said as he stopped the car at the gate. "Well, you going to get the gate?"

"I am deeply hurt that you don't think I could take that guy," Richard answered.

"Well, I guess we will never know. He is gone now, and you are getting the gate, right?" John replied.

"Yeah, I'm getting the gate," Richard said as he stepped out of the car. He walked up to the gate and opened it. John drove the Caprice through the gate and stopped on the other side. Richard closed the gate and walked to the car and got in. They drove off down a very bumpy dirt road.

"Where did you learn how to fight like that? I mean, you dropped that guy with one kick. That was awesome," Richard said as he sat down.

WILLIAM DANIEL

"Well, I learned some in the Marines, and I took some lessons for the Dallas police."

"Well, thanks."

"For what?"

"For kicking that guy's ass for me. He would have killed me," Richard confessed.

"Oh, I don't know. You look like you could hold your own."

"Well, thanks anyway for not letting me find out."

"Well, what are friends for?"

"Yeah, well. Keep going up this road. We should come to an opening," Richard said.

They continued to drive on the dirt driveway. They came to an opening. On one side were some trees and a large barn. On the other side was an open field where the grass was cut real short.

"Drive over to the barn," Richard said.

John drove the car over to the barn and parked in front of some doors. He turned off the car. Richard and he got out of the car to look around.

"Now what?" John asked.

"Help me open these doors," Richard ordered.

"You got an airplane in here or something?" John sarcastically asked.

"Actually yes. There should be a Cessna prop plane stored here."

They opened the door to the barn to see what was there. There sat a small prop plane inside the barn.

"What the hey! Whom does this belong to?" John asked.

"It's mine, actually. It's a crop duster. I own some land around here and we grow a few crops," Richard explained.

"What do you grow, pot?" John sarcastically asked.

236

THE COVERUP

"No, I grow a few vegetables that are donated to the poor. It's just a tax write-off, but it's one I can live with," Richard explained.

"Rich people like you should help the needy. I am impressed," John remarked.

"Yeah, well, helping people seems to be one of my weaknesses. I seem to find it hard to say no to someone who really needs it," Richard explained.

"I noticed that about you. Yeah, my kids would love to go to college. That is, if you're feeling charitable by then."

"Sure, hang on," Richard said as he pulled a cell phone out of the plane. He dialed a number and pushed send. John noticed it was an older style phone.

"Joshua, it's Richard," he said as someone answered.

"Aw, Senor Richard. What can I do for you, sir?" Joshua answered.

"Look, I'm taking the plane to El Paso. I'll have it back in a few days," Richard explained.

"Si, si, Senor Richard. When would you like to get it?" Joshua asked.

"Right now, "Richard replied.

"Okay, I can be there in fifteen minutes," Joshua answered.

"No, no, you don't need to come, Joshua. I have it all under control."

"Si, si, Senor Richard. Uh, will you be bringing back soon?"

"Don't worry. I'll have it back in time for you to spray the crops."

"It's your plane, Senor Richard."

"Don't worry about it, Joshua. The plane will be back in the hanger as soon as possible. Just do me one favor."

WILLIAM DANIEL

"Si, anything for you, Senor Richard."

"If anyone asks you, you never saw us, okay?"

"Ah, si, Senor Richard. I don't know where you are. And the wife wants to thank you for the birthday present. She just loves that Camry," Joshua said laughing.

"Well, you tell her for me that she deserved it. That meal she cooked me last spring was the best I ever had. And tell her that I will be back for another one soon. Give her all my love, and the kids, too," Richard said.

"Si, si, Senor Richard. The best man I ever worked for in America."

I'm the only one you ever worked for in America. I brought you over here," Richard said.

"Oh, that's right. Thank you, Senor Richard. You are good man," Joshua said as he began to sob.

"Hey, Joshua, don't go getting emotional on me here. You deserved a break and I was glad to help you."

"Okay, Senor Richard. I go now. Not crying, just eyes leaking. Must go dry. Have a safe trip, Senor Richard," Joshua said as he hung up the phone.

"That Joshua. He always makes a big deal about the birthday present I sent his wife," Richard remarked.

"What did you get her?" John asked.

"I bought her a new Toyota Camry."

"A new Camry?" John asked as if he didn't hear him right.

"Yeah, it was a new Camry, why?"

"Well, that must have been some meal."

"Not really. I have had better."

"But yet you still bought her the Camry?"

"Yeah, well, they are poor. I ran into them down in Mexico when I was looking for the Chupacabra. They helped me when

238

THE COVERUP

my jeep broke down. I told him of this project I was starting. He said he would love to come to work for me, and he has been with me ever since. He's one hell of a worker, too," Richard explained.

"You beat everything I ever met in my life. Will you adopt me, please?" John replied.

"No, you will get nothing. You can only be my friend," Richard remarked laughing.

"Just my luck."

"All right, let's get this thing outside," Richard said referring to the plane.

"What do you want me to do?" John asked.

"First, turn the car around. We'll hook a rope to it and pull it outside."

John walked to the car and got in. He started it up and turned it around to back it up to the plane. When he had the car in the right position, he turned it off. Then he got out and walked to the back. Richard was looking around the barn for a rope to tie to the car. When he found one, he walked to the front of the plane. He climbed up on a small ladder he found. He tied the rope onto a tie-down on both sides of the prop. Then he climbed down to tie the other end to the car.

"Where are you going to tie that? There's no bumper hitch to tie onto," John asked.

"I see that. Let's see. Okay, tie it to the axle or the frame underneath," Richard answered.

"See if there is something I can lie on," John said.

Richard walked into the back of the barn. He returned with a large piece of cardboard. He laid it down at the back of the car. John grabbed the cardboard and pushed it under the car. He left part of the cardboard sticking out so he could get on it. He knelt down and flipped over onto his back and scooted up underneath the back of the car.

"Find anything to tie that rope to?" Richard asked.

"Yeah, I think I can tie it to the frame at the bumper," John replied.

Richard handed him the looped end of the rope. John grabbed the rope and began tying it to the frame.

"Okay, I think I've got it," John said as he climbed out from under the car.

"Get in the car and take her slow ahead. I'll watch the plane and guide you out," Richard explained.

John walked to the driver side of the car and got in. He started the car and put it in drive. He let the car ease up until the rope was tight.

"Okay, looks good. Now ease it out while I watch the wings," Richard said.

"Here we go," John said as he pulled up the car.

"Looks good. Keep going. Easy now, the wings are at the door. Looking good. Keep going. Okay, the wings are clear. Keep going. A little bit farther. Okay, that's good enough," Richard said.

John hopped out of the car and walked to the barn to retrieve the cardboard. He took it to the back of the car and placed it under the rear. Then he climbed under to untie the rope. After he got the rope untied, he climbed out.

"I'm going to get the plane started and move it out. You take the car and pull it out some more. When I get the plane out of the way, you put the car in the barn. Then shut the barn door. This plane is a two-seater. You will get in the front seat. The pilot rides in the back," Richard explained.

John motioned that he understood and got back in the car. He started it up and pulled it out to the side. Richard climbed

THE COVERUP

into the plane and started the engine. The engine whirled and sputtered as it spun the prop. When the engine caught and was running smooth, Richard began to taxi out of the doorway. As soon as he had the plane clear of the door, John pulled the car into the barn. He closed the door to the barn and walked over to the plane.

"There are some steps on the side of the plane. Climb in and let's go," Richard shouted.

"Okay," John replied as he climbed up the plane to the front seat.

"As soon as she's warm, we'll take off," Richard said.

"Just one question. Where is the runway?"

"Runway? There is no runway."

"What do you mean there is no runway? How are we going to take off?"

"Don't worry. It's a piece of cake."

"Yeah, but don't we need a runway?"

"This is a crop dusting plane. You don't need a runway. We can take off from anywhere, on the street or a road, even in a field. It's not a problem," Richard answered.

"Maybe not for you. I hate planes, especially crop dusters," John replied.

"Why is that, John?"

"The son of a friend of mine was a crop duster."

"And your point is?"

"His son was splattered all over the side of a mountain. Bought his own plane and took off for California. Stopped at some airport with problems with the plane. After he took off from there, he was never seen again. Some hikers found him in the mountains sometime later that year!" John shouted.

Richard continued to taxi the plane to an open field. "Don't worry. I'm an experienced pilot. I've been coming up here for years to fly this plane. I like to know firsthand if the plane is in good shape."

"I'm glad one of us trusts you!"

When he arrived at the field, Richard throttled the plane to take off. The plane whizzed across the field at a high rate of speed. Then he pulled the plane off of the ground. They flew out a small distance before he made a turn toward El Paso.

"Hey, John. There are some headphones to your right. Put them on so we can talk."

"Okay," John replied as loudly as he could to get over the engine noise.

"Can you hear me?" Richard asked through the microphone on his headset.

"Loud and clear," John replied.

"We will be flying low, but don't worry. I just want to stay away from any airport radar."

"We're going to be skimming treetops and he says don't worry."

"Trust me, John. I know what I'm doing."

"That's a little harder to do than you think," John replied nervously.

"Uh oh," Richard said with a disturbing voice.

"What do you mean, uh oh?" John asked quickly.

"It's nothing. The plane is reacting a little sluggish, that's all."

"Sluggish? What does that mean?"

"All it means is it's not reacting as sharp as it should."

"So what is the problem with it?" John asked nervously.

"I don't know, yet," Richard answered calmly.

"Oh, shit. We are going to die out here!"

"You're not going to die. Trust me."

"That's easy for you to say."

THE COVERUP

"Wait a minute!" Richard said excitedly.

"What?" John replied.

"Check the meter. It should be right in front of you on the dash," Richard ordered.

"Okay, it reads full."

"No wonder she's not flying right."

"What does that mean?"

"The tanks are full of insecticide. We need to dump it somewhere. Hang on. I've got an idea," Richard said as he turned the plane north.

"What are you going to do?"

"Dust some crops."

"You know how to do that?"

"I've never done it before, but I know how."

"Oh, shit!" John repeated nervously.

"You might want to tighten your seatbelt," Richard relayed.

"Oh, shit!" John said again as he pulled the belt tighter.

"Relax. There's nothing to it. Listen, John, do you see that lever in front of you?"

"Yeah, I see it," John replied with a shaky voice.

"Okay, when I tell you, pull that lever all the way back," Richard instructed.

"All the way back?"

"Yeah, all the way back. I'll do the rest," Richard replied.

They flew for a few minutes north. Then they flew over some trees. On the other side was a field of corn. Richard took the plane down and was flying a few yards over the corn.

"Okay, John, pull the lever," Richard ordered.

John pulled the lever back as far as it would go.

"Okay, she's opened," John replied. The plane zipped across the field of corn spraying insecticide.

"What's the gauge read now, John?" Richard asked as he continued to fly the plane over the corn.

"It's almost empty."

"Okay, let me know when it gets to empty."

The plane continued across the cornfield spraying the insecticide on the corn. John paid close attention to the gauge in front of him. This way he didn't have to see what was going on outside. Soon the gauge had reached empty.

"Okay, she's empty," John said as he looked up for the first time. "Oh, shit!"

"Good, let's get out of here," Richard said as he pulled the plane up into the sky.

"Oh, shiiiit!" John yelled as the tiny plane soared into the sky.

"Relax, we've got it now."

"Oh my God, oh my God, oh my God!" John repeated excitedly.

Suddenly the plane leveled off. John became more excited. The excitement was a rush he had never felt before. He had always hated flying because of all the accidents he read about, but after dusting a crop, he was intoxicated with excitement.

"John, you okay up there?" Richard asked with a concerned voice.

"Man, I hate flying, but I have to admit, that was fun. Let's do it again," John said.

"Ha, ha, ha," Richard laughed out loud. Suddenly the plane sputtered and lurched, jerking John back and forth.

"Uh, never mind," John quickly said.

"Yeah, might better get on with this trip," Richard remarked.

"Everything okay back there?" John asked with great concern.

"We're okay. It's nothing to worry about. She just doesn't want to play today," Richard replied. He turned the plane to the west and off they flew.

Fifteen minutes of time passed before either one said a word.

"When we get to El Paso, John, I'll buy you a drink, as kind of a graduation gift," Richard said to break the ice.

"Graduation, from what?" John asked.

"From a ground dweller to a bird of prey," Richard replied.

"I don't follow you."

"The sure raw power, being the largest object in the sky at the time, to leave the ground and fly like a bird. You can't find a feeling like that anywhere else," Richard said.

"Yeah, I guess you're right about that."

"I'm glad to have shared it with you."

"Yeah, me too."

"Well, anyway, when we land I know this little out-of-the-way bar. I would like to take you there," Richard said.

"Are you going to wear that little paper dress of yours?" John asked.

"Just can't let it go, can you?"

"Well, I'm sorry, but it sounded like you were asking me for a date."

"Make one wrong move and they're on you like fleas on a dog," Richard said out loud to himself.

"I'll go, but I don't know if I will like it," John remarked.

"And why is that?"

"Well, I like my dates to dress up," John replied laughing.

"I hate you!"

"Well, I'm sorry. I just can't get that image out of my mind," John replied jokingly.

WILLIAM DANIEL

"Lord, give me the strength!" Richard began to pray out loud.

"I'm the one he needs to help. I've got this image in the back of my mind I'll never get rid of."

"I hope you get over it. Really I do," Richard replied seriously.

Time flew by as they were about to approach El Paso. It had seemed to John they were only in the sky a little while.

"We are going to land soon at a little farmhouse outside of El Paso. We will meet a farmer I know. He will loan us a car and we will go on from there to El Paso," Richard explained.

"Well, I'm glad you told me the plan ahead of time," John remarked.

"Look, things are going to get a little crazy when we get there, so I want you to pay close attention to what I say. It may sound crazy, but I know what could and may happen," Richard explained.

"Okay, you're the boss," John replied.

"Just be ready to move when I say to. I know Jack knows we are coming here. We may not be here long. The Chupacabra is due to go out again. I'm sure Jack is going to want to hold that up. I don't know if we can get a chance to see it. I would love to be able to dart it with this homing device that Professor Donner has, but I doubt we will get to see him. So I'm counting on him leaving us a message as to what to do," Richard explained.

"So Professor Donner has a backup plan?"

"Yeah, something about an old Indian. I don't know what that means, but I am sure we will find out."

"I hope you are right, partner."

"My diversion should be taking place real soon. I'm hoping it gives us a chance to get out of there quickly," Richard said.

THE COVERUP

JACK ARRIVES IN EL PASO
Chapter Thirty

At 10:45 a.m., Jack arrived at the Camino Hotel in El Paso. He emerged from a taxi and walked into the hotel. He approached the counter and rang the bell for service.

"Yes, sir, how can I help you?" the young man behind the counter asked.

"I need a room," Jack said.

"Okay, sir. I will check and see what we have."

"The manager here?" Jack asked.

About that time, a man appeared from an office off to Jack's right.

"Mr. Riley, how nice to see you again," greeted the man.

"Hello, Bob," Jack answered. Bob was the manager of the hotel.

"How can I help you, Mr. Riley?" Bob asked.

"Well, I need a room, Bob. Can you fix me up?"

"Why, certainly. Would you like your regular room?

"Yes," Jack replied.

Bob turned to the young man behind the counter. "Give me the key to room 366," Bob requested.

"Uh, sir, 366 is already occupied," the young man replied.

"Move them. Get some people up there and move them," Bob ordered.

"What shall I tell them is the reason?" the young man asked.

"Tell them there is a problem with the plumbing."

"Yes, sir," the young man answered as he picked up the phone to call for help.

Bob turned back to Jack. "No problem, Mr. Riley," he said as he shook Jack's hand.

"Good," Jack replied.

Bob turned back to the young man and took the key from him. "Here you are, Mr. Riley," Bob said as he handed the key to Jack.

"See you later, Bob," Jack said as he turned and headed for the elevator.

"Anything you need, Mr. Riley, you just call me," Bob said as Jack walked away.

Jack punched the button on the elevator and waited for it to open. When the doors opened, Jack walked in and punched the third floor button. The elevator lunged upward to the third floor. The door opened at the third floor and Jack walked out. He walked down the hall to room 366. He put the key in the door and opened it, walked into the room, closing the door behind him. He reached into his pocket and pulled out a cell phone. He began to dial a number. He put the phone to his ear.

"Anything yet?" he asked when someone answered.

"Nothing yet, sir," answered the voice on the other end.

"Call me as soon as they arrive," Jack ordered.

"Yes, sir, Mr. Riley," the voice replied.

Jack put his cell phone away and walked over to the window. He opened the curtain and looked out at the street. He then turned his attention to his watch. Realizing it was about lunchtime, he decided to go get something to eat. He

THE COVERUP

walked out of the hotel room and started toward the elevator to go downstairs. As he was walking to the elevator, a woman darted out of her room. She ran into Jack and fell to the floor.

"I'm sorry, Miss," Jack apologized. "Here, let me help you up."

Jack suddenly noticed the woman looked like Regina Barton.

"Regina," he said surprisingly to the woman.

"I beg your pardon, sir. My name is not Regina," the woman answered angrily.

"I must apologize. You look like someone I know."

"Is that some kind of a pickup line of yours?"

"I didn't mean to imply anything. I actually know someone who looks like you. I must apologize."

"That your wife?"

"I'm sorry. I don't understand what you mean."

"Is that your wife I remind you of?"

"Oh, no, just someone I know."

"A girlfriend?"

"No, there is no one."

"Good."

"I beg your pardon?" Jack replied with confusion.

"The least you could do for knocking me down is buy me lunch."

"Uh, well," Jack started to say when the woman interrupted him.

"Are you one of those guys that prefers to eat alone?"

"No," Jack said as a smile came to his face.

"Good. My name is Sandra. And you are?"

"Uh, Jack Riley."

"So, how about it?"

"How about what?" Jack replied as if he was in a daze.

249

"Lunch," Sandra said.

"Oh, sure. Why not?" Jack replied with a smile.

"Good. I am starving. Where shall we go?" Sandra asked.

"Well, I usually eat here at the hotel," Jack replied.

"Well, if that is where you want to eat, that is where we will eat, as long as they have good food. They do have good food here?"

"Haven't you eaten here before? I thought you were staying here," Jack asked.

He looked her in the eyes as if to catch her in a lie.

Sandra was too smart to let that happen. She quickly answered, "Why, of course I'm staying here. I just got settled into my room."

"Oh, I see," Jack said as the expression changed on his face, but only on the outside did the caution leave him. An experienced FBI agent never leaves his guard down. "Well, let me escort you to the dining room, Miss Sandra."

"Why, I would love to join you, Mr. Riley," Sandra replied with a smile.

Jack took her arm in his and walked her to the elevator. Jack pushed the down button on the wall. They waited for the elevator doors to open. When it finally arrived and the doors opened, they walked in. Jack pushed the first floor button on the panel. The doors closed and the elevator started going down.

"So, Miss Sandra, have you ever been to El Paso before?" Jack asked, trying to make conversation to break the ice between them.

"No, I was here a few years back, but I was just passing through. I didn't get to see any of the sites here."

THE COVERUP

"Well, let me show you around tonight."

"Oh, darn, I have this meeting to go to tonight."

"How about tomorrow?"

"Okay, that would be great," Sandra replied with a smile. She knew she would be far from here by tomorrow. Later tonight, she would board a plane and leave El Paso.

"Well, then it's a date," Jack said with a smile.

"I will be looking forward to it," Sandra replied softly.

"Me, too, Miss Sandra," Jack remarked softly.

The elevator arrived at the first floor and the doors opened. Jack escorted Sandra out of the elevator and across the room. They came to a sign which said, "Restaurant." Bob, the hotel manager, noticed Jack heading for the restaurant. He quickly walked over to where Jack was standing.

"Mr. Riley, let me get you a table," Bob said as he walked up to Jack.

"Table for two, Bob," Jack ordered.

"Very well, Mr. Riley. Give me one moment," Bob said as he walked into the restaurant to find a table.

"I'm impressed," Sandra said as she looked into Jack's eyes.

"I am, too, Miss Sandra."

Sandra had set the hook. Now it was a matter of reeling him in. All she had to do was hold his attention for part of the day, and she could slip away and disappear.

Bob came walking back to Jack. "I have your regular table, Mr. Riley."

"Thanks, Bob."

"Don't mention it. Now just come this way," Bob said as he escorted them to their table.

"I take it you have been here before," Sandra remarked. Jack just smiled as he walked Sandra to the table.

251

"Here you are, Miss," Bob said as he pulled the chair out for her. Sandra sat down and Bob pushed the chair back in a little. "Now your waitress will be with you in a moment. Can I get you something to drink?"

"I'll have a glass of tea," Sandra ordered.

"Make that two, Bob," Jack ordered.

"Very well. I will have your drinks here in a moment. Here are your menus, and your waitress will be here shortly to take your orders," Bob said. He walked away snapping his fingers at one of the waitresses. Sandra picked up the menu and began to read it.

"What do you recommend, Jack? You have eaten here before. What's good here?"

"Well, they make a good steak, but I like their spaghetti and meatballs."

"Ooh, that sounds good. I'll have that."

"You will love it."

"How often do you stay here? I mean, Bob seems to know you real well. Are you a traveling salesman or something?"

"No, I work for the government."

"Oh? What part?" Sandra asked as if she was interested.

"Now that's enough about me. I want to hear more about you," Jack softly inquired.

"There's nothing special about me. I'm just a dress designer for a large manufacturing company in New York. I'm down here to meet with some new designers for the company. That's the meeting I have to go to tonight. The company is looking for some new designs, and they sent me to look at them," Sandra explained.

"Well, that sounds interesting. You must be important for them to send you by yourself."

THE COVERUP

"Well, they trust my judgment. I've been with this company for ten years. Now I'm in charge of the new designs."

"That's great. You sound like a take-charge kinda person."

"If you don't mind me saying so, I am," Sandra replied softly.

"I just bet you are," Jack said while his eyes undressed her.

"You say the sweetest things, Jack."

Their waitress brought their drinks and placed them on the table and asked what they would like to order. Jack gave her their order and turned his eyes back to Sandra.

"You never told me your last name," Jack remarked.

"Didn't I?"

"All you told me was Sandra, which by the way, is a very pretty name."

"I'm sorry, Jack. It's Sandra Neil. Sometimes I come on too strong and I'll forget my manners. You will forgive me, won't you?" Sandra flirted back.

"Why, of course, I will, Sandra Neil. What a pretty name for a pretty lady."

"Oh, Jack, you're embarrassing me."

"I'm sorry. I can't help myself. Your beauty has entranced me."

"Jack?"

"Yes, Miss Sandra?"

"I'll be right back. I've got to go to the powder room. You will still be here, won't you?" Sandra asked softly and encouragingly.

"Why, of course I will. I will long for your return, Miss Sandra. Hurry back," Jack replied as he waved her on.

Sandra walked toward the restrooms. Jack watched until he could no longer see her. He quickly pulled out his cell phone and punched some numbers, looking toward the bathrooms to check for Sandra's return.

"Yes, sir, Mr. Riley," came the voice over the cell phone.

"Get me someone over here. I think I have been set up. Someone is trying to distract me from the chase. I want this woman I'm eating with followed wherever she goes. Put Todd Peterman on it. I don't want him doing anything but following her. Find out who she really is and report to me," Jack ordered.

"Yes, sir, Mr. Riley. I'll get him over there right now," replied the voice on the cell phone.

Jack disconnected his call and then placed the phone back into his coat. He casually looked around the room for someone watching him, just in case there were two of them involved. Cooper, he thought to himself. It has to be Cooper who put her up to this. What are the chances he would meet another woman who looked like Regina. Cooper must be trying to set me up so he can slip by, Jack continued to think to himself. He quickly pulled his cell phone back out of his inside coat pocket. He dialed a number and placed the phone to his ear.

"Yes, sir," said a voice on the other end.

"I want everybody on full alert. I think they are coming in. Remember what your orders are," Jack said and hung up. He placed the phone back inside his coat pocket. Out of the corner of his eye, he saw Sandra coming back. Like a gentleman, Jack stood up and helped Sandra back into her seat.

"Oh, thank you, Jack. You're such a gentleman," Sandra said as she sat down.

"I'm glad you're back."

"Did you miss me while I was gone?" Sandra said softly.

THE COVERUP

"Something like that."

The waitress came to their table to check on their drinks. She told them their order would be right out. Jack took a quick look around the room and turned his attention back to Sandra.

"How long do you plan on staying here?" he asked.

"I'll be in town for a couple of days. Then I have got to fly back to New York City. They'll be waiting for these new designs."

"So I only have two days to get to know you?" Jack asked depressingly.

"You could come to New York City and see me," Sandra replied invitingly.

"I guess I will have to," Jack remarked.

The waitress brought their food and began to set it on the table. Jack took another quick look around the room. He saw Peterman talking with Bob. He turned his attention to the waitress and thanked her for bringing their food and said to Sandra, "You're going to enjoy this."

"It certainly smells good," Sandra remarked as she picked up her spoon and fork. She began to roll the spaghetti around her fork and took a bite. "Hmm, that is good."

"I knew you would like it. No one makes spaghetti and meatballs like they do," Jack said as he took a bite. They began to heartedly enjoy their meal.

"So, Jack, when are you going to tell me what you do for the government?" Sandra asked in between bites.

"There's not much I can tell you. Government policy doesn't allow it. Nothing serious, just confidential information. Can't let the communist party know all our secrets, you know."

"But I'm not a communist."

"I know, but the less you know, the safer it is for you. Maybe when I get to know you better."

Jack knew he was only playing along with the game. He knew he would never be intimate with this woman. He had to play along in order for his plan to work, and if he was wrong about her, he would have a good excuse.

While Sandra and Jack continued their meal, John and Richard were landing at a farmhouse outside of El Paso. They met with the farmer to get the car and discussed the plan with him. The farmer said he was having trouble with his car and offered to take them in his farm truck.

"I've got an idea here," Richard said as he looked at a horse trailer the farmer owned.

John noticed Richard looking at the trailer. "You thinking of going in that thing?"

"Well, it might be less conspicuous," Richard replied.

"Whatever you think, partner," John answered.

"Let's do it," Richard said to the farmer.

The farmer agreed and went to get the trailer hooked up. Richard and John walked into the farmhouse. They met the farmer's wife, and she offered them some lunch. They sat down and ate while discussing the plan.

"How do we get out of that trailer without anyone seeing us?" John asked as he woofed down the meal.

"That trailer has a side door. When we get into town, we will slip out the side. Plus if we get to the city and it looks suspicious, we can abort," Richard explained.

"Well, it might work," John replied.

"Look, when we get to town, we may have to change plans. We don't know the situation with Professor Donner. If you have any doubts or suspicions, don't hesitate to tell me. We

THE COVERUP

may have to change directions several times. I need you to be in synch with me," Richard explained.

"I'm with you, partner," John answered as he finished the meal he was eating.

The farmer came in and told them he was ready. They got up and thanked his wife for the food and walked outside to get into the trailer.

"Geez, smells like a horse in here," Richard remarked.

"What did you think it was going to smell like, a rose garden?" John returned.

"I was expecting some smell but not this strong," Richard replied.

"You'll get used to it soon," John explained as he looked out the side window.

"Okay, we're ready to go," Richard shouted to the farmer.

The farmer started the truck and pulled the truck and trailer out of the yard. He drove down the long driveway until he came to the highway. He turned onto the highway, which would take them to El Paso.

The truck and trailer roared down the highway. The noise was so loud, Richard and John had to shout to hear each other.

"How far have we got to go?" shouted John.

"Not far. We are only about ten miles from the city," Richard replied screaming.

"Good, 'cause this noise is deafening."

When they reached the city limits sign, the farmer tooted the horn. Richard recognized the signal. "We are getting close," Richard shouted to John.

They both turned and looked out opposite sides of the trailer. Richard was looking out of the driver's side of the truck and trailer. He was looking for Professor Donner's signal. They passed the place where the signal was supposed to be. Richard didn't see the signal Professor Donner was supposed to leave. He walked over to the other side of the trailer.

"He didn't leave a signal!" Richard shouted to John.

"So what does that mean?"

"Means everything is okay," Richard replied cautiously.

"That seem strange to you?" John asked curiously.

"Yeah, it does. I expected to see his signal because of that incident we had at the shoe store. Very strange, indeed!" Richard shouted back.

"Do you think there might be a problem?"

"I don't know for sure, but I know Professor Donner would have left a signal if there was a problem."

The truck slowed down as they got closer into the main part of the city. "Good, we're slowing down," John said as he lowered his voice.

"Yeah, we're probably coming to the first red lights. We still have a ways to go," Richard said.

John looked out the side of the trailer and turned to Richard with his forehead wrinkled.

Richard noticed the concerned look on John's face. "What do you think?" he asked.

"I think Jack knows we are here. He must be letting us go in. It must be a trap," John answered.

"Let's play this like we saw the signal. I told the farmer to stop at the Greyhound bus station," Richard explained.

"So, what now, partner?" John asked as he looked out the side of the trailer.

"Professor Donner and I worked out a plan a long time ago. If there was something he wanted to tell me, he would leave a signal on a post. That post is right inside the city limits. It has a white paint mark on it. We put that there a long time

THE COVERUP

ago. So if I couldn't see him, he would leave a note at the bus station," Richard explained.

"You think Jack pulled the signal off?" John asked curiously.

"Maybe. I don't know, but he couldn't have gotten the note," Richard answered with great confidence.

"Why is that?" John asked.

"Last time I talked to Professor Donner, he told me he had some information for me.

He told me that he had already put a note in a locker at the bus station. It's a plan he and I came up with the first time I ran into Jack. This way if I felt uncomfortable about seeing him, I could get the information. We'll get the note and move on," Richard explained.

"That's real smart thinking, there, Richard," John said as he looked out the side window.

The truck and trailer continued to pass through intersection after intersection. They finally came to the bus station. The farmer pulled in and stopped the truck. Richard and John opened the side door and stepped out of the trailer. Richard waved to the farmer, and he drove off. They walked into the bus station, Richard leading the way to a locker at the back of the station. He took a key from his pocket and opened locker door number 99. Inside the locker was a note. Richard reached inside the locker and retrieved the note. He began to read it to himself. "Look for an Indian named Running Deer. You will find him at Burrow Hills Indian Reservation. It is located outside of Sacramento, California."

"What does it say?" John asked as he looked around the room.

"We are to find an Indian named Running Deer somewhere outside Sacramento," Richard answered.

"California?" John asked softly.

"Yes. Let's check the bus schedule," Richard said as he and John walked to the counter.

The clerk behind the counter asked if he could help them. Richard told him where he wanted to go. The clerk turned to check the schedule and turned back to Richard and gave him the departure time. Richard thanked him and took John off to the side to talk in private.

"The bus to Sacramento leaves in fifteen minutes," Richard said.

"Who is this Running Deer, and why do we have to talk to him?" John asked curiously.

"I don't know. He must have some information about the Chupacabra. Professor Donner would not have wanted us to see him if it wasn't important. Let's get the tickets and get out of here," Richard explained.

They walked back to the counter and Richard pulled out his credit card and gave it to the clerk and asked for two tickets to Sacramento. The clerk took his card and began to process his tickets. Richard turned to John and said, "If you need to use the bathroom, now would be the time."

"Yeah, where is it?" John asked as he looked around the bus station.

"It's over there," Richard replied as he pointed the way.

"Okay, be back in a jiffy," John said as he walked toward the bathrooms.

Richard turned his attention back to the clerk. He had just finishing processing his tickets. He gave Richard the receipt to sign. After he finished signing, the clerk gave him his tickets and thanked him. Richard took the tickets and turned toward the bathrooms and walked over to the entrance. Just as he arrived at the entrance to the bathroom, John was coming out. "Everything come out all right?"

THE COVERUP

"Fine," John replied.

"Good. Here's your ticket," Richard said as he handed it to John. "I've got to take care of some business myself."

"You're not going to put that paper dress on again?" John asked jokingly.

"You never stop, do you?" Richard replied as he walked into the restroom.

John stood outside the entrance and scanned the room. He saw nothing out of the ordinary. He waited a few minutes for Richard to return. The bus station clerk announced over the loud speaker, "Now boarding for Tucson, Phoenix, Los Angeles, Sacramento, in five minutes."

John turned to the restroom door to see if Richard was coming out. When he didn't see him emerge, he started to walk in. Suddenly, Richard opened the door and walked out.

"What?" he asked as he saw the expression on John's face.

"They are about to start boarding. I was just about to come get you."

"Oh, well, let's get on the bus," Richard said as he left the entrance to the restrooms.

"I got to tell you, I was a little afraid to go in there and get you," John said laughing.

"Keep it up, monkey boy," Richard remarked as he walked toward the bus.

"What?" John asked giggling.

"Never give it up, do you?" Richard asked.

"I didn't say anything about the paper dress, did I?"

"Keep it up, and I will cut you out of my will."

"I'm in your will?"

"Keep it up, fuzz ball, and you won't be."

WILLIAM DANIEL

"Please tell me what you're going to leave me. It's not that paper dress, is it?" John said laughing.

"Would you stop?" Richard said as they stepped onto the bus.

"Okay, I'll stop. Am I still in your will?"

"As long as you see to it that I live," Richard replied as he handed his ticket to the boarding agent.

"Stipulations. Always got to have stipulations, don't you?" John asked as he gave the agent his ticket.

They stepped into the bus and looked for a place to sit. Richard saw two seats at the back. He and John walked to the back and sat down. They sat quietly waiting for the bus to depart. John broke the silence. "You know anything about this Indian we are going to see?"

"No, never heard of him before. I guess it's someone Professor Donner knows. Maybe he knows something about this creature."

"You know, something about this just doesn't set well with me," John remarked.

"What's that?" Richard asked.

"Well, we know Jack knows we are here. At least we assume he knows, right?" John asked as he explained his concerns.

"Yeah," Richard interestingly replied.

"Why is he letting us go through?" John questioned.

"I don't follow you," Richard replied.

"He must know we are here because of the incident back at the shoe store. That should have pointed the direction we were heading. We know he's after us. Remember the incident back in Galveston? I would figure the bus station to be one of the places I would want covered. Yet I did not see one possible agent in that station, and here we are on the bus, and no one is stopping us," John explained.

THE COVERUP

"I see your point. It's as if he wanted us to get on the bus," Richard replied with interest.

"My point exactly," John said.

"Maybe he is watching the Professor thinking that is where he will catch us. Maybe we just outsmarted him. I mean, you've got to admit, the note in the locker was a brilliant idea. There is no way he could have known about that. Maybe we just fooled him," Richard explained his thoughts.

"With something as important as this, I would think Jack would have brought out the National Guard. He would have had the entire area covered. I mean, with a government coverup of an extraterrestrial existence, I would think that comes under national importance. Yet it's damn peculiar he didn't cover the bus station, as if he wanted us to get on this bus like you said," John curiously remarked.

"I see what you are saying, but this bus doesn't go to Nevada. That is where most people believe they are hiding an alien spacecraft. That's where area fifty-one is thought to be. He's got to believe that is where we are going. Maybe he didn't think it was important to cover this bus," Richard replied.

"Jack's a very smart man. I know, I have worked with him in the FBI. That's why they made him the director of southern operations. His ability to get the job done is what got him the promotion. I'm not sure he would have left any unturned stones in a case like this one. I think Jack has a plan, and we are following suit. I think he's following right along behind us to see where we are going," John explained his theory.

"I see what you mean. He doesn't know where we are going, so he must follow to find out. Well, that could be an advantage to us," Richard said.

"How do you figure?" John asked.

"Well, if he doesn't know where we are going, we can change directions and throw him off, sort of like a fish throws off a predator by changing directions in the middle of a chase. All we have to do is get him looking one way and go another," Richard explained.

Richard and John continued to discuss the situation. The bus roared its way toward the next destination as it left El Paso. John and Richard knew they needed to come up with a distraction plan. They needed to get Jack off their trail so they could make it to Sacramento.

"I just believe we need to get off this bus," John whispered to Richard.

"How do we know Jack doesn't have an agent on the bus already?" Richard replied softly.

"That's the bad part. We don't know for sure. However, I did get a good look at the people who got on in El Paso. I don't think any of them were agents, but I don't know about the people that were already on the bus."

"This bus stops at several cities on its way to California. We should figure a way to slip off and find another way to get to our destination."

"You mentioned Area Fifty-One. You think maybe they are keeping this creature in there?"

"My hunch says yes. I mean, what better place to hide it than on a secret military base," Richard whispered.

"How are we going to get inside a military base? If they catch us in there, we will be hung out to dry!"

"Don't worry about it. I have a lawyer who can get us out of anything. It will be all right."

"We are about to sneak onto a secret military base, and you say don't worry about it."

THE COVERUP

"My lawyer has instructions. If I turn up missing, a hoard of investigators, both news and private, will be looking for me. A public statement will be made about my quest for the truth. It will also include documented cases of my conflicts with Jack."

"And we will be dead."

"Oh, yeah. I didn't think about that," Richard replied with mixed feelings.

"That's right. We will simply disappear. Your investigators will find us, all right. Just tell them to look for us in the desert because that is where they will find us. 'Two men who got lost in the desert' is what our obituary will read!" John replied angrily.

"Well, I didn't say my plan didn't have flaws."

"Flaws, Richard. We'll be dead!"

"Okay, I get the point. There are some perils we will have to overcome, but this is not about us. This is about exposing one of the most sought-out answers of the universe. The one question on everyone's mind, 'Are we alone in the universe, exposing the government of a coverup that has gone on for a long time, bringing to light the answers people have been seeking for years, what really happened at Roswell? What is this creature called the Chupacabra?' And wouldn't you like to see Jack behind bars?"

"I would like to be alive to see that."

"I have faith in your ability to get us through that part."

"My ability? How am I going to stop this from happening?"

"Nobody knows Jack as well as you do. You know every move Jack will likely make. Deep down in your heart, I know you want to beat him. I saw it in your eyes when the three of us met in your office. I'm betting, no, I'm counting on you getting that done. I have a great confidence that you can do it. It is all in the heart, my friend. It is all in the heart," Richard confidently said.

"I guess I don't have a choice now."

"My friend, you have been waiting for this moment most of your life. Ever since you met Regina, you have fought with Jack, maybe not so much physically, but certainly mentally. You want him to go down more than I do. I think your ego demands it. I also think the better man is sitting beside me right now. I know Regina thinks so," Richard enthusiastically remarked.

"I do love that woman, and you are right. Ever since I met her, I have been at battle with my own pride. I didn't leave the FBI because I wanted to. I was forced out by Jack. The only reason I went quietly is because I do love Regina very much. Okay, Richard, we'll take him on, we'll take him on," John replied with confidence.

"That's the spirit I'm looking for. You have been carrying this burden too long. It's time you put this sucker away, my friend."

"You too, my friend. You have been chasing this creature far too long. I think it is time to expose the goatsucker. I do hope the public can handle the truth. I'm still having a time with it myself."

"I know, John. I'm impressed with the confidence you have put in me."

"What do you mean?"

"Well, here I am this rich man who drops into your life. You don't know me from a hill of beans, but yet you have stuck with me on this thing, and you don't even believe in it. I mean, not fully believe in it. You're taking me for everything that I believe in to be the truth. Most people think I'm right just

THE COVERUP

because I have money. They are just standing around waiting for a handout, but I can see that you want the truth to be known, too."

"Well, I would like to know something," John said, hesitating for a moment.

"I know, I know. It's billions, trust me."

"Uh, what is billions?"

"How much I am worth. That's what you wanted to know, wasn't it?"

"No, that's not what I wanted to know."

"Then what?"

"I just wanted to know if that paper dress comes in red. You would look cute in a red paper dress," John replied laughing.

"Morons, that's what you give me, morons," Richard said looking up at the top of the bus.

"Who are you talking to up there?" John asked while snickering.

"I ask for good people, and this is what you send me. I am disappointed," Richard remarked looking again at the ceiling of the bus.

"All right, I can't help myself, but I will try to do better," John said before he started laughing again.

"You're impossible," Richard said as he scrunched down to take a nap.

"Okay, okay, I'll shut up now," John said and then hesitated for a moment. "You really worth billions?"

"Yes," Richard replied as he yawned.

"Man, that's a lot of money," John remarked.

"Yeah, you can pile it so high, it would take all day to climb it," Richard said sarcastically.

"Man with that much money can buy just about anything he wanted," John said seriously.

267

"And I clearly have."

"You could buy yourself a whole warehouse full of paper dresses, all different colors, too. Why, you could build a paper dress factory," John remarked as he looked at Richard.

"You're despicable."

"I'm sorry. I couldn't help myself."

"Why do I put up with these morons?" Richard said softly to himself.

"Because you love us, man."

"I tell you what. You keep your eyes on what is going on. I'm going to take a nap," Richard said as he rolled over onto his side to sleep.

"Okay, partner, I'll take the first watch," John replied in a John Wayne-like voice.

The bus continued to churn its way down the long black highway. The scenery was nothing but cactus and sand. It stretched for miles away from the highway. The bus drove for hours through the desert, finally making its way into Phoenix, Arizona for a stop. It would be in Phoenix long enough to refuel and change drivers, and then it would carry its passengers to Los Angeles.

"Hey, wake up," John said to Richard as he shook him.

"Where are we?" Richard asked as he stretched his arms.

"Phoenix, I think."

"Oh. Let's get off and stretch our legs," Richard said as he got up from his seat.

"I think my butt is still plastered to that seat. I can't feel it anymore," John remarked.

"Move around a little bit. The feeling will come back to you as soon as you get your circulation going," Richard replied.

THE COVERUP

They both stepped off the bus and walked around the bus station. Richard noticed the restroom sign and headed for it. John followed close behind him. They stepped inside to take care of business.

"Hey, what are we looking for when we get to Sacramento?" John asked as he walked to the sink.

"First of all, we are not going to Sacramento. We are going to Squaw Valley and look for Indian Guide Road. That's the instructions Professor Donner left us. We're supposed to look for an old Indian named Running Deer. I don't know about this guy. I only know we will find him on Indian Guide Road. He runs some kind of an Indian cultural amusement park."

"Huh, is that one of those parks where they have the teepees set up and there are Indians running around in buckskin outfits throwing knives, hatchets and shooting arrows? At night they have the big fire act with the peace pipe. Is that what we're talking about here?" John said as he washed his hands in the sink.

"Something like that. Have you ever been to one?" Richard asked.

"Yeah, once when I was a kid. My dad took me to one out here somewhere."

"Was it this place we are going?" Richard asked with interest.

"I don't remember where it was or what it was called. Shoot, I was only five years old at the time."

"I can't remember what I was doing at five."

"That was the only time I remember my dad taking me somewhere. Most of the time he was working. Seemed like he worked seven days a week," John said very sadly.

"Is he still alive?"

"No," John said hesitating for a moment. "He died several years ago."

"Sorry to hear that, man. My dad used to take me places when I was around seven. Then it was just me and the chauffeur. Then it was just me going by myself."

"Sounds kind of lonely there, Richard."

"Mostly boring. El Chupacabra has been my escape from reality. I've put all my effort into the chase. I hope when the end comes, there will be a new adventure to begin," Richard explained.

He and John walked out of the restrooms and into the bus station's lobby.

"I hear you man. Hey, how about we get a bite to eat before we leave?" John said as he pointed to a snack bar.

"Good idea," Richard returned.

They walked over to the snack bar and ordered some food. The bus was about ready for the trip to L.A. as John and Richard got their food and sat down to eat.

"I think the bus is about ready to leave. We better finish this and get on, or they will leave us here," Richard remarked.

"Won't take but a minute for me to choke this food down," John replied as he munched down on a hamburger.

"Have you got any ideas on how we can change directions yet?" Richard asked as he munched on some French fries.

"Nothing has come to mind yet."

"Me either," Richard said as he took a bite of his hamburger.

"This bus is bound to make a few stops between here and L.A. Maybe we'll catch a break along the way," John said continuing to eat his burger.

"We will see," Richard replied.

A bus station clerk announced the bus would leave in five minutes. John and Richard finished their meal and got up and ran to get on the bus. As they were boarding, John looked at the other passengers. Their old seats were still empty, and they sat down in them. Finally the new bus driver shut the door and drove the bus out of the station and into the street. The bus made its way through the streets of Phoenix, heading for the interstate highway that would take them to L.A.

"Why don't you catch some sleep? I'll keep an eye on things," Richard said.

"Okay, I could use some rest."

"You sure could because I don't know what's going to happen between here and there," Richard seriously remarked.

"Or if it happens between here and there," John added as he closed his eyes to sleep.

"Or even where it will happen," Richard quipped.

"Yeah, well, as long as you don't pull that paper dress act again, I'll be fine," John answered with a chuckle.

"Go to sleep, you childish moron."

"Read me a story, Mommy, please," John said in a child-like voice.

"Sleep, you adolescent child," Richard said as he turned to watch the scenery go by out the window. He began to think about whether he should have brought John into this predicament.

The desert scenery passed by Richard's window for several hours. As the bus roared its way down the interstate highway toward Los Angeles, California, Richard mulled over in his mind the events that had happened. He thought about John being a married family man. He hated getting him involved but was glad to have him by his side. For the first time, he had felt like he had found a true friend, someone he could actually trust with his own life, but he kept his reservations about his safety in the back of his mind.

WILLIAM DANIEL

THE COVERUP

RICHARD AND JOHN MEET BOB GLASS
Chapter Thirty-one

The bus driver began to slow down the bus. He had to make a stop at a small bus station about halfway to Los Angeles.

"Wake up, John. We are about to stop," Richard said as he punched John on the arm.

"What? Are we there yet?"

"No, I think it's a fuel stop, or maybe to pick up more passengers."

The bus pulled into a small restaurant and gas station. The bus driver announced there would be a thirty-minute stop here. Anyone who wanted to stretch his legs should do so. John and Richard got up from their seats and stepped out of the bus. They walked around to the restaurant and went in. There they saw a young woman behind a counter with bar stools. They walked over to sit down on one of the stools. John noticed a man sitting at the end of the counter. He was dressed in Indian garments with feathers in his long black hair, a textbook picture of an Indian from a history book. The man was sipping on a glass of ice tea. He didn't look up as John was staring at him.

John turned to Richard and said, "Look at this, Richard."

Richard, sitting on John's left side, leaned forward to take a look. The man looked up from his glass of tea. He began to

273

stare at them with a cold blank facial expression. He got up from the bar stool and walked over to where John was sitting. He bent down and got right in John's face. "You Richard Cooper?" he asked John.

"Uh, no. That's Richard Cooper," John answered as he pointed at Richard. "I'm John Barton."

"Oh, name's Bob Glass. I'm here to pick you guys up," Bob said as he shook their hands.

"And take us where?" Richard asked in a shrill voice.

"Grandfather sent me to pick you guys up. I'll take you to the Indian resort you're looking for."

"How did you know my name?" Richard asked curiously.

Bob bent down close to Richard's face. "Not a good place to talk. I have a Hummer out back. We'll talk there. I'll take you where you want to go, but we must go now," Bob said seriously as he straightened up and walked out the back door.

"Man, that was weird," John said as he watched Bob walk out the door.

"Can I get you fellas something?" the young waitress said as she walked up to them.

"Oh, yeah, a large glass of tea to go, please," Richard ordered.

"Same here," John responded.

"Say, do you know that man in the Indian outfit?" Richard asked the waitress.

"Oh, that's Bob. Pay him no attention. He's just putting on an act. He runs an Indian resort and dresses up for the tourists. He's in here from time to time trying to drum up more business. I'll get your drinks for you," the waitress said as she walked away.

"That guy looked like a real Indian," John said as she walked behind the counter.

THE COVERUP

"He's a Cherokee Indian, I think," the waitress replied.

"I'll be damned. A real Indian," John interestingly said.

"A well educated one, at that," the waitress remarked as she filled their drinks. She brought them over to the counter and set them down. "That will be $2.50, please." Richard gave the waitress his credit card and waited for her to run it through the machine.

"I'll be damned, a real Indian," John repeated.

"Yeah, an educated one, at that," Richard remarked and let out a short giggle.

"Well, what now, partner?" John asked cautiously.

"I don't know, but looks like we are going with him," Richard answered.

"Don't it feel kind of weird to you? Are we sure we want to go with this guy?" John asked.

"Did you see that guy? Are we sure we want to piss him off? I mean, I like my hair, and I would like to keep it," Richard responded.

"Just feels weird to me," John remarked as he drank some of his ice tea.

"I'm sure it will be okay. Yeah, I'm sure it will be okay," Richard repeated.

The waitress came back with his receipt for him to sign. Richard signed it and gave the waitress her copy. He looked at John and said, "Are you ready for this?"

"Not really, but I guess it's a way out to the resort. I just hope he's not a Sioux Indian. You do remember Custer's last stand?" John remarked as he looked at Richard.

"You are disturbed."

"Well, I can't help it. I mean, look at the company I keep. I have an Indian who's weird and a paper-dress-wearing partner. I am beside myself," John said laughing.

"Would you stop? Come on. Let's do this."

"Okay, I'll do it, but my heart's not in it," John replied as he and Richard got up from the stools. They walked to the back door, opened it, and walked out into the blazing hot sun. There they saw the Hummer Bob mentioned. They walked over to the vehicle. Bob was in the driver seat and rolled down the window.

"Get in." Richard walked around to the other side. He opened the door to the front seat. John opened the door to the back seat on the driver's side. They sat down and shut their doors.

"I'm sorry about the act, fellas, but Grandfather said not to discuss anything until we were in the Hummer," Bob said as he turned to look at Richard and John.

"How did your grandfather know my name?" Richard asked.

"Now that's a hard one to explain. Grandfather is from the old tribe. He can see things that no one else can see. I know you white people don't understand the old Indian customs and beliefs. Grandfather is a link to the great spirits. It's hard to explain, but you will see when you meet him," Bob explained.

"Is he the Chief or something?" John asked curiously.

"No, he's a medicine man," Bob replied as he started the Hummer and turned on the air conditioning.

"How does he know Professor Donner?" Richard asked.

"Professor who?" Bob curiously asked.

"You don't know Professor Donner?" Richard answered with a question.

"No, I'm sorry, but I don't. And I don't think Grandfather does either."

"This is weird," John said.

THE COVERUP

"I know it sounds crazy, but you are going to have to trust me on this one. The spirits have told him you were coming. He knows what you want and what to give you. I know it's hard for you white people to understand," Bob replied as he drove the Hummer out of the parking lot of the restaurant and headed for Los Angeles. Three miles down the road, Bob slowed the Hummer down and turned onto a dirt road that looked like it went forever. They were about to cross the desert that seemed to have no end to it.

"Now where are we going?" Richard asked.

"Short cut," Bob answered.

"Through the desert?" John excitedly remarked.

"You white people fear the desert. Apaches lived in it for years," Bob explained.

"So you're an Apache?" John asked.

"No, I'm a Cherokee."

"Like the Apache, the Cherokees liked the desert?" John asked with great curiosity.

"Actually, we hate the desert. I prefer to sleep in a bed myself. In fact, we have a three-star hotel at the resort."

"Tell us about this resort you work at," Richard asked with excited curiosity.

"Own. I own the resort."

"You own the resort? I am impressed," Richard remarked.

"Are you trying to make fun of me?" Bob said as he continued to drive the Hummer across the desert.

"No, not at all. Please don't scalp me," Richard replied, hoping to have saved his hair.

Bob began to laugh out loud uncontrollably. "We don't scalp white people anymore," he said as he tried to control his laughter.

WILLIAM DANIEL

"Oh, sorry," Richard replied.

"Don't pay any attention to him. He's rich and doesn't know better," John explained.

"You're rich? I am impressed," Bob remarked and began laughing again.

"All right, so much for that. Tell us about the resort you own," Richard said as he crossed his arms against his chest.

"Okay. Well, we have a three-star hotel like I said. We put on these Indian shows for the tourists. They love to come up and have a chance to live like an Indian for a few days. We also have a natural spring -fed swimming pool. A lot of people come to the resort for the mineral springs in our swimming pool. They think it has some natural healing process or something. We have several teepees for them to sleep in or they can stay in the hotel. On most nights we put on some kind of Indian show. You know, we dance the rain dance or a war dance. Every other day we put on a play or two like Custer's last stand. We serve some buffalo meat as well as other Indian-type food. We have a large tourist flow every year."

"It sounds like an interesting place. Did you build it yourself?" John asked.

"No, it was all started by my grandfather. He started putting it together back in the early nineteen hundreds. My father took over when he turned thirty years old. He built it into a bigger show in the late nineteen sixties. I took over around 1985. Father took a job running a casino in Las Vegas. About the time I took over, it started to boom."

The Hummer crossed the desert with ease. Bob continued to explain the resort in great detail. Richard and John listened with great interest.

"Now wait a minute. Your grandfather started this back in the nineteen hundreds, is that what you're saying?" Richard asked politely.

THE COVERUP

"Early nineteen hundreds, yes," Bob answered.

"Why, that would make your grandfather over a hundred years old," Richard amusingly said.

"One hundred eight, to be exact."

"My gosh, is he the oldest living human being?" John asked curiously.

"No, there is a man from Japan that is 109 years old."

"And this is the man we are going to see, the man that Professor Donner recommended to me, a man who may or may not be alive when we get there?" Richard said in a disappointed way.

"Hang on there, Richard. Grandfather is not dead yet. He plans on beating that Japanese man out of that title," Bob firmly explained.

"I certainly hope so."

"I think it is impressive that he has lived that long," John interestingly remarked.

"Yeah, well, Grandfather will tell you he owes it all to peyote buttons. Just a little joke of his. Don't take it serious. He really owes it to a good living."

"That's great. I can't wait to meet him," John replied.

"And Grandfather has been waiting to meet ya'll," Bob said as he controlled the Hummer over a bump in the road.

"Now see, that's what I would like to know. How does he know we are coming?" Richard asked.

"Well, it's a spiritual thing you wouldn't understand. Trust me, it's an Indian thing."

"So you're not going to tell me, are you?" Richard asked.

"Listen to what Grandfather says. Trust in what your eyes see. Believe me, it's real. I only hope I can inherit the power after the great spirits come to get him."

"Well, I suppose I don't have much choice," Richard said cautiously.

"What is your grandfather's name?" John asked.

"Running Deer," Bob replied, taking a drink from a glass of water in his cup holder.

"So how come you don't have an Indian name, if you don't mind me asking?" John asked, looking at Bob for the answer.

"I do have an Indian name. I only use it in the show and when I'm working the tourists at the restaurant."

"So what is it?" Richard curiously asked.

"Little Deer," Bob reluctantly replied.

"Little Deer? You have got to be kidding," Richard sarcastically remarked.

"Why Little Deer?" John asked.

"Grandfather gave me the name. He still considers me to be a fawn until I become a full grown buck," Bob explained. "When I become a buck, I will inherit Grandfather's spiritual powers."

"That's interesting. You pass it on from generation to generation," John said as he leaned forward onto the back of the front seat.

"Actually, no. You have to have the spirit within you to acquire the power. My father didn't have it. Grandfather says I'm not ready to receive those powers yet, but the time grows near."

Bob brought the Hummer to a stop in the middle of the desert.

"Why are you stopping here?" Richard asked.

"Got to put some fuel in the Hummer. We are about to lose the light of the day. I don't want to have to do it in the dark," Bob explained as he got out of the vehicle.

"Need some help?" John asked as he continued to lean on the front seat.

"Thanks, but I've got it. This won't take but a minute. However, you might want to stretch your legs some before we go on," Bob replied as he got out. John and Richard got out of the Hummer and walked to the front of the vehicle.

"What do you think?" Richard asked.

"You mean about Bob?" John answered.

"Yeah," Richard quickly replied.

"Well, I don't know much about Indian spirits, but he seems to be harmless. However, we are in the middle of the desert. I don't know as we have much choice right now. Maybe we should indulge him and see what happens," John replied with some reservations.

"Yeah, he seems to be okay. At least he's taking us to where we want to go right now. I'm with you. Let's see what happens," Richard said as he looked across the empty desert.

John lit a cigarette as he stood in front of the Hummer. He looked across the deserted land as the sun was going down. "That is going to be a beautiful sunset there," he said as he took a draw on the cigarette.

"Yeah, it is," Richard replied as he watched the sun meet the earth on the horizon.

"All right, fellas, we are ready to go," Bob said as he walked to the front of the vehicle.

"How much farther is this place?" Richard asked.

"About another two hours driving from here," Bob replied as he started for the driver's side door. John and Richard got back into the Hummer where they were sitting before. Bob started the Hummer and put it into drive and took off down the dusty desert trail he had been following.

"Let me ask you something, Bob. Do you think it's safe to be driving out here at night? What are the chances we might get lost?" Richard asked as he put on his seat belt.

WILLIAM DANIEL

"Hey, don't you worry. I have been driving out here for years. I know this place like the back of my hand. We'll get there in plenty of time."

"Did you grow up around here?" John asked as he leaned against the front seat again.

"Yes, sir. I grew up right in this area. Hunted donkeys just east of here for years and prong horn antelope south of here and bear north of here. I get all of Grandfather's Indian medicines from out here," Bob explained as the Hummer climbed a small sand dune.

"What kind of things do you gather out here for medicines?" Richard asked.

"Well, there are several species of lizards and, of course, rattlesnakes. The meat is real good from a rattlesnake. Then there are the cactus buds and certain weeds that Grandfather needs. Yeah, we get everything we need right here, and it's free," Bob replied as he maneuvered the Hummer around the sandy trail.

"I've heard rattlesnake was really good. I have never actually eaten any, but I have heard it's good," John remarked.

"You've never had any rattlesnake meat? Well, I'll get you some cooked when we get there," Bob ecstatically replied.

"Great! I've always wanted to try some. How about you, Richard?" John asked as he looked at him.

"No, thanks. Something about eating lizards and snakes just doesn't set well with my stomach," Richard quickly replied.

"Come on, Richard, it tastes like chicken," Bob said as he looked over at him.

"Just give me the chicken," Richard seriously replied.

"Well, we have just about anything you could want to eat. It's not just Indian food we serve. A lot of our tourists can't

THE COVERUP

stomach that stuff, so we try to provide a variety of different foods. I prefer a good beef steak, myself."

"Now you're talking my kind of food," Richard excitedly replied.

"Yeah, well, get ready for the best steak you have ever eaten in your life," Bob returned.

"Stop, fellas, you are making me hungry!" John said as he rubbed his stomach.

"One thing bothers me about you, Bob," Richard started to say.

"What's that, Mr. Cooper?"

"You seem like a very educated man. Why do you stay?" Richard asked as he looked over at him.

"It is my destiny," Bob seriously replied. "And besides, I have seen the city life. I was in college for four years in Los Angeles. I prefer the simple life out here, where you either eat or are eaten. Much more sensible than the mind games that go on in the big cities."

"Yeah, they can get quite complicated in the city," Richard laughingly remarked.

"I prefer a smaller community myself," John said.

The Hummer spun and swirled its way along the sandy desert trail. The three men inside were bouncing off of every bump. The sun had dropped below the horizon, and Bob turned on the headlights. They continued through the desert for the next two hours, each telling stories of things that had happened to them in the big cities. Bob brought the Hummer to a halt when they reached a highway. He turned the vehicle to the left and continued on the journey to the resort he owned. As they arrived at the resort, Richard noticed one of the Indian plays being performed. There was a stage off to his right with people sitting around it. There were actors on stage acting out a play.

"That one of the shows you put on here?" he asked Bob.

"Yes, sir. That would be 'The Trail of Tears' they are playing tonight," Bob explained as he stepped out of the Hummer. John and Richard followed and closed the doors to the Hummer behind them.

"Nice place you've got here, Bob," Richard said as he looked around the resort.

"Thanks, Richard. I'm quite proud of this place. Over there is our hotel," Bob replied as he pointed to his left.

"Say, that is a nice hotel you have," John said as he looked toward the luxurious building.

"Thanks. Come on and I'll get a key to one of the rooms so you can clean up. I'll get you some fresh clothes. Then you come down to the restaurant and we'll get something to eat," Bob explained as he led them down the walkway to the hotel.

They walked up to the front entrance and went inside. Bob led them to the front desk where he retrieved a key to one of the rooms. He handed it to Richard and showed them where the elevator was. John and Richard walked over to the elevator and got in. John pushed the second floor button on the elevator. When it arrived at the second floor, the doors came open. They stepped out and looked at the room numbers until they found the one that matched the key. Richard opened the room and stepped in. John followed behind him looking around at the room. He walked over to the window to open the curtain wanting to see what view they had. Richard walked over to the bathroom to take a shower.

"Would you look at that? He's got a tennis court. That must be the swimming pool over there," John said as he pointed to an area across the courtyard.

"I'm going to take a shower first. I'll be out in a few minutes," Richard said as he walked toward the bathroom.

THE COVERUP

"Yeah, well, just don't come out of there wearing that paper dress again. I don't think my nerves could take that again," John replied giggling.

"In your dreams, pal," Richard said as he walked into the bathroom.

"It would be more like nightmares," John quickly replied.

John continued to look out the window at the scenery. He began to think about what Regina might be doing right then. His trance broke, however, when the phone began to ring. He walked over to the phone and picked it up. "Hello," he said as he put the phone up to his ear.

"Hey, John, Bob. Give me yours and Richard's measurements. I'll send a wardrobe up for you to choose from."

"Okay. Mine would be thirty-eight inch waist and thirty-six inch length. Hang on and I'll get Richard's. He's taking a shower, so hang on," John said as he laid the phone down on the bed. He walked over to the bathroom and shouted at Richard. "Hey, Bob's on the phone and wants to know what your pants and shirt size are. He's going to send a wardrobe up for us," John shouted through the door.

"My pants would be thirty-two inch waist and thirty-two inch length. Get me a medium shirt with a fifteen-inch neck," Richard shouted from the shower.

"Got it," John replied and walked back to the phone. "Okay, thirty-two, thirty-two pants and medium shirt, around fifteen-inch neck. Make my shirt a large with an eighteen-inch neck," John relayed to Bob.

"Got it. Anything else you need?" Bob asked.

"Say, Bob, can you get me some dresses around Richard's size in pink and white?" John curiously asked.

"Yeah, sure, but why? Richard's not gay, is he?"

"No, no, it's just a personal joke. Nothing serious. I just like to tease him some every now and then."

"What got this started?" Bob curiously asked.

"Well, I can't tell you because I promised Richard I would not say anything. It's just something that happened along the way. I've been riding it ever since."

"Oh, well, I guess I can help you out, but I would like to know what it is all about."

"The only way you are going to get that information is if Richard tells you himself," John explained chuckling.

"All right, I get it. I'll see what I can do. How many do you need?"

"Just a couple, two or three."

"Okay. As soon as you are ready, come down to the restaurant, and I will meet you there," Bob said as he hung up the phone.

John put the phone back on the cradle. A sinister look came over his face. He began to smile really big. He was thinking to himself of how funny the look on Richard's face would be. Man, he is going to be mad when those dresses show up. He began to giggle to himself at the hilarious plot. Figuring he would need to catch the guy with the clothes first, he headed for the door. He opened the door and walked out into the hall. Closing the door behind him, he stopped in the hall by the room door.

Waiting for the clothes to come, John began to put the plot together. First, he would get the clothes and have the guy hold Richard's. Then he would lay the dresses on the bed for Richard to choose from. He would act like he didn't tell Bob about the paper dress.

THE COVERUP

After a few minutes of waiting, a hotel employee came out of the elevator. He turned and headed to where John was standing. John noticed he had a rack of clothes on wheels. He was rolling them toward him when John went down the hall to meet him. He explained to the employee what he wanted him to do. He took Richard's clothes off the rack and handed them to the employee and pushed the cart into the room. He pulled two cute dresses off of the rack and laid them on the bed beside each other. Next he picked out the suit he would wear and laid it on the bed and pushed the rack back out into the hall where the employee was standing. He told him to wait there until he called him. He cracked the door open and waited for Richard to emerge from the shower.

A couple of minutes passed before he came out of the bathroom. He walked over to the bed where the clothes were laid out. With an angry look on his face, he picked up a white dress with pink lace around the collar. When John saw him pick up the dress, he walked into the room.

"You going to wear that to dinner?" he asked laughing.

"What the hell is this?" Richard asked with a disgusted look on his face.

"I don't know. The guy just brought it. I ran down the hall to catch him. I told him there must be some kind of mistake here," John replied trying not to burst out laughing.

"Yeah, a mistake you put him up to," Richard disgustingly said.

"What makes you think I put him up to something?" John replied with a big smile.

"You told Bob about the paper dress thing, didn't you?"

"No, hey, I didn't say a word."

"Yeah, well, somehow I don't believe you. You're just going to ride this horse until he falls over dead, aren't you?"

"Richard, I swear, I didn't say a word. He just sent it up like that. Maybe his grandfather saw it in a vision or something," John tried to explain without laughing.

"You are an embarrassment," Richard replied as he threw the dress on the bed.

"The guy said he would go down right now and get the right clothes. I'm sorry. I don't know what happened," John said as he turned his head away to keep Richard from seeing him silently giggling.

"Like I believe that," Richard replied and walked back into the bathroom.

"I'll go see what's keeping them with your clothes," John said as he headed for the door.

John stepped into the hall and burst out laughing. The employee, still standing there, looked at him with confusion. Getting control of his laughter, John thanked the employee. He took the clothes rack and pushed it into the room. By the time he got the rack back into the room, Richard had come out of the bathroom. "Here is your suit," John said as he pushed the rack over by the bed.

"Go get your shower. Maybe you can wash that devious look off your face," Richard ordered as he looked through the suits.

"That hurts, man. That really hurts. I can't believe you don't believe me. I just don't know about you anymore," John said bowing his head and walked into the bathroom. Richard turned and looked at John as he walked into the bathroom. Suddenly an enormous amount of guilt fell upon him. He was sure John instigated this joke, but on the same side of the coin, he knew he had a good friend. A warm feeling fell upon his heart and put a smile on his face. He picked out the suit he planned to wear and began to put it on when the phone rang. He walked over and picked up the receiver and said, "Hello."

THE COVERUP

"Richard, Bob. Did you get the suits I sent you?"

"Yes, I did. Why did you send up a bunch of dresses?" Richard asked. He was hoping Bob would spill the beans.

"Dresses? I don't know anything about it. Why, did they bring you dresses?" Bob replied as if he had nothing to do with this joke.

"I don't know. I was hoping you could tell me," Richard replied very curiously.

"I told them to bring you some nice suits for you to wear for dinner. However, I will find out what went wrong. It probably was a glitch in the process. You know how hard it is to find good help. I will straighten it out, though," Bob answered with confidence.

"That's all right. It's no big deal. I don't want to get anyone in trouble over it."

"Well, the reason I called was to see how long it would be before you and John are ready."

"Give us about thirty minutes. We should be ready by then."

"Okay, I will be up to get you and John in thirty minutes."

"Great. See you in thirty minutes," Richard said as he hung up the phone. He continued to put on his suit. He noticed the ties Bob had sent. He picked one of them and took a closer look. They had little Indians on them with a monogram that said, "Cherokee Hotel."

John stuck his head out of the bathroom door and asked, "Did Bob call yet?"

"Yeah, I just talked to him. Told him we will be ready in thirty minutes," Richard replied as he was adjusting his tie.

"Thirty minutes! I better get on the ball. Nice suit. What do you think of mine?" John blurted.

"Good choice. I like the shirt you picked for that suit. What is that, a cobalt blue?" "Yeah, cool, huh?"

"Iceberg, I'm telling you. One hundred percent iceberg," Richard replied in a hip manner.

John stuck his head back into the bathroom and continued to get dried off so he could get dressed.

"How much longer are you going to be in there, John?" Richard screamed through the door.

"Not long. Why?"

"Well, I've got to have time to put on my makeup."

John quickly stuck his head out of the bathroom door. "What did you say?"

"Just kidding, John. I want to see how this suit looks in the mirror."

"Oh, good. For a moment I thought..." John started to say and stopped.

"Thought what, John?"

"Oh, nothing, I guess," John replied and withdrew back into the bathroom.

Richard began to smile as he watched John return to the bathroom. He remembered how nervous John was around Ike back in Galveston. Hum, he thought to himself. I might be able to use that somewhere down the line. Paybacks are hell, he thought as he continued to tug at the suit. Richard was very picky when it came to suits. One of the things that his father always told him was, "Never let a suit make you look good. Always make the suit look good on you."

"It's all yours, partner," John said as he walked out of the bathroom.

"Great," Richard said as he darted in.

John walked over to the bed to start putting on his suit. He noticed a groaning noise coming from the bathroom.

THE COVERUP

"Something wrong in there, partner?" he curiously asked.

"Oh, this suit is awful! In fact, I don't think it's even a suit. I think it's a horse blanket or it feels like one."

"We are just going to dinner, not out on the town. Nobody's going to care what you look like in a rented suit!"

"A suit should fall upon you. This thing just hangs there," complained Richard.

"Let me see."

Richard walked out of the bathroom and faced John. "What do you think?"

"Oh, yeah. Hey, it's most definitely a horse blanket, but you make it look good," John encouraged.

"I do, don't I?"

"Hey, yeah. That horse is going to be jealous. That blanket looks better on you than on him."

Richard looked at John with a disgusted look and shook his head. "I can't go down there looking like this," he murmured.

"Come on, Richard. The suit looks fine. We are just going to dinner."

"Well, I guess I don't have a choice. Just don't let them bury me in this thing."

"You got it. Now, can we go?" John asked as he finished tying his tie. "These ties are cool. They've got little Indians on them."

"You are just too much. We can't go until Bob gets here."

"Well, when is he going to get here?"

"Be patient. He will be here in a minute. You really going to eat some rattlesnake?" Richard asked.

"Sure, why not? I have heard it is really good."

"I don't know. Something about eating lizards and snakes just doesn't set well with me," Richard said with a disgusted look on his face.

"Well, you never know when you might have to eat it to survive. I would at least like to know what it tastes like," John explained.

"Yeah, well, I don't know of too many places that don't have a hamburger stand or a convenience store. But I guess it couldn't hurt to know what it tastes like. Maybe I will try some of it," Richard replied.

"Let me ask you something, Richard. Is it the reptile skin or the fact they are a ground dweller that turns you off of it?"

"I just study them. The thought of eating them has never crossed my mind."

"Ah, it won't hurt you. Go on and try some."

"We shall see," Richard said with reservations.

"I wish Bob would come on. I'm starving here," John said as he rubbed his stomach.

"I don't know. He should have been here by now," Richard replied as he looked at the clock on the nightstand.

"Maybe we should go look for him," John said as he adjusted his tie. No sooner than John had got those words out when a knock came upon their door.

"That must be Bob," Richard said as he walked to the door to answer it. Richard opened the door and there stood Bob. He was dressed in a fine black suit with his hair combed back into a ponytail.

"Bob, come in," Richard greeted him at the door.

"You guys ready to go?" Bob asked as he stepped into the room.

"You bet," John quickly answered.

"Great. I took the liberty of ordering us all a steak. However, I did get a side order of rattlesnake for you, John."

"Hey, Bob, guess what?" John asked as he faced him.

"What?"

"Richard may try some of the rattlesnake meat."

"Really? That's fantastic. You will like it. Trust me, it's not that bad."

"We will see," Richard cautiously answered.

"Well, then, let us go downstairs, fellas," Bob said as he headed for the door.

"Right behind you, Bob," John replied as he and Richard followed him.

They walked down the hall to the elevator. Bob pressed the down button and turned to Richard and John and said, "I had the chef cook those steaks medium rare. I hope that was okay."

"Fine with me," Richard replied.

"Knock its horns off, wipe its ass, and throw it on a plate. I could eat the ass end out of a jackass right now," John candidly remarked.

Bob burst out laughing at John's reply. "Well, it's cooked a little better than that," he said, still laughing at John's remark.

"I certainly hope so, and it had better not be a jackass we are eating," Richard said with great concern.

WILLIAM DANIEL

SITTING DOWN TO DINNER
Chapter Thirty-two

The elevator doors opened and the three men stepped inside. Bob pressed the first floor button on the panel. Still laughing a little at John's remark, he turned to Richard and said, "Don't worry, we are having some fine beef steaks. I picked them out myself. I think you will like the way we prepare our steaks here."

"As long as it's beef," Richard remarked.

Finally the elevator reached the first floor. The door came open and the three men stepped out. Bob directed them to the restaurant where he had a special table waiting. They walked in and turned into a special room to one side. The table was set up with fine china and silverware. Flowers were centered in the middle of the table. It was covered with a fine white-laced tablecloth. The linen napkins had real bone holders on them. All the silverware was lined up properly. You would think the President was eating here, John thought to himself as he sat down in one of the chairs. Richard took a chair to John's right. Bob consulted with the waiter who had entered the room. He took a seat in the remaining chair.

"This is some spread you've got here, Bob," John said.

"Thanks. I love to entertain people with the finest setup money can buy," Bob proudly replied.

"These napkin holders are interesting. What are they, real bone? They look like the spine from an animal," Richard interestingly remarked.

"They are from the spine of a buffalo. We waste nothing from the animals we kill. I have a small herd of cattle and buffalo we raise for their meat. I also have some antelope, deer, and ostriches. We raise most of our meat with the FDA approval," Bob explained.

"Well, I'm impressed," John remarked as he picked up the bone napkin holder.

"Thanks. I'm glad you like it," Bob proudly replied.

"Yes, it's quite elegant," Richard remarked.

"How about a glass of wine, gentlemen?" Bob graciously asked as he picked up a bottle on the table.

"I would love some," Richard replied.

"I'm not much of a wine drinker, myself. Have you got any beer?" John asked.

"Sure, bottle, can, or draft?"

"Draft will be fine."

"Great, I'll have them bring you a glass," Bob replied as he poured Richard and himself some wine. He got up from the table excusing himself and went out of the room to catch the waiter.

"Bob is a gracious host, don't you think?" John remarked as Bob left the room.

"Yes, quite refined," Richard added as he drank some of the wine in his glass.

Bob returned to the room and sat down in his chair. He grabbed the glass of wine in front of him and took a sip. "How's your wine, Richard?" he asked as he set down his glass.

"Fine, thanks," Richard politely responded.

The waiter entered the room with a glass of beer for John. "Thanks," John said as the waiter set the glass in front of him.

"You're welcome, sir," the waiter replied and left the room.

THE COVERUP

"Our steaks will be here in just a few minutes," Bob explained.

"Great. I'm starved," John quickly remarked.

"So tell me, Richard, what business do you have with my grandfather?" Bob cordially asked.

"I don't know why we are here to see your grandfather. Professor Donner sent us here for some reason," Richard explained as he took another drink of his glass of wine.

"You must be seeking some answers to something."

"What do you know about the Chupacabra?" Richard softly asked.

"El Chupacabra, a legendary creature in Mexico and Puerto Rico, supposedly drinks blood from farm animals, also known as the goatsucker in the English translation. Approximately four foot high, hairless, leathery skin. Reported to have three claws on its hands and feet. It walks on two legs and has coal black eyes," Bob explained.

"You must keep up with the science fiction articles," Richard remarked in amazement.

"Actually, I did some studies in college on Sasquatch. I ran across an article on the goatsucker one day. It was a very interesting article, so I went on line to find out more about this legendary creature. Found some people in Mexico in a chat room who have seen it. We talked for hours about it. They really believe in this thing," Bob replied with a serious look on his face.

"I have seen it," Richard said without even cracking a smile.

"You're pulling my leg, right? Jerking my chain, aren't you?" Bob jokingly remarked.

Richard began to giggle. Then his face went back to a serious look. "I'm serious. I saw it a few years back."

WILLIAM DANIEL

"El Chupacabra? You saw El Chupacabra?" Bob answered and took a sip of his wine.

"That's right. I was on a dig down in Mexico a few years back. I couldn't sleep one night, so I went out to the dig. I sat out there just looking at the stars. This creature dropped right out of the sky and landed fifty feet from me. I swear, Bob, it had a small goat in it's arms. I saw it drink the blood from the goat. Then it tossed it aside and flew off," Richard explained.

"What did you do?" Bob asked with great interest.

"Nothing. I was frozen in my tracks. I was like a popsicle in the hot sun. Sweat was running off of me like a river. I mean, I had heard some of the stories about it, but I didn't believe them, and yet, here this thing was right in front of me. I couldn't move, I was so scared. I called the local police and they came out and took the goat away. Before he left, he told me to forget what I just saw. Things would go very bad for me if I said anything, he told me. That afternoon, they took my passport and some personal items and kicked me out of Mexico. Told me I could never go back again or they would see that I would disappear forever. So I left Mexico, and I have been chasing it everywhere I can since," Richard explained, gulping down the rest of his wine.

"Hey, wait a minute! You never told me anything about the police and disappearing forever. You never told me that part!" John said excitedly.

"Let me ask you something, John. Would you have come along if I had told you?" Richard asked.

Still excited, John quickly replied, "Probably not!"

"Then there you have it," Richard replied.

"I see your point," John answered.

"So tell me, Bob, what got you into studying Big Foot?" Richard asked.

THE COVERUP

"Well, my great-great-grandfather saw one while out picking berries one day."

"And I guess the story has been handed down for years," Richard said as he sipped his wine.

"Yeah, well, I took it upon myself to look into the stories. There have been a lot of stories written on the subject. Big Foot, the gentle giant, forest people and Sasquatch are all the same creature. All of the stories and documents point to the same description of the creature. Most of the people who have seen it believe it is real, but scientific evidence suggests that it is a figment of one's imagination. Now you have to ask yourself, 'How can so many have seen the same thing?' If Sasquatch doesn't exist, why have so many reported sightings? Are they reading this in the paper and making it up?

"Recent discoveries have uncovered a new species of ape. Gigantopithecus Blacki was discovered in Asia back in 1999. Some teeth and a jawbone were found in a cave in China. After studying the remains, they have come to the conclusion it was nine to ten feet high, weighing six hundred to twelve hundred pounds. It walked upright and had a hairy body and human-like face, hands and feet. Now according to carbon dating, this thing went extinct some five hundred thousand years ago, yet not one complete fossil has been found," Bob reported.

Finally the food arrived at the table. The conversation stopped as the food was being put on the table. There was a small plate of fried rattlesnake put in front of John and Richard. John picked one up and started eating it. "Hey, this is not bad," he said.

Richard picked up the rattlesnake meat and took a bite. "You're right. It does kind of taste like chicken. A bit more bony than a chicken, though."

"See, I told you it wasn't bad," Bob replied as he cut his steak.

WILLIAM DANIEL

"You were right, but I must find out about this steak first," Richard said as he began cutting his steak.

John ate every bite of the rattlesnake meat he had and began to cut up the steak. "That was good," he remarked.

"I knew you would like it," Bob remarked as he began to eat his steak.

Richard put a bite of steak in his mouth. "Hmm, that is good," he remarked as he chewed the steak.

"Thanks. I figured you would like it."

"Now let's get back to your Big Foot theory," Richard said as he continued to eat.

"Some of those who believe in the legends of giant wild men think they may be descendants of Gigantopithecus," Bob explained.

"But humanity knows very little about Gigantopithecus. Mostly it's guess work based on a few fossil teeth and a jawbone," Richard replied as he took another bite of steak.

"This is true. There is not enough hard evidence to support the theory. The darn thing didn't leave much of a trail of its existence. However, it must have existed. Otherwise, we wouldn't have the fossil remains that have been found," Bob explained after taking a sip of wine.

"You have a point there," Richard replied.

"There are so many things we don't know about it, like what would a twelve hundred pound, ten foot tall ape eat?" Bob remarked.

"I would think anything he wants," John remarked and snickered. Richard and Bob looked at him with an unamused look. John looked at them and smiled, but there was no reaction. "Tough crowd," he said as he waved to the waiter for another beer.

THE COVERUP

"Bamboo is what I would think. The competition for bamboo with the giant panda could be why they went extinct, or maybe the bamboo just died," Richard remarked as he picked up another piece of steak.

"That is possible. Bamboo has been known to go through a dying out cycle. Lack of food is a good explanation for extinction, but it still doesn't account for the lack of fossil remains. However, the Chinese have been using these bones in certain medicines or remedies," Bob explained as he poured him and Richard more wine.

"You think maybe they ground them all up?" Richard asked.

"That would seem very unlikely, but who knows for sure," Bob answered as he continued to eat his meal.

"Want to hear a controversial theory?" Richard seriously asked.

"Sure," Bob quickly replied.

"What if…bare with me now, what if aliens did exist? What if they were here four million years ago? Let's just say they needed a certain mineral that was here on Earth? Maybe the aliens came here to mine this mineral. It could be something that was in the meteor that hit Earth some sixty billion years ago. Now they come here and find a mammal, your Gigantopithecus Blacki, that they can train. They use them to mine the minerals that they need. If you think about it, something as big as Gigantopithecus would have to be very strong. Look at the chimpanzee. It's ten times stronger than a normal man, a gorilla maybe a hundred times stronger. What if Gigantopithecus is a thousand times stronger than a normal man? He could do the work of a thousand men. Now the aliens could mine their mineral without heavy equipment.

"What if the female species of this creature was used as a sexual partner? Maybe their genes were very close to those aliens. This would cause a branch-off that could be man's first beginning.

"Let's say after three and a half million years they mine all the mineral from here and have to move on. Let's say they take Gigantopithecus with them in large numbers. However, they leave a few for future growth, sort of like farming animals. They let them grow here and come back and take the younger ones with them. Now, if they are taking all the young ones from Earth, their population would not grow. However, if they bring back some of the species, this would keep the species growing but in controlled numbers. This could be why we don't see very many of them. Also, I don't know of anyone ever seeing a baby Big Foot, that is to say, if Big Foot is the descendant of Gigantopithecus. They don't see any need for the branch-off because they are much smaller. Maybe they leave here for a thousand years to allow Gigantopithecus populations to grow, only when they return, they find this new species has grown in population. Still, there is not a need for this smaller species, so it's no concern to them. They take what they need and move on for another thousand years or so. When they return, they find this new species has evolved into an intelligent creature. Maybe they decide to try and help this species to evolve even more."

It could explain how the pyramids got built. Maybe the aliens used Gigantopithecus to help the Egyptians build the pyramids. It's hard to believe that man could be capable of moving stones as big as the pyramids. I know it's possible, but that would take a very large workforce, or it would take some technology they couldn't possibly have at this point. If you think about it, the theory of logs and ropes moving large

THE COVERUP

stones, it would still take a long time to build the pyramids. However, a few hundred Gigantopithecus could do the work in less time," Richard explained in detail.

"Well, that is a controversial theory. If there were aliens capable of interstellar flight, I would think they would have better technology, more like, 'Beam me up Bobby-type stuff.' Like, instead of manual labor or slave labor, they would just zap the stuff right out of the rock," Bob theorized as he stuck his fork into the last piece of steak on his plate.

"Maybe they were experimenting," John remarked as he took a drink of the beer the waiter brought.

Richard and Bob stopped what they were doing and looked at John in confusion. "What do you mean?" they both asked at the same time.

"Well, I mean we do it. Where do you think a mule came from? We crossed a jack with a horse. We have crossed a buffalo with a cow. There's talk of crossing a frozen mammoth DNA with an elephant. I think we even crossed a zebra with a horse, not to mention all the crossbreeding we do with cows and horses. Then there are all the experiments that are done on all kinds of animals in the wild. We are the highest intelligent species on earth and we experiment. If there were aliens from another planet, why wouldn't they do the same things? I mean, they are obviously of a higher intelligence than we are," John answered.

A sudden silence hit the room as Bob and Richard mulled over John's theory in their minds. After a few seconds passed by, Bob said, "You know, that makes better sense than your slave labor theory, but by the same token, keeps it in tack as they could have done both."

"You are right. You did good, John. I didn't think you had it in you. Did you read that in a magazine?" Richard teasingly asked.

"No, I just came up with it," John replied as he took another drink of his beer.

"Well, you did good, partner," Richard smilingly remarked.

"I did, didn't I?" John embarrassingly said.

"Well, it certainly makes for an interesting parallel to the subject. However, you would have to prove the existence of an extraterrestrial," Bob remarked as he drank the last of his wine.

"We think the Chupacabra is an alien. He may have survived the crash of 1947 in Roswell, New Mexico. We believe that our government is hiding this creature from that crash. They just might be hiding it in Area Fifty-One in Nevada," Richard explained.

"Area Fifty-One?" Bob replied loudly.

"Not so loud. You want to tell the whole world?" Richard quickly responded.

"I've been there before," Bob whispered back.

"You have been to Area Fifty-One?" Richard asked surprisingly.

"Yes, I have been there a couple of times, not inside the compound, but close to the facilities."

"Maybe that is why we were sent here. You could lead us to the base where we could get in," Richard said as he drank the last of his glass of wine.

"Get in? Are you crazy? You try and get into that base and you will go to jail or worse! They'll kill you!" Bob replied seriously.

"Yes, I know," Richard calmly replied.

"And what do you have to say about this, John?" Bob asked, turning to face him.

THE COVERUP

"Well, I just need to get the monkey off my back, the monkey being Jack Riley," John answered softly.

"Jack Riley, the FBI director for the south. Jack is a very dangerous person to mess with," Bob remarked with serious concern on his face.

"That is what I have been telling my partner all along," John replied with a smile.

"You're looking for some serious trouble if you go against Jack Riley. I don't think that is a very good idea," Bob remarked as he sat back in his chair.

"Well, it is a little too late to back out now. The wheels have been in motion for quite some time now. Jack has been following our every move since we started. He may even be leading us to Area Fifty-One," John said as he took the last drink of his beer.

"Look, Bob, I'm not going to ask you to get involved. Maybe you could draw us a map of how to get there. That way, you won't be involved," Richard explained.

"You tell me about this exciting theory about aliens, then you tell me we have to break into a secret military base. Just telling you where this secret passage is to the base could get me in trouble. I think it is time for us to go see Grandfather. He will tell us what to do and how to do it," Bob explained as he got up from his chair. He walked out of the room with an angry look on his face.

"I think we pissed him off, Richard," John whispered.

"Do you think so?"

"So what are we going to do now?"

"I don't know. Let's see what his grandfather has to say. Then we will go from there. After all, Professor Donner did send us here for some reason. I hope it was for the right reason."

WILLIAM DANIEL

"Me and you both, partner...me and you both," John remarked as he sat back in his chair.

"As you know, I do have a backup plan," Richard explained and sat back in his chair.

"Care to indulge that plan to me?"

"Not at this moment, I don't."

"You don't have a backup plan, do you?"

"I do have a backup plan. I just don't think you need to know about it right now," Richard answered with a serious look on his face.

"You get me killed, and I will never talk to you again."

"Duh, do you think so?" Richard sarcastically replied.

Suddenly Bob returned to the room and walked over to Richard. "I have made the necessary arrangements. Return to your rooms where you will find some appropriate attire for your session."

"Look, Bob, I'm sorry if we have caused you some serious concern. I realize your situation here," Richard apologized.

"What? Are you kidding me? This is the most excitement I have had around here in years. But you do realize that I will deny any involvement in your plans. However, I must see how it ends. Let's go see Grandfather first," Bob replied as he held his arm out to suggest they leave. John and Richard got up from the table and followed Bob out of the restaurant. They walked over to the elevator and got in. Bob pushed the floor number to take them to their room. He turned to Richard and John and said, "My people will bring the clothes to your room in a few minutes. Grandfather will be waiting for us in his teepee."

"He still lives in a teepee?" John curiously asked.

"Yeah, he insists on living in the old way," Bob explained.

THE COVERUP

"That is amazing, to be as old as he is and still live in a tent," John remarked.

"A bit crazy, if you ask me," Richard said.

The elevator stopped at the second floor and the doors opened. Bob stepped out first, and John and Richard followed. They quietly walked down the hall to the room.

"Got your key?" Bob asked as he held out his hand. Richard took the key out of his pocket and handed it to him. Bob opened the door and walked into the room. John walked in next with Richard right behind him.

"As soon as we get dressed, we will go down and see Grandfather. I cannot leave your side now. Evil spirits will be all around us until we enter his tent," Bob seriously explained.

"Are you serious?" John curiously asked.

"Trust me. I have seen things that will scare the life out of you. Stick by me and ignore anything you see," Bob replied. John noticed a serious look on Bob's face as he listened to what he said.

"Okay, if you say so," Richard said with an unbelievable look on his face.

"Hear me now, and believe what I say. The evil spirits wait at his door at all times. They will not harm you if you ignore them," Bob explained.

"Like I said, if you say so," Richard replied, still with an unbelievable look.

"You, I am not worried about. John, look to me for help," Bob remarked. As soon as Bob made that remark, a knock came on the door. "That must be our clothes," Bob said as he walked to the door to open it. When he opened the door, a young man greeted him with a smile.

"Here are the clothes you ordered, sir," he said as he rolled the rack into the room.

WILLIAM DANIEL

"Thanks. That will be all," Bob told the bell boy. The young man turned and left the room, closing the door behind him. Bob pushed the rack of clothes to the middle of the room.

Richard noticed that all of the clothes were desert camouflage. "We going into the desert?" Richard asked as he looked through the rack of clothes.

"Yes," Bob simply replied.

"These are cool," John eagerly said as he quickly looked for his size.

"Let's get dressed and get on our way," Bob quickly ordered.

"I'm first," John said as he grabbed his clothes off the rack and quickly headed for the bathroom.

"Well, he's a bit anxious, don't you think?" Bob remarked.

"Why are you more worried about John with these so-called spirits?" Richard curiously asked.

"Well, John has an open spirit that can be very vulnerable. His aura alone has opened doors that are subjected to walking spirits," Bob explained like he knew what he was saying.

"You really believe that stuff?" Richard asked.

"Nah. Grandfather told me to watch him," Bob replied.

"Oh, so all that stuff was made up for the tourist?" Richard remarked as he looked at the size on the shirt he was holding.

"Grandfather does believe in walking spirits as he calls it. I just do what he says. I hope to one day understand what he means," Bob replied.

"Yeah, well, when you figure it out, let me know. I just don't believe in all that spiritual stuff," Richard remarked.

John came out of the restroom and quickly snapped to attention and saluted them.

THE COVERUP

"Are you ready for inspection, soldier?" Bob kidded.

"Sir, yes, sir!" John replied like an Army soldier. Then he dropped his saluted arm to his side.

"I believe John was in the Army once," Bob remarked.

"Yes, many moons ago," John replied as he relaxed from attention.

"Richard, it's your turn," Bob said referring to the restroom.

Richard took the clothes and walked into the restroom.

"Let me check you out there, John," Bob said as he walked up to him.

"Absolutely perfect fit there, John," Bob said as he adjusted his collar. "Listen, I want you to pay close attention to what I'm about to tell you."

"Sure, whatever you say, Bob," John replied seriously.

"When we enter Grandfather's lodge in a few minutes, I want you to keep your eyes on my boots. Pay no attention to anything you might see. Keep believing to yourself it is just an illusion. Nothing you will see is real. It's just a projected illusion to scare the tourists. It brings in more revenue every time a tourist sees something, but you trust me, it's just an illusion," Bob seriously explained.

"Yeah, sure, Bob. I'll do whatever you say," John confusingly replied.

"Don't worry about Richard. I have already explained it to him. You just take care of yourself. If you get into trouble thinking you are in reality, grab hold of me. I will pull you through it. Do you understand what I am saying?" Bob asked.

"Yeah, sure, Bob. Like I said, I'll do whatever you say," John answered.

"No matter what happens, just keep your eyes on my boots and follow my lead. Richard will be watching your back, so you watch your front. Now let me explain something about Grandfather. Trust in your heart. Whatever he tells you is real. Keep your mind focused on what he says. Grandfather is here to help you. Some of what he tells you may seem bizarre, but it is all real. Trust in what your instincts tell you to do. Remember, Grandfather is your friend. He is only going to help you, so trust in him," Bob explained.

"You got it, Bob," John confidently replied.

"Okay. See if these boots they brought will fit all right," Bob said as he handed them to him.

"All right," John replied as he took the boots from Bob. He walked over to the bed to sit down and put them on.

"Richard, you about done in there?" Bob shouted.

"I am now," Richard replied as he came out of the restroom.

"Good, my turn," Bob said as he walked into the restroom with his clothes in his arms.

Richard walked over to the bed where John was sitting. "The boots fit all right?" he asked.

"Yeah, they are great," John replied as he laced up the last one. "Try yours on and see if they fit all right."

Richard walked over and got a pair of boots and went to the bed and sat down beside John. He pulled a pair of socks out of the boots and put them on. He took the right boot and put it on and began lacing it. John got up from the bed and walked around testing the boots for comfort. Richard finished lacing up his booths and got up and walked around. "Bob sure can make a good guess at sizes," he remarked.

"Yeah, I wonder how he does that?" John asked.

"I am wondering that myself," Richard replied as he sat back down on the bed. John walked over and sat down beside him. He pulled his boot upside down to see the tread underneath.

THE COVERUP

"He must have made a lucky guess," Richard concluded.

"I think he might be a rocket scientist," John remarked as he sat his boot back on the floor.

Bob finished getting dressed and walked out of the bathroom. He walked over to the boots and picked up the pair that was his size. "The boots fit all right, gentlemen?" he asked.

"Perfect fit," Richard replied.

"How did you do that?" John asked.

"Well, it's quite simple to figure. First, you take a person's height, weight, and girth size. I then calculate those numbers into one number. Then you take that number to a chart of same size average men. This will give you the average size foot for that individual," Bob scientifically explained. He sat down on the bed and began to put on his boots.

"That is amazing. Are you a rocket scientist or something?" John asked.

"Almost was," Bob replied with some reservations.

"What happened?" John curiously asked.

"Well, let's just say they didn't want a Cherokee Indian in their program," Bob replied without really answering the question.

"You made a good guess," Richard remarked.

"Yeah, I made a good guess," Bob replied hoping to satisfy Richard's remark.

"That's what I thought," Richard said with a satisfying grin on his face.

"All right, are you fellows ready to go see Grandfather?" Bob asked as if to change the subject. He finished lacing up his boots and stood up ready to go.

"I'm ready to get this thing over with," Richard answered, still not believing in the spiritual aspects of this encounter.

"I can't wait to meet him," John replied with a smile on his face.

"All right, let's get going. I will lead, and Richard will bring up the rear. John, remember what I told you," Bob said as he began to lead the group out of the room. He opened the door and walked out leaving Richard to close it. He led them down the hall to the elevator. He pushed the down button on the wall by the elevator, and they waited for the elevator to arrive on their floor.

"How was that rattlesnake you ate, John?" Bob asked trying to get some feedback on his restaurant.

"It was real good. It does taste a lot like chicken," John favorably replied.

"How about you, Richard? Did you like it?" Bob asked as he turned to him.

"It was all right, but I have to admit, that steak was outstanding," Richard satisfyingly replied.

"Yeah, man, that steak was the best I ever had. I've got to hand it to you, Bob, you sure know how to cook," John thankfully said.

"Well, actually, I have some good chefs working for me. They came up with the formula for the best way to cook meat. I just supplied them with the incentive to do so."

"And did you initiate that?" Richard curiously asked.

"Well, I gave them a proclamation to work by."

"You told them if they didn't, you would fire them."

"Basically, yes."

The elevator arrived at their floor. The door opened, and some tourists exited looking for their rooms. An attendant carrying their luggage followed them.

"How is it going, Tommy?" Bob asked the attendant as he walked by.

"Great, sir. Hey, nice outfits, gentlemen," he remarked as he passed them.

"Forget what you just saw, Tommy," Bob relayed as Tommy walked away.

"Hey, I saw nothing at all," Tommy replied, continuing down the hall with the guests' luggage.

"You have some very loyal people working for you here," John remarked.

They stepped into the elevator, and John pushed the first floor button. Bob reached over and pushed the basement button. "We want to go all the way down. It's closer to Grandfather's lodge," he explained. The elevator doors closed and began to descend. "Yeah, well, they better be loyal, or they are history," Bob seriously answered John's remark.

WILLIAM DANIEL

THE COVERUP

RUNNING DEER
Chapter Thirty-three

The elevator stopped at the first floor. The door opened and some guests asked if they were going up. "No, sir, we are going down. I will send it back up for you as soon as we get out in the basement," Bob told them as the door closed. The elevator began to move downward again.

"Your grandfather stays in his teepee all the time?" Richard asked trying to keep the chitchat going.

"Yeah, he insists upon it. A hundred and eight years old, and he can't let go of the old way of living. Drives me nuts all the time," Bob answered perturbed.

"You would think he would freeze in the winter," John said as the elevator arrived in the basement. The door opened and they stepped out with Bob exiting last. He pushed the elevator button for the first floor before he walked out.

"During very cold weather, we literally move him to one of the rooms. He argues with me about the move all the time, but I think he knows I'm doing it for his sake," Bob explained. He led the group to a door leading outside and opened the door to let John and Richard walk out first.

Richard and John walked out of the building. As soon as they were outside, they stopped in their tracks. Not more than fifty feet away from them was an Indian teepee. It had smoke flowing out of the top. Down in front was a stone walkway leading to the entrance. Bob exited the building, closing the

315

door behind him. He stopped where John and Richard stood looking at the Indian lodge in front of them. "Shall we go meet Grandfather, gentlemen?" he said as he led the way.

They walked down to the rocky walkway with Bob leading them onto the path to the lodge. As they came closer to the entrance, Richard noticed some smoke-like elements floating about. At first he thought they were coming from the lodge, but as he got closer, he noticed the same smoke kept flying across the walkway. He thought to himself that these were some really good special effects Bob came up with. When they came to the area where the smoke kept passing the path, Bob turned to the two followers. "You're going to see some really expensive special effects. Ignore them," he said.

Richard watched as they entered the area where the smoke was. Suddenly, one flew up to him and transformed into a beautiful woman. She stared at him for a few seconds. She smiled at him as he stared back at her beautiful face. A smile came across his face as he continued to walk down the path. The floating anomaly raised her dainty little hand to her face, blowing a kiss at Richard. He began to giggle like a school child.

"Everything all right back there, Richard?" Bob asked as he looked back at him.

"Yeah, fine. Hey, can I get one of these for my bedroom?" Richard excitedly replied.

Suddenly, the beautiful woman turned into a horrible skeletal figure, sending fear all through his nervous system.

"Shit!" he shouted as fright took over his excitement. Then he began to laugh out loud.

"What's going on back there?" Bob quickly asked as they reached the entrance to the lodge.

THE COVERUP

The frightening skeletal figure floating in front of Richard turned and looked at Bob. It quickly changed back into a beautiful woman and turned back toward Richard and blew him another kiss. She turned back into smoke and floated away.

Seriously amused by the illusion he just saw, Richard smiled again. "Nothing, Bob," he replied as they stopped at the entrance.

John, having kept his head down the whole way, looked up at Bob. "What happened?" he asked, turning and looking back at Richard. He noticed Richard was smiling, and his face seemed a little flushed. He turned back to Bob, feeling a little bit lost as to what had happened.

Bob opened the tent door and said, "Enter, gentlemen."

John walked into the lodge and stopped. Richard started in when Bob stopped him at the door.

"You see something back there, Richard?" Bob curiously asked.

"Yeah, and she was beautiful, too," Richard replied, still blushing a bit.

"You liked that, didn't you?" Bob remarked as he smiled at Richard.

"I gotta get me one of those. That has to be one of the best special effects I have ever witnessed. It was so real looking. That is great stuff there."

"You cannot get one of them."

"Why not?"

"I will explain later. Let's get inside," Bob said as he motioned for Richard to enter.

Richard walked into the lodge. He saw John standing just inside the door. He stopped beside him and looked around the room. There were all kinds of Indian relics hanging from the poles that held the skins of the teepee. He noticed what appeared to be human scalps hanging by the entrance. He turned and looked at the middle of the lodge and saw an old Indian man sitting in a wheelchair in front of the fire facing them with his head down. This must be Bob's grandfather, he thought to himself. Bob stepped in and walked over to the fire. He turned to Richard and John and said, "Sit here by the fire facing Grandfather."

"All right," Richard replied as he motioned for John to sit first. They sat down on the ground covered by animal skins.

"Grandfather," Bob said to the old Indian sitting in the wheelchair.

The old man raised his head. He looked up at Bob and said, "Welcome, Little Deer."

"Grandfather, these are the two men you were waiting for," Bob said indicating with his right hand.

The old Indian turned his attention to the two men in front of him. He nodded his head to greet them.

"Grandfather, this is Richard Cooper," Bob said as he pointed at him.

The old Indian just nodded his head at Richard.

"I am pleased to meet you, sir," Richard said to the old Indian sitting in front of him.

He noticed the old Indian had beads and feathers hanging from his long stringy gray hair. His face was filled with lines of wrinkles, and his eyes were black as coal.

"And this is John Barton," Bob introduced as he pointed to him.

"Glad to meet you, sir," John nervously said as he stared at the old Indian. Bob sat down beside his grandfather facing John and Richard.

"Interesting lodge you have here, sir," Richard remarked as his eyes scanned the room.

THE COVERUP

The old Indian reached with his right hand and pulled a substance from a bag hanging on his wheelchair. He tossed it onto the fire and slapped his hands together, making a loud clap. The fire burst into a huge flame towering up to near the top of the lodge until it came back down to a low flame. Running Deer began to chant some Indian phrases over and over.

"What's his name again?" John asked Bob.

"Running Deer," Bob replied.

Running Deer chanted for a few seconds as John and Richard watched. He stopped, rolled his eyes into the top of his eye socket, and went into a trance. For what seemed to John and Richard like several minutes, they sat quietly watching Running Deer.

"Did he fall asleep?" Richard asked Bob.

"He's meditating. Give him a minute," Bob explained.

They sat there waiting for Running Deer to say something. He finally pulled his eyes back down and looked at John. Then he turned to Richard and stared at him for a moment. "You seek the creature of eternal life," he blurted.

"If you are referring to the Chupacabra, yes. I don't know about him being the creature of eternal life, though," Richard replied. "More like the killer of life, to me."

"He is not what you think he is," Running Deer quickly snapped back at him.

"I'm sorry?" Richard confusingly asked.

"He is not of this world, but he is not what you think he is. He has the power of the great spirits to bring forth life when there is none. He can heal wounds that open and bleed endlessly. He drinks the blood of animals and provides the gift of life," Running Deer explained as his bloodshot eyes stared at Richard.

WILLIAM DANIEL

"Are we talking about the same creature?" Richard interrupted.

"What you seek is there, but the answer is not the one you are looking for. You must search the people of our ancient past. We are one with the travelers and the giant ones. We share in the life-giving forces. Yet, we are different as my people were with yours in our recent past. The judgment time has come, and you must choose the right path. Our spiritual beliefs hang in the balance of your choice. Beware; the evil spirits are all around the traveler. They will stop at nothing to end your search of the truth. I will call upon the good spirits of knowledge to help you along the right path. Look within the emptiness of your heart, and the answers will be there," Running Deer explained, stopping for the moment as if to catch his breath.

"All right. If you say so," Richard unconvincingly remarked.

"Do not be fooled by the appearance of the evil ones. There are darker forces working from inside them. They have visions of controlling all the people of our great lands. It is their destiny that our freedom will die from. The great spirits have chosen you to stop them. You must not fail them," Running Deer further explained.

"Okay, whoa," Richard answered in disbelief.

Running Deer turned to John who was nervously watching. "What?" John confusingly asked as he stared back at Running Deer.

"The spirit horse will come for you. Do not follow him into the night. Do not touch him in his travel. Do not even look at him when he stands before you. He wishes to take you away from your loved ones. In the flesh, you, and you alone, must face the evil ones. You will need brave spirits to supply you with courage. They will give you the speed of lightning

THE COVERUP

and the accuracy of the rattlesnake. Only you can release their power and control their judgment. It is up to you to stop the evil one who chases you through time," Running Deer said.

He reached down the left side of his wheelchair and retrieved a peace pipe. He pulled a pouch from his pocket and opened it, pulling out a substance from the pouch and filling the pipe. He motioned for Bob to give him a lit stick from the fire. Bob reached down and pulled a flaming stick from the fire and handed the stick to Running Deer. Taking the flaming stick from Bob, Running Deer put the pipe in his mouth. He placed the fire on the end of the pipe and began to draw the air through the pipe to light the substance within. When the pipe began to produce smoke, Running Deer raised it above his head and began to chant Indian phrases over and over. Richard and John quietly watched Running Deer. When he finished chanting, Running Deer pulled the pipe down and placed it in his mouth. He drew some smoke from the pipe and removed it from his mouth. He motioned for Richard to come closer. When Richard leaned over, Running Deer blew the smoke in his face. The smoke swirled around in front of Richard and quickly went up his nose.

Startled by this event, Richard fell back to his seat. Dizzy and dazed, he shook his head to clear his thoughts. "What the hell did you do that for?" he confusingly asked.

"You are now one with the smoke of knowledge," Running Deer explained. Taking the pipe, he drew some more smoke, motioning for John to come closer. John leaned forward, and Running Deer blew the smoke at him. As it did with Richard, the smoke swirled and went up his nose. John fell back to his seat shaking his head as Richard did before him.

"Man, that was a rush," he remarked as he looked at Running Deer.

"These brave spirits I have given you will make you one with courage," Running Deer said, placing the pipe on a stone beside his wheelchair. He raised up his arms and clapped his hands together. The fire rose above their heads in a loud roar and trickled back to a small flame.

"How does he do that?" John asked, looking at Bob.

"Shhh," Bob replied.

"Go with your spiritual knowledge and courage. Make the right judgment. Trust the spirits I have given you," Running Deer said. He reached down to a pocket on the right side of his chair and retrieved a small stone. The stone had some very strange markings on it. He gave it to Richard, motioning for him to take it. Richard hesitated and reached out to take the stone. He looked at the stone and the strange markings on it. The markings were like those supposedly found at the Roswell crash. He showed them to John who looked upon them with confusion.

"So, what do I do with this?" Richard curiously asked as he looked back at Running Deer.

"Keep this stone with you at all times," Running Deer replied.

"Do you know what a wok is? It's what you throw at a wabbit," Richard said as he started laughing like Elmer Fud.

Running Deer looked at him totally confused. He reached down on the other side of his chair. Pulling from a pocket on that side, he brought out a pistol. He handed the pistol to John. "Take this gun to protect yourself. The spirits I gave you will know when to use it. Fear not their judgement for it is true and honest, even though the choices may seem wrong. Go with your heart and not your mind to make the right judgment. You will know when the right time to use it has come," he explained.

THE COVERUP

"Wow, a forty-caliber Smith and Wesson," John remarked as he looked at the pistol Running Deer had given him. "Do you have a permit for this?"

Running Deer reached down with both arms and pulled a deerskin blanket around him. "Little Deer will show you the path to your quest, but he must not follow you into the lair of the evil one. His spirits are not prepared for such a conflict," he explained as he turned and looked at Bob.

"Yeah, I'm still a fawn in Grandfather's eyes. I think too much," Bob said as he smiled.

"This gun is a little rusty. Will it still fire?" John asked as he showed it to Bob.

"Well, there is one way to find out. We have a pistol range on the south side of the property," Bob explained.

"No, there is only one cartridge in this pistol. You must save it for when you will need it," Running Deer explained.

"We could always buy some more, you know," John remarked as he opened the gun to inspect the cartridge.

"The one cartridge is all you will need. The spirits have blessed it," Running Deer explained as he leaned back in his wheelchair.

"Gee, I hope your aim is good," Richard remarked.

John pulled the cartridge from the pistol. He examined it up close to his eyes. "This bullet is a bit old and tarnished. Are you sure it is still good?" he asked as he held out the cartridge in front of him.

"Wait a minute. Let me see that," Richard requested, reaching over to John and retrieving the cartridge.

"Sure," John replied as he gave the bullet to Richard.

"This cartridge is made of silver," Richard remarked, looking at it up close.

"Are you sure?" John asked, taking it back from Richard.

"I know what silver looks like when it is tarnished. That is a silver bullet. What are we about to shoot, a werewolf or something?" Richard candidly remarked.

"The cartridge was made for the evil one, for it is his evil spirit that it can stop. He waits for you like a spider waiting for his prey. He hunts for you like a snake hunts a rat. His poison is more potent than the diamond-back rattlesnake. His spirit is more powerful than the great leaders of our lands. Death is his motive, and control is his destiny. He knows your every move by the control of many people. He must stop you from your quest. He will use all of his powers to do this. The silver cartridge, pure in its natural content, will pierce his evil heart. Fear not its tarnished appearance, for it is guided by good spirits. They will guide it to the heart of the evil one. However, only you can release their great power. Remember to stay away from the spirit horse. The traveler will bring back your spirit," Running Deer explained to John.

"I understand."

"Knowledge is the greatest of all spirits. You must use it wisely," Running Deer said as he turned to Richard.

"Why does he get the greatest of all spirits? Is it because he has money?" John jealously asked. "Maybe you should donate one of those paper things to him."

"Will this ever end?" Richard candidly asked.

"Never," John replied laughing.

"I don't know what you are complaining about. At least you got a gun. All I got was a rock," Richard remarked.

"Hey, doesn't paper cover rock?" John said smiling.

Running Deer and Bob watched as John and Richard bickered at each other.

"Just can't let it go," Richard remarked.

THE COVERUP

"You must go now, for time is not on your side. I grow weary and must rest now," Running Deer said as he laid his head back on the chair.

"Hey, yeah, sure. Thanks for everything, Running Deer," John politely said as he got up from the ground.

"Yeah, thanks," Richard said, even though he was still not sure if this was no more than a tourist trick.

"We should go," John said as he turned to Richard.

"Only reason I haven't left is because you are in my way," Richard remarked.

Bob got up from his seat on the ground. "Follow me, gentlemen," he said as he led the way out of the lodge. They walked out of the lodge and up the path to the hotel.

"What? No special effects on the way back?" Richard candidly remarked to Bob.

"What special effects?" Bob asked as he stopped at the end of the path.

"The ones we just saw," Richard said.

"You think that was some special effects you just saw?"

"Come on, you know it was," Richard replied.

"If you think that was some special effects you just saw, well, believe what you believe," Bob remarked as he opened the door to the hotel.

"You're not going to tell, are you?" Richard candidly asked.

"There's nothing to tell. You believe what you want to believe," Bob replied as he walked into the hotel's back door.

"I believe it," John remarked as he followed Bob through the door.

"You would believe anything," Richard said to John as he walked into the hotel.

325

"I will have to admit I'm following you around, chasing a creature I never saw before. The only reason I'm doing that is because you believe it, so I guess you might say I would believe anything," John remarked.

"Oh, I see. If this thing turns out to be wrong, then it's my fault," Richard replied.

"Well, I tell you what I do know. Josh Hernandez saw something that morning. He wasn't the kind of person to make up things. I also know what Tom and I saw when we went out there. I don't believe that a crazed murderer killed Josh. I think Jack did, and I think he did it to cover up something. Maybe that is your Chupacabra. I don't know, but I will tell you this. If he did, I intend to nail him for it," John seriously answered.

"Come in here, guys. We need some supplies to take with us," Bob said as he opened a side door.

"What supplies do we need, Bob?" Richard asked as he and John walked in the side door.

"First, let's get this wagon over here," Bob ordered. He pointed to a red wagon in the corner that had sideboards. They walked over and pulled the small wagon out of the corner.

"Now what?" John asked.

"Bring it over here," Bob said as he walked to the other side of the room. John grabbed the handle on the wagon and pulled it over to Bob.

"We carrying so much stuff we need a wagon?" Richard asked.

"Well, we are going to need a lot of things. The wagon is just so we can roll it out to the Hummer," Bob explained as he loaded the wagon with a five-gallon bottle of water, walking over to a cabinet and bringing out two round pointed shovels, which he put into the wagon.

"We plan on doing some digging when we get there?" Richard curiously asked.

THE COVERUP

"Yeah, we will have to dig some when we get there," Bob replied.

"What else?" Richard asked.

"Well, let's see. We better bring a pick, too. Also, I suggest that we take these snake chaps. I have run into a few diamondbacks out there. We will need a couple of flashlights and these night goggles," Bob said as he loaded the wagon with the items.

"What are we going to do, tunnel in?" John candidly asked.

"No, no. That place is on an old dry lakebed. There is an old river that goes under the compound they don't know about. The river ran dry thousands of years ago, and it left a long tunnel-like cave. I found that cave years ago when I was in college. I spent many days in there looking for fossils. One day I discovered this cave went right under Area Fifty-One, which as you know, is not supposed to exist according to our government. So I dug myself a small hole and had a peek at the compound. I was able to map an area where I could dig an opening. Before you knew it, I was walking around the facilities and nobody was the wiser. They never knew I was there. I found a badge on a coat in one of the rooms. I went all over that place except for the high security buildings I couldn't get in," Bob explained.

"But you did get in," Richard said.

"Getting in is not a problem. Finding what you are looking for, now that will be a problem," Bob replied as he loaded the wagon.

"Just get me in. I'll find what I'm looking for," Richard said.

"Well, let's see. I think we have everything we need. Oh wait, let's take some two-way radios just in case we need to communicate when we separate," Bob said. He retrieved three radios and put them into the wagon.

"Is that all?" John asked.

"Yeah, I think so," Bob replied.

"I'll pull it out to the Hummer," John said. He pulled the wagon out the door of the storeroom. Bob and Richard followed him. Bob opened the door leading outside, and John pulled out the wagon. Richard walked out behind him, and Bob closed the door.

"Which way, Bob?" John asked as he waited for him to lead them.

"This way," Bob said, pointing to his right. They walked around a walkway until they came to the end of the building. They turned left and walked around to the front of the hotel. When they spotted the Hummer, they walked over to it. Bob opened the rear door, and John put the items into the vehicle.

"All right, let's saddle up, guys," Bob said as he walked around to the driver's side of the Hummer.

"Who's that?" Richard asked, pointing to a car pulling up at the hotel front entrance.

John recognized the type of car pulling up. It was a standard issue FBI agent car. "They found us," he quickly said.

"That's not possible," Richard replied as he looked at the car.

"Get in, guys," Bob ordered.

John got in the front seat, and Richard jumped into the back. The familiar black sedan stopped at the front entrance of the hotel. Two men got out, looking around the area, and walked inside.

"We need to get out of here," John said as he watched the two men walk into the hotel.

THE COVERUP

"I'm on it," Bob replied. He started the Hummer and backed out with the lights turned off. He pulled the Hummer onto the driveway, turning the vehicle toward the highway, and drove away.

"Damn, that Jack is persistent," Richard remarked.

When they reached the highway, Bob turned the vehicle toward the east and drove away.

"I told you Jack was resilient," John said.

"Has he been following you the whole time?" Bob curiously asked.

"Yeah, seems everywhere we go, we run into one of his agents," Richard explained.

"You must have a bug on you somewhere," Bob said as he looked in his rearview mirror at Richard.

"No way. We had one earlier, but we got rid of it. We have even changed clothes and shoes. There is no way he could have a bug on us. I just don't get it!" Richard screamed.

"Informants," John remarked.

"What do you mean?" Richard quickly asked.

"Jack probably has informants in every possible exit we could have taken. Might have been someone on the bus or in the restaurant. He could have had army reserves in civilian clothes. He may be paying locals to watch for us. People will do anything for money, you know," John explained. "I hope everything will be okay at your resort."

"I don't know why it wouldn't be, as long as you're not there," Bob replied smiling.

"Yeah, well, you never know with Jack," John seriously said.

"Well, now I'm concerned. You think Jack might be causing a problem there?" Bob curiously asked.

329

WILLIAM DANIEL

"Like I said, with Jack, you never know," John replied.

"There is nothing I would like better than to take Jack down," Richard remarked from the back seat.

"Me and you both, partner."

"So, now what do we do?"

"What do you mean?"

"Well, if he is going to find us in every place we go, how are we going to get in the base without him knowing?"

"You want to know the truth, partner?"

"Yes, I would like to know."

"He already knows where we are going."

"What's that supposed to mean?"

"He knows what we are looking for. He knows where it can be found. He will be waiting there for us, unless he can stop us before we get there. Jack doesn't intend to detain us from getting there. He plans to kill us."

"Well, this just keeps getting better," Bob remarked as he continued to drive the Hummer down the road.

"All right, what are our chances of getting into the base now?" Richard asked.

"Let me tell you something, partner. He's been driving us to Area Fifty-One the whole time. I have a feeling that is where he wants us to be. That way he can kill us, and nobody will be the wiser. Your grandfather knew, Bob. That is what he was trying to tell us," John explained with a concerned look on his face.

"Ah, you think that old Indian knew something about this," Richard remarked.

"Well, I'll tell you this, Richard. If it comes down to it, I will kill Jack Riley. I just hope your lawyer can get me off," John said.

THE COVERUP

"Well, I'll tell you this, my friend. My lawyer can get you off of anything, but I hope it doesn't come down to that," Richard remarked as he stretched out on the back seat. "I think I will take me a little nap. Wake me when we get there."

"That is a good idea, Richard. Maybe you should get some rest, too, John," Bob said.

"I'm all right for now."

"You know, I was wondering about something. Isn't it going to take a couple of days to get to Area Fifty-One?" John curiously asked.

"Well, let's see," Bob replied as he pulled a GPS out of a box on the floor. He punched in the directions and waited for the results. When it had finished, he gave it to John. "That's what it looks like," he said.

John looked at the small computer instrument and read the instructions. Squaw Valley area to Nevada, it read. One thousand, one hundred sixty-nine point eight miles, two days, four hours, and eleven minutes, it read. John gave the instrument back to Bob.

"Man, it is like we will never get there. It's going to take a long time even if we drive around the clock," he remarked as he laid his head back against the headrest.

"If we drive it, it will," Bob replied with a smile.

"Uh, oh. I feel a rich man redirection coming up," John candidly remarked.

"Well, I have a friend who flies out of Lake Havasu City. We'll just bounce on over there and catch a flight out," Bob explained.

"Rich people always seem to have a friend or a plane stashed somewhere," John remarked.

"That's the perils of being rich," Bob replied smiling.

WILLIAM DANIEL

"Yeah, well, I wouldn't know, myself."

"There're other ways of being rich, you know."

"Yeah, and how is that?"

"Well, there's having a rich friend or having lots of friends," Bob answered with a grin on his face.

"Or a rich relative," John added.

"Yeah, but that's not always a good thing. I have a rich brother-in-law who wouldn't lift a finger to help a relative. He only cares about himself and his immediate family. He wouldn't even help his own father if it came down to it. Some people just don't believe in helping anyone. Then there are those relatives who would give anything to help you get a better life. My father was one of those who wouldn't help anyone. Now you take Grandfather. He would give it all to help you. If it weren't for him, I wouldn't have a pot to piss in. I have a lot of respect for him, and I would do anything for him. As for my father, he can rot in hell, and I wouldn't care. Actually, that's not all together true. Out of respect for a human being, I wouldn't want anyone to go to hell, but for the life of me, I can't lift a finger to help him. That's one of my faults I can't seem to get over. See, Grandfather forgives Dad for treating him like shit. I will hold a grudge for the rest of my life towards him, but on the other hand, I keep hoping he will change," Bob explained.

"You know, I think Richard had a lot of respect for his father and mother. At one point, he found himself mooching off of them. He completely changed his life and took on his own responsibilities. I think that is why his father left him everything and gave his other relatives nothing," John remarked as he looked in the back seat where Richard was sleeping.

"Yeah, and sometimes what some people consider taking advantage of another is actually someone helping out," Bob said.

THE COVERUP

"What do you mean?"

"Well, take Grandfather for instance. He gave me more than I can ever repay in dollar figures, but he just wanted me to have a better life. I never asked him for a dime. He just offered and insisted I take it. He told me that he would never be able to spend it all on himself and had no use for it. Now my father thinks I took advantage of him, like I'm some kind of thief. He has no concept of what it is like to be poor and unable to get a break. However, Grandfather would buy a corporation and make me the manager if that is what I wanted. My father thinks I should be flipping hamburgers to get by. Everyone is measured by how much money they have, according to him. I believe in respecting a person for his personality, not by how much money you have. You are either an asshole or you're not. I mean, just because you have money doesn't mean you have to have an attitude. Of course it also doesn't mean you have to give it away. Everybody is entitled to his or her own opinion, of course. That's just the way I see it," Bob explained.

"Well, I have always heard that money is the root of all evil. I would like to find out for myself, but I really don't want someone to give it to me like Richard got it. But it is hard to make it in today's business world," John said.

"You'll make it. You just need some confidence in yourself," Bob seriously remarked.

"That and a huge loan that I couldn't pay back."

"Well, it does take money to make money, either that or a whole lot of luck," Bob said as he turned the Hummer onto another highway.

"Yeah, I guess some people have a green thumb, and some are blessed with love," John remarked. "I do love my wife, Regina."

"I bet she's gorgeous. Got any kids?"

"Yes, I do, Bob. Two, a boy and a girl, and I love them very much," John replied with a faraway look on his face. He was wondering how Regina was and if he would ever see his family again.

"What're their names?"

"Oh, uh, John jr and Jenny."

"Got any pictures of them?

"No, I didn't bring any with me. I wish I had, though."

"So, are they with their mother?"

"No, they're with her parents at the moment."

"Good. They're safe then."

"How about you, Bob?" John asked, looking at him.

"How about what?"

"Anybody in your life that you care about?"

"No, nobody that I'm serious about."

"Why not?

"Well, I met a young lady years ago. She broke my heart. I just never found anyone to care about that much again. I just date a few ladies around the area, and I'm happy with that."

"Yeah, but there is nothing like raising a family," John said.

"Well, I always did want a family. I had the woman that I wanted to spend the rest of my life with. Wanted her to be the mother of my children. I guess she didn't want me to be the father of hers. She's married to her second husband now and has three kids. I guess she never wanted to be with me. Kind of sad, though," Bob said as he gazed out the front windshield.

"Why sad?" John asked.

"I just never could forget her. I still think of her when I'm with someone else. I guess I'm comparing them to her, maybe hoping to find that feeling again in their eyes," Bob said as his thoughts drifted.

THE COVERUP

"Well, you know, there is someone for everyone out there. You just got to find them," John explained.

"I don't think I will ever find someone to replace her. I will probably wind up marrying someone for her looks or something like that. I don't think anyone can make me feel that way again," Bob sadly replied.

"I guess Regina and I are going to have to find you and Richard someone."

"Well, you are welcome to try. I would love to forget her and move on. I think that is what she wants me to do," Bob softly said.

"Well, we will see."

"Yeah, I guess."

"Say, are we going to stop anywhere? I need a little restroom time," John requested.

"I plan on stopping at a convenience store about fifty miles up the road. We will need some gas, and I want to refill that spare tank just in case," Bob explained.

"Oh."

"Can you wait that long?"

"I think so."

"Good. I think we could all use a little short break. We've got a long way to go. I would kind of like to call back and see if everything is okay back at the hotel."

"Bad idea," John quickly remarked.

"Why's that?"

"By now, they have your phones tapped. You will wind up giving our position out," John confidently answered.

"Well, like you said, they already know where we are going. What could it hurt?"

"They know where we are going, all right. But they don't know where we are right now. If they find out, they will send

335

someone to stop us from getting there. Like Richard said, we have to keep changing directions. Keeps them off guard as to where we are exactly."

"All right. I guess you're right. I'm sure everything is okay."

"By now, they are probably questioning everyone who works there."

"I hope Grandfather is all right," Bob said as he looked out the side window.

"Hey, I'm sure he's okay. They're not going to mess with a hundred and eight-year-old man," Richard cautiously remarked.

"I hope so. I love that old man even though he is a pain in the butt sometimes," Bob replied as he reached down in the box beside his seat and pulled out a cell phone.

"What are you going to do with that?"

"I need to call my connection for our flight."

"You think that is wise? They could be monitoring your cell calls."

"I know, but they won't be watching the direct connect."

"I hope you are right."

"If I don't make this call, we may miss the flight."

"This is not another one of those crop duster planes, is it?"

"Oh, no. It's a little bigger than that."

"Good, I don't think I could have stood another flight like that."

"Oh, did you have a bad experience in a plane?"

You could say that. Richard flew us part of the way. Scared the living hell out of me."

"This should be a better flight than that. These pilots work for the government."

THE COVERUP

"We are running from the government, and you want to get them to fly us to Area Fifty-One."

"Yeah, I know it sounds a bit off, but these guys have been flying me out to certain areas for years. They are contractors paid to fly supplies to some of the bases. I get them to carry my clients out with their cargo every now and then. The owner is a good friend of mine. We grew up together. It will be all right, trust me."

"I guess you know them better than I do. Right now, I don't trust anyone with the government. I mean, we have come so far to lose it now."

"It'll be okay. Trust me," Bob said as he pushed the button on the cell phone that contacted the direct connect. "Shawn, you there?"

"Hey, Bob. It's been a long time since I have heard from you. How you doing?" Shawn asked.

"Yes, I know. I've been real busy with the resort here lately. Look, I have a couple of hot clients that need to get to South East Nevada. Got anything going that way today?"

"Well, not exactly. But I do have some parts going to Fort Hood. We could divert over close to there on our way."

"Who's the pilot?"

"Well, believe it or not, but it is Chris."

"Great, Shawn. Now I have to tell you, this is a very hot commodity. It will not set well with your bosses," Bob cautioned.

"Hey, man. I see nothing, I hear nothing, I know nothing."

"I mean it, man. You're probably going to have some repercussions from this one."

"What else is new with you? You're always doing something you shouldn't be."

"Yeah. Well, this one could get real serious," Bob relayed on the two-way.

"Well, I was thinking about taking a vacation anyway. You know, kind of disappear for a month or two," Shawn answered.

"Nothing in the flight plan, either," Bob said.

"Well, I need to go, man. I have been having some trouble with a fuel pump on my plane. We might have to divert to New Mexico if it gives us some trouble," Shawn exaggerated.

"Bless you, Shawn."

"You're going to owe me, man."

"Yeah, maybe there will be something extra in the mail for you, so you can pay for that vacation you're going to take."

"Send that blonde waitress you're always talking about. Maybe she and I can go to Tahiti for a month."

"You got it, my man. What time are we departing?"

"In about sixty minutes from now."

"Oh, shit! I don't think we can get there that quick. We're about twenty miles from Barstow. We need some downtime to fuel before we can get there," Bob said as he looked at his watch.

"Hold on a second, Bob. I hear my mechanic calling me." Bob waited for him to come back.

"Take us at least a couple of days to drive that. I hope he can wait for us," John remarked.

"Hey, Bob," Shawn called on the radio.

"Yeah, Shawn."

"Just my luck. We're having a little trouble with that pump I was telling you about. He's going to have to rig it for now. It would take at least a week to get a new one. We might be delayed for at least another thirty minutes from the original departure schedule."

"Thanks, Shawn."

"Hurry every chance you can get. I don't know how long I can hold the flight. See you when you get here," Shawn said as he ended his conversation.

"We will, Shawn."

"We're going to fly in a plane with pump problems. I don't know if I like this idea," John quickly remarked.

"He's not having any pump problems," Bob said as he turned to John and winked.

"What are you saying?"

"He's just making that up to stall for time."

"Oh."

"See, he has to report whenever his delivery is delayed. The government gets a little funny about getting their parts on time, but they do accept certain reasons, and mechanical problems are one of them," Bob explained.

"Are we going to make it in time?"

"I think so if we don't take too much time at the store," Bob replied as he picked up the speed of the Hummer.

WILLIAM DANIEL

THE TRIP OUT
Chapter Thirty-four

Bob continued to drive the Hummer at speeds just above the limit. He didn't want to draw any attention from the police, but at the same time, they needed to get to Barstow as quickly as possible. After several miles had passed, they finally made it there. They would get on Interstate Forty and get off at Trails Highway to Newberry Springs.

"Wake up, Richard," Bob said as he pulled the Hummer into the convenience store.

"Richard," John said as he shook him in the back seat.

"What? Are we there already?" Richard asked as he wiped the sleep from his eyes.

"No, just a fuel and rest stop," John replied.

"Where are we?" Richard asked.

"We're in Barstow," John answered.

"Hey, Bob, let me get that gas. Here, put it on my credit card," Richard offered.

"That's okay. I have cash. Say, Richard, have you been paying with a credit card all along?" Bob curiously asked.

"Yeah, why? Oh, shit! I didn't think about that!" Richard disgustingly replied.

"What?" John confusingly asked.

"The credit card," Richard quickly replied.

"Damn! Jack's been following us by your credit card transactions," John remarked.

"No wonder he knew where you were all the time," Bob said as he opened his door to the Hummer.

"Well, we didn't have any cash on us. We had to do something to get here," Richard said as he opened his door and stepped out.

"Well, that's got to end right now," Bob ordered.

"You're right, Bob. I guess you will have to take my 'I owe you'," Richard replied.

"I'll send you a bill. Now go use the restroom and let's get out of here quickly. We have a plane to catch," Bob said as he walked around to the gas pumps.

"Come on, Richard," John said as he started toward the store. Richard followed him into the store. They looked around for the restrooms but didn't see them. John asked the girl behind the counter, and she pointed it out to them.

"They're over here," John said. He and Richard walked over to the restrooms.

"You go first," Richard said as he leaned against the wall by the entrance.

"All right. Do you want me to make sure they have plenty of paper for you?" John asked sarcastically.

"You asshole."

"Now, Richard, is that anyway to talk to your partner?" John remarked.

"On second thought, I think I will go first," Richard said as he walked into the restroom.

"What? You don't trust me?"

"Actually, no, I don't."

"Well, I just never."

"And you never will again with me," Richard remarked as he closed the door to the restroom.

THE COVERUP

"All right. You can go first, but save me some of that paper, though," John said laughing.

John stood by the door waiting for Richard to finish. He looked outside to see if Bob had finished filling up the Hummer with gas. Bob had raised the hood on the Hummer to check the oil. After a few minutes, Richard opened the door to the restroom.

"Your turn, my friend," he said as he walked out.

"You didn't, by any chance, leave it stinking, did you?"

"No more than it already was, Bud."

"Now I'm not sure I want to go in there."

"Unlike you, my friend, I would not do such a thing."

"All right. I'm going in, but only because I have to," John said as he moved into the restroom.

"Be brave, partner."

"If I'm not out in five minutes, call an ambulance," John remarked as he closed the door behind him.

Richard looked out of the window to see what Bob was doing. He noticed him closing the hood on the Hummer. Then he watched him walk to the back of the vehicle to finish the fueling. He walked over to the coolers to find himself a drink. While he was there, he looked over the various sandwiches they had for sale. John emerged from the bathroom and scanned the room for Richard. When he spotted him at the coolers, he walked over to where he was.

"What do they have to eat?" John asked.

"Just some cold cut sandwiches."

"What's Bob doing?" John asked as he turned to look out the front window.

"Finishing up with the gas, I think."

John stared out of the window but did not see Bob. He punched Richard in the ribs lightly. "I don't see him," he said.

343

Richard turned and looked out of the window. He glanced around the Hummer but didn't see Bob. "I wonder where he went?"

"I don't know. Maybe we should go find out," John replied.

"Yeah," Richard agreed. The two men walked out of the convenience store into the parking lot. They walked over to the Hummer and looked inside for Bob.

"Well, he's not in the car," John remarked.

"He didn't even finish the fueling," Richard noticed as he pointed to the nozzle still stuck in the Hummer.

"What the hell is going on?" John asked as he began to look around.

"I don't know," Richard replied as he began to do the same.

"Uh oh," John said as he gently punched Richard in the ribs again.

"What?" Richard replied as he turned to see what John wanted. John pointed toward the side of the store building. There they saw Bob being handcuffed by two men in black suits.

John took off to his rescue as he noticed one of the men punching Bob in the stomach. When he arrived, he grabbed the man who had his back to him and spun him around. The man quickly took a swing at him with his right arm. John blocked his punch with his left arm. Then he noticed the other man reaching in his coat like he was going for a gun. John quickly drop-kicked the man in the face with his left foot making him fall to the ground. He punched the other man in the ribs with his right fist causing him to bend over. Taking the head of the man in his hands, he forced his head down against his knee. This caused the man to fall to the ground, knocking him out.

THE COVERUP

John quickly turned to the other man. When he turned to face the man, Richard jumped on him and punched him in the face several times. John relaxed and watched Richard knock out the man. When Richard realized the man was out, he stood up and looked at John. He was breathing heavily as the adrenalin was pumping through his veins.

"That was fun," he said.

"Good job, Richard. I didn't think you had it in you."

They both reached down and picked up Bob who was on his knees holding his stomach.

"Well, I feel much safer now with you guys around," Bob remarked, clinching his stomach in pain.

"Let's get those cuffs off of you," John said as he reached down to the man he knocked out. He searched his pockets for a key and came up empty-handed. "Check and see if that guy has a key, Richard."

Richard searched the other man's pockets. He found a ring of keys and handed them to John. John took the keys and found the one that opened the cuffs. They had only managed to cuff one hand as Bob had tried to fight them off.

"Let's get this off of you," John said as he unlocked the cuffs.

"What do we do with them?" Richard asked.

"Let's drag them over behind the store and cuff them to that tree," John replied as he looked around to see if anyone was watching. They dragged the two men over to the tree and placed them back-to-back against the tree. John reached into the pocket of the man he had knocked out and retrieved another set of cuffs. He cuffed the two men to the tree and threw the keys away into the bushes.

"We'd better get out of here before someone shows up," Bob explained.

WILLIAM DANIEL

"You're right," John agreed.

"Get in the Hummer. I'll pay for the gas, and we'll get out of here," Bob said as he headed for the front of the store.

"FBI agents?" Richard curiously asked.

"Yeah, let's go before they wake up," John said as he walked toward the Hummer.

Richard followed him to the vehicle and got into the back. John opened the door to the front passenger seat and sat down.

"How could they know we were here?" Richard asked.

"I don't know. Maybe they didn't," John answered.

"Well, it appears to me they did," Richard said.

"They may have just been searching. They probably got out an alert on this Hummer. These agents were just searching the area and got lucky," John explained.

"More like unlucky. Man, you dropped those two like a ton of rocks. You don't dropkick that second guy and you are dead meat. I could see he was going for a gun," Richard said, still excited from the fight.

"Yeah, but I was counting on you to grab him after he hit the ground. If you hadn't, he surely would have retrieved that gun. There was no way I could have gotten to him in time. Thanks for being there," John remarked.

"No problem, partner. Those guys are going to be real mad when they wake up."

"Jack's going to be real mad when he finds out they didn't catch us," John remarked.

"He can keep them coming, and you and I will knock them down."

"Never underestimate Jack. We have been real lucky so far," John said as he looked out the side window to see what Bob was doing. He noticed Bob was at the counter with a brown sack in front of him.

346

THE COVERUP

"Do you think he will be waiting for us when we get to Area Fifty-One?" Richard asked.

"I expect he will be," John answered, still looking out the window at Bob.

Bob finished paying the clerk at the store. He walked out of the store and headed for the Hummer. He walked around to the driver's side and got in behind the wheel. He laid a sack in the floor at John's feet.

"Get some supplies?" John asked.

"Yes, I did. I got us some sandwiches and some drinks. We may get hungry by the time we get there," Bob replied. He started the Hummer and drove out of the parking lot.

"How much longer before we get to the plane?" John asked.

"We are about twenty miles from Newberry Springs now," Bob replied as he turned the Hummer onto I-40.

"Oh, so that's where we are going," Richard remarked.

"Yeah, that's where Shawn keeps his plane. By the way, thanks for saving my ass back there, John. You too, Richard, thanks. I thought I was done for before you got there."

"Think nothing of it, Bob. We are all in this together now," John remarked.

"I'm sorry we drug you into this," Richard apologized.

"What are you talking about? This is the most excitement I have seen in years. Tell me something, John. Where did you learn how to fight like that?"

"The Marines, and I had a lot of training in the FBI."

"Well, you are very good at it."

"Thanks. It comes in handy at times."

"Okay, so what is our next move?" Richard asked.

"Well, we're going to meet a friend of mine and board his plane headed for Fort Hood. He's going to claim he is having trouble and divert to Roswell for repairs. That's where we will get off," Bob explained.

"When did you set this up?" Richard curiously asked.

"While you were taking a nap."

"Can we trust this guy?"

"Oh, yeah. He's a good friend of mine. We go way back, Shawn and I. We grew up together and went to the same college. He and I were roommates in college. We double-dated a lot and got into a lot of trouble together. I would trust him with my life."

"I hope you're right. We are too close to blow this thing now."

"Well, it was like this, Richard. If we drive out to Area Fifty-One, it will take about two and a half days. If Shawn flies us out, we will be there in a few hours. I think the risk is worth it," Bob explained.

"Yeah, you may be right."

"Trust me. I have it all under control."

"Do you think it wise to be out here on the interstate with so many looking for us?" John asked.

"No, it's not safe, but we won't be on it for very long," Bob answered.

"We might want to keep our eyes peeled for suspicious-looking cars," Richard said.

"Yeah, particularly for FBI standard sedans, huh?" Bob sarcastically remarked.

"That's right," John replied. "Not every agent drives the same kind of car, Richard."

"I guess that would be a little too obvious for them," Richard replied.

"But we can watch for any car that might make a quick turnaround," John suggested.

"You watch the front. I will take care of the rear," Richard said as he turned to look out the back windshield.

Bob continued to drive the Hummer at just above the speed limit. He was trying not to attract attention. A tractor-trailer rig came flying by them at a much higher speed. Bob decided to follow behind him. He knew if any problems came up, the rig would slow down. This would give him an early warning of a highway patrol car approaching.

"If you were trying to attract more attention, there's no better way than speeding," John remarked when he noticed Bob speeding up to get behind the truck.

"Yeah, but we only have a few miles to go, and if we get behind this big rig, we'll get there faster," Bob explained. "This will give us cover, and we'll know if something is happening if he slows down."

"Good idea, Bob," Richard agreed.

"All right, I hope nobody spots us," John remarked.

For the next fifteen miles, they followed behind the big truck. Then Bob noticed a sign on the side of the interstate. He read, "Trails Highway, One Mile."

"Okay, we're only a mile from the turnoff," he said.

"Looks like we might have made it," John remarked.

"Uh oh," Richard said.

"What?" John asked.

"I see a car crossing the median to the west side."

"Is it a police car?" Bob asked as he tried to look out the side view mirror.

"No, it's an unmarked white car. Looks like he's coming pretty fast, too," Richard relayed.

"Shoot! I thought we might at least make it to the turnoff before we got caught. Hang on!" Bob shouted.

He turned the Hummer into the passing lane and went around the big truck. He pulled in front of the truck, keeping a few yards away. As soon as the turnoff for Trails Highway appeared, he whipped the Hummer onto the exit. By this time, the car following had made it to the side of the big truck. The truck shielded them from seeing the Hummer exit. The agents continued down the interstate until they got in front of the truck. They suddenly realized the Hummer had gotten off at the last exit. By this time, they were a good five miles past the exit for Trails Highway. They had to slow down, cross the median, and return on the eastbound side. By the time they reached the exit, the Hummer was gone and out of sight.

THE COVERUP

THE FLIGHT TO AREA FIFTY-ONE
Chapter Thirty-Five

Speeding down the highway, Bob came upon an airstrip. There were several buildings and a huge cargo plane sitting on the runway. Bob slowed the Hummer down and turned onto a road leading to the runway. He quickly drove toward the back of the airplane. The closer he got, the more they could see. The plane was letting down its back door. Bob drove the Hummer onto the plane and stopped. The back door began to close as Shawn came out to greet them.

"Hey, Bob. Nice to see you again," Shawn greeted as he walked up.

"We're being followed," Bob quickly reported.

"Shit! Okay, Chris, let's get out of here now. Pronto!" he shouted on a radio he retrieved from his belt.

"There's another car coming. Do we want to wait?" Chris asked.

"No! Take off now!" Shawn shouted.

"What do we need to do?" Bob asked as he exited the Hummer.

"Here. Take these chains and wrap them around the frame of your vehicle at the front and rear. Then take the snaps on one end and hook them on the tie-downs on the floor. Let's go quickly," Shawn ordered.

He and Bob worked on the front while John and Richard tied the rear. The plane, which was already running and ready for takeoff, started down the long runway. Faster and faster it ran until it finally left the ground.

"Grab hold of something now!" Shawn shouted as the plane left the ground. They all grabbed hold of the Hummer to anchor themselves. The big plane climbed and climbed into the early morning sky. When it reached the necessary altitude, it leveled off flying east toward Roswell, New Mexico. Back in the cargo hole, the men could finally let go of the their grip on the Hummer.

"Damn, Bob. You sure know how to cut it close," Shawn said.

"Well, you know how it is. Stuff happens," Bob explained.

"How's it going? Shawn Alexandria," Shawn introduced himself putting out his hand.

"Fine. John Barton, and this is Richard Cooper," John introduced as he shook his hand.

"Nice to meet you," Shawn replied as he shook Richard's hand.

"Nice to meet you, too," Richard replied.

"You know, you're hanging out with a bad boy. How have you been, Bob?" Shawn asked as he hugged him.

"Great, Shawn, great," Bob replied hugging him back.

"Well, it's been a while since you've tried to con me out of a trip somewhere. I was beginning to think you didn't like me anymore," Shawn said. "Come on I've got some martinis in the lounge.

"Now, you know me better than that," Bob replied.

"I'll say. I've been hanging out with this guy since he was in diapers," Shawn indicated to John and Richard as he led the group into a small room.

THE COVERUP

"You've got some real bad enemies chasing you, Bob," Shawn stated as he took his glass from the table.

"You might say that, Shawn."

"Yeah, well, they just took a shot at us as we were taking off," Shawn said as he put an olive in his drink.

"You're shitting me."

"No, I'm not," Chris said. "They jumped out of the car and began firing at us with handguns," Shawn explained as he took a drink of his martini.

"Damn! I'm sorry about that, Shawn. I hope everything is okay," Bob apologized.

"I don't think they hit anything. Chris is running a diagnostic test on the systems to check out everything. These bad boys seem to want you guys real bad." Shawn began to pour the drinks for everybody.

"I would prefer a beer, if you don't mind," John said

"Sure thing, in the refrigerator behind the counter," Shawn replied.

"You don't know the half of it," Bob remarked as he sat down and placed an olive in his drink.

"Want to tell me about it?"

"Believe me, Shawn, the less you know, the better," Bob replied as he took a drink.

"Well, you know me. I'm not one to pry into your affairs. I just hope you're not in any serious trouble," Shawn remarked as he took another drink.

"Listen, Shawn. If there is any damage to your plane or you get into any legal problems over this, I want you to call my lawyer, Paul Dagget. You can find him in New York City. He's listed. He will take care of anything you might need," Richard said as he sipped on his martini.

"Richard, was it?" Shawn asked.

"Yes, Richard Cooper."

"I appreciate that. I'm just worried about my friend, Bob, though. Besides, I hope that you are gone before they catch up to me."

"Just drop us off at the first place you can find," John remarked.

"Yeah, well, I hope to drop you at a small landing strip outside of Nevada and then continue to Fort Hood where they will catch up to me. Of course, I will deny ever seeing any of you," Shawn explained.

"We really appreciate this, Shawn," Bob thankfully said.

"You will when you get my bill," Shawn replied. The light on a phone on the wall behind Shawn began to flash.

"I think you're getting a call," John remarked as he pointed to the phone on the wall.

"Yeah, okay," Shawn said as he turned to pick up the receiver.

"I hope it's not anything serious," Richard said.

"Yeah, Chris," Shawn said as he grabbed the phone receiver. He sat silently for a few seconds listening. "Okay," he replied as he hung up the phone.

"What's up?" Bob curiously asked.

"Well, it seems that someone wants us to land at the nearest airport ASAP. Chris told them he was having trouble with the radio. He said he couldn't understand what they were saying. That should buy us some time for now," Shawn explained.

"How long before we get to the Nevada border?" Richard asked.

"Well, we're about an hour and a half from there now."

"Wish you were coming with us," Bob remarked.

"You just keep your head down. I don't want to read in the news about your being shot out in the desert."

THE COVERUP

"Don't you worry. I plan on keeping out of most of this adventure," Bob said as he downed the rest of his martini.

"There was a time when we would be right up front, huh, Bob?" Shawn remarked.

"Yeah, them were the good old days," Bob agreed.

"Remember that fossil raid in Mexico?" Shawn related.

"Oh, yeah. We really surprised those thieves," Bob replied.

"Fossil raid?" Richard curiously asked.

"We were contracted by our government to retrieve some rare fossils that were stolen from a museum in Chicago. We flew down there with twelve men, a jeep, and a truck. We had planned to parachute ten men, a jeep, and a truck on sight of the hideout down in southern Mexico. Bob, here, was the last to jump. Well, about halfway down, he finds out his main parachute didn't open. Rather than go to his backup, he climbs inside the jeep and rides it down. Man, you had some guts then," Shawn explained.

"That was nothing. Tell them about the time we took some senators out in the desert."

"Oh, yeah. After that little drop, we started calling that an article seven twelve drop. Well, we were taking these two senators out for a hunt. They were real assholes, kept demanding stuff all the time, complaining about how the plane ride was rough, the drinks were weak, and the service was bad. They were constantly ragging on Bob for being an Indian, how Indians didn't belong in our society. Bob, here, decides to get them real liquored up, so he starts mixing the drinks real strong. Then he comes up to me and makes these plans to scare the living hell out of them. He had me announce that one of the plane's engines was going out, so he started screaming that the plane was going down, and we were going to have to jump.

He straps the drop chute onto the jeep and seatbelts the two senators in the jeep. Then he opens the rear door and shoves them out screaming, 'Geronimo!' Scared the living hell out of those two senators. They showed up the next day covered in puke and smelled of urine. I spent a half day trying to calm them down, they were so pissed. Then I spent the rest of the day cleaning the puke, urine, and poop out of that jeep. Man, that was so funny," Shawn explained while laughing.

"Yeah, and I remember you almost lost your pilot license over that, too," Bob remarked.

"Yeah, well, it was worth it. They were real assholes, anyway. Bob, here, disappeared for about a month. He was afraid they were going to scalp him if they caught him," Shawn said.

"Sounds like that was a little dangerous," John remarked.

"Not really. We have these special chutes for dropping heavy equipment. They floated down like a feather," Shawn replied.

"Really?" John asked.

"Yeah, there's nothing to it," Bob confidently said.

"I don't like flying much anyway. But on the way out, Richard took me up in a crop duster, and I loved it. Scared the hell out of me, but I loved it," John explained.

"Yeah, when we were swooping down on that field of corn, I was sure he was going to lose it," Richard remarked laughing.

"Are you a pilot, Richard?" Shawn curiously asked.

"Yes. I mean I can fly a crop duster or piper. Never flew a fortress like this one."

"Want to try?" Shawn asked.

"Sure. I would love to."

"Not a problem," Shawn said as he reached behind him to

THE COVERUP

pick up the phone. "Chris, Richard's going to come up front. Let him try his hand at flying the plane."

"Has he ever flown before?" Chris asked.

"Not one as big as this one. Just some small pipers and dusters."

"Well, send him on up. I could use some company."

"All right. He's on his way," Shawn said and hung up the phone.

"Gee thanks, Shawn. I've always wanted to fly one of these big cargo planes," Richard eagerly said.

"No problem. Take that door over there and follow it all the way to the end. You will come to a door that enters the pilot's cabin. Chris will take care of you."

"Great. I'll catch you guys in a few minutes," Richard said as he got up and walked out of the lounge.

"Do you think it's wise to let him fly this plane?" Bob asked.

"He'll be all right. Besides, Chris will be there with him," Shawn convincingly answered.

"Well, it's your plane," Bob replied.

"So, tell me, John, how long have you known Richard?" Shawn curiously asked.

"Oh, about two days now."

"You got a lot of confidence in short term friendships?"

"It's kind of hard to explain without getting you involved."

"I understand. I didn't mean to be nosy."

"Let's just say we are investigating a murder and a coverup."

"Oh? Are you a cop?"

"Well, a small town sheriff."

"Okay, so let me summarize this. There was a murder, and you think the government is covering up the evidence," Bob remarked.

"Well, basically yes," John replied.

"So, Richard is a cop, too?" Shawn asked.

"No. Richard is more of a crypto-zoologist," John explained.

"They study unknown mysterious or legendary creatures," Shawn remarked.

"Yeah, something like that," John replied.

"Well, now I'm more confused than before," Shawn returned.

"Don't worry, Shawn. When this is all over, I'll explain it in great detail to you, that is, if I'm still here," Bob explained.

"Now don't go getting yourself killed, Bob," Shawn remarked.

"I don't plan on being in on this one. I'm just carrying them to the place," Bob quickly replied.

"Good, because I don't know what I would do without my good friend, Bob, around," Shawn remarked.

Suddenly the plane jumped like a car running over a bump in the road.

"What the hell was that?" John shouted.

"Richard must be taking over the controls," Shawn jokingly remarked.

"Felt like we ran over something," Bob said as he reached for a towel to clean up the spilled drinks.

"I doubt it. It's probably just Richard getting a feel for the yoke. It's a little bit different flying a bigger plane like this," Shawn replied.

"I hope you're right, because that actually felt like we ran over an elephant or something," Bob remarked as he finished

THE COVERUP

cleaning up the mess. He poured the remainder of the martinis into their glasses.

"I'm sure it was nothing," Shawn calmly replied. He picked up his glass and took a sip of his drink. John had his beer in his hand when the bump occurred. He lifted it to his mouth to take a swig. Out of the corner of his eye, he saw the light flashing on the phone behind Shawn.

"I think you're getting a call," he said pointing at the phone.

Shawn turned to the phone and noticed the light was flashing. "I guess you are right." He picked up the receiver and said, "What's up, Chris?"

"Got a little problem here," Chris relayed.

"What's the problem?" Shawn asked.

"We're loosing coolant oil pressure in the number four engine," Chris explained.

"Can you see anything leaking on the engine?"

"No, I don't see anything coming off the wing. The oil pressure warning came on right after Richard took the yoke."

"What's the engine temperature reading?"

"It was climbing rather fast. I shut down the engine."

"Was that the bump we felt down here?"

"It probably was. I had to bring up the power in two and three to compensate the loss of number four," Chris replied.

"What's our status now?" Shawn curiously asked.

"Well, we can run on three, but I think we need to divert to Phoenix. We need to make repairs before we continue on. We also need to check the rest of the plane for damages."

"No, continue on to Roswell. We'll repair it there," Shawn ordered.

"Yes, sir," Chris replied.

WILLIAM DANIEL

Shawn hung up the phone and explained the situation to the others. "Do you think it's wise to continue on with damages like that?" John quickly asked.

"Yeah, it'll be fine. This plane can fly with three engines without a problem. We are only a few hundred miles from Nevada," Shawn explained.

"Whatever you say, Captain," Bob replied.

"Where are you going to land when we get there?" John curiously asked.

"There is a large landing strip just south of Nevada. It's a private farm, but the strip is long enough for us to land. Trust me. I've landed there before. I know the owner. He won't mind us stopping over," Shawn explained.

"Good," Bob replied.

"Your people can get off there and continue on to Nevada. The farm is in a very remote place, so you probably won't be noticed."

"Very good," Bob replied.

As Shawn took another sip of his martini, John noticed the phone flashing again. "I think you are getting another call," he said.

"Now what?" Shawn asked as he picked up the phone again. "What now, Chris?"

"I'm picking up some blimps on the long range radar."

"What is it?"

"Seems there's three attack helicopters headed straight for us. They're about a thousand miles out at the moment."

"Keep me informed on the loud speaker of their progress," Shawn ordered. He hung up the phone and turned to Bob, staring at him for a moment without saying a word.

"What?" Bob asked.

THE COVERUP

"Seems your friends have sent some serious equipment out for you," Shawn remarked.

"What do you mean?"

"We've got three attack helicopters headed toward us right now."

"Shit! I was afraid that might happen," Bob said as he turned to look at John.

The door to the cockpit burst open as Richard came flying through it. "Seven twelve! I think it's time for an article seven twelve!" he screamed as he entered the room.

"He's right, you know," Shawn agreed.

"I was afraid you were going to say that," Bob concurred.

"What? There's not another option?" John nervously asked.

"I'm afraid not. If you go now, there is a good chance they will not see you. I will have Chris turn on the radar jammer as soon as you drop, but we will not be able to keep it on for long," Shawn explained.

"Why is that?" Richard asked.

"Well, because they are going to want to know why it was on at this time. We can get away by saying it was an accident. That's if we keep it short," Shawn explained.

"Say the word, my friend," Bob said.

Shawn walked over and picked up the phone. He put it on the loud speaker. "Now hear this. All available hands to the cargo bay. All hands prepare for a seven twelve drop," he ordered.

"I hope you guys have the stomach for this," Bob remarked as they headed for the cargo bay.

"Is this safe?" John nervously asked.

"You'll be as safe as if you were in your mother's arms," Bob confidently replied.

"Long as your mother wasn't an ax murderer," Richard remarked.

"You going like that?" John asked.

"Don't start with me," Richard quickly replied.

"I just thought you might want to dress up," John joked.

"You belong in a rubber room," Richard quickly replied.

As they entered the cargo bay, the flight personnel were already there. They quickly retrieved a large parachute and began attaching it to the Hummer.

"Man, these guys are serious," John remarked as he watched them work.

"I need you guys to grab a couple of barf bags. I don't want to have to clean my Hummer if you have an accident," Bob said.

"Sure thing, Bob. Where are they?" Richard asked.

"Shawn, you got any barf bags?" Bob asked.

"Yeah, they are in that drawer over by the strap rack."

"Go get them, guys. And get more than one for each of us," Bob ordered.

The loudspeaker came on and Chris announced the contact was nine hundred miles and closing. Shawn walked over to the phone in the cargo bay to call Chris. "Chris, I need you to turn on the jammer at my command," he ordered.

"Roger, Captain," Chris replied.

Shawn hung up the phone and turned to Bob. "Let's get your tie-downs off," he said. They walked over to the Hummer where the men were just finishing attaching the large parachute. Shawn took the front and Bob walked to the back. They released the straps that held the Hummer in place.

"All aboard," Shawn ordered.

Richard and John got into the Hummer and strapped themselves in. Bob hesitated as he turned to Shawn. "Until

THE COVERUP

next time, my friend," he remarked smiling. Shawn gave him a halfway salute as if to say, "Good-bye." Bob turned to get into the Hummer. He noticed something on top of the parachute. "What is that, Shawn?" he asked, pointing at the device on top.

"That is an added device I came up with to help slow the descent more," Shawn explained.

"What is it?"

"It's a self-inflating helium balloon. It will inflate a hundred feet from the ground. It makes the drop a lot less bumpy upon impact."

"Does it work?"

"I don't know. You tell me next time I see you," Shawn replied smiling.

"Oh, shit!" Bob remarked as he climbed into the Hummer.

Shawn ordered everyone out of the cargo bay area. He walked over to the phone where the cargo bay door release was. He picked up the phone and told Chris to turn on the jammer. Then he put on a harness attached to the wall. He reached over to the release button and put his hand on it. He turned to the Hummer and gave a 'thumbs up' sign. Bob quickly gave the same sign in return and cranked up the Hummer. Shawn hit the button to open the bay doors for the drop. The cargo bay doors began to lower slowly. A loud swooshing sound could be heard as the doors lowered. It was the air rushing in as the cargo bay was exposed to the outside.

"Hold on to something," Bob said as he put the shifter into reverse.

As soon as the doors were open, Bob let off the brake and stomped on the gas pedal. The Hummer spun its wheels and flew out of the back of the plane. As soon as it cleared the doors, the Hummer began to fall. Attached to the parachute on top of the Hummer was a rope. It was tied to the plane. When the rope reached the end, it pulled the cord on the parachute. The parachute opened and the Hummer stopped falling and began to float.

"Damn! That was scary!" John excitedly remarked.

"Yeah, I think I'm going to need a new pair of shorts," Richard candidly remarked.

"Don't you do that in my Hummer," Bob replied.

"I was just kidding. This is actually kind of fun," Richard said.

"Yeah, it's not so bad after you get by the initial drop," John remarked as he looked outside.

"Well, it's a good thing it's still dark. You would not want to look down," Bob explained.

"How high are we?" asked Richard.

"About three thousand feet right now," Bob answered.

"You're right. I'm glad it's still dark," Richard softly remarked.

"Let's see what's on the radio right now," Bob said as he turned off the Hummer and switched the ignition to accessory. The radio came on with a hissing noise. Bob turned the tuner until he found a station.

"In the news today, a raid on an Indian resort in California went bad. Two FBI agents were killed when they tried to apprehend an old Indian at the resort. According to sources at the scene, the teepee just blew up into flames," the radio announcer said.

"The agents walked into a teepee in the back of the resort, and the next thing we knew, it was in flames," said one employee at the scene.

THE COVERUP

"No further information was available at press time," the news announcer reported.

Suddenly the radio went back to the hissing sound it was making earlier. Silence fell upon the three men floating in the Hummer.

"Sorry, Bob," John apologized.

"Grandfather," Bob said as he was stunned by the announcement.

"Yeah, Bob. I sure am sorry about this. I know how much you must have loved him," Richard added to the apology.

"Didn't you hear the reporter?" Bob asked.

"Yeah, they blew him up," Richard quickly replied.

"No, he's right, Richard. The two agents went into the tent and then it blew up," John explained.

"He committed suicide to take those two agents out. That's not like Grandfather. He's a very kind man. He wouldn't hurt a fly. Why did he do that?" Bob elaborated.

"Maybe he was trying to buy us some time," John remarked.

"Maybe, but why blow them up? He could have stalled by talking our native tongue. It would have taken them hours to find someone to talk to him. This just doesn't make sense," Bob explained. He reached up to the radio to turn it off.

Suddenly a bolt of electricity shot out of the radio. It captured Bob from his fingertips all the way down his body. Then as suddenly as it started, it stopped. Bob remained frozen in the same position he was in when he tried to turn off the radio. It was as if it had frozen him in that position. John and Richard looked at each other, still nervously shocked by what had just happened. Then as the moment passed, they became concerned for their newfound friend.

"Bob, you okay?" John cautiously asked.

There was no response from Bob. Before anyone could say anything else, the radio came back on. Only this time, it was not the radio station.

"Little Deer, it is time for you to take over. I have seen the spirit horse and have taken him by the reigns. It is time for me to join our ancestors in the holy lands. You must lead our people in the battle of right or wrong. You will now be the holy man of our tribe. I will join our ancestors and will help you with your powers. Do not mourn my passing for it is time for me to join the others with the holy spirits," Running Deer's voice projected over the radio.

At the same time the voice rang out over the radio, Bob regained consciousness like melting ice. "Grandfather," he said as he came to his senses.

"Do not fear, for your destiny is before you. You will now be the most powerful man of our tribe. Your powers will be used against evil in our lands," Running Deer said.

"But Grandfather, why did you kill those men? Will this cause extreme controversy of our resort?" Bob asked.

"Do not worry, little one. I transported the white men to a safer place before my lodging exploded. They will remember nothing of what happened. Now I must go and join the others. I will be with you always, Grandson. Whenever you need help, I will be there as your spiritual guidance. Now, Little Deer, you will be called Big Buck. Use your new powers for good. Remember, I will always be with you," Running Deer said as his voice faded from the radio.

"Goodbye, Grandfather. May your spirit horse carry you safely to the Great White Spirit," Bob replied as the radio went back to the static sound. Bob reached up and turned off the radio. He turned to John and smiled, "We are going to win. Are you ready to battle with the evil one?" he asked.

THE COVERUP

John smiled back at Bob and pulled out the revolver Running Deer had given him. "I am ready, my friend. Let's do it," he replied, letting out an Indian yelp.

"All right. Let's get it done," Richard remarked as he joined John and Bob in the Indian yelp.

It became quiet when they noticed the sun cracking the horizon. They began to look out the windows to see how close they were to the ground. Suddenly a loud hissing began as they were looking down.

"What is that?" Richard curiously asked.

"That must be that feature Shawn added," Bob replied.

"The balloon," John remarked as he turned to look at Bob. They both quickly leaned forward to look out the front windshield.

"See anything?" asked Richard.

"I don't," replied John.

"Me either. Wait a minute. I think I see some of it," Bob replied as he stretched his head between the dash and the windshield. Suddenly the Hummer jerked upwards slightly.

"Wow!" Richard remarked as the Hummer jerked upward.

"Well, that was interesting," John remarked.

"We seem to be slowing down some," Bob said as he leaned back and looked out his side window.

"Hey, look at that. You can see the ground now," Richard remarked as he looked out his side window in the back.

"Okay, listen up, guys. As soon as we get on the ground, we need to get that parachute off and the balloon down. Richard, there is a bow and arrow in the back. Get them. John, you and I will start taking off the parachute," Bob ordered.

"You got it, boss."

Richard reached into the back of the Hummer and retrieved the bow and arrows.

WILLIAM DANIEL

"Grab hold of something! We are about to land!" Bob shouted. The Hummer came to a rest with a big thud, jerking the occupants around.

"Everybody okay?" Bob asked as he unclipped his seat belt.

"Yeah, fine," replied John.

"Me too," Richard said.

"All right. Let's get going," Bob said as he opened the door on his side.

"All right. Let's do it," John said as he opened the door on the passenger side and climbed out.

"Richard, give me that bow and the arrows," Bob said.

Richard climbed out of the Hummer from the back seat and handed the bow and arrows to Bob. Bob took the bow and placed an arrow on it. He was going to shoot down the balloon. Pulling the string back on the bow against his cheek, he let the arrow fly as he released the string. The arrow took off with the force of the stretched bowstring. Flying straight and true, it missed the target, the balloon.

"What the hell! You missed it. I thought all Indians could shoot a bow!" shouted Richard.

"I am an Indian, and this is not as easy as it seems. Besides, I never could shoot one of these ancestral weapons," Bob quickly replied.

"I thought you were one of these great hunters," Richard remarked.

"I am, but I hunt with modern weapons like a rifle or a pistol," Bob replied, looking at John.

"Hey, don't look at me. I only have the one bullet, remember. That's all your grandfather gave me. That's all he said I would need," John quickly said.

THE COVERUP

"Yeah, well," Bob said as he put another arrow on the bowstring and pulled the string back on the bow against his cheek.

"Why don't you just get your grandfather to pop it?" Richard candidly remarked.

As Bob was trying to take aim on the balloon, it popped. The air rushed out of the balloon, and it came tumbling down to earth. Bob and John were stunned and confusingly turned to look at Richard.

"What?" Richard asked in surprise.

"Nothing," Bob replied as he shook his head. "Let's get this thing unhooked."

They unhooked the parachute and hid it behind some rocks. They piled some more rocks on top. The sun had cracked the horizon and provided ample light.

"We're going to be sticking out like a sore thumb in this black Hummer," Richard remarked.

"Yeah, well, if everything went like it was supposed to, they'll be in Roswell looking for us," Bob replied.

"We'd better get going before they find out we are not there," John added.

"Well, we are only a few miles from the Nevada border," Bob said as he walked to the driver side of the Hummer.

"Is that where we are going?" asked John.

"No, but it is close to there," Bob answered as he got into the Hummer.

"Where is the highway?" Richard asked.

"There are no highways or roads out here, nothing but sand and chaparrals," Bob replied.

"So how do you know which way to go?"

"Trust me. I know."

"Well, then, tell me this, Bob. How long is it going to take to get there?" Richard asked.

369

"We are about an hour's drive from the old river. Gentlemen, you are not going to believe what you are about to see," Bob explained.

"I'm still trying to figure out that electrical shock you just took. What was that all about?" Richard asked.

"Yeah, are you sure you are okay?" asked John.

"Did you not hear what Grandfather said?"

"What are you talking about? All we heard was some announcement about your grandfather's tent exploding," Richard quipped.

"That's all we heard. Then the radio went to static, and you were kind of frozen there like you were in a trance," John added.

"And you guys didn't hear anything else?"

"No, should we have?" John asked.

"You did not hear Grandfather's voice coming over the radio?"

"No, like I said, you were frozen there for a few seconds right after the electric shock," John replied after he looked at the radio.

"What happened?" Richard curiously asked.

"Nothing," Bob confusingly replied.

"Ah, come on. Something must have happened. Did you hear your grandfather talking to you from the grave or something?" Richard asked.

"I can't explain it. If you did not hear it, then Grandfather did not want you to."

"So you did hear something. Come on. Will you tell us what he said?" Richard excitedly asked.

"If Grandfather wanted you to hear what he had to say, you would have heard it."

"He's not going to tell us, John," Richard said.

"Well, maybe it's a secret, like, you know, the secret that you and I have."

"Let's get out of here," Bob said as he cranked up the Hummer and put it into gear.

WILLIAM DANIEL

THE COVERUP

JACK'S DEPARTURE
Chapter Thirty-Six

It was 8:00 a.m. back at the hotel in El Paso, Texas. Jack walked out of the elevator and approached the front counter. A young man standing at the counter smiled and asked if he could help him.

"Here, go get my luggage from my room and call me a taxi," Jack ordered as he handed the young man his key. Jack turned to the gentleman behind the counter and asked him for his bill. The man punched up his room number on the computer and printed a copy of the bill. He walked over to the printer behind him and tore off the copy and gave it to Jack. Jack took the copy and signed it and gave it back to the clerk.

As he was leaving the hotel, his cell phone began to ring. He retrieved the phone from his coat pocket and pushed the receive button. "What is it?" he asked.

"They were not on the plane, sir. Apparently a couple of our agents took some shots at his plane when he was taking off earlier today. He said they sustained some damage to one of their engines. He said they decided to divert to Roswell for repairs when the choppers caught up to him. He's hopping mad and threatening to sue us for the damages," the agent reported.

"All right. See what you can do about getting his plane fixed. Then apologize for the inconvenience. Tell him we thought we were chasing a terrorist group and send him on

WILLIAM DANIEL

his way. Send the choppers back to the place where he changed course. They must have gotten off somehow before he headed for Roswell," Jack ordered.

"A midair drop, sir?"

"Just do it!" Jack angrily said as he hung up the phone. "I know they were on that plane," he said to himself.

He walked to the front door and waited for the young man to bring his luggage. He pulled out his cell phone and began to dial a number. He placed it to his ear and waited for an answer. The phone rang a couple of times before a man answered.

"Yes, sir, Mr. Riley."

"I'm leaving the hotel now. Get my plane ready," Jack ordered.

"Yes, sir, Mr. Riley. It will be ready by the time you get here."

Jack hung up the cell phone and dialed another number. He placed the phone to his ear and waited for someone to answer.

"Hello, Mr. Riley. I will get him for you," answered a woman on the other end.

"Thanks," Jack replied.

"Jack, everything going okay?" came an answer on the other end.

"Everything is going as I had planned, sir."

"Are you heading there now?"

"Yes, sir."

"Good. Keep me informed."

"I will, sir," Jack answered. He hung up the cell phone and put it back into his coat pocket.

Jack waited for several minutes before the young man brought his luggage to him. He stepped outside where a cab had

THE COVERUP

just pulled up. He ordered the young man to put his luggage in the trunk of the cab. He stepped into the cab and sat down. He began to mull over the plan he had come up with.

"Where to?" asked the cab driver as he got back into the cab.

"El Paso International," Jack replied.

"Yes, sir," the cab driver replied as he picked up his radio microphone and relayed his direction.

The driver put the car in drive and pulled away from the hotel. The cab rumbled and rattled through the streets of El Paso. The driver was weaving and darting through the busy streets. Finally the cab arrived at the El Paso International Airport. The driver pulled the cab to the main entrance. He drove the cab to the front door and parked the cab. He got out and opened the back door for Jack to exit. Then he walked to the rear and opened the trunk. He pulled Jack's luggage out and gave it to one of the airport attendants. Jack paid the cab driver and walked into the airport to board his plane. As he walked through the busy airport, a man came out of a side door and walked over to him.

"Mr. Riley, this way, sir," the man said as he gestured for Jack to follow him.

He led him into a room that would take him to the runway. They walked through the room and out of a door where there was a car waiting to take him to his plane. The man opened the door so that Jack could get in and ordered the attendant to put his luggage into the trunk. He closed the door to the car and walked around to the driver's side. He opened the door and climbed behind the wheel.

"Your plane is ready, sir," he said as he cranked the car engine. He put the car in drive and drove over to runway three. The leer jet sat there waiting for Jack to board. The

WILLIAM DANIEL

man stopped the car beside the jet's stair ramp, got out of the car, and walked to the back door. He opened the door and Jack got out. Another airport attendant was waiting for them. He ordered him to get the luggage out of the trunk and put it onto the plane and escorted Jack to the ramp. Jack walked up the ramp, and as he boarded the plane, the man following him said, "Have a nice flight, Mr. Riley." He locked the door to the plane and ordered the ramp to be removed. Jack's pilot taxied the plane onto the runway and took off into the clear blue sky.

It was 10:00 a.m. back in the Nevada desert where Bob was maneuvering the Hummer toward a large hill of rocks.

"Are we there yet?" whined Richard.

"Gentlemen, we are there," Bob announced as he stopped the Hummer several yards from the hill.

"Where exactly are we?" John asked as he looked around.

"We are at the entrance to the river bed," Bob replied.

"Uh, Bob, I don't see any entrance, just a big hill of rocks," Richard candidly remarked.

"See that large pile of small dead trees and rocks on the side of that hill?" Bob asked.

"Yeah," Richard replied.

"That is the entrance to the cave that will lead us to the dried up river bed. Originally, it was a den for a mountain lion that I was hunting. She killed some cattle belonging to a rancher. He hired me to capture her and relocate her somewhere else. I set up a trap in there and caught her. Anyway, to make a long story short, some wildlife ranger came and got her. I was packing up my equipment when I saw a small crack in the wall. I walked over and looked into the crack. I could see a large cavern below the cave, so I brought out some digging

THE COVERUP

equipment and dug out the crack. I widened the crack enough so I could climb down to the bottom. That's when I discovered it was a large dried up river. It was so large that I widened the crack. That way I could drive my jeep down and follow it all the way to the end," Bob explained his story about the discovery.

They got out of the Hummer and walked over to the pile of trees and rocks at the entrance.

"What happened to the river? I mean, why did it dry up?" John curiously asked.

"Well, apparently the river changed course and headed up to Colorado," Bob replied.

"Wonder why it changed course?" John asked.

"Well, I think it might have split into two rivers, one running north, the other east, and then one gets bigger and drains the other. See, I investigated the beginning of this river and it narrows. The river may have split because the water flow increased, probably from increased rains and the opening didn't, so that forced the river to split into a tributary," Bob explained.

"So without the flow of the river going to the lake, it also dried up," John added.

"Yeah, that's my theory."

"Wouldn't the government be afraid of the river changing course again?" Richard asked.

"No, there was a cave-in on both ends of the river, closed the whole thing off from ever flowing again."

"Cave-in or did they close it themselves?" John suggested.

"You know, I never thought of that. They could have found the riverbed and dynamited it at both ends. That way they could insure it would never flow again."

377

"Yeah, but if they did that, it would mean they know of this river's existence," Richard remarked.

"And your point is?" Bob asked.

"Well, if they know it exists, they must know it poses a threat to their hidden base," Richard replied.

"That's true, but they do not know about this cave joining the river. Maybe they figured if they closed it on both ends, there wouldn't be a threat from intruders," Bob explained.

"Yeah, maybe you're right," Richard remarked.

"Well, let's get these rocks and trees out of the entrance before that chopper comes back looking for us," Bob said as he grabbed one of the rocks. Richard grabbed one of the trees and began to drag it away. "Don't drag it out there. Pile them up beside the entrance. We are going to have to pile them back as we get inside," Bob explained.

"Gotcha," Richard replied.

They removed all of the debris from the entrance. Bob drove the Hummer into the cave and down the sloppy ramp he built for entering the riverbed. He parked the Hummer and got out.

"Okay, let's cover the entrance back up. John, there's a lantern in the back of the Hummer. Would you get it, please?" Bob requested.

"Sure thing, Bob," John said as he headed for the Hummer's rear door.

Bob and Richard walked back up the ramp to start closing the entrance. As soon as he got the lantern, John started to follow the others up the ramp.

"Let's get this thing closed," Bob said. They started putting the trees across the entrance, leaving a small section to get back inside. John arrived and began to help with the rocks, piling them on top of the small trees. As the hole began to close, it started to get dark inside the cave.

THE COVERUP

"Where's that lantern, John?" Bob asked.

"I left it right over there by the ramp."

"Oh, yeah. I see it," Bob said as he walked over to the ramp. He picked up the lantern and turned on the igniter switch. The lantern lit up the mantle providing them with light to see. "Okay, let's finish closing it up," he said as he set the lantern down. John and Richard got the last of the trees and placed them across the opening.

"Man, I'm glad you had that lantern. Otherwise, we would be totally in the dark here," Richard said as he brushed the dust from his hands.

"Well, I've been down here a few times," Bob said as he picked up the lantern.

"Really? You can't tell it. I mean, with the big opening and the ramp designed for a huge vehicle to come down here," Richard sarcastically remarked.

"Why, Bob, one would almost think you were spying on the government," John added.

"All right, you want to know the truth?" Bob reluctantly asked.

"Yes, we would," Richard replied.

"This place is how I built the resort to what it is now. When I found this place, I began exploring both ends. What I found here was a lot of fossils embedded in the walls. Plus, I dug a lot of them out of the floor. I found a few very rare species of fish and a few mammals. I sold them to various museums for a very high price. Come on, let's get back to the Hummer," Bob said as he walked down the ramp.

"So the resort is not paying for itself," Richard remarked as he and John followed behind Bob.

"That's right."

"I thought that place looked a bit too nice for an Indian resort," Richard said.

When they arrived at the Hummer, Bob set down the lantern.

"Well, you are right," Bob reluctantly replied.

"Isn't that a bit unethical for a paleontologist to sell fossils to fund his own projects?" Richard sarcastically asked.

"Look, I'm not proud of what I did, but when my father left the resort, he almost broke the tribe. He took everything and left us in financial ruin. The place would have gone bankrupt."

"That still doesn't make it right!" Richard began to shout.

"And it was right for the white man to nearly wipe out the Indians!" Bob began to shout back in anger.

"That was not our fault. As I have heard it, Indians were nothing but a bunch of thieves and murderers!" Richard screamed back.

"My people were good honest gentle tribesmen. They never hurt anyone that didn't try to hurt them. You white people just wanted to wipe us out. We were decent human beings!" Bob angrily screamed at the top of his lungs.

"You were savages!" Richard shouted in anger.

"Hey, stop it, guys. There's no need in fighting over past history," John said, trying to calm down Richard and Bob.

"Yeah, well, I lost relatives at Little Big Horn!" shouted Richard.

"And my people were not at Little Big Horn!" Bob shouted in return.

"Look, the white man made a lot of mistakes in the past, and by the same token, so did the Indians. We can't make up for the mistakes we made in the past by fighting now. Things were different back then. Don't let the mistakes of our ancestors be our problems of today. Can't we all just get along?" John candidly remarked.

THE COVERUP

Richard looked over at Bob. Bob stared back at Richard for a moment. They burst out laughing.

"I'm sorry about what I said. I'm sure your people were kind and gentle. My people in their own way were probably more savage than I know about," Richard apologized.

"Well, I am, too. I know that the white man just wanted to civilize my people, and they were not ready for the change," Bob replied.

"There's no reason we can't put things right now," Richard remarked.

"Well, I guess I still hold a grudge for my people. Just seems to me that the white man is still trying to exterminate the Indian," Bob said as he turned down the lantern a little to conserve the gas. He walked over to the Hummer and pulled out a couple of folding chairs. He handed one to John and gave the other to Richard. Then he pulled out a bag and walked away from the campsite. He opened the bag and began to pour a substance around the campsite and Hummer.

"What's that?" John asked.

"Lime," Bob quickly replied.

"Why is he putting out lime?" Richard softly asked.

"I don't know," John whispered back.

"To keep the snakes out of the campsite!" Bob suddenly shouted.

"How did he hear that?" Richard softly asked.

"I've heard of that. Does it really work?" John shouted to Bob.

"Well, I don't know for sure, but it is comforting to believe it does. And to answer your question, Richard, remember Grandfather gave me his power," Bob replied as he continued to pour the lime.

WILLIAM DANIEL

"I didn't know he had super hearing powers," Richard candidly replied.

Bob grinned as he continued to pour the lime, spreading it wider with his boot as he walked. When he finished, he walked back to where John and Richard sat in the chairs.

"Are there really snakes down here?" Richard seriously asked.

"I haven't seen many, but I did kill a seven foot diamondback down here once," Bob answered.

"Oh, really?" Richard remarked.

"Yep. See this belt I'm wearing? Buffalo hide covered by a snakeskin. I made him into a belt. Sucker tried to bite me one day. I was digging in the walls a little ways down from here. He just happened to be hiding in some rocks there. You know, a snake that big can strike a good four feet or at least half its length," Bob explained. He walked to the back of the Hummer and put the empty sack of lime into the back and pulled out a large ice chest. He carried the ice chest to where the others were sitting. "Anyone want a soda pop?" he asked.

"I'd love one," Richard replied.

"Me too," John added.

"What would you like?" Bob asked as he opened the chest.

"Anything cold," John replied.

"Got any beer in there?" Richard asked.

"As a matter of fact, I do. You want a beer too, John?" Bob asked.

"Yeah, a beer would be great."

"That is, if you guys don't mind drinking with a dirty old Indian," Bob candidly remarked.

"One of my new best friends is an Indian," Richard replied.

THE COVERUP

"Oh, yeah? Do I know him?" Bob asked and laughed.

"You should. He was about to scalp me a while ago," Richard answered giggling.

"Well, it seems to me you were ready to cut my throat, too," Bob remarked laughing.

"Oh, no. That was just a professional observation. You know, selling fossils is illegal in the states," Richard said.

"Look, I did what I had to in order to save the resort. I'm not proud of it, but Grandfather insisted on keeping the resort going."

"Well, if I was in the same situation, I probably would have done the same thing," Richard remarked.

"Why, thank you, Richard. You're a good man. I don't care what anyone says."

"How long before we break into the compound?" John curiously asked.

"Our best bet is to wait until nighttime. Just after dark, they change the guards, and I think we can slip in a lot easier that way. Why don't you guys get some rest, and I'll take the first watch," Bob said.

"That's a good idea. I am beat right now," John replied.

"Why do we need a guard down here?" Richard asked.

"Snakes are not the only thing that like to come down here, you know," Bob answered.

"Like what?" Richard asked.

"Well, I have seen a few rats big enough to put a saddle on."

"Ouuuu, I hate rats," John remarked.

"Besides, I need to do some meditating."

"Well, where exactly are we supposed to sleep?" asked Richard.

"In the Hummer. Just shove the back seat down and there is a sleeping bag back there," Bob replied.

"Oh, no. I'm not getting in a sleeping bag with him," John quickly remarked.

"Why, John? I thought Richard was your friend," Bob seriously asked.

"Yeah, well, you weren't at the laundry mat yesterday."

"I guess I don't know what you mean."

"And believe me, you don't want to know," Richard remarked.

"If you say so, Richard, but explain it to me sometime."

"Sure, I'll tell you. When this is all over, we will all have a good laugh," Richard said.

"Okay, look fellows, unzip the sleeping bag and lay it out flat. Will that be sufficient for you, John?" Bob asked.

"As long as he stays on his side of the bag."

"You disgust me," Richard said.

"Well, I'm just not sure I trust you, that's all," John remarked as he and Richard walked to the back of the Hummer.

Bob walked away from the center of the campsite. He folded his legs together and sat down on the ground. He could still hear John and Richard bickering at each other. "You would think those two were married," he thought to himself.

"Why did you have to bring that up again! Bob doesn't know anything about that incident! You beat everything, you know that? You embarrassed me in front of Bob!" Richard argued.

"Well, I'm sorry," John apologized.

"Just get the sleeping bag out and unfold it. I can't believe you did that," Richard continued to nag at John.

Bob continued to listen to their argument until they lay down and went to sleep. Then he began to chant in a soft voice, calling out to talk to his grandfather.

It was 1:30 p.m. when John awoke from a sound sleep to the sound of Bob's voice. He rubbed his eyes in an attempt to clear them. When he was done, he looked out of the Hummer's side window. He saw Bob sitting alone, away from the Hummer. He was talking to someone, but there was no one there. He punched Richard in the side to awaken him.

"What the hey," Richard said as he awoke.

"Shhh. Look outside at Bob. He's talking to someone, but there's nobody there," John explained.

"Yeah, well, maybe he's finally lost it. Go back to sleep."

"Do you think he's talking to Running Deer?" John curiously asked.

"Maybe he's talking to the Great White Spirit. Probably wants to know what the point spread is on next week's Forty Niners' game. Go back to sleep," Richard said as he lay back down.

"I hope he's okay," John said as he lay back down.

John and Richard drifted back to dreamland. Bob continued to have his conversation with the spirit world.

It was 6:30 p.m. Time had ticked away as the events of the evening came closer. "Wake up, guys. It's almost time to go," Bob said as he punched both of them in the shoes.

"What time is it?" John asked.

"About six-thirty," Bob replied.

"I thought you were going to wake me to relieve you," John remarked as he yawned and stretched.

"Well, you guys were sleeping so well, I thought it might be better to let you sleep."

"What about you? Don't you need some rest?" Richard asked as he stretched out his arms.

"No, I'm all right," Bob replied.

WILLIAM DANIEL

"Gee, I'm hungry. What have we got to eat?" John asked.

"I have some sandwiches in the cooler. Get yourself one and let's get ready to go," Bob replied.

THE COVERUP

AREA FIFTY-ONE
Chapter Thirty-seven

There was no turning back as they were about to embark on a quest that could change the future. Bob grabbed a small shovel from the back of the Hummer. Richard and John sat quietly eating their sandwiches.

"Finish up those sandwiches, fellows. It's time to embark on Groom Lake," Bob said as he shouldered the small shovel.

"Groom Lake?" Richard curiously asked.

"That's what they call this dried up lake," Bob answered.

"Well, I'm ready," John murmured as he woofed down the last of his sandwich.

"Me too," Richard responded.

"Okay, guys, follow me," Bob said as he started walking down the dry riverbed. They walked about two hundred yards and came upon a hole in the wall of an underground river.

"Would you look at this. It's a hole in the wall," John said.

"Yeah, that's the hole leading to the compound," Bob explained.

"Did you dig that?" Richard asked.

"No, well some of it. Most of it was a washed out area, sort of like a drain plug for the lake. I discovered a few fossils in there and found myself digging it out some. This is where the floor of the lake was at its thinnest. I was rooting around in there looking for more fossils. I started digging out the roof, which is actually the floor of the lake. That's when I broke through and found myself looking at the compound of this place. I didn't know what it was at first, so I closed it back up. It comes out in an area where trash receptacles are kept. It's a u-shaped walled area, so no one can see you unless they are dumping trash at the time. I built myself a kind of plug to fill the hole. Then I went back and entered the compound. I walked around the place unnoticed. After a while, I realized this was some kind of military base. I suddenly figured out that this must be Area Fifty-One. Anyway I got out of there and never went back," Bob explained.

"How did you get away with walking around and not being noticed?" asked Richard.

"Well, I found this room that had a lab coat with a badge on it. I put on the coat and nobody asked any questions. In fact, they would say hi to me as they walked by."

"So how are we going to know where to go?" John asked.

"Richard has that knowledge. Grandfather gave it to him back at the resort," Bob replied as he started up the hole.

"I hope he's right," Richard remarked as he looked at John.

"Me, also, partner," John agreed as he adjusted the gun stuck in his pants behind his belt.

"You know, if we get caught with that thing, we are dead meat," Richard remarked.

"We'll see to it that we don't get caught," John replied.

"That's easy for you to say," Richard remarked as he grinned slightly.

Bob reached the top of the hole about twenty feet from the floor. He pulled the plug he had placed there. He stuck his head out to see what was happening in the compound. Suddenly he heard a loud roar coming at him. He quickly closed the hole back with the plug.

THE COVERUP

"Shhh!" he said to the others below. He heard the rumbling of one of the trashcans. Someone was dumping some trash into the receptacle. He listened as the individual finished and walked away. Then he carefully pulled out the plug again and stuck out his head. Noticing that it was quiet on the compound, he pulled his head back in and replaced the plug. Then he climbed down the hole to where the others were.

"What did you see?" Richard asked as he appeared from the hole.

"Well, it seems quiet. There was a custodian dumping trash, but he went back inside," Bob explained.

"So now what?" John asked.

"Okay, let me draw you a map of the area," Bob replied as he dropped to his knees on the ground. He drew a rectangle shaped building and put a u-shape on one side. On the outside of the front wall of the u-shape, he drew a door. "Okay, casually walk around this wall to this door. The guards will not think there is a problem if you act casual. They will think you are dumping trash. Open the door and go inside like you own the place. Once you are inside, you are on your own. I suggest finding a room that has lab jackets or at least a badge. No one will suspect you if you have a badge on," he explained.

"Sounds simple enough to me," Richard said.

"Once inside, let Richard guide you to the right places, John. Just trust him. He knows where to go."

"Okay by me."

"Okay, good luck, guys," Bob said as he stepped out of the way.

Richard climbed up the narrow hole. He pulled out the plug and handed it to Bob. Then he squeezed his skinny body through the hole. When he was out of the hole, he looked around to see if anyone was coming. He motioned to John to follow him. John stuck his head out of the hole. He had to squirm his way out. When his shoulders were through, he climbed out.

"All right, are you ready to do this?" Richard whispered.

"Let's do it, partner," John replied softly.

"Follow me, and remember, act casual. Hey, put that gun under your shirt so no one can see it," Richard said.

"Gotcha," John replied as he pulled his shirt out of his pants.

"All right, let's go," Richard said.

He and John stood up and casually walked around the wall to the door. Richard opened the door and they stepped inside. John closed the door behind them softly. Richard surveyed the area and motioned for John to follow him. He led John down the hall until they came to a door with the number one hundred fifty-two beside it. He stopped and put his hand on the doorknob. He looked both ways before he opened it. He stuck his head in and looked around the room. There was no one in the room. He turned to John and said, "In here." He opened the door and walked in with John following him. He softly closed the door behind him to keep from attracting attention.

"So far, so good, huh," John remarked.

"Yeah. Look, there're some lab coats on that rack over there. See if there are any badges on them," Richard said.

John walked over to the rack and looked through the coats. "There's nothing here," he said.

"All right. Bring the lab coats. We'll have to take our chances without them," Richard said as he opened the door slightly. He looked out into the hall to see if anyone was there before they exited. John walked over with two lab coats and handed Richard one of them. Richard took the coat and put it on, and John put on the other one. Richard opened the door and walked out into the hall. John walked out behind him. They stood in the hallway and looked both ways to see if anyone was coming.

"This way," Richard said as he motioned for John to follow.

They started walking down the hall for a few yards. Suddenly a door in front of them began to open. They froze in their tracks as two men came walking out of the door.

"Oh, excuse me," one of the men apologized for running into John as he came out of the room.

"That's quite all right. Hey, how are you doing?" he quickly said to the other man. He walked over to him and hugged him. As he walked away, he said, "Good to see you again."

John and Richard could hear the two men talking as they walked away.

"Who was that?" the first man asked.

"I'm not sure what his name is," the other one replied.

"What was all that about?" Richard whispered to John.

"Look," John said as he held up a pair of badges.

"How the hell did you do that?" Richard asked as they continued to walk down the hall.

"I've arrested a few pickpockets in my time. Learned their tricks of the trade along the way," John replied as he handed Richard one of the badges.

"Well, it sure paid off this time," Richard remarked as he placed the badge on his lab coat.

"I agree, partner," John replied as he placed his badge on his coat.

As they walked down the hall, they came to a T intersection.

"This way," Richard said with confidence as he pointed to their right. They turned and walked down the hall waving at people as they passed them.

"This is easier than I thought it would be," Richard whispered as they continued down the hall.

THE COVERUP

THE MEETING
Chapter Thirty-eight

Richard and John walked down the hall for a couple of hundred feet before coming to a secured door. "Security alert. Only authorized personnel allowed beyond this point," the sign read on the door.

"This is the place," Richard said as he opened the door slowly, peeking in to see if anyone was there. He couldn't see anyone inside and opened the door the rest of the way. He and John walked in and looked around the room at a lot of technical equipment. Across the room, they saw a large picture window. Leading the way, Richard walked over to the window to look outside. John cautiously followed, looking all around at the equipment on the counters.

"There he is!" Richard shouted as he looked through the picture window.

John walked over to the picture window to get a look. "Well, I'll be damned! It does exist. And it looks just like Josh described it to me the day he died," John remarked, peering through the picture window.

"Yeah, I told you it was real," Richard replied.

"And you were right, partner. Forgive me for ever doubting you," John said as he stared at the creature crouched in the corner of this tiny room.

Suddenly the door they had entered was opening and in stepped a woman in a white lab coat. Richard and John quickly turned to face her. John had pulled the pistol he was given from his belt. He noticed the woman was reading something and didn't see them yet. Richard noticed the woman had long flowing light orange hair. He figured she must be in her mid to upper thirties. He was entranced at how beautiful she was and couldn't take his eyes off of her. When the woman finally looked up from the paper she was reading, she saw John and Richard standing there. She noticed that John had a gun pointed at her.

"Who are you people? What are you doing in here? This is a restricted area," the orange haired woman asked.

"Stay calm. We mean you no harm," John replied as he lowered the pistol. He quickly put the gun into his back pocket.

"Oh, yeah? Well, you had better have a good explanation for being in here. You stay right there. I'm calling Security," the woman said as she headed for a phone on the counter in front of her. John quickly ran over and grabbed the phone from her. The woman, feeling threatened, punched John in the jaw. She proceeded to do so again, but John caught her arm and stopped her.

Richard slipped in behind her and grabbed her, pinning her arms. "A little feisty, isn't she?" he remarked as he held the woman tightly.

"I don't think Professor Donner expected this," John remarked.

"You know Professor Donner?" the orange haired woman asked as she calmed down.

"Yeah, are you our inside connection?" Richard asked.

"I had talked to Professor Donner a while back about the situation here. I didn't think he would send someone in here. How did you get in?" the woman replied.

THE COVERUP

"First things first. I'm Richard Cooper and this big tall man is Sheriff John Barton," Richard introduced.

"I'm so sorry. I'm Professor Melinda Leyland. Just call me Melinda. Everybody does," Melinda replied.

"Melinda. That's a pretty name for a pretty lady," Richard said, laying on the charm as if he had found his soul mate. Melinda began to turn red with embarrassment as she grinned at Richard.

"Uh, Richard," John said, trying to break the romantic tension.

"Huh? Oh, yeah. We got in here with a little help from a friend, but that's not important at this moment. Getting out is what's important," Richard babbled.

"You break into a highly secure government military base and you don't have a plan to get out," Melinda sarcastically remarked.

"Well, it wasn't exactly planned. We kind of winged our way through getting here. We've been through quite a bit in the last few days," Richard explained.

"Yeah, especially with Jack on our trail the whole way," John added.

"Jack Riley?" Melinda asked.

"Yes, you know him?" Richard asked.

"Jack Riley is out of control. That is why I went to Professor Donner. He's turned this operation into his own military project. We have a chance to do something good for humanity here. However, Jack has turned it into a military weapon, and he has the approval of the President," Melinda replied.

"I don't understand. How could the Chupacabra be used as a weapon?" Richard curiously asked.

"Yeah, what's he going to do, produce an army of goatsuckers to suck the blood out of the enemy?" John candidly remarked.

"Look, you don't understand. This creature is more than a blood-sucking varmint," Melinda replied.

"All that I believe is that he's one of the aliens that crashed here in 1947," Richard said as he released Melinda and walked over to the picture window with John and Melinda following him.

"So you think this creature is one of the aliens that crashed here?" Melinda asked.

"He is, isn't he?" Richard asked.

"No," Melinda replied.

"Then if he's not, what is it?" Richard asked.

"That's what we thought we were chasing," John added.

"Okay, let me explain this from the beginning. First of all, yes, the crash of 1947 was real. There were four aliens in that spacecraft. Three of them died on impact. The fourth was still alive and well. The military arrived at the scene to find this gruesome discovery. The alien that was alive was running around screaming while clutching a box in his arms. There were three bodies that were torn apart somewhat. Then there was this space ship that was embedded in the side of a hill. Bits and pieces of the ship were all over the place, just like it was reported in the newspaper the next day. Two of the military men who were the first to arrive were stunned at the site. They just stood there looking at it in disbelief. A third man, an officer, arrived seconds later. He looked around at the scene and ordered one of the men to get that box. He believed the box must be important, seeing as how the alien didn't want to give it up. The man struggled with the alien but could not get the box away from him. The officer grabbed a rifle from the third one and hit the alien in the head with the butt. These aliens were four to five feet tall with heads larger than ours. We did not find out until later that their skulls were very thin. The

THE COVERUP

blow to the head killed the last one on impact. However, he did retrieve the box which is right here," Melinda explained as she pointed to a box on the counter.

"At first we had no idea what this box was. We could not open it or figure out what its function was. But in the mid 1960s, one of our scientists discovered a hidden panel. There were several buttons, and he took a chance and pushed one. As it turned out, this box is the aliens' survival kit. The button he pushed turned out to be a locator beacon. They also discovered a button that opened the box. Inside they found a leather-like egg.

I didn't start on this project until the mid eighties. Most of what I'm telling you comes from notes of former scientists who have worked on the project. The box was in a lab in Pennsylvania at the time being studied. They were afraid to push any more buttons because they did not know what would come out of the egg. There were other things going on in the mid sixties, the assassination of President Kennedy for instance. Some time after they had pushed the first button, an acorn-like object fell upon the earth near a small town in Pennsylvania. It turned out to be an alien shuttle. In this small spacecraft was Nelly, as we have come to call her. See, we have found out that when they turned the beacon on, the aliens sent out this creature you call El Chupacabra," Melinda explained in great detail.

"I don't understand. How could this blood-sucking creature be a survival kit for these aliens?" Richard remarked.

"Well, I'm getting to that part. See, we found out that this creature has fangs that are hollow. She was very young when she landed here, so we thought maybe she would drink some goat's milk. She was a very gentle creature, much like a pet dog or cat, despite her hideous appearance. One of our attendants brought in a goat to milk. He put the goat in her cage and went to get a bucket to milk her. When he got back, he found the goat lying on the floor dead. It was completely drained of its blood. Nelly was standing over the goat, her fangs dripping of blood. The attendant became quite frightened at the carnage and ran out leaving the door open. Nelly escaped the cage, and as you can see, she has wings. She flew off the base here and attacked some local ranchers' cattle. We tried to capture her without alarming the public. She is very fast and elusive, and they had no success in catching her, but the strange thing is, she came back to this military base like a homing pigeon. Anyway, after she returned, she was put into a secure cage. Shortly after her return, she produced a jelly-like substance, sort of like a honeybee makes honey for the hive. We began to study the substance, but we had no idea what it was. The studies went on for years. They couldn't link this substance with the survival of the aliens in a stranded situation. In the late nineties, we were given permission to use death-row inmates for experiments. This, of course, was voluntary by the inmates as opposed to being put to death. Well, one inmate was given the substance to see if it had any reaction. Nothing happened to him, and the study seemed to be a failure. The inmates were being put back on death row. The inmate we had given the substance decided to try to escape. He broke out and got into the compound and attempted to climb the fence. One of the security guards shot him as he was climbing the fence. He fell to the ground with a bullet wound in his leg. We carried him to the infirmary where the bullet was taken out and the wound sowed up. He was placed in a secure room and watched constantly by the security guards. The next day, I went in to see how his wound was doing. I was quite surprised to find that the wound was completely healed. There was no trace of a wound at all. Even x-rays didn't reveal any kind of tissue damage. We decided to test it on other wounds and diseases. We brought more inmates that had different problems, and they were all cured. Then one of our doctors had a daughter who had contracted a brain tumor. We took a chance the substance would cure her. The next day she was running all over the facilities just as healthy as she could be. Everything was going good with the study until 1999. Everyone we had treated died that year. It was a devastating setback to the study. Here we thought we had found a cure for every kind of disease that humans encounter, but it looked like the substance had failed. We were at a loss and had to go back to the beginning," Melinda explained.

"Even the little girl?" John sadly asked.

"Even the little girl died. We had her frozen just in case we found the problem and could revive her. I went back and studied my notes on all the cases we had tested. Then it hit me one day that the substance may be too pure, so we started to dilute it and started our study over. It was a miraculous recovery for the substance. All of the patients we administered lived without any problems," Melinda excitedly explained.

"What about the little girl?" Richard asked.

"Yeah, were you able to bring her back?" John curiously asked.

"Well, we started to study the possibilities of bringing people back to life who have died. We took inmates who were electrocuted and tested the product but to no avail. I made several adjustments to the substance but nothing was working. However, I think we may have found the problem. We are working on it now but have yet to test it. See, most of the subjects that we tested were dead for several hours. We think that it might work if the subject just died. We are getting ready to test it sometime this week. We have an electrocution subject and a lethal injection to be performed here this week. I have high hopes that the substance will work," Melinda replied.

"That is a truly remarkable story, Professor Leyland," Richard remarked.

"Yeah, I can't wait to hear the ending," John added.

THE COVERUP

THE SHOOTOUT
Chapter Thirty-nine

The door to the laboratory where John, Richard, and Melinda were discussing the Chupacabra suddenly opened. Jack Riley and two FBI agents, with their guns drawn, casually walked in.

"Well, well, well. What have we here? A pair of lab rats and a mad scientist," Jack sarcastically remarked as he strolled into the room.

"Jack, how nice to see you again," Richard candidly replied.

"Yes, it is nice to have finally caught you two rats in my trap," Jack said as the two agents stepped to his side with their guns pointed at John and Richard.

"You knew we were coming here all the time, didn't you?" John curiously asked.

"No, I drove you here. It was my plan to get you two in here and dispose of you at my leisure," Jack confidently replied.

"I told you he knew where we were all the time," John said to Richard.

"Yeah, well, he's not going to get away with it. My lawyer has orders to launch a full scale investigation if I should die," Richard confidently remarked.

"Oh, you mean this lawyer," Jack said. He pulled from his inside coat pocket a newspaper article. He walked over to Richard and handed it to him.

401

WILLIAM DANIEL

Richard took the article and read it. The headline read, "Controversy Surrounds Sudden Death of New York Lawyer; The sudden death of New York lawyer, James Baker, has a cloud of mystery surrounding it. His cleaning lady, Joan Purifoy, found James Baker dead in his office yesterday. Mr. Baker appeared to have been shot several times in the chest. The investigators found a gun lying beside the body. After running a check on the weapon, they have determined the gun belongs to a Richard Cooper. Cooper, an inherited millionaire, was a client of Mr. Baker's."

"According to this you killed him, or at least they made it look like you did. However, at the time they say he was killed here, you were doing the paper thing. There is an eyewitness to that," John said as he took the clipping from Richard and read it.

"Oh, yeah, the little old lady. She died in a freak car accident," Jack sarcastically added. "That poor lady. I didn't think even you could stoop so low," John remarked as he gave the article back to Richard.

Suddenly the motion-censored camera overlooking the compound came on, and everyone turned his or her attention to the monitor. A naked Indian covered in war paint ran across the screen. He was screaming Indian yelps and shaking a spear as he ran through the compound.

"What the hell is that?" Melinda curiously asked.

"That would be a last desperate attempt of a Cherokee Indian," Richard said as he and John looked at each other.

"Go and get him. Bring him here so he can die with his friends," Jack ordered the two agents at his side. While Jack had his attention with the two agents, John slipped his hand behind him. He pulled the pistol from his back pocket and put his thumb on the hammer.

THE COVERUP

"Jack, this is not necessary. We can keep them here where they can't talk," Melinda desperately pleaded.

"Professor Leyland, I would think you should be more concerned with what is going to happen to you. You have become a great security concern to this project," Jack replied as he motioned for the agents to go.

A scared and concerned look came over Melinda's face. "Look, Jack, she was forced to tell us what was going on. She's not any part of this," Richard said, trying to take the heat off of Melinda.

"Thanks, Richard, but I think this coverup is going deeper than you think," Melinda replied.

"Good perception, Professor," Jack said.

"What exactly is this all about, Jack?" Richard curiously asked.

"Sure, why not, seeing as how you are both going to die. We are planning to put together an army that can never be stopped, an army so great that it never has to be retrained, no more anti-war marches by young men who don't want to fight for their country, an army that can take over the world and create world peace by domination," Jack explained.

"Sounds a lot like Adolph Hitler to me," John remarked as he waited for Jack to drop his gun for a moment.

"Hitler's beliefs were not wrong. He just didn't have the army to do it. Extermination of all the parasites that control this world is my vision," Jack said as he reached behind himself to close the door.

"Jack, don't do this. The project can go on with them here. We can let them work on the project," Melinda pleaded her case.

"I'm afraid not, Professor. You see, the less people who know, the better," Jack replied.

WILLIAM DANIEL

"So you're just going to take over the world, maybe become some kind of dictator," Richard remarked as he started to inch his way around to his left. He figured if he could draw Jack's attention away from Melinda and John, John might get off his one shot.

"You can't imagine the vision I have," Jack replied.

"Oh, I don't know. I could vision some seriously sick stuff," Richard sarcastically remarked.

"You think I'm sick. Sick is the terrorist that threatens our everyday life. Sick is these goody two-shoes that can't see death as a means of cultivation. In all animal society, the sick and weak must die for the healthy to live," Jack explained as he followed Richard around the counter with his gun.

"What about the President? What does he think of your plan?" Richard quickly asked, trying to cover up his movements.

"Our President is in favor of this plan. Only he thinks he will be in charge of the world. I have other plans," Jack replied.

"You plan on killing the President, too?" Richard asked, inching a little farther around the end of the counter.

"He's a little wimp of a parasite himself. He wouldn't have the guts to take over the world. That's my vision, not his," Jack explained.

"So he doesn't really know about the world dictatorship you have planned?" Richard asked, moving another step.

"No, he doesn't," Jack said.

Noticing Richard had moved away from the others, Jack ordered, "Get back over there."

John realized it was now or never. With one quick and smooth motion, he pulled the pistol from behind himself. At the same time, he cocked back the hammer, pointed it at Jack,

THE COVERUP

and fired. He wasn't quite quick enough to catch Jack off guard. Jack saw him moving his arm out of the corner of his eye. He turned and managed to get off several rounds before falling to the floor. John had hit him right between the eyes, but Jack had managed to put one bullet into his chest right where his heart was. John fell to the ground and lay motionless, blood pouring out of his chest onto the floor. The sudden shock of the gunfire and the shattering glass behind John caught Melinda by surprise. When the smoke cleared and her senses came back, she saw Richard on the floor holding John in his arms.

"Don't die on me, John! Stay out of the light! Don't touch the spirit horse!" Richard screamed.

Melinda looked on in disbelief at what had just happened. "Oh, my God!" she cried out.

"John, please don't leave me! You're the only true friend I have! Professor, do something, please!" Richard screamed.

"Hold on," Melinda said as she ran over to a small refrigerator in the corner. She pulled out a small vile of the substance she was working on. She opened a cabinet and took out a syringe and put the needle into the end of the vile and drew out a full syringe of the product. She dropped the rest onto the cabinet top and ran over to where Richard was holding John. She quickly knelt down onto the floor and held the syringe in front of John's chest.

"Thanks, Professor," Richard said, tears running down his cheeks.

"Please, call me Melinda. You know, Richard, there is no guarantee this will work. The product hasn't been tested, yet," Melinda said as she held the syringe in her hand.

"Give it to him, Melinda, because there is no way I'm letting him leave me now. It's just got to work," Richard replied.

"I guess we've got nothing to lose by trying," Melinda said as she stuck the needle into John's chest. She pushed the plunger down until the entire product had been delivered.

"Thanks, Melinda," Richard said as he held onto John and whispered into his ear. "Don't leave me, you bastard."

"Are you two an item or something?" Melinda asked.

"Oh, no. He's just my best friend, that's all," Richard quickly replied.

"Good, because I kind of like you," Melinda softly said.

"Me?" Richard confusingly asked.

"Yes, you," Melinda replied, smiling prettily.

"This is hardly the time for romance," Richard remarked.

"I'm sorry. You're right. Let me get someone in here to move him to a room," Melinda said as she got up from the floor. She turned and ran out of the lab to get some help.

"Definitely cute," Richard remarked to himself as she ran out of the room. He looked over at Jack lying on the floor with a hole between his eyes. "You sure got the bad guy with a good shot, partner."

Melinda reappeared with two men holding a stretcher. They quickly brought the stretcher over and placed John on it.

"What about him?" one of the men asked as they lifted John off of the floor.

"I don't think he can do us anymore harm. Take him to a room and get an IV in him. When you are done, come back and move that monster to the freezer. Then get one of the custodians to come clean this floor," Melinda ordered.

Richard got up from the floor and watched as they took John out of the lab. "So, now what?" he asked.

"We call the authorities and explain the incident," Melinda replied.

"Yeah, I guess you are right," Richard said as he stood beside Melinda. Suddenly he heard a moaning sound. He turned and looked at Jack lying on the floor. Then he turned his head slowly to the shattered window behind him.

"What?" Melinda asked as she noticed some concern on his face.

"Oh, no," Richard said as he walked over to the window. Melinda followed him to see what was wrong. Lying in the corner of the tiny room was Nelly, the floor covered in her blood. She had been shot from one of the stray bullets.

"Oh, no! She's dying!" Melinda said in a sad voice.

"Quick, give her one of those shots!" Richard remarked.

"I'm afraid it won't help her. See, she produces the product, but the product will not affect her in any way," Melinda explained.

"That's a damned shame," Richard remarked.

"Come on," Melinda said as she led Richard into the room where Nelly was. Melinda squatted down to the floor and held Nelly's head in her hand. Nelly looked up at Melinda with her big black eyes. With her last breath, she let out a murmuring last groan and passed on.

"Goodbye, Nelly," Melinda softly said as she laid her head on the floor.

"I'm so sorry, Melinda," Richard apologized.

"It's probably best for her. Come on. Let's check on John."

"This is all Jack's fault. I should let you revive him so I can kill him," Richard said.

WILLIAM DANIEL

THE COVERUP

THE FUNERAL
Chapter Forty

Two days later at the Quasar Villa Cemetery, Regina sat quietly all dressed in black wearing white gloves. The black veil covering her face was hiding the tears running down her cheeks. The preacher offered a prayer to end the services and asked for the people to bow their heads. Regina bowed her head clutching a white rose in her right hand. Richard, sitting to her left, was holding her other hand. As the preacher finished with the final words of the prayer, he motioned for them to rise. He walked around to the other side of the casket. Walking down the line saying words of encouragement to each one in the front line, he stopped at Regina and talked softly to her before departing back to the other side. Regina stood there for a moment with her head bowed. With Richard holding her arm, she placed the white rose on the casket. She lowered her head as Richard escorted her to his black limousine. Reporters were lined up around the car. Cameras were flashing as pictures were taken of them entering the car. Richard put Regina in the car and walked to the other side. The reporters were screaming, "Mr. Cooper, can you give us some insight as to what happened?"

"No comment at this time, gentlemen," Richard replied as he got into the car. As soon as he sat down, he told James, his chauffeur, to take them to the Barton house. The car pulled out from the cemetery and onto the highway. For the first few minutes, they sat quietly thinking to themselves.

"Everything is going to be all right," Richard said as he broke the silence.

"I hope you're right," Regina said as she wiped the tears from under her veil.

"I will take care of everything. I don't want you to worry," Richard replied.

"Mr. Cooper, you have a phone call," James announced on the intercom.

"Don't worry. Everything is going to be okay. Hello," Richard said as he picked up the car phone.

"Mr. Cooper, everything has been taken care of like you asked. Is there anything else I can do?" the President asked.

"I think you have done quite enough as it is, Mr. President," Richard sarcastically replied.

"Look, Mr. Cooper, as I told you before, I had no idea what Jack was up to. He was acting on his own accord. He was told to keep you out of the picture. I never gave him permission to kill anyone. He did that on his own accord," the President replied.

"That's not what I heard. I was told that you and General Rumsfield encouraged him to do it. Did you know that he planned to kill the two of you and take control of the project himself?" Richard screamed.

"Look, I know Jack was out of control. I had some CIA agents watching him."

"Well, you didn't stop him before he did all this damage!"

"Okay, maybe that was an error in my judgment, but the fact remains you cannot tell the public. It would be very devastating to our nation."

"And I told you I would decide that when the forty-eight hours were up."

THE COVERUP

"Okay, Mr. Cooper. The fate of our nation lies in your hands."

"No, the coverup since 1947 lies in my hands."

"This nation cannot survive without a government to run it. The people who are under its rule trust us to handle things for them. They look to us for guidance and protection. If you expose that coverup, this country will fall apart. No one will ever trust our government again. There will be chaos everywhere, and it will be at your hands," the President explained.

"Like I said, forty-eight hours, Mr. President."

"Your time is almost up, Cooper. Be a man, make the right decision."

"Good-bye, Mr. President," Richard replied as he hung up the phone.

"You're making some powerful enemies," Regina remarked as she looked out the window of the limousine.

"He's just an elected official. He can be impeached just as easily as he was elected," Richard replied.

"Well, don't let me tell you what to do," remarked Regina.

The car turned and drove down Main Street. There were people lined up on the street waving as the limousine drove by. It turned onto Fuller Street and drove until it came to the Barton house. The driver pulled the car into the driveway lined on both sides with reporters.

"Oh, Richard, I can't deal with this now," Regina said as she looked out the window.

"It's okay. I will take care of it," Richard said as he opened the car door and exited.

"Good luck with that one," Regina replied.

Richard walked around to the other side of the car to let Regina out. Reporters were screaming his name and asking for a statement. He opened the door and took Regina by the hand. She stepped out of the car as the cameras began to flash. Richard escorted her to the house as policemen held back the reporters.

When Regina was in the house, Richard turned to face the reporters. "A statement will be made later today. We have no other comment to make at this time," he said as he closed the door.

Regina walked into the hall and turned to enter the kitchen. Richard followed but stopped at the door to the kitchen. He watched as Regina removed her veil and placed it on the kitchen table. She walked over to the refrigerator and opened it to get a carton of milk. She placed the carton on the table and turned to the cabinets to get a glass. Opening the cabinet, she pulled out a small glass and placed it on the table. She opened the carton of milk and poured some into the glass and placed the carton back into the refrigerator. She picked up the glass and took a drink, and when she finished, she placed the glass back on the table. As she lowered her head, she began to weep. Richard walked over to her side and took her into his arms.

"Don't worry. Everything is going to be all right. Trust me," he said, trying to comfort her.

Regina slowly peeled herself from Richard's arms and walked out of the kitchen, picking up her veil as she passed by. She turned and walked down the hall to her bedroom. Richard followed but stopped at the door. Regina walked into the room and headed for her dresser. She placed the veil on top and removed her gloves, placing them in the top drawer. Richard, still standing at the door, watched as she began to lower her head to cry again.

"It's time you know," he said as he watched.

THE COVERUP

"Yes, I know," Regina replied as she reached up and removed her earrings. She placed them in her jewelry box on top of the dresser. She walked over to the bed and sat down on the edge. With her back to Richard, she leaned forward and kissed John on the forehead. John Barton, lying in the bed on his back as if he was in a coma, did not move.

"John, wake up. Please wake up," Regina said as she shook him lightly, but there was no reaction from the seemingly lifeless body lying before her. She shook him a little harder. "John, for God's sake, wake up!" she said as she pleaded for a reaction. She had performed this act several times before in the past forty-eight hours. Like before, there was no reaction. She was afraid she had lost him forever and began to cry, laying her head on his chest. Suddenly through her tear-swollen eyes, she saw one of John's fingers move. She quickly pulled herself up and began shaking John again and again. "Wake up, baby," she said as she shook him lightly.

John's eyelids began to flap open and shut several times. He was trying to adjust them to the light. Finally, they opened wide and cleared so he could see. "Water?" he asked when he finally cleared his eyes.

Regina grabbed a Styrofoam cup with a straw in it from the nightstand. She had kept it there full of ice water in case John awoke and was thirsty. "Here, baby," she said as she held the straw to his lips. John took the straw and drank a few sips from the glass.

"By any chance, would you know who scotch-taped my tongue to the roof of my mouth?" John asked as he let go of the straw.

"Oh, baby! I'm so glad you are awake," Regina said as she put her arms around him and hugged him.

"Oh, baby! I just had the most weirdest dream you have ever heard," John said in a scratchy voice.

"Honey, there is someone here that wants to see you," Regina said as she sat up.

"This dream was so real, like you wouldn't believe it. Who is it that wants to see me?" John asked. Regina got up from the bed so John could see.

"How are you feeling, partner?" Richard said as he stood in the doorway.

"Ah, gee wiz, I might have known you would ruin a good fantasy dream," John sarcastically replied.

"Welcome back to reality," Richard said.

"So the dream was real. Well, tell me, how did it come out seeing as how I missed the ending?" John sarcastically asked.

"Well, let me sum it up for you. You killed the bad guy, and he killed you. The Chupacabra brought you back to life, and the government buried Jack," Richard briefly explained.

"And what about Bob?" John asked.

"Bob wanted to be here for when you woke up, but he had some urgent business to take care of. He was here all day yesterday but had to fly back. He plans on coming back later today. He was anxious to talk to you when you woke up," Richard replied.

"What about El Chupacabra?" John asked.

"Nelly caught one of Jack's bullets. She died shortly after you did. Regina and I buried her in your cemetery and put up a headstone with the name, Nelly Barton, on it," Richard answered.

"Wait a minute. You gave that hideous creature my name?" John shouted as loudly as he could.

"Well, Regina thought it might be appropriate seeing as how she saved your life," Richard replied.

"She did?"

"Yes," Richard replied.

THE COVERUP

"How?"

"Well, remember the product Melinda was working on?"

"Yes," John cautiously answered.

"Well, she gave it to you."

"Uh, but I thought that product was unstable."

"Oh, no, no. Melinda says she has found the answer to the problems," Richard replied.

"Melinda? Since when did we start calling Professor Leyland by her first name?" John curiously asked.

"Well, ever since you died, I guess," Richard replied grinning from ear to ear.

"This is great. Now we can have barbecues and nights out on the town. You're going to love married life," John excitedly remarked.

"Wait a minute. I didn't say I was marrying her."

"Say, Regina, I've got to tell you what this guy did in a laundry mat," John started to say.

"Are you going to start that again?" Richard asked before they both started laughing.

THE END

Made in the USA